# *The*
# MOTION
# PICTURE
# TELLER

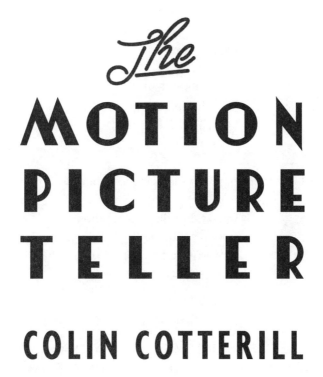

# The
# MOTION
# PICTURE
# TELLER

## COLIN COTTERILL

SOHO
CRIME

Published by
Soho Press, Inc.
227 W 17th Street
New York, NY 10011

Library of Congress Cataloging-in-Publication Data

Names: Cotterill, Colin, author.
Title: The motion picture teller / Colin Cotterill.
Description: New York, NY : Soho Crime, [2023]
Identifiers: LCCN 2022024746

ISBN 978-1-64129-435-5
eISBN 978-1-64129-436-2

Subjects: LCGFT: Novels. | Classification: LCC PR6053.O778 M68
2023 | DDC 823/.914—dc23/eng/20220524
LC record available at https://lccn.loc.gov/2022024746

Printed in the United States of America

10 9 8 7 6 5 4 3 2 1

My thanks to my Thai friends who encouraged me to go ahead with this project and to my longtime editorial readers with their sarcastic but always relevant comments over the years. My love to Kyoko, my wife and best friend, and a passing wag to our nine mentally challenged dogs.

# ACT 1
# Bangkok 2010

# PROLOGUE

*There were two worlds. There was the real world, where Supot delivered letters for the Royal Thai Mail service, where everyone he met was an unlikely character even for fantasy. In this world, teenagers dropped lighted matches into post boxes; elderly transvestites invited you in for coffee and romance; paving stones subsided beneath your feet, leaving you ankle deep in muck; monks smoked a joint before heading off on their alms rounds; and office girls paid homage to the plaster elephants at the concrete altar in front of the department store, then returned to instant noodles and cheesy television soaps in their windowless rooms.*

*There was that world.*

He was six paces into Nisomboon's yard before he realized what he'd done. It was an increasingly common bout of stupidity. He should have rung the bell and had the owner come to the gate. Or, even better, he should have stayed in bed. All around him like slow-breathing land mines were the mid-siesta bodies of nine dogs, semi-rehabilitated and doubtlessly dreaming of postal worker kebab even then. They were probably rabid ex-street mongrels with issues, each with the capacity to rip the flesh from his bones. But they slept in peace in the midday heat under the shade of the sprawling banyan tree. There was hope.

He completed the walk to the house more silently than

any postman in the history of mail delivery. He placed the letter on the step of the open front door, then turned on his heel and prowled back toward the gate . . . and safety. Were it not for the clash of keys in the bunch on his belt, he might have got out of there unscathed.

*Then there was the* intended *world—one that beckoned from a cruel distance. The world of motion pictures, where he spent his only truly happy hours. Where Brando pads his cheeks with cotton wool and Kelly risks pneumonia in the rain. Where Lang introduces the serial killer, Godard highlights the dangers of romance, Fellini encourages decadence, and Akerman demonstrates the beauty of housework. Where women are stabbed in the shower, seven men overthrow an army, and a computer takes over a spaceship. A world where anything is possible and preferable.*

He sat beside Ali—his best friend—a spicy fish ball on a skewer poised at his lips. He had no idea what the actress was saying—she was speaking French, the language of seducers—but she was saying it so beautifully that he didn't want to insult her by reading the Thai subtitles. Not while she was up on the screen acting her French heart out for him. He could pick out a semblance of a plot: there was some problem with her schoolmaster husband. Some deal going down with the man's minor wife. But Supot could read that later. It didn't matter. For now, he was in the trance of delight, riding around on this cinematic carousel for an hour or so. The truly great films could keep a person engrossed whether they were in Thai or Icelandic or Mauritian Creole. Language was superfluous, a supplementary bonus to a man who loved film.

If Supot Yongjaiyut had shown any aptitude at all, a mere glimpse of skill as a filmmaker, actor, or even a lighting technician, he would have lived contentedly in the world of cinema. But he was without hope. Hopeless, some might say. He'd trawled down through his depths of creativity and imagination and found not one modest shoal, not one squirming sprat of aptitude. In fact, considering the natural ability of his mother, Oi, he even left the plausibility of genetic transference in tatters. She had been the talent of the family, and she'd kept her genes to herself.

Supot couldn't complain, though. Oi undoubtedly loved her children. Where other mothers might have given themselves to an unsuitable replacement husband for their benefit, Oi never did. She vowed never to leave herself dependent on a man again. She worked two jobs and dedicated herself to doing the best for her kids—sending them to a good school and having plans for their futures. During the day she clerked in the office of a river barge company. At night she made tiny clay models at home to meet orders from Central Department Store.

She molded little market people, bunches of fruit, carrying baskets, and sleeping dogs between her clever fingers. She painted them with brushes as fine as a baby's eyelashes, varnished them, and baked them in her old Chinese oven. Every evening, Supot and Tam would finish their homework and sit on either side of the table watching her, wondering whose mother this woman was. If she was really theirs, they thought, surely, they would have inherited something of her. Surely, she wouldn't have produced these two clumsy people with hands like hoofs.

Supot and Tam tried. Goodness how they'd tried. They turned out whole tribes of deformed elephant-man market people and dogs as ugly as congealed mucous. They painted eyes that filled up whole heads and bananas that contaminated all the fruit around them with their hepatitis yellow.

Oi always giggled at their efforts, not to embarrass them, but because she was realistic. There's no justice done in telling your children lies. Very soon they all saw the funny side, and their clumsiness lost its stigma. She told them that the Lord Buddha shared abilities around. She admitted she had certain gifts, but that her children had other skills to make up for those they lacked. To this day Supot was still searching for his prowess.

Now, he was thirty-two, reasonably good-looking as far as postmen went, but somewhat economical when it came to facial expressions. The span between boredom and shocked horror was barely perceptible, no more than an eyebrow shift. He had feelings as deep as any, but they rarely inconvenienced his face. To the customers on his route, he often seemed to be drunk in thought, philosophically high, even on days when he was as empty-headed as an egg puppet.

If you asked, he would tell you he had a mental disability. He was the first to confess to it. He didn't need to compare himself to the genius of his film idols or even to normal thinking folk he met every day. Standing alone on a street corner, he could feel it. He probably should have qualified for a disability pension, but his defect wasn't listed in the postal service manual. Otherwise, he could have collected his compensation check alongside the armless and the legless. Supot, "the original thoughtless."

Memories from his childhood would suggest he once had an imagination, or part of one at least. He could remember sitting with Oi sharing theories about where his father might have gone in his hunt for a heart. The heart-hunt series had been Supot's last original work. It had grown out of Oi's telling him how a glittery lady had stolen the heart of her husband. To a three-year-old, the image of his father traveling around Thailand trying to get his heart back had been as vivid as the golden roof of the Grand Palace across the Chaophraya River. Together, he and Oi sent the treacherous man on mythical journeys through dark northern forests and sandy southern islands. Never did the man find his heart. Never did he return.

But imagination had left Supot somewhere along that journey, and now he could barely come up with excuses for being late to work. Naturally he had no less of a capacity for lying than any, but once a man convinces himself he can't do a thing, no amount of counseling will make him believe otherwise. He'd been a postman for almost ten years. But if you asked him what he did for a living, he would answer that he was working at the post office "for the moment." It wasn't a career. It was just a job he did while he waited for his "big something."

The setting for Supot's unwanted life in late 1996 was a suburb called Bangkok Noi—Little Bangkok. In the mind of someone who hadn't been there, the name probably conjured up an image of a quaint place with narrow streets and flower boxes. And there could have been a time in Thailand's past when that was how it looked. It had once sat immune like a foreign land on the west bank of the river. But Greater (and uglier) Bangkok soon gobbled it up. Bangkok Noi turned from a destination to a transit route. It was sliced through, hemmed in, and overpassed from all directions. It ended up caged like a dove in a latticed concrete dome. It was blinded in a fog of exhaust fumes, and its song couldn't be heard through the relentless noise of traffic. If it hadn't been for the river at its back, the suburb would certainly have died without a trace.

But people like Supot, those who had been born there,

had gone to school there, and lived all their lives there had a strange ability not to see the concrete crowding in on them. There were still little streets here and there, and canals with pink orchids drooping over them. If that's all you bothered to notice, that's all there was.

A tall thin man in a pirated Abibas T-shirt was walking along the racks of videos like a person of knowledge at a gallery. He read the details on the spines and nodded recognition. At that pace, assuming he didn't take time out for meals or toilet breaks, it would've taken him four and a half days to read to the very last title. Ali couldn't wait that long.

"Can I help you?" Ali said.

The man looked up, surprised. "Ah. Yes. I'm looking for something, you know . . . happy."

"Um. Happy," said Ali. "Now there's a concept. Happiness, you do realize, is relative."

"Eh?"

Allah was, without question, living inside Ali. He could feel His presence, and he was delighted to have Him. But He wasn't alone in there. There was a devil in Ali too, and that beast took over the reins more often than Ali would have liked. It wasn't clear whether Allah stepped out from time to time and the devil took advantage, or that this was the normal process of Islamic Enlightenment, the constant juxtaposition of internal goods and evils. On this particular evening, with a monsoon rain beating against the shop window, Allah was not at home.

"Well," said Ali, "I mean, for example, what makes Saddam Hussein happy could be something dark, something sinister, like Tarantino."

"Taran . . . ?"

"He may see humor in John Travolta accidentally blowing a man's head off. Blood splattering the interior of the car."

"I—"

"Teacher Pratheep, our very own senator with a social conscience, on the other hand, may find happiness in something lighter. Perhaps the softer but no less biting wit of Woody Allen or Jacques Tati. Just how happy are you planning to get?"

It was apparent from the pause-button expression on the thin man's face that he had no idea what Ali was talking about. Ali was used to that.

"In fact, I was looking for something by the Mom Jokmok comedy troupe from Channel Seven," said the man. "The ones with the bald midget. You know them?"

"And that would make you happy?" Ali asked.

"Oh, yes."

"Right, then. Over there on your left, you'll find the complete gallery of their greatest works. They produce a new tape every eleven minutes. Take your pick."

The man couldn't have been more excited if he'd discovered the gold left behind by the Japanese invaders in the Second World War. He started to study the spines Ali had pointed out.

"There are so many," the man said. "Which one would you recommend?"

"Recommend?" Ali put his finger on his cheek and considered the choices like a gourmet going down a menu. "I think number nine. That's probably your style. It has a very nice selection of fart jokes."

Going with Ali's suggestion, the tall, thin man brought his choice to the counter, paid his fifty-baht rental fee, and was allowed to take advantage of the week's special: a copy of *Seven Samurai* to take home and watch absolutely free of charge. There wasn't much hope, but Ali never gave up on his life's mission to elevate the tastes of his regular clientele. Every now and then one would emerge from the darkness and be dazzled by the brilliance. Most, however, would come back and tell him why they hadn't found a fondness for the "foreign muck" he'd given them. He really understood how the Mormon fellows must feel; they ding-dong their way from house to house, enjoying only abuse and failure in the hope that one day they might stumble upon a convert. Ali was the Mormon of motion pictures.

The tall thin man left . . . happy. Happiness was what he'd come for, and happiness was what he got. One more satisfied customer for Ali's Video Rental. As the door shut, the bell tinkled. It was a real bell, not like the electric burp at the 7-Eleven. It was genuine brass caressed gently by a tongue of rubber every time the door opened and closed, making a tinkle like ice in real cut glass. Its infrequent sound rankled the nerves of Ali. Twenty-five customers from nine to nine was a good day.

Ali had bought the place knowing he would never make money out of it. He'd sat his stunned mother down at the kitchen table one day and told her, "Ma. Money shouldn't be a reason for doing things."

That message had come as a surprise to his ma because she'd spent a lot of money sending him to do the MBA at Bangkok University. It wasn't the most prestigious MBA of the ninety or so on offer around the country. Nor was it the cheapest. But it was good enough to give him the acumen he needed to make his family wealthy.

He'd learned everything the university expected of him and one thing it hadn't. He learned that he didn't like making money. He learned that gratuitous wealth was un-Islamic and unnecessary. The national MBA philosophy was, "Amass lots of money and use it to amass lots more." When you made too much you had to change your lifestyle, so it didn't look like excess. It was like having a suit that was too big for you and putting on weight to fit into it.

He lied about his doubts when the faculty gurus asked him; he feigned avarice and passed second in his class. He'd had offers from greedy companies with logos and retirement plans, and he'd turned them all down. When the family asked him what he'd decided to do, he took them all to the high street and pointed to the spot where his share of grandpa's inheritance money had gone.

They called the imam to the house that same evening. He was a dry-skinned elder with penetrating eyes that peered out through a curtain of unruly brow hair, an Asian Gandalf. Islamic holy men don't perform exorcisms as such, but it was obvious, even to him, that the boy was possessed. This was Thailand before the economic tiger was cruelly spayed. It was unimaginable a smart young Thai with an MBA wouldn't want to climb up on its back and ride on into glorious capitalism.

It was a month before the family gave up on him completely. It was as if he'd gone into an asylum. They would talk about him in the past tense, even though he was still living at home with his ma. They'd talk about how successful he could have been, if only . . .

Ali was as content as an aardvark in an ant farm. He had everything he needed: his own shop with a small viewing area where he and his best friend, Supot, could spend endless hours watching films; a girlfriend called Kwang, whom he'd been dating since primary school and would one day marry. *Probably*. He had a steady if not spectacular income, a good face with a structurally sound jaw, and his faith and health. Nothing about his lifestyle was likely to give him a heart attack. All he had to do was wait for his "big something."

The bell tinkled.

"Hey, Islam."

Supot stood sweating in the doorway of the shop. He had a bandage, speckled with blood, on his right hand. Ali ignored it. Supot had a historical collection of such mementos.

"Go away," said Ali. "We don't want your type in here."

"I don't have a type," said Supot. "I'm a one-off."

"You're sweating all over the mat."

"Right. I'll go. But that means you won't ever hear about my date last night."

"Ah, yes. Then you can stay. But come completely in. You're letting out the AC."

Supot glanced outside before entering. The street was clogged with traffic. His post office Honda was parked at the curb on a "No Parking" yellow line. He'd always considered himself to have the same privileges as an ambulance. The saddlebags were bursting with mail eager to be delivered. He walked to the counter and sat on one of the barstools across from Ali.

"This is Miss Yakult we're talking about. Right?" said Ali.

"Anjira."

"Lovely name."

"Lovely girl, if you can ignore her mouth."

"Oh dear. Did we have problems?"

"She has no sophistication. No culture."

"Pot, you didn't take her to the film festival, did you? I thought we agreed you wouldn't."

"*Schindler's List.*"

"Now, what type of girl wouldn't want to eat popcorn and drink Coke whilst watching an enjoyable film about genocide?" Ali reached down to the bar fridge. "You want a soy milk?"

Ali emerged with a large plastic bag pregnant with fresh soy and wrestled with the rubber band that held it shut.

"Not while I'm on duty," said Supot. "Are you listening?"

"Yes."

"I thought a bit of culture would be nice for a girl who stirs yogurt all day. Thought it would give her a chance to escape, you know?"

"But?"

"She said it was boring."

"Oh."

"She said there was too much talking and not enough jokes."

"Uh-oh."

"She asked me why I didn't want to see a Thai film, and why we had to see a film that was, like, a hundred years old."

"It was released a couple of years ago."

"I know. You don't have to tell me. It's the film noir thing that confuses these factory girls. Anything black and white has to be older than they are. And she said Spielberg ought to have made the film in Thailand."

"I believe they considered resetting it in Phuket," said Ali. "Sun, surf, and carnage."

"She said . . ." He put on a Yakult factory girl accent for Ali's benefit. "'Who can read subtitles that fast?'"

They laughed at her expense.

"The poor thing," said Ali. "I feel sorry for anyone you take to the movies."

He transferred the entire half-liter of soy into a glass that had a capacity of 450 milliliters. Supot already had his emergency hand bandage at the ready and dammed the flood before it reached the edge of the counter.

"Given your disturbing obsession with film," Ali continued, "how could you take a girl to the cinema on a first date? You're asking for trouble. I don't know why I'm mocking her. It's you I'm worried about. You should take her to Lumpini Park and pedal around in one of those little boat things. Have a conversation. Get to know her. Find out what type of films she likes."

"Being in the cinema didn't stop her from having a conversation."

Ali sucked conditioned air noisily through his teeth. "Really?"

"I had to move away from her."

"It's an illness," said Ali. "Don't blame her. She was probably deprived of breast milk as a baby. I'm sure she didn't realize she was trespassing on sacred ground. So few people do. To most of them, it's just an excuse to get out of the sun for a couple of hours. They aren't like you and me, Supot. They don't need film to stay sane. We're the weird ones. We're the addicts. They should be feeling sorry for us."

Supot climbed down from his stool and walked to the door. "I don't think so. I'm starting to think there are only one or two cultured people left in this world."

"You going to see her again?"

"No."

"Go on. Give her another chance."

Supot opened the door slowly and watched the rubber caress the bell. *Tinkle.*

"I need something more than a Yakult girl, brother. I need . . . Gene Tierney."

Ali nodded in agreement.

"Okay. We'll go and dig her up at the weekend. I'll bring a shovel."

"Ali. Ali. I don't want her now. I want her then when she was still a goddess."

The bell tinkled again, the door shut, and Ali watched his friend climb on the post office Honda, kick at the pedal six times, and speed off into oncoming traffic. The shop was filled with a concert of angry horns.

There were probably no more than twenty Thais in the entire country who'd know who Gene Tierney was. Ali had eight of her films on Beta. The whole back section was full of classics: American, European, Asian, all subtitled in Thai. Many originated from the good old days when foreign embassies had cultural budgets and could translate and subtitle their country's classic movies. A subtle cultural invasion. There were one or two customers who borrowed them regularly, but most couldn't be bothered to read the translation. "If you're going to read for two hours," they'd often express, "you might as well buy a book."

Ali and Supot had seen every one of them at least twice. Ali watched, once reading, then once more to look only at the film. Supot enjoyed the film first then read the subtitles in round two. You'd think they'd have incidentally learned the languages by doing that. But they didn't. Not even English. Ali once heard about the "silent period," where little children listen to a language but aren't ready to speak. Then one day they start babbling as if they'd known it all along. He figured he and Supot would wake up one morning fluent in half a dozen languages.

Ali had films with Thai voice-overs. To him and Supot,

they were like temple walls with spray paint graffiti. Two Thai men read all the actors' parts, and two women read for all the actresses, children . . . and animals. They held their noses or gurgled saliva to broaden their limited range of character interpretation. That made the original performers sound like they were suffering from nose and throat infections. Those four Thai actors were shameless. He could never forget Claudette Colbert sounding like a Hualamphong station announcer in *It Happened One Night.*

From that day on they pushed the mute button as soon as they discovered a film dubbed in Thai. Better to be silent than to be offensive.

Most evenings and weekends Supot came to help out in the shop. He never asked to get paid, and he knew he wouldn't if he did. Ali barely made enough to cover the bills. Then there was the forthcoming investment in CDs. Tape was at the end of its regime. There wouldn't be half a generation before grandchildren started asking, "What's in that black plastic box, Grandma?" Videocassettes would take their place in museums alongside records and gas TVs that had to be warmed up before the picture arrived.

Ali considered slowly bringing in DVDs and VCDs, even though Bangkok Noi people weren't about to give up their video players without a fight. They knew as soon as they'd saved up and bought their state-of-the-art DVD player, the Sony bloodsuckers would come out with something new. Technology was always one step ahead of your salary.

There's a scene in *The Blob* where the actual blob blobs around in a trancelike state, bumping into furniture and gas pumps. It starts off as a cute little baby blob but gets bigger and bigger, eventually eating everyone in Pennsylvania. When Supot first saw that scene, it reminded him of himself as a postman. The army could have fired missiles at him while he was on the job, and he wouldn't have noticed till he got home and saw the burn marks on his uniform. But even as a postman blob, he was a hundred times better than Supot as a teenager with no hope, left behind by his mother. He missed her. Oi would tell fantastic stories while she molded her little clay people. There seemed to be no end to her imagination. She'd take her children on incredible journeys to places that she would fashion in her head. She'd give birth to creatures that even great poets like Sunthorn Phu couldn't have imagined. She could turn the sound of a crash from the street into a drama of foreign spies and government agents. She never told the same story twice and never once disappointed with the ending. Supot and Tam were two of the few children in their school that looked forward to going home in the evening.

When Supot was fourteen, Oi had died. TB suddenly took her voice first, then the rest of her. She'd had no time to plan for the children. She wasn't supposed to die. She just had to get over a cough that didn't want to go away. In Bangkok a cough wasn't such a rare thing. A lot of people wouldn't have been themselves without their coughs. She didn't have time to see a doctor, but when she couldn't put it off any longer, it was too late.

Supot could see no reason to stay in school once Oi was gone. He didn't see it as betraying her. He just didn't have any other option; he had to keep himself and Tam alive. There were no other relatives to take them in. He portered at the cloth stores in Chinatown for a few years and worked odd jobs. But he wasn't much of a breadwinner. They were forced out of their house after only six months for not keeping up with the rent, and Tam left school at thirteen. By fourteen she was living with a boyfriend of sorts, technically a pedophile; a definition that was often glossed over in the land of smiles. But, either way, her life no longer headed in a forward direction. She had no dreams or ambitions, no goals, no hope.

Supot did short stints at more jobs than most. He didn't settle into any of them. He'd lost touch with Ali for most of that time and didn't know where his friend was or what he was doing. Then, one day he'd been walking along the high street and happened to be looking at the posters in a video shop. The big movie marketing firms had gone out of their way to make Hollywood blockbusters more appealing to a Thai audience. A full-bosomed, bikini-clad Sandra Bullock helplessly entangled in a net in a film about identity theft. Batman sporting a whip with his arm around a bikini-clad girl in a movie subtitled *The Man in Leather Loves Forever*. And a movie about an adorable baby pig retitled *Don't Let Them Cut Me Up in the Abattoir*. The poster showed little Babe being rescued by yet another bikini-clad girl built not unlike Sandra Bullock.

There was a bang on the window. Ali had pushed his nose

up to the glass and breathed a cloud onto it. He wrote "dick-head" on it with his index finger. That encounter was the turning point in Supot's life. There were those who believed if he hadn't met Ali that day he would have landed with a bad crowd, taken up drugs, and flushed himself down that drain that claims all the defeated young men.

There was no question in Ali's mind that Supot would come to work with him in the shop. Supot didn't know then that his friend had to borrow the money for Supot's salary from his ma. It was just a stroke of luck that he could suddenly do something he liked and get paid for it. He'd worked at the shop for a year. It was enough to help him get his life together. He'd found somewhere to live and, inadvertently, fell in love with films. They weren't a complete replacement for Oi's stories, but movies certainly filled a gap in his life. Ali introduced him slowly to all the Thai stars and directors. Then Ali weaned him on to big-name foreign films and ultimately to the old classics he came to love.

Supot eventually realized what a sacrifice Ali had made for him and set about paying him back. He studied for the Royal Thai Mail exams and took a job at the district office. It wasn't a cause for celebration, but it did bring in a living wage, and he still had Ali's shop for his distractions. Once the debt was cleared, he lovingly volunteered his free time to help out his friend. Being a postman was an intermission between films. He blobbed around on his Royal Thai Mail service Honda, then got off and blobbed around some more on foot until all the letters were gone. There was nothing about the job to tax his mind. He didn't have to think about anything most days. Once in a while, however, the unexpected happened, and he always yearned for those days.

Supot had been expecting the axe fight between old Mrs. Wangkum and her husband for quite some time. She baked sticky rice in bamboo for a living. Supot often passed her in the yard and watched her cut the bamboo to length with her axe. Her husband, still not old enough to know better, was having an affair with a fifty-year-old lady who swept the streets. Both women dipped into their unspectacular pay packets to stop him from getting thirsty for Thai whisky.

Supot knew there'd be a boil-over, especially given that the sweeping lady cleaned the street in front of Mrs. Wangkum's house and had a habit of singing country songs with Mr. Wangkum's name substituted in for that of the lover. When Supot arrived at the house on a day that, unbeknownst to him at the time, would have a remarkable effect on his life, there was a small audience of neighbors gathered in front of the Wangkums' place. They were listening to the obscenities issuing forth from the woman's mouth inside the house. Her husband appeared to be sobbing and begging for mercy.

If Supot hadn't had a registered letter that needed a signature, he would probably have walked on by. Domestic violence wasn't one of his strong points. But nothing interrupted the Royal Thai Mail. Not then anyway. He pushed through the crowd and knocked on the door frame. As he wasn't able to interrupt Mrs. Wangkum from her tirade, he knocked louder and called out, "Registered letter!"

Mrs. Wangkum, in a fit of fury that filled the onlookers with terror, came running to the front door with hatred still in her eyes and the axe raised above her head. There was no blood on it yet, so Supot assumed Mr. Wangkum was still in one piece. The idea that he was in danger himself didn't enter his head. Or perhaps it did, and he didn't care. Maybe being sliced down the middle was his big something.

This was one of the rare occasions he exceeded his duty as an operative of the RTM. He told her she had to sign for the letter and held out the pen. He showed no fear because he felt none. It caused her a moment of indecision. She asked him to hold the axe while she took the receipt pad and pen and signed. He could have just handed her the letter and the axe and gone home, but he didn't. He slipped off his boots, stepped inside the house, and went to make them all a cup of tea.

Mr. Wangkum was cowering in the corner of the kitchen when Supot entered, weeping like a baby. Supot didn't actually say anything to the couple. What would a man with no imagination say in a situation like that? The three of them sat on the couch, drank their tea in silence, then he left. In the street he handed the axe to the local headman and walked off.

Anything interesting happen at work today?" Ali asked.

Supot told him about the incident with the Wangkums. He told it without embellishment or exaggeration. He told it as he saw it in his mind's eye and seemed surprised when Ali said what a heroic act it was.

"Nothing heroic," Supot confessed.

"Why did you do it, then?" Ali asked.

"I had a registered letter. They fine you at the post office if you deliver them late. If they'd taken away Mrs. Wangkum for axing her old man, I'd have to spend half a day at police headquarters trying to get her signature."

"What a job you've got yourself, Supot. Move on. You can't be a postman all your life."

"Why not? You can be a video rental pauper all your life."

"That's totally different. We poor people don't get attacked by axe murderers and mad dogs."

The speckled bandage on Supot's hand was now grubbily gray.

"Just mad Welsh tourists," said Supot.

Ali nodded. For a few months, he'd been toying with a film script that he hoped might one day make him famous. There had been many such fizzled-out startups. It opened with a handsome Muslim man named Ali, being randomly attacked on the street as he walked in front of a bar. That was the total sum of its progress. Ali had only recently admitted the aggressor might have been Welsh. Up to this point, Supot wasn't sure how much of the story was based on truth, since his friend had sported a head bandage for a week. There had been an incident with a foreigner, of that he was sure, but Ali had given a dozen or so versions as to what had happened. He said he was seeking credibility.

"Right," said Ali. "I've been contemplating that. I think I've worked out the moral elements. He isn't attacking me, per se."

"This isn't going to be political, is it?" asked Supot. "You know, political films have a short shelf life."

"Then let's call it a cultural exposé. I'm walking past a street side bar. It's two o'clock in the afternoon and there are half a dozen foreigners drinking there. One is sitting on a stool overlooking the street. I smile at him, and I ask him how he is."

"In Thai?"

"In Thai. But I say, *'Sawat dee crap?'* and he thinks I've said something else. Something disgusting in Welsh. It's a common mistake."

"No, it isn't."

"All right, it isn't that common, but he's drunk, and he's depressed because his girlfriend has just left him. One of the girls in the bar explains what I'd said, and he's immediately filled with remorse. So begins our relationship. What do you think?"

"It needs a bit of polishing."

"Right."

"And you do all this in English?"

"Naturally. We can't expect tourists to speak Thai, can we?"

"And just to think, only a month ago you couldn't speak a word."

"It came flooding back to me from those four English lessons we had at elementary school."

"Then I'm in luck. Tonight, ladies and gentlemen, we are honored to present a film in that very language. *The Big Sleep.* You can translate it for me."

They were already in the premiere opera supreme seats at the back of the shop. The seats were stuffed purple armchairs, the type you might find in a museum at the palace. They'd rescued them from a skip outside an old Chinese colonial home that was being pulled down. Once Supot and Ali had gassed the creatures living inside, there was hardly a thing wrong with them. They'd wheeled them the ten blocks it took to get to the shop. They were so big they didn't fit through the door without taking the castors off. It was all worth the effort, though, like watching films in heaven, wrapped in clouds. There was only a shower curtain separating their crammed, windowless alcove from the cluttered shop. A total area no more than the size of a squash court, but it was their nirvana.

This was it. This was what they loved about the shop. The six and a half customers they averaged a night gone. The almost English WE ARE CLOSE sign on the door. The lights out. This was their time to get lost in a film.

"You ready?" Ali asked. He held the remote in his hand like a weapon and threatened the player with it.

"Yes, sir," said Supot. "You had a pee yet?"

"All clear." Ali pressed the button, the blue rectangle flicked to gray, and the opening credits began to roll.

They regarded all the films with deference. They weren't allowed to speak or run out in the middle. The shop would have to be burned to the ground in a slum fire to make them interrupt the showing. They treated the performances like stage plays, where the actors could look down and see who was crunching peanuts or slurping Sprite. There had to be mutual respect. Even if they didn't understand the words. Even if the subtitles didn't make a jot of sense. There still had to be respect for the craft of the performers.

They never worked out who murdered who and who survived in *The Big Sleep,* but it was still one of their favorites. If Humphrey Bogart were looking down from the stage, he would have seen Ali living his role for him, miming his tough-guy scenes, aping his facial expressions.

Supot had been lost in the aura of Lauren Bacall from the moment she appeared on-screen. From the moment she said . . . whatever it was she said. He was hooked like a Mekong catfish. She had style. She wasn't Gene Tierney, but she had something better. Bogart once said she made love to the camera. As Supot was standing immediately behind that camera, he was indirectly being made love to by Lauren Bacall. She must have known what effect she was having on the men in the cinema. Supot's horny, heartless father probably sat at the Lido dribbling down his pencil tie whenever she appeared. That would have been pornography in his father's day.

They weren't sure who was to blame for not locking the shop door that night. Given the trouble that started because of it, it was costly, not in terms of money, but in terms of people's lives getting rearranged. In terms of nothing ever being the same again.

They were lost in the film. Philip Marlowe's big gun was blasting so loudly they didn't hear the tinkle of the bell. The man made it all the way across the shop and was standing so close they smelled him before they saw him. They certainly heard him.

"Hey, you two."

When people say something made them jump, it's an expression. They don't actually mean they jumped. It's modest hyperbole, an exaggeration to make a point. But when that greeting came from a previously empty space behind Supot and Ali, there was a plausible gap between their backsides and the stuffing on the opera supreme seats.

Standing behind them was Woot, one of the sorriest street tramps you could ever hope to avoid on a dark night. He donned what once might have been a combat army uniform but was now so black it could only offer up camouflage after a bush fire. He wore his unkempt hair on the left and his only flip-flop sandal on the right. He had a beaten-up Singha beer carton under his arm.

Supot and Ali shouted together, "WOOT!"

Supot was taking deep breaths to slow his bucking heart. "Woot, you frightened the bloody life out of me," he said.

Woot smiled with the last stubborn tooth still squatting in his otherwise vacated mouth. "Sorry. I didn't realize you two was having one of your . . . intimate moments."

"How did you get in?" Ali asked.

"Well, I had planned to waft through the glass window like a radio wave, or squeeze through the air vent like a lizard, but then I thought twice about it and came in through the door instead. I thought you'd be more pleased to see me. I've bought you some stock." He walked over and plonked the old cardboard beer carton on the small table between the chairs.

The scent of him turned the air putrid. It was as if a corpse had dropped from the ceiling and was decaying there in front of them. Ali switched on the light. He apologized to

Humphrey and Lauren by *wai*'ing a prayer at them before pausing the film.

"You should be ashamed of yourself, creeping around like that," said Ali. "Is this found stock, borrowed stock, or just plain stolen stock?"

A look of wounded indignation came over Woot's face. "Don't be rude," he said. "These are from my own personal collection. I've decided to part with them. It breaks my heart, but with the advent of new technology, I feel the need to take a step up."

"Really? And there we were believing you didn't have a TV," said Supot. "Or electricity."

"Or a house," said Ali. He'd managed to get his pulse rate below a hundred. He peeled back the flaps of the box and took out the videos.

Woot, slighted beyond repair, made to grab them back. "I could take these elsewhere, you know?" he said.

"Somewhere like the police station?" Ali suggested.

Supot took the last of the cassettes from the box and shook his head.

"They aren't stolen," said Woot. "You are a wicked boy. Wicked." He gestured dramatically to the sky. "I call upon the spirits of Bangkok Noi to come and haunt your shop and you in it."

"Really? Well, thanks. I could use the extra customers." Ali wasn't too disturbed.

Supot threw down the last of the stock and collapsed back into the opera supreme. "This is all crap," he said. "We don't want it."

Woot's jaw dropped. "Come on, Pot. I got it from a professional man. That's all quality film in there."

"No, it isn't. It's crap. Here, take it away."

Woot was devastated. They knew he didn't know anyone

else in the entertainment business. He'd been sure the two "weird boys" would give him plenty for his windfall.

"Guys. Help an old man out, won't you?" He coughed and churned up something deep in his lung.

"You just brought down the spirits of Bangkok Noi on my shop," said Ali. "Allah won't like that. Why should we help you?"

"All right. All right. I'll call them off." He fell to his knees and looked up at the white halos around the fluorescents. "Spirits. Do not fall upon these two good men, because they are going to give me . . . one thousand baht to save my wretched life."

Supot laughed. "One thousand baht? For all this second-hand junk? We could buy new ones for that."

"I don't make that much all year," said Ali. "Here." He reached into his pocket and took out a scoop of loose change. "Take this and never haunt my shop again." He handed the money to Woot and returned to his chair.

Woot knew it wasn't a lot, but he counted it to make sure.

"Two hundred baht? Two hundred baht? Be reasonable. The box alone is worth that much."

Supot picked up the box and threw it at him.

"Good. Then you can take the box back and sell it. Good night, Woot," said Ali.

"Good night, Woot," said Supot.

Woot looked indignant. "If I starve to death tonight, it will be a lump of granite in your souls forever."

He shuffled out of the shop grumbling, but with a smile on his tooth. Even though his body left, his essence would stay around for days. Once he'd gone, Ali started to go through the swag.

"How did we do?" Supot asked.

"We just robbed an old street person. I hope you're pleased with yourself."

Ali couldn't believe what he was seeing. He was tempted to run after the old bum and give him more money. This was theft, plain and simple. They stood on either side of the heap, checking that the tapes inside their cases were those advertised on the covers. They all seemed to match, and their condition was surprisingly good, considering they'd lived in a damp cardboard box for goodness knew how long. Ali's pulse was back in the nineties.

"Wow, Supot," he said. "There are two oldies: *The Blue Angel* and *Persona,* but most of them are film-award winners from last year: *Rendezvous in Paris, Ulysses' Gaze, Underground, Wild Reeds.* All of it's European. Collector's heaven. Where did a homeless bum like him get all this? I'm excited, Supot. I'll have to ask my imam if I'm allowed to feel like this."

"You know, Ali, we shouldn't get too excited just yet."

"Why not?"

"You remember what happened with the classics we bought at Chatuchak Market."

"What happened? The films were all in good shape. They didn't have voice-overs."

"Right. But they didn't have subtitles, either. To this day we don't know what the heck *Naked Lunch* was all about. And we had to corner a French professor at Chula to explain the finer points of *Mon Oncle.* There are a dozen films here. If they haven't got subtitles, we'll—"

"All right. All right. I get it."

Ali *wai*'d again and ejected Humphrey, laying him respectfully back in his container like an undead corpse into a coffin. He replaced him with the first of the new arrivals: *The Blue Angel,* which neither of them had seen. Given the identity of the female lead, their motivation was obvious. Instinctively, they turned off the light, sat back in the seats, and watched. The screen remained black for some time, then followed the opening credits to the overture of "Falling in Love Again."

"See? No subtitles," said Supot.

"It hasn't started yet. Be patient."

**INT. BUSY TOWN SQUARE — DAYTIME**

VILLAGERS ARE MILLING AROUND, BUSILY. SOUNDTRACK OF DUCKS BEING MANHANDLED AND GENERAL BUSTLING.

"Can't see any subtitles," said Supot.

"Look," said Ali. "It's a market. Nobody's saying anything important. Just calm down and watch."

Supot calmed down, but it was obvious they'd selected the wrong film to check on subtitles. The scene cut to a professor's sprawling but untidy home office. A maid entered and said something like, "Breakfast, professor." No subtitles. Supot was about to mention the fact but was shot down by Ali's glare. In fact, it was twelve minutes into the film before anyone managed a sentence, and another three before Ali was convinced. But by then they were into the movie and, as Ali said, "Who needs subtitles when you can listen to Marlene Dietrich sing in a frilly swimsuit?"

It was after midnight when the closing credits and the boys' eyelids began to roll. They'd loved the film but had no idea what it was all about. They began loading the cassettes into a lockable cupboard. Ali had read about all the films but had seen only two of them. Out of all the videos, only one was a mystery offering. It was in a plain white box. The title was written in felt pen on the spine.

"What's this?" Ali asked.

"*Bangkok 2010*," Supot read. "Never heard of it. Must be a documentary. Or a home holiday video."

"Doesn't really fit in with this lot, does it?" Ali tossed it to one side and went back to stacking the new cassettes. "You fancy a couple of days off work?" he asked.

"I always fancy a couple of days off work," said Supot. "But I've had my quota this month, and we aren't into the third week yet."

"You want to see the end of Humphrey?" Ali waved the remote.

"No, I've lost the mood now, and I'm buggered. We can finish it tomorrow . . . if Lauren can ever forgive us for pausing her." He stood up and stretched himself painfully like a man eight times his age. "I have to get up and be abused by the mail-receiving public tomorrow."

Ali looked up at the store clock over the counter. "Today."

"Shit. The job's bad enough when I've had a full night's sleep."

At six-thirty, Supot sat on a little stool sorting mail. He wasn't nearly awake enough to do it properly. Beside him sat Chet, a real postman—fast, efficient, proud of his light brown uniform and his long service bar. Thirty-five years in the Royal Thai Mail with only two days of absence. He stopped at one white packet with an address sticker attached.

"Pot. This look like cocaine to you?" he asked.

Supot licked his finger, dug his fingernail into the parcel, and tasted it. "Could be."

"They get more brazen every day," said Chet, then threw the letter off to one side and carried on with his work.

Supot looked around at the mountain range of mail they still had to sort. "There's a lot today," he said.

"No more than usual, boy."

The open post office sorting room backed onto a humble garden at its rear. Beyond was a white wall that hid the neighboring tofu factory from the eye but not from the nose. There was a concrete bench in the yard, but Supot couldn't recall anyone ever sitting on it. He put that down to the myna bird droppings and the fact the only view from the seat was of the water tank. But, every day, Chet voluntarily tended the garden and shared the chilis that grew there with his fellow postal workers. Supot stopped to watch the old man work. He was always amazed; Chet was like an efficient piece of high-tech machinery. Grab, look, sort. Grab, look, sort.

Supot didn't have much of an aptitude for being a post-man. He worked with people like Chet, who were natural at it. It was as if they'd been born with a frank stamp instead of a birthmark. They smiled and whistled and patted little children on the head. They knew every street, knew all their customers by name, and gave advice about muscle aches and lottery numbers. Supot wasn't that type of postman. He just delivered letters.

"You like this work, don't you?" said Supot.

He knew "like" was a poor choice of word.

"It's an honor to handle the mail," said Chet. "My family's worked in the post office for four generations. They were all so proud when I passed the entrance test. Weren't you?"

"I was amazed."

"See? You can't get a better job. You get to use your brain. You get exercise. You get to meet famous people. You get to—"

"Who?" Supot asked.

"What?"

"Famous people. You said you get to meet famous people. I've never met anyone famous. Who have you met?"

"They're everywhere."

"They are not. Who?"

"Movie stars."

Now, that really was a joke. Movie stars in Bangkok Noi. Supot couldn't imagine Thai tourists on open-top bus trips around that grimy suburb spotting the homes of the stars. Looking at little celebrity maps. He laughed.

"Name me one."

"What?"

"Name me one famous movie star on your round."

"Anchalee Anonruk."

Supot leaned back on his stool and almost toppled over. "Liar. Anchalee Anonruk does not live around here."

Anchalee was Thai cinema royalty. She'd appeared in twenty or more films in the seventies and early eighties and was one of the great presences of the Thai silver screen.

"Really, she does," said Chet. "Over on Soi 22. Narok Thani. Number 21B."

It wasn't till after his shift that day that Supot could get to Narok Thani, number 21B. It wasn't on his route. It was a bizarrely remarkable and embarrassingly small house. Greek pillars that could easily have held up the lintel of the Acropolis were supporting a Perspex porch roof. Each corner had its own gargoyle. A small brook with a water wheel and stepping-stones trinkled around the yard. It was as if the owners had spent all their money on the accessories and were forced to live in the packing case they'd arrived in.

He stood in front of a large, locked fret-iron gate. In his mind he had the standard shot of Anchalee Anonruk in one of her trademark glamorous roles: big hair, thick makeup, Darlie toothpaste smile. Getting a glimpse of her would really make his day. He unwrapped the bandage from his dog-ravaged hand and dropped it in the garbage bin in front of the house. First impressions counted.

A frumpy old maid in curlers and pink Chinese pajamas was out in the yard dishing up dinner for an overweight shih tzu and sweeping up its droppings with a straw broom. She looked over at Supot and noticed he had a letter in his hand.

"Is that for here?" she asked.

"No," he replied. He had no intention of being diverted from his mission by a woman who wore bed attire in the early evening.

"You got a letter there for this house?" she persevered and walked toward the gate, wiping the sweat from her hands down the leg of her pajamas.

"No."

"What's that in your hand then?"

"It's a 3HH 7d." He looked past her to the upstairs window. There was movement. He felt sure the actress was looking down at them. She'd soon join them to sort out the confusion.

"Is that like a letter?" the maid asked.

"Yeah. It's like a letter, but it has to be delivered personally to Ms. Anchalee," he said.

She held out her hand through the bars like one of the sad monkeys at Dusit Zoo and spat out her gum.

"Right. Give it here then. That's me."


Ali and Supot sat cross-legged on the floor, indexing the new videos and putting them on the classics shelf. The collection was becoming quite impressive—a modest altar to the golden ages of cinema. Ali was still disturbed by the news.

"I can't believe it," Ali said.

"I couldn't."

"Like a common housewife."

"Like a common maid. It was humiliating. And you should have heard the language she used when she found out the envelope was empty. I don't know. One of our biggest stars. How are we going to have our own Joan Crawford, our own Greta Garbo, when our top actresses sweep up their own dog shit?"

"Exactly. I bet Greta Garbo employed a person just to clean up after the dogs. A team perhaps."

"I know for a fact she didn't use foul language in public," said Supot. "We need people like that. It's not like our big stars can't act . . ."

"Some can't."

"Right. But it's not just the acting we're talking about here. Acting's important, but there's . . . something else you need to be a star."

"Presence."

"Charisma."

"Can you imagine Marlena Dietrich putting out her own garbage?" said Ali, pinching his nose between a thumb and forefinger.

"It would never happen."

"Never."

They were warming up now, heading toward a familiar finale.

"There has to be some magic the actor brings to the screen. It shouldn't be like working in a bank, having lunch in the market, taking the bus home," said Ali.

"It has to be your life," said Supot. "You're carrying the hearts of every one of your fans around in your soul. You as a person no longer exist. You are above the earth like a rainbow. You certainly don't sweep up dog poo."

"Exactly."

They worked in silence for a minute or two.

"I get the feeling we've had that conversation before," said Ali.

"It sounded familiar."

They never made a difference, these discussions. Neither disagreed with the other. Movie stars were gods. If this were the tenth century, they'd be sacrificing virgins and sheep to them. Actors could and *should* do no wrong.

Supot had the *Bangkok 2010* boxed tape in his hand, wondering where to put it. "What do we do with this?" he finally asked Ali.

"I guess we'll have to take a look at it," Ali told him. "See what it is. Then we'll know where it goes."

"Okay. I'll take it home and watch it there. I'm too depressed to stay here."

"You can't just walk out on me like that. Do you want to get yourself fired?"

"First you pay me, then you can fire me."

"Oh, yeah. Here. This'll cheer you up before you go. I've been working on it all day. I have a scene two for my movie script."

"Have we agreed on scene one yet?"

"Pretty much. But scene two is a hit. I get a phone call from the British embassy. You remember the tourist?"

"The one that brained you with a stool?"

"That's the one. They tell Ali—our star—they tell him the Welshman is still filled with remorse for what he did."

"Wait. Why does he have to be Welsh?"

"Because he was."

"Was what?"

"Welsh."

"Right."

"He wants to make amends," said Ali.

"Money?"

"Better than that. You know? The guy feels so bad about hitting me with the stool that he wants to help out at our house. Volunteer work."

"Doing what?"

"Not sure yet. Maybe, you know, plumbing?"

"What does your ma say?"

"She's all for it, as long as he doesn't stay overnight."

"Nice. Get it on paper while it's fresh."

Ten minutes later, Supot was on the bus. He could have walked home in twenty minutes, but it wasn't as if he'd get any health benefits from a stroll. The smog never really went away. The streets weren't as clogged at night, but the cars were liberated by that fact and got out of second gear whenever they could. Most accidents involving pedestrians happened between 10 P.M. and 4 A.M. in Bangkok Noi.

He must have dropped off for a while because he had a nightmare about a love scene starring Anchalee Anonruk looking like a maid. Her dirty, garbage-covered hand caressed the cheek of her handsome leading man. Little scraps of vegetable rinds and chicken skin were left there. Her maid-like unmade face leaned into a kiss. Her teeth were crimson with betel nut. Supot pulled out of the dream just in time before they kissed. His bus stop sped past on the inside lane.

"Wait. Wait. I'm getting off."

The maid incident had left a deep impression on him. He wasn't sure he could ever watch a Thai film again. He'd developed a nervous Indian head shake because of it. He still couldn't believe it. He walked up the staircase and along the balcony to his bachelor apartment. It was only a bachelor apartment because he lived in it. The place next door had a couple with a baby. It was the same small rectangle as his, but that was called a family unit. They all had one main room with a double bed and a couch, a pokey little kitchenette at the back, and an even pokier little bathroom with no bath. The back balcony wasn't broad enough to stand with your feet facing forward, and the view was of an identical building. It was like looking in a huge mirror, but for the fact that he wasn't in the reflection.

He rented. He admired watching his wages soar off into the pocket of a rich speculator. But the good point was that he had no obligation to keep the place neat and undamaged. The door key found its way to the front of the bunch. He still hadn't forgiven them for the dog massacre. He rattled the door open.

"Honey," he said. "I'm home. Oh. I forgot. I'm not married."

It was Michelle Pfeiffer's line from one of the Batman movies. It was the only English phrase he'd ever bothered to learn, so he said it every time he came home. The neighbors probably thought he was married to a foreigner. Or mentally unstable. In the shower, as usual, he acted out the scene from *Psycho* using a toothbrush, pretending his arm was someone else's. So, on some official scale of palpable sanity, he was probably nuts.

Even though he wasn't planning to sleep, he put on his bed singlet and shorts and watched the kettle boil. He supplemented a double helping of Wai Wai instant noodles with peanuts. They were as close to vegetables as damn it.

He put the *2010* video in the player, sat on the sofa, and, as luck would have it, dropped the remote into the noodles. While licking it clean, he accidentally activated the machine. Supot rarely did things the way human beings were programmed to.

*Bangkok 2010* seemed to be a movie. It was obviously a rough cut that wasn't prepared for the stores. There were no ads or warnings that the FBI would shoot him if he was showing it in public. A countdown appeared on the screen.

"All right, *Bangkok 2010*. Let's see what contribution you have to make to the reputation of Thai cinema."

The opening credits started to run. The director was called Ketgaew. Supot had never heard of him, but the start was good. It was a clever technique. Dark shadows of shuffling people dragged the titles back and forth across the screen. Each caption was erased by another shuffling person dragging their own caption in the opposite direction. It was polished, unusual, unexpected, shot in black and white . . . mostly black.

"Hm. Clever," mumbled Supot. "Couldn't afford color, eh, Mr. Ketgaew?"

He read down the credits. "I've never heard of any of you lot. Must be amateur hour."

*Bangkok 2010*

## 1 EXT. OPENING SCENE — EARLY MORNING

```
A gloomy black-and-white art nouveau
Bangkok. The skyscrapers are obviously
a beautifully painted backdrop, but the
heavy smog makes them hard to see. The cam-
era is at street level, looking up to
show a lot of depressed people walk-
ing to work. All of them are wearing
smog masks and unusual clothes. Unmov-
ing, futuristic traffic, sleek and shiny
like rocket parts, clog the street. The
vehicles aren't clearly visible through
the fog, but the drivers are so comatose
they could be corpses.
```

"Brilliant. I like that," said Supot.

## 2 CU. WATERPROOF BOOTS. TRUDGING THROUGH ANKLE-DEEP POLLUTED WATER.

```
They step over sandbags into the door-
way of a large high-rise building.
After the figure has gone in through
the door, the camera pans upward to the
sign, MINISTRY OF SECURITY.
```

## 3 INT. LOBBY — DAY

The feet step in through the doorway and walk along a line of shoes on racks that have the sizes on them like bowling shoes. The feet step out of the boots and into a pair of high-heeled shoes. That's the first indication that this is a woman. The boots are left in their place. We follow the feet toward a counter, where they stop.

Off camera, in Thai, a man's voice says:

> **RECEPTIONIST**
> You got an appointment, citizen?

The voice of the mystery woman, also off camera, answers:

> **SIRILUK**
> I sure do, handsome. Citizen Siriluk 81,988. Eight hundred hours. To see Captain Nikom.

A few seconds pass while the man looks up the name.

> **RECEPTIONIST**
> I see it. Go on up. Forty-seventh floor. Room 47X.

**SIRILUK**
Thanks, darling.

**4 INT. CU. HIGH-HEELED SHOES.**

The feet, walking elegantly now in the heeled shoes, go over to the elevator and step inside. The lift door slides down like a guillotine.

The screen splits, one camera travels to the top of the skyscraper from the outside, a second camera scans slowly up the body of the woman. She's wearing a very stylishly cut skirt suit, the type Joan Crawford would wear, but silver. Her slim, muscular stomach is exposed, and a ruby stud decorates her navel. By the time the camera reaches her face, the wait has been worth it. The total effect is complete.

She's stunningly beautiful. Her long hair cascades down either side of her face in glossy ebony waves. Her eyes are those of a puma. Her smile is perfect. She's holding a compact mirror to her face. On the mirror is a small pile of dark powder that she gathers into the center of the glass. She lights it with a lighter and inhales the smoke. It's obviously a stimulant. She shudders from the hit.

Her voice is gruff and sexy.

**SIRILUK**
(under her breath)
That's better. Now I can handle
your shit, Comrade Bundtut.

She studies her face in the mirrored
elevator and nods her approval.

Supot was frozen. The noodles dangled from his fork—he hadn't eaten a single strand. His eyes bulged at the amazing woman he was seeing on the screen.

"Who . . . are . . . you?"

She only answered indirectly. Her name in the credits and in the film was Siriluk. It was the name of Supot's first girlfriend in primary school, so it was significant to him. But it wasn't that connection that had him entranced. He knew he was witnessing the birth of a Thai diva. Everything he loved about stars in Western films was there on the screen in front of him. She had a natural presence. She was remarkable.

The film lasted ninety-eight minutes. Ninety-eight minutes Supot never wanted to end. The abandoned bowl of Wai Wai instant noodles sat untouched at his feet. On the screen the final scene sadly arrived.

**61 EXT. BALCONY SCENE — DAY**

Tears are pouring from Siriluk's eyes
as she sits crumpled and bruised on the
dirty ground. She sobs her last line.

**SIRILUK**
No. It wasn't supposed to end
like this. God help us all.

CUT TO FINAL CREDITS
ROUSING MUSIC PLAYS
THE END.

Supot, crumpled and inwardly bruised on the sofa, tears pouring from his eyes, exhausted from the emotional ride, applauded.

"Wow."

He got to his feet, grabbed a pen and paper, and paused the tape, so he could write down the names of the actors and crew. They were mostly Thai. He *wai*'d them.

"Thank you. Thank you very much. Thank you, Kn. Vongkot. Thank you, Kn. Siriluk. Thank you, Kn. Sunisa. Thank you, Kn. Khanthon. Thank you, Kn. Chiangkoon . . ."

He put the list to one side, sighed, and stared at the snowstorm on the screen. He wondered whether the television was aware of what had taken place in that small apartment on that peculiar day. If it had any human traits at all, it would never forget the night *Bangkok 2010* made its debut in their lives. There was no way to end the delight. No way to go to bed. No way he could sleep. He listened to the distant hum of traffic crossing the Phra Pinklao Bridge and the frustrating tutting of his ceiling lizards. He rewound the tape and restarted the miracle.

As always, Ali arrived at the shop on his motorcycle at a quarter to nine. He'd prayed for world peace and happiness at the mosque that morning but, as far as he could recall, hadn't asked for an unexpected delivery from the postal service. Supot, in shorts and a Red Bull running singlet, was curled up on his doorstep. Ali went over and prodded him to see if he was dead. The body moved.

"Allah, help us. What are you doing here? Why aren't you in your secret postman disguise?"

Supot came around slowly and painfully like a shipwreck victim impaled on coral. "I'm off sick," he said.

"You look sick, man. You look like you spent the night in a spin dryer. What the hell happened to you?"

Supot fumbled around on the step behind him. After a slight moment of what appeared to be panic, he found and held up *Bangkok 2010* in a transparent plastic bag.

"This happened to me, brother."

"Eh?"

"I've watched it four times." He creaked to his feet and grabbed his friend by the shirt collar. "Now, you're going to watch it."

Supot was nervous. It was like asking someone to read a story you've written. You want them to like it, but you're afraid they won't, which would inevitably break your heart. That was how he watched *Bangkok 2010* that morning—one eye on the screen and the other on Ali. The signs were good because Ali didn't seem aware he was being watched. Neither did he appear to be breathing.

A customer made the mistake of coming into the shop during this first public showing of *Bangkok 2010* in hopes of renting a romantic video for her aunt and herself to watch before lunch. Supot and Ali did not hear the bell as she entered. So, she went back, opened and closed the door several times to alert them of her presence. They were obviously quite deaf. So, she shouted, "Excuse me!"

Not only did the two rude men not turn around, but one also said, "Shhh."

The other went so far as to tell her to go away. She was taken aback but undaunted.

"I want something by . . ."

"Go away," said Ali. "Can't you see we're watching something?"

She fled in a steam of anger, vowing never to be seen again at Ali's Video Rental. Ali didn't care.

"Go and lock the door, Supot."

"You lock the bloody thing. It's your door."

"I'm busy."

Supot reluctantly ran and locked the door as quickly as he could. He knew the film only too well already, but every time he watched it, he saw something new. He wondered if anyone had ever starved to death from enthrallment, dazzled to malnutrition by cinematic magic, not realizing they hadn't eaten for a week.

Ali barely moved. When they arrived at the final scene, Supot lip-synced with Siriluk, not waiting to spoil it for Ali.

*"No. It wasn't supposed to end like this. God help us all."*

Once the music climbed to its peak and the credits rolled, Supot stared grinning at Ali, who looked like he'd finished in a medal position in the Olympics marathon.

"Wow."

"That's what I said."

"It's brilliant," said Ali.

"Isn't it?"

"It's a mixture of present and past and future, and . . . some other time too. The filming's incredible. They make black and white look sensational. And they can all act."

"I've got a serious thing for the actress."

"Me too."

"You leave her alone. She's mine. Plus, you're engaged."

"Kwang's got nothing in writing."

Ali was still watching the credits. "Who are all those people? I've never heard of any of them."

"That's just it." Supot pulled a crumpled sheet of paper from his pocket. "Look here. I've copied down the names of everyone: the actors, the director, camera, sound, everyone. The movie production was dated 1996, but I don't know any of these people."

Ali took the list and scanned down the page for a familiar name.

"I bet they're all from Hong Kong and are pretending to be Thai . . . for tax purposes."

Supot looked at him to see if he was being serious. You never could tell with Ali.

"There are a few foreign names here," said Supot. "All I can think of is that they're Thai film school graduates that got together to make a movie . . . a *great* movie."

"Then why didn't they release it? It hasn't been at the cinemas. I haven't seen it advertised, and it isn't on our video lists. Thai audiences would love it."

"Perhaps they haven't released it yet, but they plan to. It isn't that easy to distribute a new film without financial backing. What if they're holding it back and this is a leaked copy?" Supot stood, went over to the little kitchen area, and held up a pack of noodles. "You want some breakfast? I'm starving."

"No, thanks," said Ali. "We all had poached eggs and fried bread for breakfast this morning."

"Wouldn't it be something if we can get in touch with these people, you know?" said Supot. "We could get to be fans before they're famous. We'd be like pioneer groupies." He started preparing the noodles, but his slow morning mind wasn't taking in information as quickly as his ears.

"Poached eggs and fried bread? Your ma run out of rice soup?" Supot said, finally catching up.

Ali walked over to join him.

"Dylan, the Welsh volunteer, was at our front door at six. He still needs some training. But he cooks great. We'll teach him to make Thai food. He taught my aunt how to shear a sheep using her poodle as a model."

Supot raised his eyebrows. Ali called his style "method screenwriting." You had to live the story you were creating. Supot could never tell what was real and what was imagined. But he worried that Ali might have the same problem. Supot decided he needed some quality control on his product.

"I've got a few queries about this screenplay of yours," said Supot.

"Ma's going to get him to fix the back fence," said Ali, ignoring him.

As the noodles slowly turned into food, Ali looked across at the dull TV screen. It was hard to imagine it had been the site of such an earthshaking event.

"You don't suppose we could watch this just one more time, do you?" Ali asked.

"Absolutely."


For Supot, it became a strange fixation to solve the mystery of *Bangkok 2010*. A detective story without a crime. There were thirty-some names on the production credits. Somebody had to know one of them at least. You couldn't make a soap commercial in Thailand without somebody in the industry knowing about it. At least that's what he thought.

He didn't really need an investigatory excuse to pay his two baht, climb on the ferry, and cross to a different type of Bangkok on the far bank. He knew the pollution didn't stop at the river, but it was a pollution steeped in history over there. After the ferry ride, he walked beside the whitewashed wall of Thammasat, under flame trees that had been there when the fathers of the fathers of great Thais studied at the university. The royal poincianas had been there before Thammasat was a university at all; they had been there since the founders of the city first laid out the plans for a place of canals and wide avenues to replace the previous capital at Thonburi.

After a wheezy jog, he arrived at the green rectangle of Sanam Luang, where festivals were staged in the day and country people camped at night. He took a left and avoided death by traffic, more by luck than judgment crossing over to Chotana. He smiled at the braless backpackers picnicking on the central reservation. They saw his uniform, thought he was a policeman, and smiled back. By the time he found the National Film Archive building, he was in a happy state of mind.

That happiness didn't last long, though. The archivist was a long-haired but elderly man who spent several minutes looking down the list of names Supot had copied from the video. He read a name, looked up at Supot, then read another name. This continued until the archivist had arrived at the bottom of the list.

"Exactly what kind of film is it?" he asked.

"It's a kind of spy movie, set in the future."

"Do you have it with you?"

"No."

"Then you'll have to bring it in. If I see it, I'll know for certain whose work it is. I don't recognize anyone on the list. Perhaps they're using false names."

"Why would they do that?"

"I don't know. Film people can be a little weird at times."

Supot was getting one of his intuition tingles. It happened when he was around people his heart didn't want him to trust. "Just bring it in. I'm here every day. We can watch it together." He reached over to his desk and held up a pencil to his jotter. "Write down your phone number and I can call you if I get any ideas."

"I don't actually have a phone."

"Mobile?"

"No."

Instead, Supot promised to bring the tape in the next week. He felt a little uneasy at the man's persistence. Even as Supot was leaving, the archivist called out, "What post office are you based at?"

Supot pretended not to hear. He didn't want strangers turning up at work. And there was something possessive, something territorial about his feelings too. It was his secret, his mystery, *his* movie. On his way back to the ferry, he stopped off at Thammasat and was immediately aware of two things. Firstly, the female students had that poise that comes from studying in one of the country's most prestigious universities. Most of them were only a year or two out of high school, but they were already ladies. His heart fluttered about in his chest as he tried his best to have his smile returned. Which brought him to his second observation, each one of them furtively glanced at his uniform and avoided his eyes: he was not the step up in society they were hoping for.

There was no security at the Humanities building, and he asked the students where he might find a teacher who taught film. He was directed to the common room where a dozen or so professors were winding down after a heavy day of what he called eggheadery. He approached one who was closest to his age, a man with styled hair and an uncreased shirt.

"Excuse me," said Supot.

"Ah, you don't need to bring that up here," said the *ajan.* "You could just leave it at the office downstairs."

Everyone expected Supot to be delivering mail. He

wondered what the reaction would be if someone in a naval uniform turned up on campus. Would they expect the sailor to have his boat moored out front?

"I'm off duty," said Supot.

"Oh, sorry," said the man. "What can I do for you?"

Supot told him the fundamentals of his story and showed him the list of names. The *ajan* seemed fascinated but confessed he didn't recognize anyone. He called over a colleague, a pretty, middle-aged woman in a traditional Thai skirt. Only sophisticates and hotel employees bothered to dress that way. Modern Thai women considered it passé. It was a fact that saddened Supot, who was enchanted by women in *phasin*. Neither she nor the man had ever heard of a production like *Bangkok 2010*. They knew of no other works from the director or the producer.

"You might want to try the film archives down on—"

"Just came from there," said Supot.

"It's a fascinating mystery," said the woman. "If there's no record of it in the archives, it can't be that old. I've been teaching film and drama here for ten years. There aren't that many Thai films produced in a year to get lost in the deluge. I would certainly be interested to see it."

"Me also," said the man.

But still, Supot was loath to share his treasure. He took the *ajans'* phone numbers and promised to contact them next time he was in the city. He doubted he'd keep that promise. As he boarded the clunky old ferry, he made a decision. He didn't want film experts crawling all over his *2010*. He could come back if he needed help, but for some reason he couldn't tie down, he had a feeling that the Thammasat *ajans* and the old man at the National Film Archive weren't being totally honest. Or, at least, they weren't telling him everything they knew.

It was about 10 P.M. when Supot was down at the back lots off the deep lanes of Arun Amarin, one of the main roads that strangled Bangkok Noi. All around were the ever-present sounds of traffic and the warring of dogs. Without the benefit of light, Supot found himself stumbling over a dumping ground of broken bottles and black plastic bags full of matter that squelched and crunched. He had to rely on staying close to his guide, a street boy he'd singled out and offered fifty baht to help him out. The kid tiptoed through the garbage and pointed to a pile of junk that leaned up against a graffiti wall. Supot gave him his money, and the boy walked off looking at it, imagining what ills it could do him.

Supot went over to the pile of junk, which turned out to be Woot, leaning drunk against the wall. Woot had lost his dignity many years before. There were those who remembered him as a family man. He'd had a small house, a small wife, and a Ford Anglia that belonged to his old English employer. But the wife and the car were only briefly in Woot's hands. When his employer returned to England, he'd taken Woot's wife with him.

As soon as Woot realized the car was compensation for the woman he loved, he drove it into a canal, where it probably still lingered to this day. Thus, began his romance with rum and his hatred of foreigners.

"Woot." Supot leaned over him and shouted. There was no reaction. "Drunk old Uncle Woot."

Woot crawled out of his stupor like a thick maggot oozing out of an apple hole. "Just leave the room service outside," he slurred. "I'll pick it up after my shower."

"Right," said Supot. "But don't blame me if the cockroaches get it first."

Woot focused on his visitor.

"Pot? Is that you? What a surprise. If I'd known you were coming, I would have tidied the place up a bit. Did the maid give you something cool to drink?"

He pulled himself up to lean against the wall. Supot helped. His eyes were getting used to the darkness. He looked around at the sad landscape.

"Which one of these piles of debris is your home, Woot?"

"It's a time share, young Pot. Me and my fellow street adventurers cannot be tied down to one abode. We just look in through the flap, and if there's nobody inside, we curl up and go to sleep. Such is the magical life of the gypsy. But I'm sure you aren't here to discuss my living conditions."

"You're right. You remember that last batch of films you brought into the shop?"

"I didn't steal them. Really, I didn't, Pot."

Supot cleared a space and sat down on a decommissioned washing machine. Woot slid back down the wall. The man gave off the type of stink you'd expect from someone who hadn't changed his clothes for a decade. Supot had anticipated that. He rubbed Tiger Balm ointment onto his top lip the way a country coroner might do at an autopsy.

"Relax," said Supot. "I haven't transferred from the post office to the police force yet. I don't care how you got them. I only want to know where you got them from. It's important."

Woot appeared to think long and hard about this, then

finally said, "I'd love to help you. You know I would, Pot. You know it's been difficult since the brain operation. The surgery was almost a complete success. But the consulting neurological surgeons all agreed that it would be almost impossible for me to recall historical facts as long as my crania is in need of a constant source of lubrication."

"Would splashing it with water help?" Supot asked.

"It has to be internal, Pot. Normally they used this very expensive chemical to steep my brain in. But . . ."

"Oh. You mean this." Supot reached into his post bag and produced a bottle of Saeng Thip rum. "I don't suppose this would do?"

Woot lit up like a carnival bulb. He grabbed the bottle. "I don't know, Pot. But it's certainly worth a try. What a coincidence. You been talking to the surgeons?"

Woot started to unscrew the cap, but Supot stopped him.

"Yeah. I've been talking to the surgeons." Supot pulled two full plastic bags from his pack. "But they said you can only soak your brain on the condition you fill your stomach at the same time. I'm afraid it's all healthy stuff. They were right out of garbage bin slops. I hope you don't mind."

Woot dipped his dirty fingers into the bags. "Oh, Pot. Such a kind boy. If you weren't so ugly, I'd swear you were the son I gave away at birth." He successfully unscrewed the top of the bottle and took a swig. "You know, it's coming back to me already." He looked around. "No ice?"

Ali sat behind the counter, splicing broken tapes. Supot sat opposite on a stool on the customers' side. They watched as a small, dark, shadowy figure in a towel hat, his collar turned up to hide his face, walked slowly past the window.

"He must be getting tired out there. That's his fifth lap," said Ali.

"Should I just go out and tell him?"

"No. This is a valuable learning experience for him. Finish the story. You went to the dead guy's apartment . . ."

"Yeah. So, I went to the dead guy's apartment and met the landlady. She was the one who'd called Woot over and told him to take away all the stuff she couldn't sell.

She said the guy had been staying there for almost a year. The dead guy. Not Woot."

The character with the towel hat walked slowly in front of the shop again, paused, and looked in.

"He was a quiet, polite fellow," said Supot.

"Woot?"

"No. The dead guy. Pay attention. His name was Vong-kot, like the *2010* producer, but his surname was different. I bet it was him though. I just bet. He paid the rent on time. He didn't have any visitors. Kept himself to himself. She—the landlady—had had no idea he was sick. He didn't smoke or drink. He was out every day, but she didn't know where he went. She felt sorry for him. She said he was a sad type of person. He just wanted to be alone. They didn't talk much."

"I wonder what he did every day," said Ali.

"Now, from there, as Inspector Clouseau might say, 'The trail is not 'ot anymore.' The landlady found him dead on the staircase one morning. She wanted to get in touch with the relatives to take care of the body. But when she went into his apartment, she couldn't find a—"

The bell tinkled, and they looked up to see a shadowy figure walk into the shop. He was a boy, about thirteen. The same mysterious figure who had stalked them for half an hour. He had a penciled-on mustache. He ignored Ali and Supot and pretended to be looking at the shelves. Ali smiled.

"Can I help you there, sir?" Ali said.

The boy shook his head and they left him to browse and build up steam for the big question.

Supot lowered his voice to finish the story. "They couldn't find any papers. No ID. No passport. Nothing. It was like he just"—he hummed movie-intense music—"came from nowhere."

Ali joined Supot in adding movie climax music to increase the tension. "I don't know where to go next. I'm stuck."

He held the tape ends for Ali to splice, and they followed the journey of Pencil Mustache to the rear of the shop.

"So, how's Dylan, the Welsh volunteer?" Supot asked.

"Ah. Dylan. Right. It's terrible. He ran off with my aunt. They took the poodle with them."

"Just like that?"

"Yeah. We found the ladder at her bedroom window in the morning. She left a note on the pillow."

"Too bad. What did your uncle say?"

"He was quite upset."

"Only upset?"

"Devastated?"

"No. It doesn't work."

"It doesn't?"

"Not if anyone knows how peculiar-looking your aunt is. Go back to the part where he was making you all breakfast. That was still plausible. I don't think anyone would believe him running off with your aunt. She's seventy-two?"

"Fifty-nine. She could be younger in our film. We could get Mai Charoenpura and Sinjai Plengpanich to play her and my ma."

"If your aunt's going to be young enough to run off with a tourist, that would make Ali, the handsome Muslim, about twelve years old."

"Shit. This isn't as easy as it looks. Can't we just steal ideas from someone else's movie like everyone else does?"

Before Supot could respond to his friend, they were interrupted by Pencil Mustache, who stood watching them. He had his head tilted forward. Only the mouth and the laundry-pen mustache were visible beneath his floppy hat. He attempted to speak in a deep voice.

"Ahem. Me and the other men at the snooker club would like a couple of . . . sex films. You got any?"

Those organs within Ali and Supot that were given to bursting from laughter were pushed to their limits.

## 4 INT. OFFICE BUILDING — DAY

Siriluk leaves the elevator on the forty-seventh floor and walks along the hallway to room 47X. She looks at the number but doesn't go in. Instead, she continues to the end of the corridor and enters the emergency stairwell. She walks up the

stairs four more floors to the fifty-
first and carefully opens the door to
see an armed guard facing the lift with
his back to her. She creeps quietly
along the corridor and checks the number
51X on one door before proceeding. When
Siriluk enters, a secretary at a large
desk stares up through her pince-nez
and looks her up and down disapprov-
ingly.

SECRETARY
And who do you think you are,
waltzing in here unaccompanied?

Siriluk ignores her, walks directly to
the door of the inner office, opens it,
and steps inside without knocking.

SIRILUK
It's okay. I'll let myself in.
Thanks.

5 INT. BUNDTUT'S OFFICE — DAY

Comrade Deputy Field Marshal Bundtut is sitting signing papers behind
a vast desk. He is a handsome thirty-
five-year-old in a formal futuristic
semi-military/police uniform. He looks
up from his work quite composed.

**SIRILUK**

How are you, Captain Nikom?

I'm your minor wife assignment
for the second trimester.

I must admit, you're a lot better
looking than the geezers they
normally saddle me with. It's my
pleasure to please you.
Would you like to see what you're
getting?

Siriluk starts to unbutton her top
and smiles beautifully. The secretary
finally catches up with her and pushes
in front of her.

**SECRETARY**

You can't . . .

I'm so sorry, Comrade Deputy
Field Marshal. She just walked
past me. I couldn't . . .

**SIRILUK**
(looks surprised)

Deputy Field Marshal? Oops.
Almost my lucky day there. My
mistake.

The guard walks in. The secretary is angry with him.

> **SECRETARY**
> (to guard)
> What exactly do you think you're doing out there? You just let any little tramp walk in off the street? Get her out.

The guard grabs Siriluk's arm a little too roughly. She looks him in the eye.

> **SIRILUK**
> Oh, but you're so strong. I love a man who has muscles as a substitute for brain matter. I hope my arm isn't bruising your hand.

Siriluk swings around and knees the guard in the groin. He drops to the floor. The secretary appears embarrassed.

> **SECRETARY**
> (to Siriluk)
> Get out this minute.

Through all this, Bundtut has been sitting bemused but moderately amused.

**BUNDTUT**

Would anybody care to tell me
what this morning's cabaret is
all about?

**SECRETARY**

I'm sorry, Comrade Deputy Field
Marshal. She just . . . just—

The secretary is about to burst a lung,
but Siriluk cuts in.

**SIRILUK**

I think we should give the skinny
bitch a rest and let the tramp
have a say.

**SECRETARY**

Why you . . .

The secretary goes to slap the invader,
who turns her cheek to her. The con-
frontation is interrupted by a smiling
Bundtut.

**BUNDTUT**

Miss Ohd. Let the tramp have a
say.

The secretary is torn between anger and
deference. Siriluk calmly walks to the
guest chair and sits down. She crosses
her legs elegantly.

**SIRILUK**

Thank you so much. This should be
simple enough to resolve. Thence
I can get on with my allotted
business. Some gorilla's twin
brother downstairs sent me up
to room 51X to meet my allocated
master, Captain Nimit. I
apologize that your receptionist
has the brain of a bean, but I'm
just following orders. I'm sure
you know what that's like. I
hardly deserve this treatment for
someone else's mistake.
(pause)
Now, I'll go straight back down
and get the right room number.
Excuse—

She's about to stand when he speaks.

**BUNDTUT**

You're a minor wife cadre?

It's apparent from Siriluk's demeanor
that she isn't proud of her status.

**SIRILUK**

Comrade Siriluk 81,988. Grade C.

**BUNDTUT**

That seems rather a low grade.
Grade Cs are usually reserved for

flawed women. Minor wives that
look . . . well, that look like
you are usually grade B2 at the
very least.

**SIRILUK**
Well, then I suppose I must be
flawed, my sweet Field Marshal.
Perhaps I've rudely exhibited too
much of an independent spirit for
the taste of some bullies in your
ministry. Perhaps the insecure
men of Security are happier with
a silent bedmate than with a
partner with a mind.

The secretary can take no more.

**SECRETARY**
Watch your mouth, girl. Your
fault is between your ears. Don't
you realize who you're talking
to?

Siriluk continues to stare at Bundtut.

**SIRILUK**
Are you somebody?

Bundtut can no longer hold back his
smile.

**BUNDTUT**
I don't know. They tell me I'm
the Vice Minister of Security.

Siriluk returns his smile.

**SIRILUK**
Is that important?

Bundtut laughs. The secretary is exas-
perated at the girl's stupidity. She
turns to the recovering guard.

**SECRETARY**
(to guard)
We've had enough. Take her
downstairs and see what you can
do about getting her license
revoked.

The guard escorts Siriluk away while
she hums the Thai version of "We Shall
Overcome" and looks back at the field
marshal. The secretary turns back.

**SECRETARY (CONT'D)**
Comrade Deputy Field Marshal,
I can't tell you how sorry I am
about that. I don't know how it
could have happened.

Bundtut still has the smile on his lips.
He ponders matters for a moment.

> **BUNDTUT**
> Captain Nimit. What section's he in?

> **SECRETARY**
> Captain Nimit? He's in Interrogation and Coercion, sir.

> **BUNDTUT**
> Send him up.

> **SECRETARY**
> Surely, you're not . . .

> **BUNDTUT**
> Yes?

The secretary is defeated but not surprised.

> **SECRETARY**
> Nothing sir.

> CUT TO:

**6 INT. SIRILUK'S APARTMENT**

Siriluk is in an empty, boxlike windowless room. It looks like a cell, but it's actually her apartment. She's still dressed the same, but she's lying on the bed with her shoes on, looking at the ceiling. Her packed suitcase is beside

her on the floor. She's chanting quietly
to herself.

### SIRILUK
Come soon, my knight. Come rescue
me. Come soon. Come. Come on.

There's a doorbell chime to the tune of
"The Red Flag."

### SIRILUK (CONT'D)
Bravo.

She jumps up, goes to the door, and
practices her "surprised" face before
opening it. A uniformed officer and an
adjutant are at the door.

### SIRILUK (CONT'D)
Yes?

### OFFICER
Are you Comrade Siriluk 81,988?

### SIRILUK
Yes. But my friends call me
Eighty-eight.

### OFFICER
Oh, a smartass. Come with us.

### SIRILUK
Where are you taking me?

                    OFFICER
The Deputy Minister of Security
wants to see you.

                    SIRILUK

Me? Why, goodness. What would
such an important man want
with me?

                    OFFICER
              (smarmily)
I can't imagine.

Siriluk goes to get her suitcase. The
men watch her the way men do, in a lascivious kind of way.

              OFFICER (CONT'D)
What grade of minor wife are you?

                    SIRILUK
Heading for A-plus by the looks
of things.

The officer pats her ass as she passes
them. The camera focuses on her face. We
see a brief glimpse of the puma in her
eyes.

Supot lip-synced the famous final line from *2010*. "'No. It
wasn't supposed to end like this. God help us all.'"

The closing music came up and Anjira sighed. She was

sitting beside Supot on his vinyl couch. Her mascara had run from the tears, and she looked like Freddy Krueger, but she didn't seem to have noticed. Supot looked at her. She was still transfixed by the closing credits.

"Well? What do you think?" he asked. No sound came from her. "About the film."

She looked at him. He wanted to laugh at her mascara but didn't.

"It was terrible."

Supot was stunned. "Terrible?"

"What they did to her. It was really terrible."

"Right. But I guess you liked the film . . . right?"

She turned toward him to speak earnestly. "Supot. When you invited me here to your place to watch another film, I didn't believe it. I thought, 'No. Surely Supot wouldn't pull another trick like that depressing German movie on me.' I assumed that had been a lesson to you. I just assumed you wanted to, you know, fool around a little bit to make up for it.

"So, when you put on this video, I have to tell you, Supot Yongjaiyut, I was on my way out the door, never to see you again. Really. I thought you must be some kind of weirdo. I don't just fool around with everyone, you know? I get a lot of offers from the boys at Yakult. But you know I have a soft spot for a man in uniform. I'm quite fond of you, but I was still leaving. Then the film started, and I couldn't get my legs to walk out the door. I was . . . what do you call it? I was hypnotized."

Supot looked at her for a few seconds. "That means you liked it, right?"

"It was wonderful. It was like . . . like magic."

He looked as pleased as if he'd written and directed the film himself. He slid his arm along the back of the couch behind her. "So. You want to . . . fool around now?" he asked, still aglow from the umpteenth viewing of *2010*.

Anjira paused for a moment, seemed to be thinking about it. "Nah. I'm not in the mood now. You want to watch it again?"

The Nung Thong Film Company was three large concrete buildings in a compound between private houses deep on a lane off Sukhumvit Road. Supot went there straight from work. He walked into a reception area that didn't have a receptionist. Two men were crouched over a dismembered editing machine at the back of the room. They didn't notice Supot.

"Excuse me," Supot said.

The men peered up like surprised rabbits but looked back down again when they saw the uniform.

"Just leave it on the desk over there," one said.

"Leave what?"

"You didn't bring mail?"

"No."

One of the men stood and went over to him. "Then what do you want?"

"I need to ask you about Mr. Vongkot Aromdee. You did the final print on his video here. You're mentioned in the credits."

In fact, the Nung Thong Film Company hadn't been mentioned in the credits. No film company was credited, but Supot and Ali were playing a hunch. The cassette containing the copy of the film was new. The date stamp on the box was three months ago. Vongkot had been in Bangkok for all that time and left his apartment regularly. What if he was traveling to a production company to work on his film in a lab? What if the original footage on film was converted to video there? What if the original film was locked up in a cupboard at one of those production companies?

This was the sixth production lab Supot had been to in Bangkok, and he was getting used to the blank stares he'd received at all of them.

"Vongkot what?" asked the man, running his finger down the list of appointments in a ledger.

"Aromdee," said Supot.

"What's your business with him?"

"No business," said Supot. "He's just dead is all."

The room flickered to life under the fluorescent lamps. It was a well-equipped modern lab with expensive film, editing, and treatment equipment. Thailand had become something of a regional hub for foreign movies, and these state-of-the-art studios had mushroomed. The walls were white, like in a private hospital ward. There were two AC units. Supot was impressed. The man who'd led him in was the manager. He'd been sorry to hear about Supot's uncle's death. Ali had suggested the subterfuge. Thais were very sympathetic to relatives of the newly departed.

"So, you see," said the manager. "This is all we are. We rent out these rooms and the equipment. If they don't have technicians, we hire them out too. But mostly the film people come here to do the final work on their productions. As long as they can afford the rental and look like they know what they're doing, we don't disturb them. Your uncle ordered in some pretty sophisticated equipment. By the look of him, he could afford it. Money didn't seem to be an object. He was using this room for about five months. But I have no idea what they were doing in here."

"They?"

"There was another guy. I guess he was a technician.

Young fellow, maybe in his twenties. Can't remember his name. You probably know who he was."

Supot kept quiet.

"They finished a couple of months ago," said the manager. "I didn't notice any celebrating. Odd that. Most people are pleased as piss when they finish a production, but those two just paid up and walked out like they were on their way to a funeral." He realized what he'd just said. "Oh, shit. Sorry. I didn't mean anything by that. Just slipped out."

Supot shrugged to show it was a forgivable slip. The manager continued. "From what you say, it looks like he passed away just a bit after he finished working on the film. Too bad. I'm sorry. Was it any good?"

"Excellent."

"Shame."

"Do you know what happened to the original film?" Supot asked. "He didn't have it with him when he died."

"Really? There was nothing left behind when he completed his work. I guess you'd have to talk to the young fellow about that."

"In fact, I can't imagine who the young fellow might be," said Supot. "I don't suppose he left any contact details?"

"Not that I . . . No, wait. I think you might be in luck. They misplaced a piece of equipment that was their own property. Our lads mixed it together with our stuff when they were clearing up. The young fellow said it wasn't vital, but if it showed up, they'd be grateful if we could give them a call. They gave me a phone number. Now, where would I have put that?"

He went to his desk and opened a filing cabinet that apparently contained just that one piece of paper.

"We don't abuse trees much down here," said the manager. "All our notes go straight to computer. Don't know why

I bothered to buy these damned cabinets. They're pretty much just for show. Your uncle's assistant seemed as much of a technophobe as your uncle. Neither of them had phones. So, it was odd they'd be able to work on the movie." He handed the note to Supot.

There was a number followed by three English letters.

"He said he didn't have a phone, but this was his sister's number," said the manager. "Said she'd pass on any messages."

Supot couldn't erase the grin from his chops on his way home. He kept taking the note out of his pocket and rereading it. It wasn't a challenging read, but for Supot it might as well have been the original screenplay of *Some Like It Hot*. Those three letters held him spellbound all the way to his dismal apartment. He hurried to copy them into his notebook for fear they might disappear, but they were still there when he took his last glimpse before he went to bed. L . . . U . . . K . . . LUK: the most common Thai nickname for women whose full name is Siriluk.

## 21 INT. COFFEE SHOP — EVENING

We are in a crowded, dark, bohemian coffee shop. There are couples, mostly men in uniform and older men with younger pretty girls. Siriluk, in a beret and dark glasses, sits at a corner table. She's sipping a cocktail from a coconut shell. She's joined by two unattractive women. They seem nervous to be there. Siriluk, on the other hand, is perfectly calm. One of the women, Soupah, appears

to dislike her. The larger of the two,
Boss Lady, leans into Siriluk's ear.

**BOSS LADY**
Are you in?

Siriluk nods.

**SIRILUK**
It was all a little too easy.
But perhaps I'm being paranoid.
Sometimes I forget how much of
this regime is just show.

**SOUPAH**
I assume you've been able to stay
over at his place already. You've
had enough time.

**SIRILUK**
Not yet. Not overnight. But I'm
not pushing it.

**SOUPAH**
You do know we're on a deadline?

**BOSS LADY**
Soupah. Give it a rest.

**SOUPAH**
I'm just stating a fact.

**SIRILUK**

You can't rush these things.

**SOUPAH**

Enjoying it, are you?

Siriluk pulls her glasses down her nose and glares at Soupah, then turns back to Boss Lady.

**SIRILUK**

It isn't as much fun as I was expecting it to be. This Bundtut character isn't one of the worst.

**SOUPAH**

You aren't falling for the guy, are you?

**SIRILUK**

There must be something between love and hate in your tiny mind, Soupah. When I'm about to destroy someone, I find it's easier if he's a complete bastard. Bundtut isn't.

**SOUPAH**

They're all basically the same. As long as the uniforms are in control, our Thai sisters will continue to be sex slaves forever. You really have to learn

to stop looking at the guy inside
the uniform.

**SIRILUK**
You think so? You think if we
overthrew the security agency
and put in men in gorilla
suits they'd be any different?
It's power and influence we're
fighting here, not shiny buttons
and medals. To defeat these
people, you have to see inside
their heads. If it isn't a
security agent, it could be a
man with the biggest gun, or
a man with the biggest wallet
. . . and eventually, it may not
even be a man.

Soupah looks at Boss Lady and laughs.

**SOUPAH**
I'm not sure we've got the right
woman for this mission.

Siriluk has had enough. She huffs and
looks Soupah in the eye.

**SIRILUK**
You're right. I tell you what.
Why don't you go in and do it
yourself? A little bit of makeup
and a push-up bra, and who knows

what you could achieve? They
might not even notice that chip
on your shoulder.

That pushes Soupah over the edge. She
loses it and squares up to Siriluk,
knocking over their drinks. Some coffee shop patrons look over. Boss Lady
and Siriluk laugh to make it look as if
it was a joke. Soupah is incensed and
storms out. Boss Lady appears embarrassed.

### BOSS LADY
Isn't that marvelous? We can't
even keep order in our own ranks.

### SIRILUK
I don't understand why she's
always like this around me.

### BOSS LADY
Really? Have you ever looked
at yourself in a mirror? You're
gorgeous. You know you are. Every
man you've brought down has
been insanely in love with you.
They've given up everything to be
with you. And now here you are at
the top of the heap.

**SIRILUK**

It can't be jealousy.


**BOSS LADY**

Not as such. It's just that what
you do . . . the way you use your
body to get results, it's the
maximum sacrifice.

So few of our sisters would be
able to do that, and there are
those, like Soupah, who see you
as an outsider. A different
species. But those of us who
know the real you, we all
have absolute faith in you.
We wouldn't have selected you
otherwise. You've proven your
value to the movement too many
times already. Just get the
access codes and get us into the
computer system. Then you can get
out of that awful place.

**22 INT. APARTMENT — AFTERNOON**

Bundtut's apartment is sparsely deco-
rated, but the taste is expensive. He
is fabulously wealthy, as are all his
fellow officers. He has several million
bahts' worth of art just around the bedroom.

Siriluk is in the bed under a single sheet. Her arms are on her knees. Her chin is on the backs of her hands. She's smiling at Bundtut as he does up his uniform buttons in the mirror.

> **BUNDTUT**
> What are you grinning at, monkey?

> **SIRILUK**
> Can I ask you something?

> **BUNDTUT**
> No.

> **SIRILUK**
> How many minor wives do you have?

> **BUNDTUT**
> One hundred and fifteen.

Siriluk whistles with admiration.

> **SIRILUK**
> To tell the truth, I wasn't expecting that much honesty.

> **BUNDTUT**
> My mother taught me to tell the truth when dealing with matters that aren't worth lying about.

                    **SIRILUK**
And you can satisfy that many?

                    **BUNDTUT**
Do you have any doubt?

                    **SIRILUK**
Not after the last two hours.

Bundtut comes back to sit on the bed and
puts a hand on her neck. He says something into her ear.

                    **BUNDTUT**
                    (whispers)
Tell you the truth, I haven't
actually met most of them. I only
know I have a hundred and fifteen
because it's in the tax statement.
Most of them are farmed out to vis-
iting politicians and businessmen.

                    **SIRILUK**
Are we being recorded?

                    **BUNDTUT**
Why do you ask?

                    **SIRILUK**
I'm just wondering why we're
whispering.

                    **BUNDTUT**
It's more romantic, don't you
think?

                    **SIRILUK**
So, we're not?

                    **BUNDTUT**
Bugged? No. All we have is the
camera in the living room. But I
do have a hand camera if you're
into show business.

                    **SIRILUK**
Pervert.

Bundtut kisses Siriluk long and passion-
ately until Siriluk pulls away.

              **SIRILUK (CONT'D)**
Well, how many of the hundred
and fifteen have you actually
fertilized to produce babies for
the regime?

                    **BUNDTUT**
How many?

Siriluk nods. Bundtut leans forward and
looks up under the sheet.

              **BUNDTUT (CONT'D)**
You got anyone else under there?

Siriluk giggles and pulls the sheet down, then shakes her head.

> BUNDTUT (CONT'D)
> Then I guess you're the sum
> total.

> SIRILUK
> Oh. Give me a break.

Siriluk snorts in ridicule.

> BUNDTUT
> No. I'm serious.

Bundtut gives Siriluk a look that can only be genuine.

> SIRILUK
> Is this one of your mother's
> matters that aren't worth lying
> about?

> BUNDTUT
> I guess I'm just one of those
> old-fashioned family types. My
> mother was with my father for
> forty-two years. She was the only
> lover he ever had.

Siriluk looks as if a serious accident has happened before her eyes. But Bundtut's already standing and un-creasing his tunic, so he doesn't see her reaction.

> ### BUNDTUT (CONT'D)
> Stick around. We'll eat when I get back.

> ### SIRILUK
> (surprised)
> You aren't throwing me out this time?

Bundtut turns and kisses her before heading out.

> ### BUNDTUT
> My throwing arm's starting to get weak.

Once Bundtut is gone, Siriluk bangs her head on her knees several times.

> ### SIRILUK
> Damn. Damn. Damn. Damn.

Siriluk takes a deep breath, which is full of emotion, wraps the sheet around herself, stands, and walks to the living room. She leans in the doorway in one of those *Vogue* poses and looks up at the CCTV camera on the wall.

> SIRILUK (CONT'D)
> (under her breath)
> Hi, viewers. Welcome to Siriluk
> time.

CUT BRIEFLY TO:

23 INT. TECH OFFICE — SIMULTAENOUS — DAY

One CCTV monitor in a bank of many.
We see the same shot of Siriluk posing
POV camera.
A uniformed technician is watching her.
He zooms in.

> TECH
> Hello, hello. Just look at you.
> Oooee, I want to be a minister
> when I grow up. Wow.

With his zoom control, the tech tries
to keep up with Siriluk waltzing around
the room.

Eventually he finds her at the refrigerator taking out fruit. She picks up a
knife, spears a slice of mango, bites on
it, and resumes her waltz. The technician loses her again.

> TECH (CONT'D)
> Damn. Where are you, sweetheart?

CUT TO:

**24   INT. APARTMENT — AFTERNOON**

Siriluk stands directly beneath the camera in a blind spot, reaching up and unscrewing the camera bracket with her knife.

The unit drops, hanging from one screw and dangling straight down.

She walks into the center of the room and looks around the walls.

> **SIRILUK**
> (whispers)
> Now, sweet Comrade Deputy Field Marshal. Why would you need a camera in this room?

Siriluk goes to one revolutionary wall poster and looks behind it. She then lines up the original camera position with a second poster. Behind it is a wall safe. She pumps her fist into the air.

CUT TO:

**25 INT. TECH OFFICE — SIMULTAENOUS — DAY**

A wider shot of the bank of TV monitors. The technician has called in a supervisor. All they see from the camera feed is a shot of the carpet. It no longer responds to its controls.

> **TECH**
> One minute she was walking around. Picture was fine. Next, this happened.

The supervisor picks up a mobile, pushes a speed dial number, and waits.

> **SUPERVISOR**
> Get building security up to Minister Bundtut's condominium right now. Break down the door if you have to. I want to know what's happening in there this minute.

> CUT TO:

**26 INT. APARTMENT — AFTERNOON**

Booted feet rush out of the elevator and up to a door. One man goes through the skeleton key cards and opens it. They burst in. Siriluk, still in her sheet, is draped over the sofa, sexy as hell, eating mango with a knife. The head of security looks at the dangling CCTV camera.

**GUARD**
What the shit happened to that?

Siriluk smiles at him.

**SIRILUK**
Can't say I know, General. One
minute it's up there intrusively
following me around. The next
it's dangling, limp, and useless.
It just has to be male. But
what do I know? I'm just a minor
wife cadre. Ask the technician
that put it up. Tsk. Tsk. Thai
workmanship has really gone down
the drain.

The guard and head of security look at
Siriluk suspiciously and lustfully. She
holds up the plate of mango.

**SIRILUK (CONT'D)**
You want a piece of this?

Early the next morning, Supot was blobbing in the post office sorting room. He looked across at Chet as always, with his usual admiration. The old man's hands were sorting letters as if he were on fast forward. Supot, on the other hand, sorted one letter a minute.

"You ever make a mistake, brother Chet?" Supot asked.

"Yeah. I made one in 1987. But that was because of the language. I never make mistakes in Thai. English can be a bugger."

"What do you do with anything you can't read?"

"File it in RG224E—foreign languages. Indecipherable."

"We got a file like that?"

Chet nodded toward the garbage bin across the room. For the first time, Supot noticed a faded *RG224E* written in whiteboard pen on its side.

"Right," said Supot. "That's where I've been filing them too. Glad it's official." He thought for a minute. "Chet?"

"Yeah?"

"You know a lot of stuff, right?"

"Yeah. Almost everything."

"Well, what do you do if you want to phone someone and the operator tells you they have an unlisted number, but you want to phone them anyway?"

Chet looked up from his sorting and licked his mustache. "Can't you write and ask them for their number?"

"I don't exactly have an address either."

"How the hell did you find out they've got an unlisted number without an address?"

"My sister's boyfriend's next-door neighbor works for the Telephone Organization of Thailand. She traced the name to a list of ex-directory customers. But she was denied access to details."

Chet mulled it over without slowing down with his work, then said, "Them having an unlisted number generally means they don't want just anyone phoning them. You know that?"

"I know. But just suppose it was something really important."

Chet stopped work and went over to Supot with a knowing, fatherly look on his face.

"This wouldn't be a matter involving a young lady we're looking for, would it, young Pot?"

Supot looked off into the distance. "Yes. It would."

"Then I think there might be a way."

The Bangkok Noi postmaster was out of his office for the afternoon. It officially had something to do with mail security and unofficially had something to do with golf. Supot was sitting cross-legged on the floor behind the big metal desk. It hid him from view from the corridor outside, but he had to keep his voice down on the phone.

"Thank you."

While he was waiting to be transferred, he looked carefully around the desk and through the glass office interior window. He could see Chet talking to the secretary. She was obviously trying to get into the postmaster's office, which Supot currently occupied. The timing was lousy. Supot's call went through. He looked at the sheet of paper in front of him and put on his most refined accent.

"Ah, yes. Good day. This is Postmaster Wossayot speaking, from Bangkok Noi Sub District Office. I was just—... What? ... You do? ... Well, yes, of course, I remember you too."

Supot was shocked and embarrassed. This was going to be harder than he'd expected. He didn't know his boss and the TOT head were acquainted. His only good fortune was the poor quality of the phone line. He really wasn't cut out for lying. He looked for help in the script that Chet had written for him.

"The mid-summer conference?" said Supot. "Right . . . Yes, we did, didn't we?" He laughed unconvincingly. He had a clear view of Chet failing to stop the secretary from walking to the door of the office. Desperate, it appeared the old man had feigned a heart attack, and the girl went running back to him. At least Supot hoped it was feigned. The girl and another person helped carry him offstage. Supot returned to his script.

"Okay," he said. "I won't keep you longer than necessary. I know what a dedicated man you are. Running the TOT isn't like managing a noodle stall."

The telephone boss gave that more of a laugh than it deserved, but it encouraged Supot to forge ahead, even though he was having trouble reading the old man's handwriting.

"We have a little problem here, you see. We've just had a parcel returned. It's labeled URGENT MEDICINE, so I know it's . . . urgent. But it's been returned with 'recipient unknown.' We tried to call the recipient at her last known number, but she's moved, and her new number is ex-directory. If she isn't dead already—from not getting her urgent medicine."

He took a deep breath.

"I'd really like to get in touch with her. You can understand I need to get this *urgent medicine* to her before it's too late. We need a mailing address. You can imagine how . . . urgent this is, for lack of a better word."

The writing had become illegible. He listened patiently to the voice at the other end of the line.

"Of course, you're quite right," said Supot. "It isn't strictly following the rules. So, let's just forget the whole thing and— . . . What? . . . You will? That's most sensitive of you. I put you down as the sensitive type as soon as I set eyes on you."

Supot gave him the details and asked him to fax that information to his right-hand man, Mr. Supot, who handled all the . . . urgent cases. He gave the fax number and thanked him.

"You really are a lifesaver, Nop . . . What? . . . ehr, Pon. Right. See you at the next conference. Look forward to it. Bye."

He collapsed back onto the floor, drained of emotion but proud of himself in an odd way. A successful lie is every bit as impressive as the truth.

Ali and Supot were on the premiere opera supreme seats at the back of the shop in front of the TV screen, but it was blank. Supot was clutching Ali's mobile phone as if it was an ancient Khmer relic. Ali was reading to him from an old school notebook.

". . . And it wasn't my aunt, see. I made a mistake. It was my sister. Dylan fell in love with her while they were collecting chicken eggs in the backyard to make breakfast. I've dropped the bacon joke. Bad taste. But, of course, despite their love for each other, there are all the pressures of cross-cultural relationships. That's why . . ." Ali looked at Supot, who was fixated on the phone and the piece of paper in his hand. "You aren't listening, are you?"

"I am. You don't know the difference between your aunt and your sister, and you don't actually have a sister anyway."

"Oh, Pot, Pot, Pot. It's a film. I can have as many sisters as I want. Asanee Chotikul can play the part." But this wasn't a day to be talking screenplays. "Oh. For the sake of Allah, phone the woman, why don't you? You're squeezing all the power out of my mobile there. I'll pay for the call. She's in Chiang Rai, not Chicago."

"It's not the money. It isn't that easy, Ali."

"And why not? Apart from the fact that she's a beautiful talented actress and you're an average-looking penniless postman and she'll laugh in your face."

"Oh, that was good. Really filled me with confidence, that did."

"Supot, she isn't famous yet. This would be her first fan call. She'll probably get a kick out of it. Take you on as a love interest."

Throughout this conversation, they weren't taking much notice of the customers in the shop. When two youths were sure Ali and Supot weren't watching, they surreptitiously began putting videocassettes into their backpacks.

"That's the problem, brother," said Supot. "I don't want to be one of her fans."

"Oh, help me. You haven't got yourself into a *Roman Holiday* fantasy here, have you?" said Ali. "Please tell me you haven't."

When Supot didn't respond, Ali did a passable impersonation of Supot at his most pathetic. "'*When she gets to know me, she'll love me too.*' Crap. Beautiful princesses only fall in love with lowlifes if it's in the script. It only happens in movies, Supot. Even then you have to look like Gregory Peck."

"It doesn't have to be love. I'd like to know her as . . . as a friend."

Ali put his hand on Supot's cheek. "You poor, pathetic, sad, hopeless, helpless, meaningless romantic you. Forget it. Now . . ." He looked again at the small CCTV screen beside the large TV. It was the nearest thing to a security system the shop had. "If we don't get these two assholes right now, I won't have any stock left and you won't have a non-paying evening job. You ready?"

"I suppose so."

They both took deep weight-lifter breaths, let out ancient warrior war cries, and ran back into the shop. In their hands were large chunks of two-by-fours. The youths were sure their end had come. They dropped their packs full of videos and escaped into the street. Ali and Supot stopped in the doorway. The adrenaline rush had been good for Supot. They put their arms around each other and said good evening to a nervous old lady walking past.

"We are two tough hombres," said Supot.

## 44 INT. MINISTRY OF SECURITY — NIGHT

Background music. The skyline is lit up with rooftop neons. Siriluk is sitting on Bundtut's lap in his office at the Ministry. Their life together over the past six months has been idyllic, but the time has come for Siriluk to complete her mission.

Bundtut obviously has work to do but is torn between that and flirting with his woman. He persuades her to go away, and she sulks and slouches off reluctantly. He points to the clock and lets her know he won't be long. She grabs a magazine from his coffee table and goes to the secretary's office. (She left work a long time ago.) At the doorway she plays goodbye games, blowing kisses, peeking around the doorframe, flashing a leg, until he throws a desktop toilet roll at her and laughs.

Once she has closed the connecting door, she hurries through the outer office and peers into the corridor. The armed guard is facing the elevator, practicing a kind of slow-motion tap dance. She slips into the room directly opposite, checks that there is no camera, and sits at a huge computer that takes up one entire wall of the room. The room is only illuminated by the external rooftop advertising outside the window. Siriluk takes the dildo from her purse and unscrews the end. It contains a roll of paper and a cigar-shaped gadget, which fits into one of the computer's slots. She turns on the computer and taps in the code written on her paper. Within seconds, an expanse of data lights up the screen and her face. She prods the memory button, and the memory light comes on to show it's recording. She looks toward the door and contemplates the implications this will have for Bundtut. But her duty is to her sisters.

When Bundtut comes out of his office, he can't see Siriluk at first. The camera sweeps around to see Siriluk sitting at the secretary's desk, wearing her glasses and impersonating her. The camera pans to Bundtut's face, who looks at her with admiration and undisguised love.

*My dear Siriluk,*

*I am sorry to disturb you. You don't know me, but I am an admirer of your work. I think your acting ability is tumultuous. I have seen Bangkok 2010 over thirty times, and every time I watch it, it says something different to me. It is the finest film I have ever seen, and I am something of an authority on cinematography.*

*My name is Supot, and I am in the communication business. I am thirty-two and I was born in the year of the dragon. So, I am steadfast and resolute in action. I am kind to animals and children, but I confess I don't necessarily like them much.*

*I have a telephone number for you, but I do not want to disturb you unless I have your permission. I shall leave this message at this juncture and send the letter. I hope to hear from you at your convenience. If you don't feel like replying, I suppose I understand. I still think you are the best Thai actress I have seen.*

*And you are in good shape too.*

*Sincerely and with respect,*
*Supot Yongjaiyut*

The ferry wasn't too crowded. On Sundays you didn't get the lemmings going to work. Just tourists and residents from upriver going into the city for the day. Supot and Ali, even by their own admission, were looking too cool. Surf shirts and gelled hair. They sat at the window seats and leaned out to watch the amazing life in the Chaophraya River. Well-kept wooden huts. Wat Arun. A fat foreigner sunbathing. In the tourist brochures, they called the Chaophraya

River "timeless." But that wasn't true. The Chaophraya is a calendar of passage from a mellow history to a hectic present. It showed the scars like an old soldier boasting of his wounds at the end of a night of Mekhong whisky. The river carried effluent and chemicals out to the gulf. It tolerated four-stroke engines on noisy longboats. It gently buffeted the bloated carcasses of dead animals and the occasional person against the concrete pylons. It was greasy and thick, and children who somersaulted into it did so at great risk to their futures.

But to Ali and Supot, it was a time warp that carried their sailing ship to a futuristic mecca or some such mixed metaphor they couldn't ever settle on. Ali, in his own mind, had reached a crucial point in his homemade screenplay, but Supot was of no help to him. He was lost in his daydream, rehearsing the words he might say when he first meets Siriluk. He unfurled his tongue like a Great Dane on the back of a pickup truck, and unwisely caught warm spray from the bouncing boat.

"What if Dylan and my sister elope on the Chaophraya Express Boat?" Ali asked. "We could put in artistic shots of the river."

"They wouldn't be able to elope very far, would they?" said Supot.

"Pakret. Then a bus to the airport."

"You realize if they get on the airplane, that's the end of your film."

"Why?" Ali asked.

"Budget limitations. We can't afford to go anywhere."

"Right. But let's assume one of the big studios picks it up. We could go to Florida as advisors."

A blindly romantic couple sped past in a Pepsi longboat. They ignored the diesel fumes and gazed with passion into each other's eyes. "You know? Maybe I'm trying too hard for them to have a romance. Maybe she could just shoot him over some love problem," Ali said.

Supot laughed. "They say screenwriters iron out all their own traumas and hang-ups by putting them in the scripts."

"Are you suggesting I've got a love hang-up?"

"I don't know. How long have you been dating Kwang?"

"Not that again. Kwang? Twenty-two years." He waved at some sort of duck who was ensuring himself a short life by swimming in the murky water. "You aren't suggesting that's abnormal now, are you?"

"You date a girl since primary school—you love her—but for some mysterious reason you can't quite bring yourself to marry her. I don't see anything abnormal in that."

"I told you. It has to happen first."

"What?"

"Our big *something*."

"Let's be honest here. We aren't really looking very hard for our big 'somethings,' are we? We aren't going to find our big 'somethings' on the Chaophraya ferry. We aren't going to find them shopping at Siam Square. You give yourself one day off and you spend it with a moron instead of your loved one."

"You can't go looking for a big something, Supot. It comes looking for you. It'll happen. I'll get it out of my system, and me and Kwang will get married and have eight good little Muslim kids. Kwang understands."

"You sure? She'll be eighty-two by the time the eighth child comes along."

"Tell me something here, Supot. Based on two failed dates with a Yakult factory worker and a very unhealthy and disgusting stalker affair with an untouchable movie star, you're suddenly giving *me* advice on love. You think you're qualified?"

"Don't you bring my Siriluk into this. I bet she's my big something."

The boat pulled away from Tha Chang Pier, temporally divorcing a confused Chinese couple. The boy at the stern yelled to the boat pilot, who threw the ferry into reverse and chugged back for the laughing wife.

"It's been over a week," said Ali.

"She'll write." Supot stared dreamily out across the metallic gray water. "I know she will."

Ali leaned over the edge and pretended to vomit. The sweet old tourist lady beside Supot handed him a plastic bag for his friend and smiled.

"I get that way on boats too, love," said the old lady.

Supot smiled. She'd probably said something profound.

Supot looked off into the distance. He knew Ali was right. He always was. Big somethings came looking for you. He knew it was dangerous to be making a connection between real life and fantasy. He'd thought about it a lot. It was like time travel. If you were to go back and try to change your past, you'd probably end up with two heads or be somebody else. And, by the same principle, you can't go reaching into fiction and pulling people out just because you feel like it. You'll end up with two heads just the same. He'd thought about it a lot but not necessarily with any common sense.

Supot and Ali had a good day in the city. They were ten years old again, playing truant from school just like in the good old days. They had a fast-food repast that was 80 percent junk and took in two movies. Going to see a film in a crowded theater was like sharing a meal. It was brotherhood and sisterhood. It was a basic animal instinct to want to partake in pleasurable experiences with members of your own pack. That's why cinemas hadn't all closed down when video was invented.

But there's always the odd rogue stray in every pack.

Ali and Supot sat with their popcorn in the front row of the rear section. The position provided legroom but didn't force them to crick their neck looking up at the screen. The theater wasn't full, but the film was well attended. A thinking crowd all but one.

The film started, and the friends were just getting into it when . . .

*Ring, ring, ring!*

"Allo. Mee? How are you? . . . I'm good . . . No, I'm at the cinema . . . No, it doesn't matter . . . Yes . . . Yes."

Sometimes you have to be cruel to be kind, even to members of your own pack. Ali and Supot looked down in frustration, then at each other. They reached into the emergency packs resting at their feet and pulled out the two mini water cannons they always took to the cinema for sad situations just like this one. They located the mindless fool and blasted her in unison. She was confused to find herself in a rainstorm in the middle of a theater.

"What? . . . Eh? . . . No, why?" she said into her phone. She was soaked, and in a chilly air-conditioned theater, that could be quite a serious thing. She could likely catch pneumonia and die. A puff of smoke came either from her head or from her crippled mobile. There was quiet but polite applause from the other viewers. One or two people hurriedly switched off their own phones. Supot and Ali settled back to their film. The last of the cinema samurai.

On the Monday morning, Supot was loading his post bag. One envelope was bigger than the bag by a couple of inches. He made several gentle attempts to insert it and eventually decided to fold it once despite the DO NOT FOLD sticker. What harm would it do? The crack of whatever was broken inside was louder than he'd expected. But at least it now fit. He wasn't a good postman, but he did solve problems.

By now, he'd all but given up on hearing from Siriluk. Of course, he was already madly and crazily in love with her just as Bundtut had been, but he thought there'd be snow on the Golden Mount temple before he'd get a letter from her. And it might have been easier for all of them if she hadn't written.

With his bag sorted, Supot was ready to go out when one of the other postmen sorting letters turned to him and said, "Pot. Didn't know you could read. You've got a letter." He held one up and Frisbee'd it in the direction of Supot.

Supot juggled and caught the small pink envelope. He looked in amazement at the return address. His knees gave way, and he squatted on the floor. His hands were shaking too badly to open the letter. Somehow, he managed to detach the penknife from his utility belt and sliced open the envelope. He unfolded the single sheet of thick northern *sah* paper and noticed the writing—small and neat. He started to read.

*Dear Khun Supot,*

*Thank you very much for your kind letter. It came as an incredible shock to me. I have no idea how you found me.*

Supot staggered to a bench, where he took a few seconds to compose himself. The other postmen noticed the reaction and feared the worst.

"Bad news, Pot?" said one.

But Supot could hear nothing. He read on.

*I have so many questions for you. Where did you find 2010? Is it a copy, or is it the original film? Has anyone else seen it apart from you? If your answer is yes, how many people have seen it?*

*I don't know you at all, Khun Supot, but I'm going to ask you a very big favor. If you have 2010 with you now, please, can you get it and keep it safe? I want you to promise me that nobody else will watch it, and that no copies are made of it. Can you promise me that?*

*This probably sounds very strange, and I'm afraid I can't explain anything to you right now. You'll just have to trust me that it's for the best. I have to trouble you to write to me again with the answers to my questions. I'm sorry to be so secretive. I hope we can become good penfriends.*

*With very best wishes and thanks for your nice letter,*

*Siriluk*

It was a happy Supot delivering mail that day. He stopped to read the letter from Siriluk a dozen times. Even at Ali's shop that evening, unraveling miles of spaghetti-looking tangled videotape that someone had returned in a plastic bowl, he was still grinning.

It was during the untangling task that Ali put down the letter and said, "I don't believe it."

"Does this count as a big something?"

"It's bigger than big. It's extra-large big."

"Cool, isn't it?"

Ali did his movie sleuth voice. "Cool indeed, my dear friend, but look how the mystery deepens and thickens with every clue that's unfolded. 'I want you to promise me that nobody else will watch it.' How mysterious is that? What do you think she's trying to hide?"

"She can't tell me. I bet it's a copyright thing. I bet they can't release it till it's registered or something. Probably Vongkot dying wasn't part of the plan and it wasn't supposed to be shown to anyone yet. Suddenly this top-secret production is out in public and they're all shitting themselves."

Ali watched Supot getting entangled with the tape. "You want some tomato sauce with that?"

"I wrote back and told her everything," said Supot. "I'm sure she'll be grateful that I'm not going to take *2010* to the movie registration secret police. I'm like a co-conspirator now. I bet she'll let me in on the secret as soon as she knows she can trust me." He looked down at the tape, a knot in his hands. It amused him that someone could tie a knot in a tape inside a cassette. "*And* she wants to be friends."

"Hmm. I wonder why she's so easy," Ali said. "You know, I bet she's a transvestite."

Supot raised his eyebrows. The knot was all but out. Normal viewing would soon be returned.

"But if she was a transvestite . . . and she looked the way she does . . . I wouldn't care," said Ali. He draped the tape over his head like a wig. "Come to me, Supot, my love."

"Wait," said Supot. "That's it. Dylan, the Welsh volunteer, falls in love with your sister, but it turns out that your sister is really your brother in a dress."

"I don't believe it," said Ali. "That's the first idea you've offered for the screenplay. In fact, it's the first sensible idea you've had since I've known you. This actress worship is good for you. And you may just be onto something there, brother." He reached for his notebook and started writing. "They go to the British embassy and the Welsh department doesn't know if they shouldn't give her a visa because she's a Muslim or because she's a transvestite. It could be a very emotional scene. And you're the one who gave birth to the idea. You know, I'm not sure how long I can cope with you being in a good mood, Supot. You normally swear and spit when we get tapes back in that condition. You aren't going to unravel the whole lot, are you?"

"It may take time, but I shall not let a hundred meters of videotape get the better of me. Patience, my dear friend, is one quality we Buddhists have in unlimited supply."

Allah, in revenge and in one of His well-known playful moments chose to snap the tape at that point.

"Shit," said Supot.

*Dear Supot,*

*I was so happy to hear back from you so soon and very relieved to know the tape is in safe hands. I can't tell you how much it means to me to know it will not be shown around to anyone. You are one of the very few people to have seen it, so I am pleased to hear that you liked it.*

*You are so kind to talk positively about the role of Siriluk. It always concerned me when leading ladies were too stiff on-screen, trying too hard to win over an audience with their looks rather than their ability to act. 2010 was the first film produced by our group, so all the performers were still developing their skills. It's very pleasing to me to hear that the film has made you and Khun Ali so happy.*

*What branch of communication are you in, Supot? I'm afraid I don't know very much about technology. New advances are happening so fast. How do you spend your free time? Life is very quiet here in Chiang Rai. But it's nice to still be surrounded by nature. I hope you are well.*

*Your friend,*
*Siriluk*

*Dear Siriluk,*

*I was ever so excited to hear from you again. I think you are not stiff at all. You're easily the unstiffest and most natural*

*Thai actress I've ever seen. I am your number one fan. I noticed you didn't really answer any of my questions about the film and the stars. But that's okay. How long will we have to wait before the film is released and you start to do the promotion and ads and stuff? I can't wait to see you and Khun Bundtut arriving at EGV Grand in your big black limo. You make such a striking couple. Is he your boyfriend? I have a license if you need a driver.*

*I have a confession to make to you. The field of communication I'm in is called "postman." I hope that doesn't shock you too much. You probably thought postmen couldn't write grammatically correct letters like this. Postal work is only my job. It isn't my life. I don't know if you've been here, but Bangkok Noi, where I work, is surrounded by big, noisy highways and overpasses. The only way to escape is by river. It's only two baht to cross over the Chaophraya to Thammasat and Sanam Luang. That's as near to nature as I can get. I'm sure Chiang Rai is more natural than Sanam Luang.*

*As to how I spend my free time, well, that's a whole different story, which I'll save for my next letter. But I'll give you a spoiler first by telling you I'm still single and looking for that perfect woman. I hope you are well, and I look forward to hearing from you soon.*

*Your forever admirer,*
*Supot*

Ali and Supot were playing a video game when two girls came into the shop. Ali looked up and abandoned the game. Under his breath, he whispered to Supot, "Act handsome."

Supot looked up to see that one of the girls was Anjira. "What are you doing here?" he asked.

Ali seemed impressed. "You know them?"

"Yeah. This is Anjira, the one that couldn't keep up with the subtitles."

Ali went around the counter to welcome her like an honored guest. "Miss Anjira, I'm so delighted to meet you at last. I've heard so much about you." He glanced at Supot. "But I don't think you're plain looking at all. I think you're quite lovely. Welcome to my shop." He *wai*'d her much too politely. She and her friend *wai*'d back.

Anjira looked disdainfully at Supot. "Why aren't you as polite as your friend here?" she asked, then turned back to Ali. "This is my friend Pim. She's at Yakult with me. She's in aluminum foil caps."

"I'm sorry to hear that," said Ali.

Supot didn't like the idea of this girl being within the walls of his temple. There were long-standing in-house rules, but there was also more to it than that. In his mind he was in a relationship with another woman, and to him, this counted as an act of infidelity toward Siriluk.

"You trying to get her fixed up?" Supot asked Anjira. "It won't work. He's got a fiancée."

Ali looked ashamed, but Anjira seemed to be used to the lack of good manners from her sometimes-boyfriend.

"She's already got enough problems with men," she directed at Supot. She then turned to Ali and said, "No offense meant."

"None taken."

Supot continued to be rude. "So, what do you want?"

By the looks of it, Ali continued to be ashamed. "I'll have to give you lessons in charm sometime," he said.

Anjira sat on one of the stools. Her friend still hadn't spoken. She seemed embarrassed to be there.

"Pim here's got problems with the manager of one of the aluminum foil plants," said Anjira. "He expects her to . . . well, it's just like Siriluk in the film. Ali, have you seen *Bangkok 2010*?"

Ali nodded with enthusiasm.

"Then I don't need to go into detail about what the creep wants from Pim, do I?"

"Indeed not."

"He keeps telling her he can get her fired if she doesn't. Says he's got influence at Yakult. I told her about how Siriluk gets the better of all them slimy men and refuses to take any of their crap, even if they've got so much money it flows out of their assholes. If you'll excuse my filth."

"Good for you," said Ali.

But Anjira was in attack mode. "Siriluk was one of us," she said. "Illegitimate daughter of a minor wife. Her mother had no rights, no say, no hope. She struggled to raise her daughter in a society that looked down on her. Put her into a temple school where even the nuns were second-class citizens. Her mother got the clap and didn't have money for medicine, so she died in her thirties. Siriluk swore revenge on the system. I told Pim all this, but she needs to see the film for herself."

"Ahh," said Ali.

Supot reanimated at the mention of the viewing. "Oh no," he said. "That's out of the question."

"Why?" Anjira asked. "It's urgent. It's a matter of life and death, I guess. Not just for Pim, but for a lot of the girls we work with. They take a lot of shit from the men there, and they think it's normal. They think they're supposed to do what the bosses tell them, in the factory and after hours. They need a leader, a heroine. They need a Siriluk. That's why they have to see this movie."

"I can't—"

"Perhaps one more person wouldn't be too serious," Ali interrupted him.

"I promised."

"You're known to be unreliable."

"Siriluk doesn't know that."

He and Ali glanced at Pim, who was looking particularly vulnerable.

"Oh, all right. Just once, though. And don't tell anyone I let you." Supot was a sucker for red-eyed women.

## 51 EXT. CAR ON HIGHWAY — DAY

A futuristic car, the type popular with thirteen-year-old boys who got their thrills from TV puppet shows, is speeding along an almost deserted elevated

expressway. The landscape beyond is bare
and brown. The camera pans down to a
ground-level road shrouded in smog.

Bundtut, with one arm around Siriluk, is
steering with a PlayStation-like control
in his other hand.

Siriluk looks content.

The camera pans to a trunk shot of both
of them.

> **SIRILUK**
> At last, we're out of bloody
> Bangkok.

Bundtut isn't really concentrating on
his driving. He often looks at his woman
in the mirror.

> **BUNDTUT**
> I'd forgotten what it was like to
> have a couple of days off.
> > (smiles)
> Feels good.

> **SIRILUK**
> So, you aren't angry at me
> anymore?

Bundtut laughs.

**BUNDTUT**

I was never angry at you. I'm
just not used to having a woman
bully me, that's all. My mom
used to do it pretty well. But I
didn't get to spend any time with
her once I turned eleven. They
shipped me off to a residential
Security Council Corporation
high school. The production line
at the minister factory starts
early, you know?

**SIRILUK**

They knew you'd be a minister
even then?

**BUNDTUT**

There was every chance. Right
genes. Right social class.

**SIRILUK**

Too bad. I think you would have
enjoyed childhood.

Bundtut looks at Siriluk and smiles.

**BUNDTUT**

Did you?

**SIRILUK**

I had a blast. But, of course,
I had everything going for me.

Wrong genes. Wrong class. Wrong
gender. Naturally, there was no
point in sending me to school.
So, I worked the fields. All that
bending down—that's how I got
thigh muscles like this.
                    (grabs her thighs)

Siriluk then realizes she's been saying too much and immediately changes the
subject.

                    **SIRILUK (CONT'D)**
Ooh look. A tree. Where are we?

                    **BUNDTUT**
Lopburi.

                    **SIRILUK**
Man, there used to be a lot more
trees this close to Bangkok.

                    **BUNDTUT**
You must have a good memory.

We see the bare landscape outside the
car. Siriluk tries to look down to
the lower road. Her breath steams up the
window.

                    **SIRILUK**
You ever driven on the public
highway?

**BUNDTUT**

Of course. When I was a student,
they had us mix with the
riffraff. Didn't like it. It's
been awhile. The military doesn't
let us use public roads unless
they've been cleared of traffic.

**SIRILUK**

The poor bastards. We get to
Singburi in three hours on an
empty road, and it could take them
up to two days in a traffic jam.

There's a hissing sound and Siriluk
turns to see Bundtut, who's pretending
to spray from an imaginary aerosol can.

**SIRILUK (CONT'D)**

What is it? We got bugs?

**BUNDTUT**

Worse than that. I don't know for
sure, but I thought I heard the
buzzing of anarchy in the car.
You hear anything?

Siriluk looks out the window. She appears
embarrassed at her overenthusiasm.

**SIRILUK**

I used to be one of those poor
bastards. It's got nothing to

do with anarchy. It's all about
hemorrhoids. You sit on hot
plastic for twenty-four hours,
and you end up with an ass like
an orangutan's.

Bundtut laughs so heartily he almost
loses control of the car.

> SIRILUK (CONT'D)
> Steady, Mr. Minister of Vice.
> Let's get there in one piece.
> You're quite sure we'll be alone
> at this place? Our coitus won't
> be interruptus by annoying
> phones, as per usual?

> BUNDTUT
> I guarantee it. I didn't tell
> anyone where we were going. The
> secretary was mad as hell, but
> she couldn't tell me she was.
> We've escaped. It's just you
> and me.

Siriluk kisses Bundtut on the cheek.

> BUNDTUT (CONT'D)
> What was that for?

> SIRILUK
> Just to let you know I accept.

**BUNDTUT**

Accept what?

We see a flagged Benz pass them in the opposite direction. Bundtut gives the Security Council salute.

**SIRILUK**

Any proposals you feel like making this weekend?

**BUNDTUT**

Anything?

**SIRILUK**

Anything within the realms of decency and, perhaps, one or two proposals in the outer suburbs of indecency.

**BUNDTUT**

Would that include? Marriage?

She laughs.

**SIRILUK**

Huh. You wish.

**BUNDTUT**

You think you could do better?

The atmosphere changes. Siriluk is suddenly aware that the man beside her has left the world of banter and is asking a serious question. She's felt it coming for a while. She is uncomfortable but surprisingly elated. She's been with him for seven months, and during that time, the role she played has taken over the real Siriluk.

She loves him. It is written all over her face.

> **SIRILUK**
> I know there's a housekeeper
> at the chalet, but do you think
> I could do some cooking this
> weekend?

> **BUNDTUT**
> Is that your way of changing the
> subject?

> **SIRILUK**
> Perhaps.

> **BUNDTUT**
> Why would you do that?

> **SIRILUK**
> (nervously)
> Why? Because you're making fun of
> me. I don't like it.

**BUNDTUT**

What makes you think I'm not
being serious?

**SIRILUK**

Stop it.

**BUNDTUT**

So, if I asked you to marry me,
you'd say no?

**SIRILUK**

Why would somebody like you want
to marry somebody like me? It
doesn't make sense.

**BUNDTUT**

I disagree. I think it makes
perfect sense. We're good
together.

**SIRILUK**

I'm a whore.

**BUNDTUT**

Through no fault of your own. And
there's so much more to you than
that. You have a brain. You're
bold. You're brave. You see
something you don't like, and you
call it out.

> **SIRILUK**
> And you think all the generals
> would allow you to marry below
> your station in life?

> **BUNDTUT**
> I don't care what they like and
> dislike. Most of them have one
> or two legal wives among their
> stables of minor bitches.

> **SIRILUK**
> What happens when they kick you out?

> **BUNDTUT**
> I'd struggle by on my thirty-
> million-baht pension and raise
> alpaca.

Siriluk looks out of the window and
shakes her head.

> **SIRILUK**
> Sounds like I'd be marrying a
> loser.

> **BUNDTUT**
> (laughs)
> No man in this country is going
> to lose his job for romantic
> indiscretions or poor judgment in
> the bedroom. They might disagree
> with my choice, but they need me.

I'm reliable. They've invested in
me. I'm the future.

**SIRILUK**
And how do you see that future?

**BUNDTUT**
With you beside me and four or
five little Bundtuts running
around our feet.

**SIRILUK**
No, I mean, the future of the
country with you at the wheel.

**BUNDTUT**
There's no need for you to worry
about that. We have our plan for
the future mapped out.

**SIRILUK**
So, I'd be more behind than
beside. You wouldn't want
feedback from that little woman
in the bedroom?

Siriluk goes silent. Bundtut looks at
her and notices one single tear rolling
down her cheek.

**BUNDTUT**
What's wrong? You look sad. Did I
say something I shouldn't have?

**SIRILUK**
No, Bundtut. That's exactly what
I needed to hear you say.

                              CUT TO:

Car passes camera and heads off into the
distance.

It was 1 A.M., and it felt like it. Ali was sweeping; Supot was clearing up. They were alone in the shop. The girls had just left. Ali didn't seem to disapprove of the invasion of their space nearly as much as Supot.

"Well, that was very pleasant," said Ali. "We should have screening evenings with pretty young ladies on a regular basis. It could become a Bangkok Noi cultural event. We could have a festival."

Supot wasn't really listening to Ali. Instead, he decided to respond with what was on his mind. "You know, Ali? I bet there are a lot of girls in the same boat as young Pim. Pushed into corners they can't get out of by manipulating old bastards with a bit of money and a horn. That manager's got a wife and three kids; he's old enough to be Pim's granddaddy, and he's still blackmailing her for sex. I thought we left that kind of thing behind in the sixties."

"Don't you believe it, Supot. I bet there are even more minor wives around today than there were then."

"What happened to women's liberation?"

"When you've got enough money to pay the rent, feed the kids, and pay your college fees, then you can afford to be liberated. How many women have that luxury? Don't they teach you anything at the post office? Supot, it's too late to solve the plight of our downtrodden Thai sisters. Let's go home."

"Just doesn't seem fair."

Supot noticed the *2010* video box beside the TV.

"I want that to go in the safe, Ali. Before you know it, we'll have the entire staff of Yakult and every minor wife in the country in here queuing up to watch it."

Supot picked up the box. It was too light. "That's odd." He reached into the cassette player, but it, too, was empty. "You seen the cassette?" he asked.

"Yeah. It's in the box."

"You wanna bet?"

"Sure it is." Ali came over to look. "I put it in there myself . . . Oh, shit."

It was eight-thirty the next day before Supot could get through to Anjira at Yakult. Supot was in a phone box, sweating through his uniform, trying to be heard over the noise of the traffic. His motorcycle full of letters was parked at the curb behind him.

"No. Anjira. A N J I R A . . . No, I don't. I don't know what section she works in. I never— . . . . Isn't there someone you can ask?"

A barefoot street Rasta man wandering along the curb found the motorcycle full of letters blocking his path. His hair was matted like something you'd find in a blocked drain, and he was dressed like a fisherman. As he didn't get any letters himself, he obviously saw this as a good opportunity to catch up with the news. He took one out of the pouch, sat on the curb, opened the envelope, and started reading. Supot had his back to him.

"Look. It's urgent . . . What? No, I can't tell you. It's top secret . . . Thank you."

Supot, waiting for Anjira to come on the line, decided to put in more coins, accidentally dropped one, then spotted the thief. He struggled to open the door.

"Hey, you. What do you think you're doing?"

The Rasta man ignored him.

Supot didn't know what to do. "Put that back," he shouted.

A voice emerged from the phone. "Yes?" The phone cord was

too short to reach the man. Supot tried to grab the letter but didn't want to let go of the phone. "That's government property. I'll— . . . Hello? Anjira? It's Supot. Listen. Did you or Pim take home the *2010* video? . . . . Well, what about Pim? After you left, it was gone. It's important. I'm not supposed to let anyone else see it."

The Rasta man finished the letter and took another. Supot was getting mightily frustrated. "Look. I gotta go. What time do you finish work? . . . Okay. Go find Pim and tell her I'll be around after work to get the tape. She'd better have it. Tell her it's urgent . . . Yeah."

The Rasta man had taken another handful of letters and was walking off along the curb. Supot hung up and ran after him, not sure what his tactics should be in such a situation. He perhaps expected some form of retaliation. Some defensive ploy. He was even prepared to engage in fisticuffs. But he hadn't anticipated the Rasta man's actual response. The would-be thief turned to face the advancing postman, smiled, untied the drawstring on his Thai fisherman pants, and let them drop to the pavement. There was no other layer of undergarment and, as Supot recounted later to Ali, no bull at the annual plowing festival could have boasted such an impressive package. It wasn't admiration. Supot felt sorry for him, having to lug around such a heavy burden all his life. He doubted there was enough blood in the man's skinny body to ever engorge the beast. So, it was out of sympathy that Supot abandoned the chase and left the poor man to his plunder and his skin-headed albatross.

## 54 INT. CHALET BEDROOM — DAY

The shot opens with the rain pelting against the window, then the camera pans around the empty bedroom. It settles on a letter and a chocolate on the pillow of the bed. We hear the apartment door open and close. We hear the voice of Bundtut returning from his run.

#### BUNDTUT
Ah, I needed that. I love running in the rain. Siriluk . . . Luk?

Bundtut, wearing soggy running gear, walks into the bedroom and sees the note. He sits, dries his hair with a towel, eats the chocolate, and opens the letter. Siriluk's voice begins reading the contents of the note.

#### SIRILUK (V.O.)
My love, this is a coward's letter. I can't look into your eyes when I tell you my story. By the time you read it, a great deal of damage will already have been done. Your position and possibly your life are in great peril.

CUT TO:
SECURITY FOOTAGE

Security people are in front of the mon-itor bank reviewing old CCTV recordings. They watch Siriluk's arrival that first

day at the Ministry. The CCTV recording shows Siriluk changing her shoes
and talking to the reception guard, then
walking up the stairwell to the fifti-
eth floor. We see the footage of her in
Bundtut's apartment.

                              DISSOLVE TO:

CAMERA is a single frame of her with the
fruit knife. The technician saves and
enlarges the shot. We see her leaving
Bundtut's secretary's office one night,
then appearing in the computer room seen
from a hidden camera inside the computer. While he's watching this last
video, the supervisor gets on the phone
and begins to describe what he's seeing.

BACK TO SCENE

FRONT ANGLE. CU. BUNDTUT'S FACE.

            **SIRILUK (V.O.)**
    Thanks to information I gathered
    from your apartment and your
    office, my sisters and I were
    able to access the payment
    accounts of all the minor
    wives on your ministry lists.
    Today, as you are well aware,
    is salary allocation day. When
    some nine hundred thousand minor

wife cadres went to collect their quarterly allowances at government currency centers, they found they had each received a substantial raise.

CUT TO:

**TELLER SCENE**

A sister arrives at a high-tech office. The cashier can't believe what he sees on the screen, so he reinserts the ID card.

CAMERA PANS OUT.

Confused, the cashier hands over the larger amount.

The sister is shocked and thrilled.

BACK TO SCENE

> SIRILUK (V.O.)
> As you were unavailable today, there was no one to countermand your orders, so every currency center paid out according to the computerized instructions. They had to accept your verification code.

TRACKING SHOT OF BUNDTUT

Bundtut rushes to his home computer
and checks the figures to confirm what
Siriluk has written. His department is
indeed ruined. His head falls forward
against the computer screen.

CU OF COMPUTER SCREEN

> SIRILUK (V.O. CONT'D)
> Your generous allowance increases
> were so substantial that most of
> the women are now in a position
> to pay off their debt and be
> relieved from their minor wife
> bonds. You see, my love? Money is
> power for everyone.

**55 INT. SIRILUK IN CHALET BEDROOM — DAY**

Siriluk places the letter and the chocolate on the pillow of their bed. As
she runs her hand over the sheets, she
starts crying.

BACK TO SCENE

> SIRILUK (V.O.)
> The responsibility for this mess
> sadly falls upon you, my darling.
> That is my dilemma. You see,
> I have no need to act now, no

reason to pretend. I hated our
day at the lake together today,
as I knew it would be our last.
Although this love affair of ours
began as a fraud, it eventually
became real. I surprised myself
and fell in love with you.

                              CUT TO:

Siriluk passes through the gate of the
Chalet Resort, smiles at the guard, and
crosses the street to the cab rank.
She's about to get into a taxi when
three black Daimlers speed to a halt,
blocking the path of the taxi.

Men in security uniforms stream out. The
head agent stands in front of her and
gives her a back-hander across the jaw.
She's floored. The agents pick her up
roughly and drag her to the car.

                **SIRILUK (V.O.)**
Love really is an awful emotion
but totally addictive. I
understand now why so many of our
sisters lose their minds to you
menfolk. I had never experienced
such a feeling, and it hurts
like no weapon I know of. In
destroying you, I am destroying

a part of myself. I can only hope
that this letter gives you enough
time to save yourself.

                              CUT TO:

## 56 INT. UNDERGROUND CELL — NIGHT

Siriluk is dragged to a dark underground
cell and thrown inside. The shadows
around move toward her. She comes around
slowly and looks up to see that she is
sharing a cell with a number of low caste
males. One hideous old man is already
caressing her leg.

The others seem to be fighting over her.
When she realizes what is about to happen to her, we see the horror.

CU ON HER FACE.

### SIRILUK (V.O.)
My sisters would have me believe
that you are a fundamental
male. That as I aged, you would
naturally lose feelings for
me and seek a younger version.
That inevitability has kept me
strong and allowed me to complete
my mission. Saying sorry is
worthless, I know, considering
what I have done to you. But I

can bequeath you every ounce of
love that my heart has begrudged
me all my life until you came
along. I hope it can mean
something to you.

                              CUT TO:

Bundtut, head down, sitting on the edge
of the bed with the letter at his feet.
When he finally stands, his face is
strong and resolute. He changes into his
uniform, straps on his gun, and rushes
out of the chalet.

              **SIRILUK (V.O.)**
And so, I kill you, my love. But
I will never love another.

Yours always,
Siriluk.

Supot was sitting on the perimeter wall when the Yakult workers left their factory at the end of the shift. They walked like extras in the *Night of the Living Dead* but without the invigorating lust for blood and human entrails. Without any human emotions whatsoever. He jumped down when he saw Anjira and Pim in their Yakult uniforms and hurried over to them.

Pim quickly handed him the video, and said, "I wasn't stealing it. Really, I wasn't. I was going to take it back to Ali's shop tonight."

Supot took the cassette, relieved to be reunited with it.

"That's all right," he said. "No harm done. At least I've got it back."

"It's just . . . it was so important, you see?" said Pim. "Anjira was right. When you watch that movie, it gives you strength to be brave. To stand up for yourself."

"I know."

Anjira took his arm. "We're going for a drink, to celebrate?"

"Nah. I gotta work in the shop. Ali's waiting for me." He pulled his arm free. "Better be going. See y—" But before he could leave, he saw that Pim was about to cry.

"That's why I did it," she said. She couldn't hold back the tears.

"Did what, Pim?" he asked. "Pim? What did you do?"

Anjira put her arm around her. "What did you do?"

"At . . . at . . . at lunchtime, I got the technician in the advertising department to make copies for the other girls in the aluminum tops section."

"You what?" said Supot. His expression changed slightly, an indication that he was annoyed, possibly steaming inside. "The other . . .? Just how many copies did you make exactly?" he asked.

Pim could only cry.

"You're frightening her," said Anjira.

"Really? I'm frightening her? I tell you, being frightened is the best that she can expect if we don't get those tapes back. Pim? How many copies did you make?"

Through her tears, she smuggled out a number.

"Eight."

## 57 INT. JAIL RECEPTION CONSEC.

Bundtut walks past two confused security guards, who follow him to the sergeant's desk. The sergeant is young but seems to be in control. When the sergeant sees the Vice Minister, it's clear from the expression on his face that he's conflicted. He dismisses the guards with a nod and salutes Bundtut.

BUNDTUT
Where's the girl?

SERGEANT
Girl, sir?

                    **BUNDTUT**
Siriluk, 81,988. They told me
upstairs she was brought here.

                    **SERGEANT**
Sir, I've been told there's to be
no access . . .

                    **BUNDTUT**
And the rank of the officer who
gave that order?

                    **SERGEANT**
Captain, sir.


                    **BUNDTUT**
And the rank of the man standing
in front of you here?

                    **SERGEANT**
Comrade, I was told specifically
to give you no access.

Bundtut steps close to the sergeant and
lowers his voice.


                    **BUNDTUT**
Okay, son. Here's what's
happened. It won't be announced
until later today, but there's
been an attempted military coup.

The captain that brought the girl
here was one of the ringleaders.
I'm revoking all his orders.

### SERGEANT
I don't know, sir, perhaps I
should call . . .

### BUNDTUT
We don't have that much time to
waste, son. The woman in the
cell has the names of all
the collaborators. That's why he
wanted her locked away. I take
full responsibility. It's time
for you to decide which team
you're on.

Bundtut calmly takes out his gun but
does not point it at the sergeant.

### BUNDTUT (CONT'D)
I know you can't be proud of
locking up a woman in the lower-
caste male cell. Tell me that's
by the order of someone you can
respect.

The sergeant blushes.

### SERGEANT
No, Comrade. It is not. But I . . .

Bundtut reholsters the gun. He and the sergeant glare at each other. Finally, the sergeant picks up a wad of key cards and leads Bundtut down into the cells.

CAMERA rises to show us that the exchange has been witnessed on CCTV.

CUT TO:

The cell door opens and the sergeant and a guard, with his own gun drawn for safety in that dangerous place, lead Bundtut inside. By the light of a small flashlight, they make out the crumpled body of Siriluk in the shadows. Her clothes are ripped and in disarray.

Bundtut goes to her and kneels over her.

**BUNDTUT**
(whispers)
Oh, my love. What have they done to you?

He looks around at the relaxing inmates, who turn away innocently. Bundtut is shaking with hatred. He lifts Siriluk's body gently in his arms. She's half-conscious, but she looks up at him as he carries her out.

**SIRILUK**
Are you going to kill me?

They leave the cell, following closely
behind the camera to show Bundtut's
dismay.


## TAPE FOUR: 20:40 HOURS

Supot, in full ceremonial dress postman's uniform, was
standing with Ali, who was wearing an ill-fitting suit, trying
to fix his tie, in the shadow of a low-budget housing complex.
Every other streetlamp was inactive, and the moon was hidden somewhere behind the smoke and pollution of the day.

"You sure I have to do this?" Ali asked.

"Brother, brother, brother," said Supot. "You know me. I
couldn't act my way out of a plastic bag, otherwise I'd do it.
You have all the skill, all the imagination. You can get away
with it." He held up a list of addresses. "Besides, we only have
five addresses to visit. I got three of the video copies before
the girls left the factory. We have to do it tonight before they
get a chance to make any more."

The knot in Ali's tie looked like a ginseng root.

"I'm losing valuable income by closing the shop for a
whole night," said Ali. "Who's going to compensate me for
that?"

"When DreamWorks buys the *Dylan the Welsh Volunteer*
screenplay, we'll be so rich, we won't need our three and a
half customers a night."

"That's true," said Ali. "Let's act."

They walked in an official manner up to the door of one
cramped terraced house. There was no bell, and the door

was loose on its hinges, so Supot knocked. An older man in shorts and an off-white singlet came to the door. Supot saluted while Ali *wai*'d.

"Good evening, sir," said Ali. "I am Inspector Bradit from the Post Office Video Inspection Division." He flashed a card. "Does a Miss"—he looked at his list—"Kesinee live here?"

The old man looked at him for a moment, then said, "That was an ATM card."

"What?"

"That card you just showed me was an ATM card."

"No, it wasn't?"

"Yes, it was. There's nothing wrong with my eyes."

"Really?" said Ali. "Oops. Wrong card." He pretended to be going through his wallet for the official POVI ID card, when a girl came and stood beside the man.

"What is it, Dad?" she said.

Ali abandoned his search. "Ah. Are you Kesinee?"

"Why do you wanna know?" the old man asked.

"Today you received a video from a Miss Pimpaporn. Nickname Pim. Is that correct?"

"Well?" said the girl.

"I'm afraid it was an unlawful recording and—"

"Unlawful? People copy videos all the time," she said.

"That's why we're clamping down," said Ali, then turned to Supot.

"There you are. An epidemic of illegal activity." Supot looked sternly at Kesinee. "As part of the Interior Ministry clamp-down against civilians blatantly infringing copyright laws, we are obliged to reclaim all illegally copied videos and begin the process of the payment of fines. I'm sorry."

Supot and Ali waited on the step when the girl went inside. She was gone a long time. The father stood guard but said nothing.

"What did you mean when you said Dylan has to be Welsh because he was?" Supot asked Ali while they waited for the copy of the tape.

"The tourist who hit me was wearing a WALES FOREVER rugby shirt," said Ali.

"Kwang said you just started wearing a head bandage for no particular reason."

"She knows nothing about the film industry."

"But did that really happen?"

"Does it matter?"

"I guess not," said Supot. "But it's getting a bit creepy. And . . ."

"And what?"

"And you'd have a better chance of selling it if he was American," said Supot.

Ali chewed it over. "I suppose he could have been an American wearing a WALES FOREVER rugby shirt."

"There you go," said Supot, still not knowing the veracity of it all. "Art and business in perfect harmony."

A few minutes later, Kesinee brought out the video and gave it to Ali. Supot saluted, as did Ali. Kesinee and her father did the same. Ali and Supot turned and walked in an official manner from the house.

Once out of earshot, Supot leaned toward his friend. "You're good at this."

"I am." Ali grinned from ear to ear.

Four more tapes remained.

## TAPE FIVE: 21:02 HOURS

Supot and Ali stood outside an open door in an uninspiring apartment second-floor hallway. The neighbors on either side had come out to see what "she'd done this time." "She" opened the door just wide enough for Ali to see her nose with its rather uncomfortable-looking nose ring. She didn't speak, so Ali gave his spiel, but the nose showed no reaction.

"Do you understand?" Ali asked.

There was still no reply.

"She won't answer you," said one of the nosy neighbors. Almost every room on the floor had now spewed out its occupants.

"She's from the northeast," said one, which made it sound like she was from another country.

"Keeps herself to herself," said another.

"Not the sociable type."

Within minutes, the girl had been put on trial by the second-floor community for being antisocial. Ali wondered whether they had enough rope for a lynching. Supot felt sorry for the girl and took it upon himself to clear the floor and give Ali a better chance of rescuing the tape.

"Listen up," he said, and looked at the names on his note board. "I'm sure we all want to get this over with as soon as we can and get back to our TVs. We'll get to all of you in time."

"All of us?" said a woman.

"Of course," said Supot. "I'm sure you've got nothing to worry about. You look like an honest crowd. We just need to check that your videos are legal and that there are no bootleg copies or homemade recordings from the TV."

He was confident they'd all have TVs and video players. For the folks of this social background, the first salary check would procure them a TV; the second, a player. The middle class had its priorities.

"Wouldn't want to have to fine any of you, would we?" he added.

There wasn't exactly a stampede of people returning to their rooms to hide their videos. Rather, one by one they slipped back inside and, soon, the hallway was all but empty.

"Good job, Supot," said Ali.

Unnoticed, the girl with the nose ring had retrieved her version of the *2010* video and was holding it out through the gap. They never did see what she looked like.

## TAPE SIX: 11:26 HOURS

Ali, Supot, and a pretty plump girl sat on her couch watching *2010*. She'd insisted they watch it one last time before they confiscated it. Supot looked at his watch and showed Ali the time. Ali shrugged. Like the apartment building of the girl with the nose ring, this room seemed to be somewhat beyond the means of a Yakult girl. He had to assume somebody else was paying the rent.

The girl was explaining a point from the film, a point that Ali and Supot understood all too well. But it was clear from the defiant look on her face and the set of her jaw that she was not seeing the film as mere entertainment. Fortunately for Supot and Ali, her political stance was interrupted by the sound of a car horn. The girl went to the window, and Ali and Supot followed.

A black Benz was parked below. The window of the car wound down, then an elderly man in the driver's seat poked his head out. He looked up at her and angrily signaled for her to join him, pointing to his watch. The girl made a rude sign and shouted insults that he would have been unable to hear. But her intent was unmistakable. Ali and Supot heard the words clearly, and even they were red-faced. The man looked amazed and drove off. Ali and Supot watched as he almost took out a roadside dried squid seller before vanishing into the night. The three figures in the window stood staring long after he'd gone. Something profound had just happened.

## TAPE SEVEN: 01:00 HOURS

There was no door to the tall thin girl's house. The entrance was blocked with a sheet of plywood. It seemed she relied on an elderly pit bull to keep out intruders. But when Ali and Supot arrived, the dog wasn't remotely interested in them; he just snored loudly in its dotage. They slid the plywood to one side and took off their shoes, even though the floor was dirty. They apologized to the girl, who was sitting cross-legged on a mat eating noodles. They hadn't realized it was so late. She told them not to worry because she'd just returned from her second job. She was, she said, "a waitress at a sleazy bar in the city." She readily confessed that if she were better-looking and had cleavage, she would have preferred to be on the stage holding onto a pole. "Much better money for a girl with a figure," she said.

Ali and Supot began to explain about the tape. The girl laughed and pointed to the other side of the room, where her toddler sat in a makeshift crib playing with *2010*. It was a brand of spaghetti that was already familiar to them. It was unwatchable.

## TAPE EIGHT: 02:17 HOURS

A gritty-looking young woman in curlers stood in the doorway with her arms folded. She was wearing pajamas with a Disney *101 Dalmatians* cartoon theme. It made her look like a huge four-year-old. They'd woken her, and she didn't appreciate that. She was the type who needed all the beauty sleep she could get. Ali ended his act with a confident plea for the return of the tape. The girl thought for a while, then shook her head. She wouldn't part with it, she said. She slammed the door in their faces. They looked at each other, shocked, and sat on the step outside.

"I'm tired," said Ali. "Can't we just forget this one?"

"You know we can't, brother. I promised Siriluk."

"She'd never know."

"She'd know when there were suddenly a few thousand bootleg copies of *2010* on the market," said Supot. "She'd know it was me who broke my promise. She'd hate me."

"Well, there's only one solution to this dilemma."

"What's that?"

"Turn out your pockets."

The girl was not prepared to come to the door a second time, so the financial negotiations were conducted loudly and long-distance between the door and the back bedroom. Everyone in the building would have been forced to listen to the dealings. At last, they settled on a figure that would leave them with only the taxi fare home. She told them to slide the notes under the door, which they did. And nothing happened.

"Do you think we've been robbed?" Ali asked.

"Young lady," Supot shouted.

There was no answer.

"Are you going to give us the tape?" Ali asked.

There was no reply."

"You should know we have recorded this entire interaction on video camera," Ali lied.

There was another minute of silence before . . .

"Hold on to your horses, I'm counting," said the girl.

"She's counting," said Ali.

"There were only ten banknotes," said Supot.

"She sticks tops on bottles for a living," said Ali. "She's not a banker."

Back at the video shop, Ali and Supot were drinking Lactasoy from cartons. There were eight *2010* videos piled on the counter in front of them. Ali, with his tie around his head, was tired but still obviously on a high from the performances.

"At a moment like this, I would expect myself to be moaning and complaining about the humiliating, not to mention illegal activity you forced me into tonight," Ali said.

"But?"

"But I confess I found it stimulating."

"You're a good actor, my friend."

"I am indeed. I'm a natural. I'm going to rent myself out to film companies. Maybe this was the big something I needed. I'm certainly going to play myself in the *Dylan the Welsh Volunteer* movie."

"Who is currently Randy, the volunteer from Texas."

"Yeah. Right."

Supot walked over to the comfortable chairs and started rearranging them.

"You could play my transvestite sister," said Ali. "We'll say she was damaged in an earthquake and lost all the movement in her face . . . What are you doing?"

"It's three in the morning."

"I didn't ask you what time it was."

"I'm getting ready for bed. It's morning. I start work in two and a half hours. I'm already in uniform. You have instant noodles. I'm not going home." He settled down on the chairs. "Sweet dreams."

*Dear Siriluk,*

*I'm sorry to write again before you have a chance to answer my last letter, but it's been almost three weeks since I heard from you. I'm worried in case you caught malaria and are in bed alone. (I mean with no one to look after you.) I've heard there are a lot of mosquitoes up there because of all that greenery. Thank goodness we don't have that many trees here in Bangkok Noi.*

*I just want to say, don't worry about answering the questions I asked. I'm too nosy. Forget I asked. Really. I wanted you to know I'm taking good care of 2010. It's in safe hands. No problem here.*

*Perhaps you'd be interested to hear that there's a lot of concern around the subject of minor wives here in Bangkok. I'm sure if young women could see 2010 it would motivate them to be independent and not let men take advantage of them. I was wondering whether you would ever consider making it available to young women.*

*I would never take on a minor wife, and not only because I can't afford one, I'm not sure I'll even find a major one. The girls here are very nice and some are very beautiful. But I'm hoping to meet an elegant and sophisticated woman with talent—someone like you. You are really special and, to tell the truth, I can't stop thinking about you. I hope you don't mind me saying that.*

*I'd better get this letter off to you now. You know how bad the postal service can be. If you've got malaria, it might cheer you up to get a letter from your special penfriend in Bangkok Noi. Of course, I'd prefer you not to have malaria.*

*I end here and look forward to receiving your letter.*

*Your devoted supporter and holder of the only copy of 2010,*

*Supot*

# ACT 2
# THE MOTION PICTURE TELLER

Nine weeks went by without Supot hearing from Siriluk. He had written six times in total. The last four were registered and express. He went over and over the contents of his second letter—the first one she didn't reply to. He probably knew deep in his heart what had led to her silence. That was the letter in which he broke the news to her that he was a postman. That had to be it. It was stupid. What classy woman would want any sort of relationship with a postman? It certainly isn't something a girl would boast about to her movie star friends.

The day arrived when he was left with little choice. His contact at TAT had given him the number and an address for Siriluk's cell phone. Writing letters hadn't worked. He'd avoided thinking about the next option for all that time because . . . well, because he was himself. He was boring. Insufferable, some might say. In a letter you could paint over faults like that, but in real life, live and in color, you were exposed. You had to be responsive. You had to have confidence. You had to be brilliant in some way to distinguish you from other suitors.

He rehearsed for a month. He drew up dozens of scenarios, directions their phone conversation might take. Questions she might ask to throw him off. Personal questions that deserved personal responses. He sat through a dozen classic comedies: *Duck Soup, Some Like It Hot, Bringing Up*

*Baby,* and the like, and jotted down witty remarks he could make to lighten the dialogue. When it came to the day of the call, everything was covered apart from spontaneity. He decided it wasn't something you could prepare for, so he would do his best to avoid it.

The phone only rang three times before a female voice came over the line and smashed against his heart like a defibrillator.

"Khun Siriluk?" he said. "I'm sorry to disturb you. This is your long-distance friend Supot." He spoke fast, eager to get words on the table, but the voice ignored him.

"The number you are attempting to call is no longer registered," it said.

"No," he said. "That isn't possible. I'm trying to—"

"The number you are attempting to call is no longer registered."

"I just need to—"

"The number you are attempting . . ."

He engaged the recorded message for another five minutes until it ran out of steam and left him listening to a continuous apiarian hum. He called again, just to be certain, and again, and again. But the message didn't change its tune, and Supot did not have the opportunity to release any of his lines. The exchange left him in a funk that he couldn't find a way out of.

The rainy season arrived with its usual inconsiderate timing. The monsoons always pissed him off, but this year was worse than ever. The river overflowed and the smelly high water filled the lanes and hid the potholes. The pavements reverted from concrete to mud overnight. Cockroaches seeking higher ground ran through the spokes of Supot's motorcycle wheels, and the drenching rain soaked through to his underwear. His fake leather boots became soggy, and the peak of his cap drooped over his face as he watched the addresses on his envelopes slowly blur themselves away in the deluge. It was a thoroughly appropriate rainy season for his mood.

Ali had been right. Supot was suffering from *Roman Holiday* syndrome. He'd really wanted something to happen between himself and Siriluk, and when it didn't, there was no point to the movie. Audrey Hepburn has her fling and moves back into the palace. And that's it. We catch a glimpse of Gregory Peck in a public toilet masturbating as he thinks about what might have been. That was real life.

Supot needed Ali more than ever about that time. But he'd lost him too. In a way that was Supot's fault. The scam they pulled to get the videos back really put Ali in the mood to be an actor. His confidence was blooming. He'd gone for auditions for bit parts in films and, one day, a local company had called him back. He was exactly what they were looking to cast for a small part in an upcoming Thai movie. He and Supot had once tried to calculate the percentage of Thai films that were either ghost stories or tales of unrequited teenage love. They had wondered whether audiences flocked to them because it was what they were hungry for, or whether it was the only fodder they were fed. But there was Ali, cast as a young schoolteacher in *Zombie High School Prom.* He even had a few lines before being decapitated. The irony had apparently evaded Ali.

Right through to the going-away party, Supot had convinced Ali he was delighted for his friend. He wanted to hear all about it upon his return and go through all the photographs together. It was a great thing, but it hurt. If trauma had a scale, losing Ali at that moment would have settled somewhere between losing a leg and going blind. It wasn't a catastrophe, but it was certainly domestic upheaval. It wasn't just because he suddenly didn't have a friend to bring down daily with his depressing news. It was because Ali had chosen this particular time to do something alone that Supot should have been doing with him. It was something he'd always dreamed of but had known was beyond his capabilities. He could never be an actor. He should have been happy for his friend, but he wasn't.

Something strange happened to Supot. He could no longer stand his life. He hated the mail service. Every step on every route, every sleeping dog, every stupid question from every stupid householder. It all came crashing down on him like a poorly constructed building in an earthquake. For a good misery buzz you needed passion, and he'd never reached that extreme. The suicide scene in *Romeo and Juliet* had baffled him. He always got a laugh out of it. He was sure he'd never be that brokenhearted to take his own life because of a failed romance. But now he had doubts.

There was one day in October when the only way his customers would have received their mail was with a fishing net. On the canal bank, a soaked Supot sat all afternoon in the pouring rain, smoking cigarettes and flicking letters into the water. It was a latter-day *Krathong* festival, where the candle and flower floats were replaced by packets of sweets from the northeast and love letters to girls who would never know. Anyone who saw him that afternoon avoided him. Not only because of the menacing look in his eyes, but there was also something feral about a uniformed man crouching in the damp grass. It was his last day as a postman. He'd slipped a note under the door of the shuttered video store before he left. He wasn't sure he would ever come back.

There's usually a line between doing insane things and

actually being insane. On that occasion, the line got rubbed out in Supot's mind. There was only one thought, and nothing about it was rational. In the West, perverts were put in jail for stalking actresses. Supot used to say what pathetic losers those guys must be. You always think badly of pathetic losers until you become one yourself.

No. He didn't care whether they arrested him, or shot him, or chemically sterilized him to make him safe for society. He was in love. It was a horrible feeling. He wouldn't recommend it to anyone. He just needed to hear the words, "Don't bother me, postman," from Siriluk's own mouth, and see the look of disgust in her eyes. That would have been enough to get him unstuck from the muddy fictional romance he'd found himself in. He decided to let fate decide whether they should be together.

It would be surprising and perhaps intriguing to learn that Siriluk shared some common ground with Supot. Like the postman, she had never known her father, and they both mourned their absent mothers. At their compound, she was surrounded by artists and artisans, actors, and those with limitless imaginations. Hers was a commune of the arts. Despite her obvious abilities, by comparison, she considered herself lacking. She had no belief in herself. To Siriluk, her looks meant that nobody would take her seriously as an actress. Yet, the fact that she would choose not to act at all had astounded everyone. They believed that if it was in the blood, it was impossible to ignore.

She sat beside Ting, the headwoman of the commune. The old woman's white hair was piled on top of her head like a triple vanilla cone. It was the hour before sunset, the magical time when light cast an eerie pallor across the landscape. It was a time when secrets begged to be told. From her bamboo veranda on the crest of the hill, they could see the sprawling longan orchard. It stretched out all the way to the opposite hill, which seemed content with its humble pomelo and orange groves. Macadamias and mangoes lined the flanks. Not surprisingly, Ting had named her home Fruit and Nut Villa.

"Of course, Luk, it's your decision," said Ting. "You're free to come and go as you wish. This is no stalag."

"I know."

"But how do you think it will solve the problem of the letters?"

"I can't pretend I know the answer to that," said Luk. "He has the address. There's every chance he'll find his way here one day. We both know what that would mean."

"It might not be as bad as you believe."

"And it could be worse."

The old woman poured them more chamomile tea from the hand-crafted pot.

"My intuition tells me it's a disaster waiting to happen," said Siriluk. "I need to deflect him somehow. The only way I can do that is to go to Bangkok and talk to him. Persuade him not to come."

"He certainly seems infatuated," said the woman. "Six letters in two and a half months?"

"We've all read them. There's no question. And having a crush like that makes us do ridiculous things."

"I'm not sure your letters to him helped the situation in any way."

"What do you mean?"

"They were deceptive," said Ting.

"I could hardly tell him the truth, could I now?"

"Have you told your mother?"

"She knows nothing."

"I think that's best," said the woman. "How will you explain your absence?"

"I'll tell her there's an audition," said Luk. "In her troubled mind, I'm still the leading lady in *2010*. She's desperate for me to accept a new role."

The dusk bats were beginning their early evening foray. Their shadows scythed back and forth across the veranda.

"Do you have somewhere to stay?" asked the woman.

"I was hoping I might be able to use the condo."

"Of course. It's just sitting there, empty. Moo bought it with the money he inherited from his father, so we'd have somewhere to stay in the capital. Of course, he never got to use it. The idiot died before the papers were finalized. His timing was always lousy."

Luk smiled and sipped her tea. "We all miss him," she said.

"With Gan passing last year and Vongkot leaving us a few months back, it's starting to feel like the top end of our world here is reaching its use-by date. I won't be far behind them."

"Ah, don't say that, Ting. You'll outlive all of us."

"You're nervous."

"What makes you say that?"

"It's not like you to drop in a random cliché like that."

"Clichés are clichés because they're the most economical way to get the job done. In my opinion, they get a bad rap."

The woman laughed.

"You have a lot of your father's traits."

"So they tell me."

The old woman bent down and retrieved an old metal biscuit tin from under her seat. She opened it, took out a wad of banknotes, and handed them to Luk.

"You'll need this. There's nothing free in Bangkok. I doubt you'll get away with bartering mangosteens for a taxi fare. How long do you think you'll be staying there?"

"As long as it takes, I guess. Long enough to be sure he knows how hopeless the whole thing is. I have to fall him out of love."

It had started as a chill on the day Supot launched the Royal Thai Mail on its journey downstream. A hot shower, a mug of Ovaltine, and an early night, and it might have remained just that: a sniffle. But when a man feels sorry for himself, it's natural for him to self-harm. He'd sat on his narrow balcony in his damp clothes that night drinking rum and Coke. He wasn't a drinker, so it was more of an act of idiocy than a celebration. The alcohol deleted any immunity his body could offer.

Yet, deep in his influenza funk, he'd left his apartment the next morning, launching himself into another Bangkok Noi downpour. He wore a plastic poncho that was barely waterproof and carried his post office bag on one shoulder. He hailed a *tuk-tuk* at the end of his lane and set off for the bus station, where he bought a ticket to the north. He sat at the terminal with a few dozen passengers and watched the girl clean the interior of the orange Chatchai coach. He felt sorry for a bus that seemed to have no chance to rest. He coughed into a sarong he'd wrapped around his lower face to protect the other passengers from his cold. His nose dribbled, his head throbbed, and every muscle in his body ached. The woman who sat beside him had apparently lost some mystical lottery and would no doubt infect everyone in her village after their night together.

It probably didn't occur to him that his life might be

in danger. He wouldn't have known that over a hundred thousand Thais died of flu every year and that he'd done everything possible to join them. He mistakenly believed that the Fisherman's Friends he sucked during the journey would be some magical antidote to death.

Siriluk walked the puddle-bound streets of Bangkok Noi in her Wellington boots. It had been a last-minute decision to pack them, but they and her Wall's ice cream umbrella turned out to be her wisest choices. Despite the incessant rain, she could taste petroleum in the air. She was used to long hikes through jungled landscapes, hours of absorbing nature. But here in the dirty city, the fumes weakened her. Walking was a chore. Nature was gratuitous. Embarrassing plants in concrete pots seemed to mock her as she passed. She could see no way for the sparse vegetation to apportion the correct amounts of carbon dioxide and oxygen to satisfy nature. Bangkok was undergoing a slow extermination of its population.

Siriluk had three addresses for Supot from his letters. The first was that of a video rental shop on the high street. The shutter was rolled down to hide the door and was fastened with an embarrassingly small padlock. The windows on either side were plastered with movie posters and Siriluk couldn't help but to study them in detail. She'd heard of a number of the films, seen some, but didn't expect to witness such posters in a Thai shop window. They were beautifully designed and advertised in foreign languages like secrets.

The lights were off inside, and there was no movement. She was about to walk away when she spotted a small note at knee level.

*With apologies to our regular customers, this shop will be closed for a month from October 20th to November 21st. We're off to make a movie, Ali Choangulia.*

The second address on Siriluk's list was that of what must be the postman's apartment. The gray building had possibly been white in its heyday, but mold and inclement weather had turned its walls blotchy and its demeanor melancholy. The reception area was an airlock between two glass doors. Neither of them was locked. A bank of mailboxes overflowing with junk occupied one wall and a RESPECT YOUR BUILDING sign the only feature opposite. Through the inner door she found herself on the ground floor corridor with white doors on either side. It reminded her of a mental hospital dormitory she'd once visited with her mother in Chiang Mai.

She climbed the stairs to the third floor where room 3D stood out from the rest. It was the only happy door in the building, adorned with movie posters and flyers. The door handle sprouted out of an alien's rear end. She knocked. There was no reply, but she heard a shuffling in the room opposite. She turned in time to see a brief shadow pass over the peephole. She knocked once more on Supot's door then turned and knocked on the one with the shadow.

"Excuse me," she said. "I'm looking for—"

The door opened and jammed briefly in the frame. A middle-aged man stood there in full Chelsea Football Club uniform. From the size of his paunch, it was apparent he didn't actually play for the team.

"He's not there," he said, looking her up and down.

"Any idea where he is?" she asked.

"He's gone to make a movie."

"Really? Where?"

"Hollywood, I guess," said the man. "Nice boots."

"Thanks. How do you know he's making a movie?"

"I'm looking after his cactus," he said, as if that explained everything.

"I don't—"

"I came home this morning . . . I work nights, you see? And there was this cactus in front of my door with a note asking me to water it while he's gone. I always thought the point of having a cactus was that you didn't have to water it, but what do I know? He said he'd collect it when he comes back from making a movie. Didn't say where. You his girlfriend?"

"No."

"You got anyone?"

"Yes, thanks. What about his job?"

"The post?"

"Yes."

"No idea. Took leave, I guess. We're not exactly close, you know? Not buddies, you might say."

Without being asked, the man went back into his room and returned with the note. The one thing Siriluk noticed was that the handwriting was not Supot's.

Siriluk waded back to the condo through the ever-deepening flood water. In some places the grimy slush threatened to overflow into her boots. In others, residents had made stepping-stones from chairs so they could enter their property. Some had inflatable boats in their garages, others settled for a zinc bathtub. Bangkok residents had become used to the ravages of nature. Theirs was a city that had been planned and built on a network of waterways surrounded by fields to absorb the water. Once the developers took over from the planners, the system failed, and Bangkok started to sink.

At the compound condominium, Siriluk had a hot shower to remove the pollutants and helped herself to the noodle selection in the kitchen cupboard. She didn't know what her next move should be. Where could she find Supot? The note in his friend's shop window had said he too was off to make a movie. Perhaps they'd gone together? Tomorrow, she would focus her attention on the owner of the shop and his family. Somebody must know where they'd gone.

The orange bus took fourteen hours to get to Chiang Rai. It felt more like the twelve days it might have taken in a *2010* traffic jam. He felt every bump, every swerve. His body ached as if he'd been trodden underfoot by yaks. His face scarf was damp from snot and sweat. He sat shivering on the concrete bench at the bus station with barely enough strength to get to his feet. The phlegm churned in his chest like gravel in a crusher. The sign above him said WELCOME TO CHIANG RAI, but the place was no more or less welcoming than any of the towns the bus had stopped in on its way north. The other passengers had found their way out of the bus station, leaving one solitary postman.

"Need a ride, brother?" came a voice.

Supot looked up to see a sinewy, dark-skinned man in a navy-blue shirt and pink Bermuda shorts.

"You know Bang Maprao?" Supot asked. His own voice frightened him. He was Linda Blair in *The Exorcist*. Probably didn't look unlike her either.

"Know it like the hairs on my chin," said the man.

Supot noted those few hairs that barely constituted a beard.

"How far is it?" he asked.

"Not far," said the man, grabbing Supot's bag and heading for the car park. Supot took a deep breath, found his feet, and staggered after him. He caught up with him standing beside a rusting bicycle *samlor*.

"You're joking," said Supot, looking around for something with an engine. But this was the last cab on the rank.

"Not at all, brother. Me and Pam here have covered every inch of this province. There's not an address we don't know, not a shortcut we can't show you, not a pothole we can't avoid."

"You heard of Nirvana?" Supot asked.

"The commune or the state of happiness?"

"I'd settle for the commune right now."

"Know it, brother. Know it well. I'm out there all the time. Climb aboard. Your pack's loaded already."

Supot had trouble focusing on his bag, which was attached to the canvas roof with a bungee cord. The rider helped him onto the seat, straddled the saddle, and strained to reach the pedals. But once engaged, those scrawny legs built up quite a head of steam.

The rider's idea of "not far" was a stretch. Time seemed to slow down in Supot's mind as they left the suburbs and headed off along the highway. He ignored the metallic screams of pickup trucks passing a whisker from their wheel hub and fell into a blurry coma. Somewhere along the journey they left the main road and began to climb hills. He was jarred awake by the unfamiliar sounds of creatures. Crows cawed. Cicadas screeched. The rider wheezed. The chain squeaked. And all these sounds came together in a sort of dirge that made Supot smile. Hours might have passed, or just minutes, but the sun was still high in a sky that was bluer than any he'd seen at home.

The *samlor* stopped in the middle of a paved but seemingly untraveled road. The rider helped Supot to the ground and unfastened his pack.

"We're here," he said.

"I don't . . . I don't see anything," said Supot.

He was so weak he could hardly stand. All around him was a lush forest that trespassed onto the road here and there. He recalled the scene in *Misery* when the unconscious author is found beside the road and is dragged to the house of a psychopath.

"Are you going to just leave me here?" he asked.

"See that pathway?" said the rider. He pointed to an area where the vegetation had been somewhat cleared. At that point there was an incongruous mailbox. "That's your Nirvana."

"There's no sign," said Supot, still holding on to the frame of the *samlor*.

"Yeah, I get the feeling they aren't so in love with strangers."

"How far's the commune?"

"Not far."

Supot had become color blind on the way and had trouble distinguishing between the banknote denominations. He may have paid too much, but neither he nor the rider cared.

The *samlor* man looked him up and down. "You want me to wait?" said the rider.

"No, thanks."

The *samlor* turned around and headed back in the direction from where it had come, but being without it was disorienting. He had nothing to hold on to. He was in the middle of an empty road with jungle all around him; jungle that had started to move, the greens blending together. He could no longer see the clearing or the mailbox. No longer stop the trees from jogging rings around him. He could no longer prevent the sun from spreading into the shape of a frying egg. The last he remembered was the tarmac of the road rushing toward him and the crack of his head against it.

It was cold and desolate in Supot's coma. Sometimes there was just blackness. Then there were voices, men's voices.

"Well, he's not dead," said one.

"That's a relief," said another. "There'd be all that paperwork to take care of."

"How did he get here?"

"I'm told they made a litter out of bamboo and dragged him."

"Unusual that. The hero usually marches in on two feet brandishing a sword."

"It would have to be a horse."

"Brandishing a horse?"

"Heroes no longer walk, you fool. You, of all people, should know that."

There were several confusing exchanges like that, sound only. Then there were the dreams. There was one where he was in a poorly lit room and Siriluk was sitting on a chair beside him, reading him a story. She was wearing one of her costumes from *2010*. Her hair was blow-dried and sparkly. She smelled of eucalyptus.

He tried to say, "Ma, tell me another story," but nothing came out of his mouth. And then she was gone.

There was another he remembered well. He was in the body of old Woot. Only his face gave away the fact that he was Supot. A limousine pulled up in the slum and the rear window wound down, revealing Ali, who had become a superstar of the silver screen. He threw an almost completely melted Kit Kat bar at the bum version of Supot.

Supot attempted to shout, "Ali, it's me," but, again, his

voice was inaudible. Most of his coma reveries were silent movies. It was surprising.

Finally, he awoke one day in a bright cottage surrounded by knickknacks and bizarre sculptures. He was lying on a soft bed with images of kittens on the sheets. An electric fan bathed him head to foot in cool air. The smell of baking wafted its way through the air.

"Hello?" he said and was pleasantly surprised to hear his own voice. He felt weak, but his mind was more alive than it had been for most of his stay on earth. He tried to sit up, but it became apparent that his muscles hadn't been used for some time. He wondered how long he'd been there in that nice room. He tried again.

"Hello?"

This time, a woman of about sixty popped her head around the doorframe. Her hair was gray and thick as a horse's mane. She wore dungarees and a plaid shirt. The outfit was topped with a green hospital mask.

"Well, at last, Mr. Supot," she said. "We thought you'd never wake up."

"Is this Nirvana?" he asked.

"Why, yes, in both respects."

She turned and shouted, "Malee, go tell Ting that our visitor has regained consciousness."

"Yes, Granny," came the out-of-sight response.

"You'll have to excuse the mask," said the old lady. "But you did bring some nasty germs with you from Bangkok. Out here in the wilderness, we don't have resistance to a lot of city illnesses. We didn't want an epidemic, did we now?"

"How close was I to not making it?" Supot asked.

"Hard to tell. Probably, one night in the rain would have polished you off. It gets cold up here in the mountains. But two robust hill-tribe girls found you and dragged you here.

You had a fever and a temperature of forty-something. You were probably heading for pneumonia. We couldn't get you to a hospital, so they brought you here."

"Are you a doctor?"

"More like a witch doctor but without the curses and voodoo dolls. We grow all our own naturopathic medicines, but I have a stash of antivirals for cases that can't wait for Mother Nature to cure. I suppose you could say I saved your life . . . if you want to be dramatic. My name is Chawalee."

Supot thought about that for a while.

"Thank you," he said.

"You're welcome."

"In fact, the reason I came here was—"

"Ah, we don't want to hear about that," came a voice. Through the open door walked a woman Supot guessed to be in her early sixties as well. She also had a fine head of white hair and was tall for a Thai. She kicked off her sandals and walked over to the bed, where she stood, hands on hips, staring down at the patient.

"I'm Ting," she said. "I'm currently the leader of this commune. And you are an intruder."

"I know," he said.

"As soon as you're well enough to walk, you'll be leaving."

"I thought communes were places of peace and love," said Supot.

The witch doctor subdued a laugh.

"I came here to meet someone," said Supot.

The two women exchanged a look that Supot noticed.

"Who?" asked Ting.

"Siriluk," said Supot.

"Have to be more specific than that," said the headwoman. "We have half a dozen Siriluks here. It's a common enough name."

"Siriluk Pamang," said Supot.

"Ah, then you've wasted a trip. She doesn't live here anymore."

"But I wrote to her here just a few months ago."

"I don't know about that. Perhaps someone forwarded it to her."

Supot felt a weight heavy as an old refrigerator in his chest. He struggled for words.

"Do you know where she went?" he managed after some time.

"No idea," said Ting. "All right. I have a lot to do. Glad to see you're better. But I don't want you walking around annoying people. Understand?" And with that, she turned and left.

The witch doctor shrugged.

"She's adorable," said Supot.

"She's an amazing woman," said the witch doctor. "She and her husband started this place thirty years ago. We're self-sufficient on most things, and what we can't grow we barter for."

"Are you communists?" Supot asked.

"Well, that depends."

"On what?"

"Whether you think communism is nice or nasty. I personally think it's lovely."

Supot rearranged himself on the mattress. There were few muscles that didn't cause him pain. There was a pile driver throbbing in his head, and he was aware that he could sink back into the mire at any minute.

"You know Suriluk, right?" he said.

"Oh, look, Supot—"

"Why is this such a difficult question?"

"It's not the question that's difficult. It's the answer."

"What did she do that was so terrible you can't tell me?"

"Nothing. Look, you need to rest. We'll have a talk when you're feeling better."

She handed him a glass of water and held out two small earplug-sized lumps of something organic. She gestured for him to swallow them. They burned a little on the way down but felt good in his gut. And as he thought about his insides, he forgot completely what he'd been talking about and rejoined the spirits of the unconscious.

"He's here."

"What?"

"Your postman turned up here half-dead with a fever. He barely made it."

"Damn. I was afraid of that. I should have called you sooner. Yet another case in favor of mobile phones."

"There's nothing so urgent that you need a ringing tone in your back pocket shocking you to death," said Ting. "This good old immobile phone has served us beautifully all these years."

"So, you wouldn't consider this call 'urgent'?"

"The postman being here in itself isn't necessarily an emergency. We just need to get him out before he learns anything."

"I'll take the bus back tonight."

"I . . ."

"What?"

"I told him Siriluk didn't live here anymore," said Ting.

"Oh, how sweet that you two should have already started a dialogue on the subject."

"It wasn't much of a dialogue. 'Siriluk' was the first word he spoke in his deliria. I think if you were here, it would be very hard to convince him to leave. You have to agree, we want this over with as quickly as possible.

Just stay there. Enjoy the condo for a few more days. Go see some films. Eat junk food. Breathe some carbon dioxide."

"How long will it be before he's well enough to leave?"

"He can already make it to the bathroom on his own, I'm told."

It was midday. A time that Supot traditionally hated. The hour when the concrete capital had absorbed its share of blazing sun rays and had started to pay the city back. Invisible plumes of heat rose from the sidewalks. Clouds of unbreathable air. Saggy people shuffling off in their lunch breaks to sit on uncomfortable stools under tin roofs for twenty minutes of tasteless noodles that begged for spicy sauce and just made everyone sweat to hell and back.

But here in Chiang Rai, midday was more than tolerable. The air was breathable. He might even have called it pleasant. The heat was crisply therapeutic, and there was a breeze escaping from the forest that wasn't exactly cool, but cheerful. He inhaled its rural bouquet as he sat crumpled on the wooden veranda of the witch doctor's house.

Chawalee was usually close by, but Supot had awoken that morning, alone but for the ceiling lizards. He knew for the first time that he was going to live. All the signals of his previous awakenings had been ominous, the almost imperceptible shaking of the head of his doctor, the pains of toilet helplessness, the memory in-and-outs. But this time was different. Chawalee wasn't home. It had taken him some ten minutes to drag himself to the door and another one or two minutes to lower himself inelegantly onto the creosoted deck. He'd never felt so out of touch with his own skeleton. He'd never claim to have been in shape, but all those years of pounding the pavement for the Royal Thai Mail had given him some bulk. Yet here he was, struggling to scratch his own nose, wondering how he might ever get to his feet.

"Well, look what the crocodile dragged in," came a voice.

Supot looked up to see two old fellows in floppy straw hats walking toward him.

"I'm told he was ravaged by buxom hill-tribe girls," said one.

"Is that true?" asked the other. "Did they have their way with you and dump you here with us?"

"No," said Supot.

The men stood below his balcony and smiled up at him.

"Oh, well said," said one. "And they tell us postal workers have no sense of humor."

Supot was lagging way behind and realized he'd been visited by these two before.

"I don't . . ." he began.

"Your girlfriend not here?" asked the other.

"My?"

"Your own personal Dr. Zhivago," said one. "No, that doesn't sound right. Why is there never a literary female doctor on the tip of one's tongue when one needs one?"

"Anyway," said the other, "literary name or not, how is she?"

"You mean . . . ?" said Supot.

"He means, in the sack," said the other.

"In the . . . ?" said Supot, lost beyond help now.

"Yes, son," said the first. "We know what you city boys get up to when you're alone with fairly attractive mature women."

"I would never . . ." said Supot.

"Never say never, son," said the other. "Once you've tried

elderly, you'll never . . . Damn. Nothing rhymes with 'elderly.' Never mind. I'm Wen. This is Seksan. I'm sure you'll have heard of us."

"Or not," said Seksan.

"They said we shouldn't talk to you," said Wen. "There was a meeting about it."

"But we're the rebellious types," said Seksan.

"Black sheep," said Wen.

"Small flock. Naughty as shit."

"They said that you being here was explosive."

"Potentially life-threatening."

"But to two crustaceans like us, that wouldn't be such a disaster."

"Not so bad at all."

"Because we've been here thirty years, and life can be dull as Hades."

"And a bit of stirring might just bring the sweet lotus to the surface."

"But we'll let you enjoy your uncomfortable seating position. We'll come back when you're feeling completely one hundred percent yourself and are able to make sentences of more than three words."

"We live in hope," said Wen.

And, jauntily for gentlemen of certain ages, the odd couple headed off. Supot watched them go, stop, and turn around. Seksan said, "Whatever you do, don't go near the green house at the edge of the macadamia orchard."

"Whatever you do," said Wen.

Supot knew that hearing was invariably the first sense to die in the elderly. What they said next was probably meant to be out of earshot, but there was nothing wrong with Supot's ears.

"Think that did it?" asked Seksan.

"Should have," said Wen. "If he's got any sense of mystery at all."

The head of the commune had told him not to walk around annoying people. The inhabitants had been ordered not to speak to him. Now there was a green house he shouldn't go to. In a movie, that would have been plot device overkill, but real life wasn't interested in positive reviews. It was clear to him that there was a lot going on around him he wasn't supposed to know about. Siriluk no longer lived there, but it seemed to him that his relationship with her, however nonexistent, had poked a stick into a wasp's nest. He'd already shed every facet of his insignificant life, so he literally had nothing to lose.

That's when he decided to act. He didn't have the imagination to pull it off himself, so he called upon the skill of Kevin Spacey, who had died impressively in a frightening pandemic film called *Outbreak*. Supot and Ali had watched it at the Scala. Despite feeling fine, Supot feigned those same terminal conditions. He made himself pale with the help of Prickly heat powder and had the witch doctor convinced he'd relapsed. He no longer had the strength to stand or walk. So, for the time being, at least, there was no fear that he might wander around the commune talking to people.

Nirvana relied on power from a generator, and that life-giver was turned off at 9 P.M. From then on, the moon was left to do her job alone. In the crescent phase there was no moonlight to guide the footsteps of anyone foolish enough to be out at night. But there was nowhere to go, nothing to do. Supot checked the other room where Chawalee and her granddaughter slept together on a futon. He helped himself to a flashlight that spent its nights beside the door awaiting an emergency. The bamboo steps creaked as he climbed to the ground, but the sound was absorbed by nature's choir all around. Supot had always questioned the need for nine hours of sleep. But he was coming from a background of karaoke lullabies, squealing brakes, and screaming wives. Being rudely awakened was a part of being asleep.

In the rolling hills of Chiang Rai there were no security problems, so there were no aging night watchmen, no guards doing a second shift after a day of pizza delivery. You could walk around without the fear of being challenged. He aimed the flashlight at his feet so as not to disturb the sleeping communists, and he set off to learn the lay of Nirvana. There was clearly no grid, barely a straight line in sight. Some rich benefactor had clearly donated a large tract of hilly land and laid no rules on the beneficiaries. It would have been a nightmare to deliver mail here. Houses and huts and shacks faced this and that direction with not a path or a lane between them. Fruit bushes and flowers spread like weeds with no respect for domain. If a hut proved to be too small, the owner would attach another room to its backside like a cubic barnacle. And every building was painted with no consultation on color coordination. Recycled garbage totem poles sprouted in every open space. It was an art installation that people lived in.

He'd heard chickens and dogs during his convalescence and was expecting to be confronted on this journey. There were creatures there in the shadows, but they merely watched him pass. It was as if a stranger with a flashlight was not enough of a threat to warrant a bark or a cluck. They had been programmed not to disturb their owners unless it was imperative. Supot had never given off urgent vibrations. There was the odd moment when he thought he was being followed, but he saw nothing. He passed a meeting hut with a conical grass roof and no walls and came to a wooden sign that read FRUIT AND NUT VILLA in front of the largest of all the buildings. But he didn't see a green house. He was ashamed to admit as a city boy he wouldn't know a macadamia tree from a coconut palm, but he did know his nuts. After ten minutes, he found macadamias dangling in bunches from a sprawling tree. Nestled in a grove of them was a small green house on stilts. There were no lights or sounds from inside. Considering the buildup he'd been given, it was a disappointment. He wondered why he was there. What did he expect? But at least he'd found his target. He could come back some other time.

He was about to retrace his steps when he saw a tiny red glow in the moon shadow of the porch. The light vanished, but he could just about make out the shape of a person, small as a child, no more substance than a coat hanger. The red cigarette glow returned. There was a puff.

"Smoking is only a bad habit if you plan to stay alive at the end of it all," came a woman's voice, deep and crunchy.

Supot was embarrassed. He was intruding. He avoided shining the flashlight in her direction and turned it off. And there they were. Two shadows staring at each other in the night like ninja gunfighters.

"Sorry," he said.

"What for?" she asked.

"I don't know."

"I was hoping I might get a look at you," she said.

"You know about me?"

"Word spreads around here like butter in a hot wok, even when nobody talks to you. It's a miracle."

"They told me not to come to your house."

She laughed. It was the sound of coffee beans in a blender.

"So, you shouldn't have," she said.

Supot's eyes were getting accustomed to the dark. There

really wasn't much of her. The glow of the cigarette held at ear level hinted that she might have been bald, or wearing a swimming cap. Neither made sense.

"Why not?" he asked.

"We're dangerous."

"How so?"

"We kill people."

Supot looked around for accomplices.

"Why?" he asked.

"It's a knack."

"Do you have a list?" Supot asked.

"Of what?"

"People you plan to kill."

For no particular reason, she made the sound of an owl. "You're a peculiar one," she said once the impersonation was complete.

"I've heard that."

"Would it help us to have a list?" she asked.

"Might help me," he said. "At least I'd know how far down the list I was. How much time I had to get away."

She laughed again, and two small eyes lit up at her feet. Supot stepped back in surprise. A cat, gray now but probably white as coconut in daylight, changed its position on the balcony and went back to sleep.

"We don't know enough about you to kill you yet," said the woman. "I heard the macadamia pickers say you were a postman, that you'd come here from Bangkok. That you were dying. It appears you didn't. You might have to fill in the missing pieces for me."

"I came to—"

"Oh, no, boy. Not now. It's far too late for stories, and I must arrange for them to be here to listen. Come tomorrow. Bring an offering."

"What kind of offering?"

"Something personal. Something you treasure, if possible. They won't keep it. It's the rules. We have to have rules, right?"

The next morning Supot woke up feeling surprisingly refreshed despite his late-night stroll. He could smell food cooking. He wanted to help, leap out of bed and do the housework, wash his sheets, fluff the pillows. But he still needed the scope that being too ill to move afforded him. Shortly after, a girl of about fourteen came into his room carrying a tray. She was wearing a surgical mask as the witch doctor had done. He vaguely remembered her from his feverous period.

"Do you think you can eat today?" the girl asked.

"Tell me again who you are," said Supot.

"I'm Kruamart. Chawalee is my grandmother."

"Right," he said.

She put the food on a side table and helped him sit up. She was strong as a buffalo.

"You need to eat to build up your strength," she said. "Your medicine is in the beaker there. Gran upped your dose. She's surprised you aren't getting better. Do you need help to eat?"

"I think I can manage."

"Good."

She put the tray on his lap.

"Could you do me one last favor?" he asked.

"Yes?"

"When I arrived here, did I have a pack? A post office bag?"

"Yes."

"Do you know where it is?"

"Yes . . . maybe."

"Could you get it for me?"

"I . . . er . . ."

"Something wrong?"

"I should ask Gran."

"Ask her what?"

"If I'm allowed to give it to you."

That decision seemed to take a lot longer than was necessary. It was evening by the time the witch doctor arrived carrying Supot's bag. He opened it. The reason for the delay was immediately apparent.

"Where is it?" he asked.

"Where's what?" said Chawalee.

"I think you know what's missing from this bag."

"I was assured this is everything you arrived here with—clothes and a book, toiletries and various odds and ends."

"There was a video," said Supot.

"Oh, I know nothing about that. Perhaps you should ask the women who brought you here."

"You really think hill-tribe ladies who went to the trouble of dragging my emaciated body six hundred meters over rocks would go through my pack and steal a video"—he held up his wallet—"and not take this?" He opened it to show a few thousand baht notes and an ATM card.

"Look, Supot," she said, "I'm just an herbalist with a few dubious medical certificates. Don't expect me to explain the wonders of the world."

"I need to speak with Ting," said Supot.

"She's a very busy lady."

"Then, how about this? If she'll agree to talk with me and answer one or two simple questions, I promise I'll leave tomorrow and never come back."

"You're in no condition to travel."

"I'll take the risk."

"All right. I'll ask her. But I . . . What are you staring at?

"You. You're not wearing your mask."

"Oh, shit. You're right. I must have forgotten it in all the confusion."

Supot's unexpressive face was moderately contorted.

"What is it?" she asked.

"It's just . . . just that I've never seen your face before. It's . . ."

"Gorgeous?"

"No, well, maybe that. But, for some reason, you remind me of my mother."

"And they wonder where all the romantic men have gone."

"It's a compliment. She was beautiful."

"Then, I forgive you."

"Sorry."

"I'll go see Ting."

"Thank you."

"You wanted to see me?" said Ting a few minutes later. "I hear you'll be leaving us tomorrow."

Supot smiled. "I've never felt this unpopular," he said.

"That's hard to believe," said Chawalee with a smile.

"It's nothing personal," said Ting.

Chawalee had set out six foldable chairs at the end of the bed. She and Ting were seated in two of them. The other four were occupied by what looked like a council of elders. They all wore surgical masks and reminded Supot of the scene in *Death by Hanging*, where the observers witnessed the failed execution.

"Isn't it?" said Supot.

"Of course not," said Ting.

"I came here to meet Siriluk," said Supot. "She doesn't live here anymore. That should have been the end of it. I recover. I thank you all. I leave. But that's not how it turned out."

"What do you mean?" asked Ting.

"A veil of silence has been lowered upon this village." He couldn't recall what movie the line was from, which annoyed him, but it was a damned good line.

"That's nonsense," said Ting.

"Is it?" said Supot. "If you had nothing to hide, I'd have been allowed to talk to people who knew her here, perhaps find out where she went. But you told me not to talk to anyone. You banned villagers from contact with me."

"This is a private place," said the headwoman. "We don't want outsiders coming here polluting our lifestyle. We value our privacy."

"Yeah, I get that," said Supot. "But something smells bad here. For example, are you planning to give me back my video?"

"What video is that?" asked Ting. There came a mumble from one of the old men.

"The one that used to be in my bag," said Supot.

"You probably dropped it on your way here," said the mumbler.

"It's an official post office letter sack with double buckles," said Supot. "Things don't fall out of it."

"I assume you had permission to walk away with government property?" said the elder.

"Oh, now what?" said Supot. "You're going to rat on me to the post office?"

"Look," said Chawalee. "Can't we all be nice to each other on Supot's last night here? We'll look around and see if we can find the video, and perhaps, we can come up with a forwarding address for Siriluk. How's that? Now I think my patient needs his rest."

There were reasons for Supot not mentioning the green house in the macadamia grove. The old lady there was certainly odd, but he got the feeling she'd be the one person he'd get any information from. Then there were the two old fellows who'd led him to her: Wen and Seksan. They didn't seem like the obedient sorts. But the only way to find them again was through the macadamia lady. And everything relied on one last late-night walk through the compound.

There had been a rainstorm that day. It was brief, and the sky had soon regained its swimming pool hue. The evening cicada string section was replaced by the toady wind instruments, which gave way to an eerie silence. There were puddles on the ground, patches of mud here and there. But the air smelled clean with promise. His postman sense of direction took him directly to the green house, which was just as dark and silent as it had been the previous night. There was no cigarette glow from the porch. No sign of the old woman. He wondered if she'd forgotten their appointment.

"Take off your shoes and come in," came a voice.

That was when he first realized he wasn't wearing any. Being barefoot had been so natural. In Bangkok, walking without shoes would have been like a cannibal hot coal initiation ritual, braving the broken glass, the dog shit, the engine oil, the concrete paving stones baked in the City of Angels kiln. Here, his bare feet were enjoying the soft, muddy earth and the grass. He wiped them on a mat by the front door and knocked.

"I'm here," he said.

"I guessed as much."

When he entered, the woman was in the process of lighting a circle of tea light candles with a taper. They gave off just enough light for him to make out the contours of her old face. She was, indeed, as bald as a cue ball. He thought he saw years of misery etched on her face, even though she was smiling. That smile was another matter.

"When will the others get here?" he asked. "You said—"

"They're already here," she told him.

He looked around but saw nobody; a situation that might have frightened a man who hadn't watched endless hours of haunting and horror. Once you've spent a night at Amityville, real life was tame by comparison. His mind was too busy working out which camera angles would best capture this mysterious scene.

"Okay," he said.

"I know you don't see them."

"No, but there are a lot of people I don't see."

"You're strange, aren't you?"

"I guess."

He could see clearly now that all the candles were lit. The woman was wearing an elegant *phasin* skirt and a white blouse, and there may have been a hint of rouge on her lips.

"Did you bring an offering?" she asked.

"Not the one I wanted to bring," he said. "They stole that."

He reached into his pocket and produced a Royal Thai Mail hat badge circa 1950. Postal worker Chet had given it to him on the occasion of Supot's thirtieth birthday. The old man had no family, no kids, legitimate or otherwise. He probably saw this gesture as highly symbolic, a treasured possession passed down to a young postman. Perhaps he even saw Supot as the son he didn't have, an heir. Supot, on the other hand, saw it as a worthless hunk of rusting junk. He'd pinned it to the inside of his pack to appease Chet but had forgotten about it. He decided that it qualified as a treasured possession, at least to somebody. He handed it to the woman, who placed it carefully at the focus of the circle. She looked around, nodding at empty spaces.

"They approve," she said, and smiled once again.

Hollywood might have given this shriveled old maid a mouth of missing incisors and bloodred betel nut gums, but her teeth were neat and chalky white. There was something too perfect about them. He imagined them smiling back at her from a bedside beaker. But those teeth made him feel more comfortable looking at her—they gave her a sort of charm.

"Sit down, postman," she said.

There was no furniture, so he sat cross-legged on the floorboards opposite her.

"We've been looking forward to our story," she said.

"I confess I'm not much of a storyteller," he told her.

"Nonsense. Everyone has untold numbers of stories inside them. All you have to do is coax them out."

He heard a scratching sound from somewhere deep in the shadows. He hoped it was the cat.

"What was it they stole from you?" asked the woman.

"A video. It wasn't in my bag when they returned it."

"What was on it?"

"A movie."

"Ah, then it doesn't surprise me," she said. "They're all addicted to films here. Every night of the week is movie night in some hut or another. It's a disgusting waste of a grown-up's time."

"You don't like cinema?"

"No."

It was the type of "no" that signaled the end of a topic.

"Then I doubt you'll like my story," said Supot.

"Why so?"

"It's mostly about a movie."

"Oh, what a disappointment. Nothing else?"

"And a girl."

"Ah, now you're cooking with soy oil. Romance. Let's focus on that, shall we? Start whenever you're ready. We'll try to keep quiet."

Supot was aware that many of the best stories began with a prologue, and he felt that the old woman would benefit from hearing one. He told her a little about the life that he and Ali lived in Bangkok Noi, about their relationship with films and how it conflicted with his real life as a postman. He told her about the night they were watching *The Big Sleep* and Woot arrived with his cache of films. He told her there was one video, a Thai production that they'd never heard of. In fact, nobody they asked had heard of it. Without any great expectations, he'd watched that movie and had been left stunned. It was the greatest thing he'd ever seen. The lead actress was astounding, a true goddess of the silver screen. Her name was Siriluk.

The old woman grunted, stood, and walked to the small kitchen area at the rear of the shack. He assumed she was going to make them a drink, a snack perhaps.

"Do you think we don't know where you're going with this?" she said.

"I don't think so," said Supot. "How could you?"

Her back was toward him, but he could feel a change in the atmosphere. There was a biting chill to her tone.

"Did they think I might be seduced by the voice of a handsome postman? Did they think you might be able to remove the curse? Huh?"

"Who . . . ?"

She turned and the light of the candles flickered in the blade of the knife she held. He'd seen somewhere that in the event of being attacked by a tiger you just hold your ground, look confident, and take a step toward the beast. Ninety percent of the time the tiger will back off, fearing that you have some unknown power. But you can never be sure when you've run up against that ten percenter.

The old woman ran at Supot. She plowed through the candles, sending them flying in all directions. He considered taking a step toward her, but that thought was brief. She slashed at the air. In the film version of this scene, the weapon would have been a clever, the kind of weapon that would take off an arm with hardly any effort. This woman's knife was of a modest size, but it was honed down to a sharp point. The tip of the blade was awfully close to his shirt. He turned and ran for the door, which he'd conveniently left open, and stumbled down the steps, kicking the cat as he went. He ran toward the macadamia grove before looking back over his shoulder to see how close she might be. There was no sign of her. He leaned against a tree to catch his breath and try to make sense of what had just happened. She'd gone from Jekyll to Hyde in the flicker of a flame. Surely her dislike of movies was not motive enough to slice him open. She was clearly quite mad.

He heard the popping of bamboo before he saw the flames. The wooden hut had caught fire, he assumed, as a result of the strewn candles. Despite the rainstorm that day, the little house was easy tinder for the flames.

"Oh, shit," he said, and called on what little energy he had left to go back to the shack. The old lady wasn't outside. The place was burning like a pyre. Flames lashed out through a side window, and the damp grass of the roof produced billows of smoke.

He called out, "Old lady. Old lady."

It must be said that he entered the shack without thinking, because if he had given it any thought at all, he would have stayed outside. Even when he reached the little balcony, he still had time to retreat, but he couldn't bear the thought of the old lady burning to death inside indirectly because of him. One step through the door and he was confronted by a wall of fire. Nothing could have survived it. He was overcome both with emotion and with nausea, and in seconds he felt himself falling onto the hot bamboo slats.

He came to, wrenched from sleep by a bout of his own coughing. The sun through the window told him it was late afternoon. He was back at the witch doctor's place, but there was nobody with him.

"Hello?" he called out.

The effort had him hacking up soot. Chawalee appeared from the balcony, not wearing her mask.

"Are you doing everything you possibly can to kill yourself?" she asked.

"Is the old woman dead?" asked Supot.

"They didn't find any remains, so we're assuming she got away."

"What? Where would she go?"

"Oh, she has her hiding places. Abandoned resorts and caves and the like. She doesn't spend much time in the compound."

"She tried to kill me."

"I doubt that," said Chawalee. "She's frightened the living daylights out of a lot of us, but she hasn't actually murdered anyone yet."

Chawalee took his pulse and felt his forehead.

"How are you feeling?" she asked.

"How did . . . how did I get out of that house? All I remember is the fire and the smoke."

"You've met Wen and Seksan." It wasn't a question. "They've been tailing you for the last couple of nights. Fortunately, they saw you climb the steps and go inside. It's lucky your center of balance is in your backside, otherwise you'd have fallen into the flames. As it was, you fell back onto the balcony, and they dragged you away."

"So, they would have seen the old lady escape."

"There used to be steps at the rear of the shack. She probably took those."

Supot shook his head and considered all the information he'd been given.

"I need to see Seksan and Wen," he said.

"You'll get your chance later. I've been given the task of assessing your physical condition. If you're well enough, you're invited to attend a town hall meeting tonight."

"What's the topic?"

"You."

"You mean people finally get a chance to talk to me?"

"From what I've learned about you, I think you'll need to prepare yourself for something of a shock. They seem to think you're ready to hear the truth."

And that was all she'd tell him. The granddaughter brought in food, which he ate between coughs, and they found him a set of clothes that were roughly his size. He bathed and cut his unruly hair. It was eight before they sent for him. The granddaughter called to him from the front yard.

"Uncle Supot, can you come?"

He followed her barefoot across the compound, feeling surprisingly nervous. It was like going for an interview for a job he knew nothing about. By the time they reached the grass-roofed meeting area, the butterflies were colliding inside him. It seemed that everyone in the commune was there, young and old. They were seated on parallel benches like schoolchildren, facing a huge blackboard that had nothing written on it. The elders sat on chairs directed toward the audience. There was one empty seat beside them. Ting gestured for him to sit there, but before doing so, he scanned the onlookers until he saw the two men, Wen and Seksan, who had saved his life the previous night. He gave them a most respectful *wai*. They seemed embarrassed, but they returned an edited version of the gesture.

As Supot took his seat, a hush draped over the meeting like a fine mushroom net. It was as if someone more worthy of silence had arrived. Ting stood and leaned on the small desk in front of her.

"Brothers and sisters," she began. "This is our unexpected, unwanted visitor, Comrade Supot."

The audience wasn't sure whether to clap at this introduction. The result was a brief, microwaved popcorn round of applause. Supot was equally confused.

Ting continued, "Comrade Supot arrived here with a mission and a video. The content of the video was a film called *Bangkok 2010*. All of you have heard of this film and know its significance. It is because of this film that we are all here today."

Supot sat aghast. He looked across the lake of faces and wondered for the first time whether *2010* had spawned a cult. From there, his imagination took him to Jonestown and Kool-Aid, and a fear for his own life. He noticed that all the elders and a number of older audience members still wore surgical masks. Given that he had probably infected half the commune with his Bangkok germs, he felt it was disrespectful for him not to be wearing one also.

"It was our intention," Ting began again, "to treat Comrade Supot's illness and send him off without sharing the ethos of this community. We have always been careful to avoid contact with the outside. But I'm afraid we underestimated Comrade Supot's resourcefulness. We should have been more aware. He had already used his skills to find us and had risked death to come here. Thanks to interference from one or two of our senior members"—Wen and Seksan stood and took a sarcastic bow—"Comrade Supot heard about our friend in the macadamias and contacted her. We are not to know how much he learned from her, or her from him, but we must assume that our pact has been compromised. Short of killing Comrade Supot and feeding him to the pigs, we have no choice but to let him in on our secret."

There came a ripple of laughter, but Supot was certain a pig breakfast had been considered at some point. He was still uneasy about this whole thing. He needed Ali beside him, counting the evil cult leader clichés, questioning the acting ability of the extras, reworking the whole "postman in Nirvana" concept. But he was alone and confused and, admittedly, still a little afraid.

"Comrade Supot," said Ting, "let us begin with a test of your observational skills. Dr. Chawalee, would you please stand?"

The witch doctor smiled, took off her mask, got to her feet, and took a bow.

"Have you seen this woman before?" Ting asked.

"Yes," said Supot. "She was looking after me."

"I mean, not here. Somewhere else."

The witch doctor still reminded him of his mother, but perhaps not so much now in this artificial light. He shook his head.

"Then let's try somebody else," said Ting, turning to the

elders. "Comrade Soop, would you be kind enough to stand and remove your mask?"

The elder beside Supot did as he was asked. He turned to the visitor, smiled, and shrugged, but, once again, Supot shook his head. He had no idea what he was supposed to be seeing or for what reason. The game was too complicated for him.

"Too subtle?" said Ting. "Let's go with all of our original commune-founding ladies and gentlemen."

The remaining elders and a total of sixteen members of the audience got to their feet and removed their masks. They were all elderly, but not to the point of impending decay. In fact, they were a healthy bunch of specimens, perhaps in their sixties. There was evidence of hair loss and wrinkling, possibly a little overweight, but Supot could see no canes or walkers or wheelie oxygen tanks. There was no need for them.

"Just tell him, for God's sake," shouted Seksan.

"How about this immortal line from yours truly?" said Wen in a high-pitched voice. "'Are you Comrade Siriluk 81,988?'"

"You're assuming Vongkot didn't cut that line out," said Seksan.

"You can't be serious," said Wen. It was the most moving two minutes in the film.

It was the sound of Wen's voice rather than his face that triggered a recollection in Supot's brain. Wen's was a whiny, annoying squeak. Ali had commented on something similar during one of their later viewings. He'd asked why they'd choose an actor with a squeaky voice to play a heavy. They'd concluded it was deliberate.

"Maybe 'whiny' was what the director had been going for," Supot had argued. He'd repeated the line that night in Ali's shop using the same high-pitched voice.

And he repeated it now.

"'Are you Comrade Siriluk 81,988? What grade of minor wife are you?'"

"Excellent memory," said Seksan.

"But . . . how?" said Supot. "How could you know that line if you haven't seen the film?"

He looked more carefully at those standing, and one by one their faces found a perch in his memory. His gaze landed on one man, taller than anyone else, skinny as a hat stand. He saw him fuller, broad-shouldered, in medals and a helmet. Could he have been the prison guard who took Bundtut to rescue Siriluk? No, it was impossible. He turned to the witch doctor. She was nothing like his mother. The reason he'd recognized her was that hers was the face of the resistance leader in the nightclub. How many times had he watched that scene?

"You're the boss lady," he said.

"I'm disappointed you didn't recognize me," she said.

"You can't . . . it can't be," said Supot.

"Yet here you have it," said Ting. "You've entered a world that you thought was fantasy, but here it is, in real life. Welcome to *2010*."

Now the applause was genuine and overwhelming. When it had died down, the actors introduced themselves, one by one.

"I am Noon Khanthon. What's my role?" said one man, offering a sort of test.

Supot recognized the name and the features of a young man he had seen in the film. He homed in on the role. "Public Official Sahai Pridyathorn 242," said Supot with a smile.

The audience clapped again.

"Aha. Our only devoted fan," one woman said.

"I am Picha Nakhorn Than," offered another of those standing.

Supot put some thought into it, but it finally came to him. "Right," he said. "Sound. Special effects."

"Spot on." The man laughed. "Plus, three heavily disguised cameo performances, each worthy of an Oscar."

The meeting had turned into a television quiz show with an enthusiastic audience.

"You weren't the waiter in the nightclub?" said Supot.

"No. That was me. Wittayakorn, Lek," said the man beside him.

"And I was Minor Wife, Level C, flawed," said one pretty, old lady.

"Kn. Chiangkoon?" said Supot.

"Nickname Gai. At your service."

They continued to introduce themselves and joke and laugh. Supot knew them all so well as young actors. It was odd to see them so much older than him, but, still, he had a feeling of camaraderie. There were many questions still to answer. He considered the possibility that they were still young but heavily made up to fool him. But who would go to such lengths?

"No," said Supot. "You couldn't possibly have made a film like this all those years ago. We would have known. We would have recognized the shortcomings."

"We made it in 1965," said Ting, still standing. "We were in our late twenties and early thirties."

"It couldn't have been made in the sixties," said Supot. "The computers. The modern technology . . ."

"It was all science fiction when we made it," said Ting. "It appears we anticipated modern science quite accurately."

"But that film quality. Those techniques. There's no way. We would have known."

"Then you obviously aren't the expert you claim to be," said Chawalee. "Perhaps, if it had been made in Thailand, you would have noticed. We certainly couldn't have made a film of that quality here in those days. There weren't the facilities or the personnel. But in Europe, there were."

"You made a Thai film in Europe?"

"Sweden, to be exact."

"You made a Thai film in Sweden in the sixties? The market for Thai movies must have been huge over there in those days."

"Ah. Good," said the witch doctor. "Sarcasm. You've obviously recovered."

"Perhaps you'd be interested to learn some of our history," said Ting.

"Please," said Supot.

The onlookers made themselves comfortable. They were hearing a familiar story. The cast members took their seats.

"We were young students from good families back in 1958," she began, "when General Sarit staged another Thai coup and began a political revolution that affected so many lives. His clampdown on communism, the 'dark evil,' was without mercy. Intellectuals with left-leaning ideas were a threat to the new order. These young artists and writers and thinkers suddenly became the enemy in their own country. Those of us that could afford it went to study overseas, and we waited for a chance to return and to get our lives back. The *2010* group chose film as our diversion and found ourselves in Stockholm. We studied under the contemporaries of the great Swedish director Ingmar Bergman.

"The regime in Thailand we thought would soon fall continued for many years. We were granted asylum because of our political beliefs. We stretched out our studies to graduate-level then post-graduate, until all of us had reached the highest levels in our respective fields of expertise. As a thesis for our studies, we put together a screenplay for a bizarre film called *Bangkok 2010*. It started out as a jokey response to the news that Thailand's new field marshal had a stable of eighty mistresses. It was to be a kind of satire. But it grew inside us like a cancer. As we were writing it, we realized the power of art over politics. The project turned into a way of expressing our frustrations. All the exiled Thai students in Sweden contributed their skills to the one unique practical thesis, and the result was the film you, Comrade Supot, have watched twenty times, and us, not once. We changed our names in the credits, for obvious reasons. All but Vongkot, who was determined to go down in history."

"Why the hell didn't you want anyone to watch it?" asked Supot.

The audience muttered its discomfort.

"I'm afraid that is a question we can't answer," said Ting. "We took a vow of silence on the matter. We've told you as much as we are able to."

Through all of this, one overwhelming matter had blocked every thought, every question in Supot's mind. He'd expected his heart to be broken in a traditional way. That would have been bearable because the cinema prepared a man to deal with heartache. But the implications of what he was learning this night were too vast to take in. His only way of dealing with trauma had always been to pretend he'd misunderstood the plot. If it was important, he could always come back to it, rewind, and go through it at a pace best suited for a man of his limited wisdom.

In the meantime, he could focus on minor details.

"Why, I . . . Are you allowed to tell me why Kn. Vongkot went to Bangkok?" he asked.

Ting held up her hands in submission.

"In our ranks in Sweden there were four older members. They were our teachers—Vongkot, Gan, and my sadly departed husband, Moo. One more, Chavalit, left early and gave himself up to the military junta here. The former had been a film director who'd been forced to leave Thailand before us. He became the producer of our film. He and Moo came from very wealthy families. In our absence, his people bought this land as a home we could return to when life became less suffocating in Thailand. Almost everyone involved in *2010* relocated here when the government declared an amnesty. That was almost thirty years ago. And here we still are."

"Do you know what happened to Chavalit?" Supot asked.

"He spent some time in jail, was rehabilitated, and I hear he's at the—"

"Film Archives Department," said Supot. "I met him."

"He wasn't that popular," said Wen. "We had suspicions he was the one who alerted the military to what we were doing in Sweden. We had no proof."

"What about the film?" asked Supot.

One of the elders, Chakra, a stockily built man with a shaved head, took up the story. "Vongkot was a stubborn old man," he said. "Ours had been just a student project. He had a foolish idea that *2010* could have been the pinnacle of his career. It most certainly was not. He did much better work in Europe later. But for some reason, he wished to preserve our film for prosperity. That's why he risked everything, returned to Thailand, and worked on the raw footage. He had inoperable cancer. He knew he was dying, and he would listen to nobody. He completely ignored the curse."

"There should have been a clap of thunder at that point," shouted Wen from the gallery.

"Comrade Wen, you're out of order," said Ting.

"Why don't we talk about that curse?" asked Seksan, his partner.

There were snickers from some of the others, some uncomfortable muttering. Supot was even more confused.

"Curse?"

"There is a curse," said the elder beside him. "It's a childish idea that got itself embedded a long time ago and became real. It is believed that anyone involved with a completed version of *2010* will fall victim to the curse. We warned Vongkot."

"He was seventy-five and suffering from cancer," said Chawalee. "I don't think a curse had much of an influence on that outcome."

"Then there was Supot," said the elder.

"Who survived," said Wen. "That fact should serve to quell any notion of a curse, don't you think?"

"He almost died," said Chakra.

"Look," said Wen. "I think there are enough intelligent, rational people in this hall to put nails in the coffins of both the curse and the pact. I, for one, would like to see *2010* in its completed form."

"As would I," said his partner.

There was an unexpected chorus of "me too" and another round of applause.

"You have no authority to allow us to ignore the pact," said Chakra. "There was a vote."

"And some of the people who took that vote have passed on to that other Nirvana," said Seksan. "I say it's time for a new vote."

"Hear, hear," echoed the crowd.

Supot and Chawalee were walking back from the meeting. Being himself had exhausted the postman.

"Was all that because of me?" he asked.

"Do you really need to ask?" said the woman. "Your

knowledge of the movie and your familiarity with the characters endeared you to the audience. There's no doubt your presence in the commune has sparked new interest in *2010*. And why not? It was the film that gave birth to this community. We original members of the group moved here, mated, and started an alternative lifestyle because of it. I'm not at all surprised they voted to watch it. It's a historical record."

"I think some of the elders hated me for it," said Supot. "That grumpy old bastard Chakra had his nose turned up at me the whole time."

"Some of the elders hate everybody, him especially. He instigated the attempt to keep you away from us. He was afraid you'd influence the younger members of the community. Old people don't like change, but never you mind. We'll die off, and the next generation will step up. They'll sneak in mobile phones and computers, and next thing you know, we'll be just another suburb in an expanding metropolis."

"Do you want that?" asked Supot.

"What I want doesn't matter. I made the mistake of having six children. By the time they reached their teens, this place was already their past. They didn't have despots and Sweden and *2010* in their development. They dreamed of modernity. All of them left."

They arrived at the witch doctor's house. Supot took a breather at the top of the stairs.

"Do you have the energy to sit and have a drink with me?" she asked.

"I'm not much of a drinker," said Supot.

"That's all right, Supot. It's not much of a drink."

And that was how they started on Chawalee's new batch of langsat liqueur. They sat together watching the fireflies dance their jig. They enjoyed the silence for a while.

"I'm surprised you resisted the temptation to ask about her," Chawalee broke in.

"Her?"

"The woman you came here to see."

"Well, it turns out she doesn't exist. Nothing to ask."

"Oh, she exists, Supot. You know she does."

"I knew the moment they broke the news about what happened in Sweden all those years ago. I'm ashamed I didn't see it, or rather, that I ignored it. When I was with her, I noticed her teeth."

"Her teeth?"

"They were in such good condition, so perfect I assumed they were false. But I get it now. The teeth are all that remain of the woman I fell in love with. The reason her smile made me feel uncomfortable was that it was all that remained of her. She looked after her mouth and let the rest of herself go to the devil."

"She's the result of three decades of self-destruction."

"What happened to her?"

"I can't tell you. They voted on seeing the movie, not on canceling the pact. There are reasons for that. You can't vote out a promise."

"There really was nothing else left of her," said Supot. "Even deep in her eyes there was no memory of the actress I came to see. Why did she pretend she didn't know why I was here?"

"She didn't."

"We wrote to each other."

"No, you didn't."

"Somebody faked her letters?"

"No, your letters were answered by Siriluk, just not the Siriluk you met last night."

"I don't understand." He helped himself to another liqueur and topped up Chawalee's glass.

"Siriluk had two children, twins. One boy and one girl. She named the boy Bundtut and named the girl after herself. Those were the years before she lost her mind completely. She was still in Europe with other family members at the time. Eventually they found their way to us. But she was already quite far gone. The boy lived here until he reached his teens, but he could no longer stand to watch his mother's mind corrode. He became a film technician. It was he who worked with Vongkot to edit the film in Bangkok.

"His mother never really formed a bond with us. She soon grew apart from the commune. What friendship we'd developed in Sweden had disappeared. She ignored us. She turned to opium to escape reality and stopped looking after her health. She befriended strange men, offered them sexual favors to keep up her supply. She started to go on long walks, usually naked. Gone for days. She'd turn up at villages and frighten the children. She stole things from poor country folk who had no valuable possessions.

"Only Siriluk, the daughter, stayed on to help her. She was . . . has been incredibly patient with the old woman but caring for her has taken a toll on the girl as well. The mother ceased to recognize her own daughter. The old woman would tell people young Siriluk was a famous actress. Some of us were certain she thought the girl was herself years before. She'd tell people Siriluk was off making films, appearing in television dramas. It was as if she was a fan of her own daughter. Young Siriluk has sacrificed her life to look after a person who doesn't know her."

She paused and sipped her drink to give Supot time to take it all in.

"When your letters arrived," she continued, "it was young Siriluk who wrote you back. We had to be sure you had the only copy of *2010*. That was good news. But it also meant you had our address, and there was nothing to stop you from turning up here. Siriluk went to find you in Bangkok to persuade you not to come here. Some of the elders were convinced that your presence would destabilize our group. What if the film was copied and became popular? What if news reporters came to interview us? The Chiang Rai authorities know that we're here, of course. They accept us because we are largely anonymous, invisible. We're not insurgents. We do no harm. But what if we became famous and fans conducted pilgrimages to visit us? What if we became visible? Ours is a fantastic story. Just think of the headlines, COMMUNIST MOVIE STARS HIDE OUT IN NIRVANA. It's the sort of fame nobody wants. It would kill us."

"You've put a lot of thought into something that might not happen," said Supot. "I have . . . *had* the only copy of the film. I didn't show it to the media. And what if I had made it public? How do you know the country would take to it? It's a bit sophisticated for your average Thai viewer."

"You've seen it, Supot. You talked about it in your letters. You know what effect it would have."

Supot nodded. "It would be a sensation," he said. "You're right. So, why did you change your minds and let me in on your secret?"

"As opposed to feeding you to the pigs?"

"I get the feeling that's still an option."

"The elders decided you'd be less of a threat if you understood the situation. If you were on the inside. And then there's Siriluk, the nutty one."

"She thought you'd sent me to her place. Why would you?"

"There are those of us who believe she needs to talk about Sweden. If what happened there was the cause of her madness, if it was the reason she started to live with demons, then only addressing it could help her. She's suppressed the whole of her past. She needs to find herself again. We've tried, all of us. As soon as we mention *2010* . . . well, you've seen for yourself. That's how she reacts to everyone, her daughter included."

"She seemed perfectly nice right up to the point where she tried to gut me with a knife," said Supot.

"I know. Inside, I'm sure she's still one of us. We were so strong back then—rebels, convinced we could change the world for the better. We shared an ideology. Our time in Europe showed us how a country should develop. Making *2010* brought out all that was good in us. We truly loved each other. We were unselfish, supportive, faithful. We were Thais proud of our kingdom. I believe watching the film would bring back all those feelings."

"Did you see it?"

"You mean, after it *accidentally* fell out of your bag?"

"Yes."

"No, it went straight to the other elders. Chakra took charge of it. And I don't think they've watched it either. It's probably in a safe somewhere."

Supot let a firefly land on his palm. It basked in its own glow.

"You don't think Siriluk will go to the viewing?"

"Not a chance in hell."


Supot slept well that night and half the following morning. He walked around the compound met by "hello" and "how are you?" He was a temporary celebrity, like the television stars, famous for being nothing in particular. But he wouldn't refuse any sort of fame. By afternoon, the clocks had almost stopped ticking. Time leading to the world premiere of *Bangkok 2010* had slowed to a crawl. The film was scheduled to start at seven. There was no red carpet, so they'd settled on a walkway of hemp rice sacks leading up to the meeting hall. The compound newsletter writer interviewed guests as they arrived and commented on their fashion choices. Naturally, the event was black-tie. The glitterati improvised with grass skirts and daisy tiaras. Chawalee's granddaughter had presented Supot with a length of bicycle inner tube.

"What do I do with this?" he'd asked.

"It's a tie," she said. "They won't let you in without one."

She was wearing a batik sarong tied at the waist with a length of rope. Her shoes were four sizes too big for her and their heels stuck in the mud, but she refused to take them off. Chawalee was wearing an actual dress fastened at the back with enormous safety pins. Her headwear was a folded newspaper pirate hat.

They left early so they'd have time to stop off at Wen and Seksan's place for cocktails. The old fellows lived in a fussy, pastel-shaded house with a space beneath for socializing. They'd been a couple, in the romantic sense, for over forty years. It was a love that showed no sign of aging. They'd probably been cantankerous even before they were old enough to get away with it. They'd prepared an alcoholic fruit punch concoction that went straight to everyone's brain. As Wen said, had anyone been wearing socks, those socks would certainly have been knocked off by the brew.

The high alcohol content meant the group arrived at the meeting hall in the perfect frame of mind for a premiere. Still, Supot confessed he couldn't have felt more nervous if he'd directed the movie himself. The air was clammy with apprehension. An usher with a small flashlight showed them to their seats. Supot had the chair of honor in front with the elders, some of whom had yet to arrive. The blackboard had been covered with a white sheet that would serve as the screen. Beside him was a hewn log coffee table upon which sat the video player and the projector. All they were missing was a video.

He looked around at the excited faces and a creative display of banana leaf bonnets. There were thumbs up and air punches offered in his direction. Beside him, Chawalee was waving at a chubby woman four rows back.

"I didn't think she'd make it back in time," said the witch doctor.

"Who's that?" he asked.

"Your penfriend."

Supot took a second look.

"My . . .? That's Siriluk?" he asked, unable to keep the surprise from his voice.

"Expecting something else?"

"I don't know," he said. "I suppose I was expecting her to look more like her mother . . . used to."

"Genes are mysterious things," said Chawalee. "Her brother's a hunk. But young Siriluk is more a victim of her upbringing than anything else. The kids had no discipline at home. When the mother took to opium, the daughter started a relationship with food."

Supot looked back at her and returned her wave. She had a nice smile and bad skin.

"I imagine that's your second disappointment," said Chawalee.

"What do you mean?"

"Once you gave up on the mother, I wouldn't be surprised if you'd fantasized about falling in love with the daughter."

"That's ridiculous," he said, but she'd hit the proverbial

nail on the proverbial head. He bemoaned his own lack of depth and transparency.

"I'm glad to hear it," said the witch doctor.


The scheduled screening time arrived and departed with no sign of Ting and the video. The boisterous crowd had run out of funny lines and had resorted to slow handclapping and whistles. These turned to ironic cheers when the head-woman and two elders arrived empty-handed. Ting held up her palms. The audience muted.

"I'm afraid there will be no viewing tonight," she said, immediately drowned out by a booing crowd. When the sound subsided, she added, "Or any other night."

"Why?" called the crowd.

"Perhaps Comrade Chakra can best answer that question." She gestured for Elder Chakra, who had arrived with her, to step forward. He did so reluctantly.

"As an elder," he said, "it is my responsibility to—"

"Speak up," shouted one frustrated audience member.

"As an elder," he repeated, "it is my responsibility to consider the well-being of all of our brothers and sisters for the long run. Sometimes, it is necessary to make unpopular decisions."

"Just stop talking and show us the film," shouted Seksan to loud cheers from all around.

"There . . . there is no film," he said.

"What are you talking about?" said Wen.

"Tell them," said Ting.

The elder studied his sandals for a brief moment before speaking up. "I . . . it has been destroyed. For your own good."

An angry murmur bubbled around the meeting hall.

"You destroyed the only copy of *2010*?" said Seksan.

"You'll come to thank me," said the elder.

"We'll come to lynch you," shouted Wen.

"And you did this without consulting the other elders?" said Chawalee.

"You would have voted against it."

"That's what voting is all about," shouted Seksan. "So one idiot doesn't make damned fool decisions on behalf of the majority. It's why we have a committee."

"Is it repairable?" someone asked.

"It's burned," said the elder. "Melted."

The gala event had become a wake. The guilty elder slumped in his seat. Some people stood but nobody left. It was as if they were awaiting a miracle. Chawalee turned to Supot. "How well do you really know *2010*?" she asked.

"Very well," he said. "Why?"

"Because it would appear the only surviving copy of the movie is inside you."

"How does that help?"

She put a hand on his. "In the old days," she said, "traveling storytellers would go from village to village. All the villagers would gather in a place like this, and the storyteller would sit them down to enjoy tales of adventure and mystery. The young girls would fall in love with the heroes. The children would have nightmares when they were visited by the storyteller's monsters. Men would dream of travel to far-off lands on sailing ships."

"Are you thinking of calling in a storyteller to sort this mess out?"

"We already have one."

He looked her in the eye and smiled and shook his head. She smiled back.

"That's not funny," he said.

"Not meant to be. You've seen the film so many times you must know the dialogue by heart."

"I'm not a storyteller. I have no imagination."

She laughed. "You don't need one. You just need to describe what you see in your memory. You say what the characters would say. Maybe put on an accent here and there."

"I can't."

"Look around, Supot. Look at all these disappointed faces. You could cheer them up. They want to see *2010*, and they can see it through you."

"I don't know."

"And think how proud your mother would be."

"My mother?"

"Didn't you say she was a great storyteller? A skill like that doesn't fade away. It travels down through generations. You have her ability inside you. It's just that you haven't unlocked the place it's stowed away in. It'll come."

Before he had a chance to argue, Chawalee stood and called to the unsettled audience.

"Brothers and sisters."

"Don't," said Supot, but it was too late.

"There is no video," she said. "We can't watch the movie on the screen as we'd hoped. But there is a way to experience *2010*. We can hear it from the heart of its greatest fan. Supot is here, and he has watched it many times. He will tell us *2010* from his memory."

A National Football stadium–sized crowd could not have produced such volume on game day as was issued forth in the meeting hall of Nirvana. Chawalee reached for Supot's hand and walked him through the benches to a spot directly under the cone of the roof. Someone put a stool behind him, and the onlookers began to rearrange the benches, so they could look at their motion picture teller.

Supot was surprised at his own reaction. He should have been embarrassed. He should have stood his ground and refused. He didn't want to disappoint all those people, but something had occurred to him quite clearly. He would tell them the story of Siriluk and Bundtut because he knew he could. He'd never been more confident about anything in his life. And he'd already told the movie to himself as he walked his postal route, rode the ferry, lay in his steamy apartment waiting for sleep. He'd forget bits here and there, mix up names, remember small scenes out of order. But that wouldn't matter. He loved the movie, and he would do it justice. And he could think of no greater gift than to share it with the people who had conceived it.

He sat on his stool.

There was a polite silence.

And he began.

*"The opening scene is a dark, depressing modern Bangkok. Skyscrapers everywhere. But it's so smoggy you can't really make them out. We're at street level, watching depressed people go to work. They're all wearing smoke masks and weird modern clothes. There's a traffic jam of cars of the future. The drivers are so comatose they could be dead bodies. It's a horrible place."*

And with just that, the audience was already rapt.

"How long are you planning on staying here?"

"As long as it takes."

Supot was seated on the bank of an artificial pond observed by three headless concrete flamingos. The HAPPY HOME RESORT sign had broken in half, leaving just the HAPPY HO. He was grasping a tree branch with a string fishing line looping down into the murky water. He had an empty basket beside him.

"You do know there are no fish in this pond?" she said.

"It's a learning process. I'm coming to terms with nature. Soon I'll be living on raw mice."

"A movie?"

"*Never Cry Wolf.*"

"Haven't seen it," she said. "What made you think I'd be here?"

"Reported sightings. You're a bit like Bigfoot. This was one of the places you were spotted. I chose to stake you out here because of its luxury. It has beds."

"With crabs."

"We can learn to live together."

Siriluk, the mother, had taken up a position behind Supot on a rickety old bungalow balcony. He turned to look at her and smiled.

"What's that?" he asked.

"What does it look like? You never seen a rifle before?"

"Where did you get it?"

"Stole it."

"Is it loaded?"

"You'll find out."

Despite the fact the gun was aimed in his direction, he laughed and shook his head. It was the first time he'd seen Siriluk in daylight, albeit rapidly approaching dusk. The low sun reflected red off her bald head. She wore white like a nun and seemed to have more meat on her than at night. Even so, she couldn't have weighed more than ninety pounds. The coconut-white cat was at her feet.

"I did some investigative journalism," he said.

"Good for you."

"I checked the list."

"The hit list?"

"It turns out you and your ghostly friends haven't actually killed anyone."

"So?"

"So, I probably overreacted when I ran screaming from your cabin. We could have avoided burning the place down."

"It had termites anyway," she said.

"You're all cock-a-doodle and no do."

"Did you pick that one up at elementary school?"

He stood and tossed his unproductive fishing rod into the pond. Even though the rifle was still trained on him, he walked up the bank to where she was sitting.

"Did they send you after us?" she asked.

"Them again? Why do you assume I can't make my own decisions? I've been here at this dump for four days. Doesn't that show some determination?"

"I know how long you've been here," she said. "I've been watching you. You really are an awful woodsman."

"Really? You've been watching me struggle and didn't think to help me out?"

"I thought you'd be more placid once the malnutrition set in."

He ignored the gun and sat on the deck a few feet from her. He'd seen a lot of crazy people. Capital cities attracted them like flies to a corpse. Some were downright dangerous. Others made him sad. But this little woman was in a category all of her own. She had wit and wisdom, and it made him wonder whether this whole crazy lady routine was part of some long-term act.

"So, Comrade Supot, why are you here?" she asked.

"I'm putting off a move back to Bangkok," he said.

"No, I mean here at Happy Ho."

"To see you."

"Here I am. You have something to say, say it."

"Last time I tried to talk to you, you came at me with a knife," he said.

"It was just a small knife," she said. "If I'd been serious, I would have chased you with a scythe." She lowered the rifle.

"Thank you," he said. "Why have you decided to show yourself today?"

"I felt like a chat," she said.

"In spite of me being a commune spy?"

The cat stood, sauntered across the balcony, and curled up at his feet. He wasn't that fond of cats, but he considered this a tactical necessity.

"You came back," she said.

"From where?"

"The night of the fire. You were clear of the hut, but you went back inside."

"I wanted to rescue my post office hat badge."

She smiled.

"You could have been killed."

"It was an antique."

Her gravelly laugh echoed through the hills. She reached into her shoulder bag and retrieved a squashed pack of cigarettes. It took her some minutes to get one lit. She didn't offer him one. It was the first time he'd noticed her trembling hands. One drag on the cigarette and the shaking stopped. It must have been another five minutes before either of them spoke again.

"I was there, you know?" she said.

"Where's that?" he asked.

"At the telling."

He was truly astounded at her confession.

"*2010?*"

"You have a good memory."

"I screwed up a few times. The audience was forgiving."

"They loved it."

"I didn't see you there," he said.

"I was in a tree."

"Of course you were. Why did you attend?"

"Nobody's ever considered saving my life before. It gave me a little buzz. I suppose I was indebted to you."

"So, you were just being charitable."

"That's right."

"Nice of you. What did you think?"

"You want a review?"

"Just a personal opinion."

"Why should I tell you?"

"You'd never seen the movie. I'm curious what you think."

The cat jumped up onto Supot's lap and looked up at him as if he should have felt gratitude. He resisted the urge to swat her off.

"It was like . . . like a primer," she said. "A two-dimensional undercoat. An actual movie tells you what to feel. It does most of the thinking for you. Puts ideas into your head. But your telling made us all work. We had to paint and decorate your words. It allowed me to step out of the movie and look at it through your eyes. I needed that."

He subconsciously stroked the cat. She purred. He liked the feeling. It might have even explained why people bothered to keep cats.

"Nobody would tell me about the curse," he said. "Or the pact."

"I'm surprised they still have some moral responsibility," she said. "The pact was a committee decision. The curse? I suppose the curse was my idea. I decided that just in case the pact wasn't binding enough, even the most cynical person in the country has respect for the spirit world. They're happy to break a contract but wouldn't consider cheating the demons."

"Is that when you started living with them?" he asked.

"Oh, no. They've been with me since Sweden, Mr. Supot."

"So?"

"So, what?"

"Are you going to tell me?"

"Tell you what?"

"Why nobody has been allowed to watch one of the most brilliant Thai movies ever made. Why nobody can talk about it. Why everyone escaped to the hills and turned into hermits."

She got to her feet untidily. He was afraid she was about to leave him, but she went to the railing and leaned against it. It barely held her weight. She took two deep drags of her cigarette and flicked what was left into the pond.

"Is this your final scene?" she asked.

"What?"

"When they make a movie of your life, Supot."

He laughed at the thought of it.

"If anyone was stupid enough to do that, they'd have to skip over the first thirty-two years," he said.

"So, when would it start?"

"I don't know. Perhaps with me sabotaging the Royal Mail. Or no. I guess it would have to start with old Woot selling us the videos. Or with me taking *2010* home and becoming a different person. And, yes, your story would be somewhere near the end. Sort of a denouement."

"So, you're saying your film wouldn't be complete without my story?"

"The reviews would be awful."

"You'd finish with this scene? Me leaning on a rickety railing smoking a cigarette?"

"We'd need a few short scenes after it to find out what happened to Ali and me. I guess I'd need a sort of final ending, Hollywood rather than Paris. The French are into dark conclusions. After watching an hour and a half of me, I doubt the audience would stand for the protagonist putting a rifle in his mouth."

"And what becomes of me, Supot?"

"Everyone finds out you're only pretending to be a nutcase, and you step back into mainstream society. You open a souvenir crystal stall at Chatuchak Market, meet a mature Lithuanian, and settle down to domestic bliss."

"You're a very strange man."

"You've said that."

"Will I have to be dressed the whole time?"

"If we want to avoid an R rating."

She laughed again and lost control of her lungs. He considered stepping over and slapping her on the back, but the cat was too comfortable.

"You really have no respect for mental illness, do you?" she said once she'd calmed the cough.

"I do," he said. "I watched *One Flew Over the Cuckoo's Nest* five times."

"I don't know that one either. I stopped watching movies in 1965."

"See?" he said. "Life does it again. Here we are arriving at a perfect segue. And I say, 'Why did you stop?' and you say . . ."

In fact, she didn't say anything, not for a while. Supot let her chew things over. The insects chirruped; the banana leaves flapped in the wind. The cat farted. Siriluk looked up at a lone cloud shaped like a koala.

"His name was Ketgaew," she began.

"Field Marshal Bundtut," said Supot.

"Of course, you'd know that. It was 1965. I was twenty-four and pure and fresh as Swedish snow, but perhaps not as virginal. We were away from the restrictions of Thailand, and I felt that I could love him openly and be seen to be in love in ways I couldn't here. We lived together. It was blissfully sinful, but in Sweden, it didn't seem in the least abnormal.

"We all worked so hard on the film. It was our fight. Our weapon in the war against tyranny. Most of us were headstrong artists without any clear philosophy. But Ketgaew was a leader. He was the only one of us who proudly boasted publicly to being a communist. It was his aim to return the film to Thailand and distribute it as a tool to raise the masses. To end the curse of coups by the police and the military. It seemed like every few years another gang of uniformed despots would take over and line their pockets.

"Ketgaew and I had been lovers for six years, and it was still every bit as magical as at the start. But he was tired. He was the director and the main actor. Perhaps that was why he wasn't as attentive to detail in the last few days. We all chipped in to do everything that needed to be done, but he worked harder than any of us."

## 60 INT. BUNDTUT'S APARTMENT — DAY

Siriluk and Bundtut are in each other's arms on the bed, both fully dressed. She has bruises on her neck, dried blood on her face. Both are crying as they know they have to part. She kisses him one last time and rises painfully. She squeezes his hand for the last time, and he watches her go to the back emergency exit, turn, and salute her lover, then walk out.

There's nothing more to be said.

It is the last we see of her.

Bundtut slowly and deliberately puts on his full dress uniform jacket. The Security Force Secret Servicemen are knocking at his door. From their numbers, it's obvious they've come to arrest him. Someone brings a battering ram. Bundtut looks around his room, steps through the open window and onto the balcony.

CAMERA pans a long shot that shows us he is on the fortieth floor. He looks

```
back as the SS break in through the
door, and, still crying, he steps into
thin air.
```

"It was the final scene, the suicide where Bundtut throws himself from his apartment balcony down to the street below. We were all exhausted. We should have gone home and shot the final scene the next day, but we thought we were super-human, and there was only one main shoot left to do.

"The last scene was to be dramatic and realistic. He would crash through the glass roof of a city bus. Of course, it was special glass. It broke easily. But, to get the effect right, per-fectionist Ketgaew insisted on doing the stunt himself. There was a platform set up about ten feet over the bus. He was to leap off the platform. We had a Swedish stunt specialist who made sure it would be safe. How to fall and all that. He offered to disguise himself as Bundtut and do the stunt for us. But Ketgaew refused. It would be replayed in slow motion allowing for a close-up. It had to be him, he said. It was going to be the defining moment of the film. The defeat of the enemy. We had one camera beside the bus, another on the platform showing the fall from above, and a third was inside the bus to film him breaking through the glass.

"We only had the one glass roof, so everything had to be perfect with just one take. I assume everyone was so con-sumed by the filming techniques that none of us bothered to double-check the details. We'd talked. We'd all talked about how safe we were from Thai government agents in Sweden. There were reports of the assassination of other dissidents in England and a lot back here in Thailand. But at the time, it seemed unlikely to us that they would bother to watch us. We were just students. But Ketgaew wasn't very circumspect. He was writing articles criticizing the regime and using his own name. The release of *2010* would certainly have been damaging too.

"We had no proof the murder was committed by an agent of the junta. We never did discover who was responsible. We couldn't believe it was one of our own people. Everybody loved Ketgaew. But someone had inserted a dozen thirty-centimeter fisherman's needles through the underside of the top mattress. They were the sort used to sew nets, but they'd been sharpened to a fine point. You wouldn't have noticed them by just moving the mattresses. When he landed . . ."

She was shouting now. Supot wondered whether it was a way to purge herself of her demons.

"When he landed, one of the needles pierced his thigh," she said. "Another went through his heart. The doctors said he wouldn't have felt very much of anything.

"The final scene of the film, where I say the line, 'No. It wasn't supposed to end like this. God help us all.' That wasn't acting. That was my reaction to my lover's death."

The small bell over the door was caressed by its leather strap and a voice from the back room shouted, "I'll be with you in a minute."

It wasn't the voice he'd expected to hear, but instead, the gnarly voice of a woman. He walked around the shelves taking note of the new arrivals. The classics corner had swollen, titles he'd never heard of donated, he'd been told, by Ali's new movie crowd. They were giving up their Beta and VHS and moving on to a peculiar phenomenon called compact disks. He was hoping it wouldn't catch on. He ran his finger over the familiar video boxes—*The Bicycle Thief, Hiroshima Mon Amor, Das Boot.* So many good old friends and so little time.

The woman came out of the back room and stopped in surprise.

"Supot?" she said.

"Kwang."

He wasn't sure what he expected from her. She wasn't the type who'd run up to him and throw her arms around him. Neither would she *wai* politely to someone like Supot, whom she'd known, good and bad, since elementary school. If anything, she looked disappointed to see him. Perhaps she wondered whether he was there to reclaim his best friend: her fiancé. She and Ali had been officially engaged for five months. Supot had read about it in one of Ali's monthly letters to Chiang Rai. Supot had written back offering his congratulations, did his best to sound sincere. But he knew that she considered Supot to be a loser. She blamed him for taking up so much of Ali's time. Time that should have been hers.

"How's Chiang Rai?" she asked with no enthusiasm.

"Clean," he said.

"Are you here for the wedding?"

"I'm not . . . it's not really my thing."

"So I recall."

"I did bring you a wedding present, though," he said and hoisted a large plastic bag onto the counter.

"It's fruit," he said. "Picked it all myself yesterday. One night on the bus to mature. Should all be ready to eat."

"Thank you," she said unconvincingly.

They stood staring at each other for a while.

"Where's . . . ?"

"He went to the bank," she said.

"With a mask and a gun?"

"No."

There, that was what confounded him. How could Ali choose a woman with no sense of humor? It was unforgivable. How could you go through life explaining punch lines?

"I have to . . ." she said, pointing to the rear.

"Go ahead. I'll make myself useful."

He'd noticed some titles were out of order alphabetically and started to rearrange them.

"Ehr, *Khun* Supot," she said. "I'd rather you didn't touch those."

"But they're—"

"I have a system," she said.

He held up his hands, wondering what system trumped the alphabet, but he said nothing. It was almost her shop, after all. He sat on a stool at the counter and browsed the *Thai Rat* newspaper. A cup of coffee would have been nice. A glass of water after the sweaty walk from the ferry even better. But he had to settle for a headline.

GORY GUN RAMPAGE IN CHINATOWN.

It would have made a good movie title. He was down to the description of the fifth victim whose "head was blown right off," when Ali walked into the shop. He threw himself at Supot. The enthusiasm overwhelmed the visitor. They hadn't seen each other for over a year. Ali and the shop were the only things he missed about Bangkok Noi, and Ali and the shop clearly missed him back. He had a lump in his throat when he said, "You'll have to let me go eventually."

"You'll never guess where I've just come from," Ali said.

"The bank?"

"Damned good guess. Do you know why I went to the bank?"

"Something to do with money?"

Ali released the hug but held on to his hand.

"All that fresh northern air has made you intelligent," he said. He reached into his shirt pocket and pulled out his bankbook. He flipped it open to the last active page. "See that?" he said. "The last deposit."

"I don't remember you ever making a deposit in a bank before," said Supot. "Let me see. Holy cow. Two hundred and eighty thousand baht? Where did you lay your hands on that sort of money?"

"The cinema industry."

"They pay extras that much?"

"No, that paid shit," said Ali. "It didn't take me long to get the acting bug out of my system."

"So . . .?"

"You remember Dylan?"

"Dylan who?"

"Dylan the Welsh volunteer."

"Your never-to-be-finished screenplay?"

"That's it. I finished it, and Grammy Film bought it."

"You're a genius," said Supot, and they hugged again.

"I had to make one or two changes to the last draft I showed you," said Ali.

"Like what?"

"Like he's not Welsh anymore."

"Probably for the best," Supot agreed.

"And it no longer has anything to do with me or my family."

"Is there anything left?"

"And it's set in Singapore."

"No transvestite sister?"

"Sorry. I know you were hungry for that part."

"I'll get over it."

"But, as of today, I'm a professional screenwriter. They like me. They've asked for another script."

"Got any ideas?"

"In fact, I do," said Ali. "But I'd like to talk to you about it."

"We have to celebrate tonight," said Supot.

"I . . . ehr . . ." Ali looked to the rear of the shop. "We have a sort of family thing tonight. Can't get out of it."

"Really?" said Supot. "Then we'll have to settle for a very long cup of coffee with a little dribble of something stronger. Let's go."

Ali noticed the plastic bag. He peeked inside. "Wedding present?" he guessed.

"Call me sentimental." There was a cactus beside the plastic bag. "I see your ugly plant survived."

"I went to your place to collect it when I came back from the movie shoot. That's when I found out you'd left town. It still had my note to you attached. Your neighbor gave it to me. He said you didn't water it."

"It's a cactus," said Supot. "They're never really happy unless they're dying of thirst."

"I'm assuming you won't be sticking around for the wedding," said Ali.

"It's not really—"

"—Your thing. I know. No problem. I wouldn't have gone to yours either."

Tik's Coffee Emporium was eight tables in an open-fronted shophouse ten down from the video store. It's where Ali and Supot used to hang out to escape the pressures of entrepreneurism. It had nothing in common with Starbucks. The coffee was filtered through what looked like an old sock, and you could stand a teaspoon in the sludge at the bottom of the mug. But it gave you a buzz and Tik would throw in a shot of Mekhong whisky if you asked him nicely. After catching the owner up on news, Ali and Supot were left alone to talk films.

"We just found out something before I left the commune," said Supot. "You know Vongkot was based in Europe and just came back here to put *2010* together."

"Right."

"Well, it turns out we've found the completed film version of the movie."

"You don't say."

"He had family over in Germany. It appears once it was edited, he sent the finished film to them. They contacted the commune. There were two copies. They're sending one to us."

"So, they'll get to see their movie after all," said Ali.

"There are those that won't watch it. Siriluk for one, but,

yes. They'll get their world premiere after all. You don't seem that happy about it."

"Do you think they'll put copyright restrictions on it?"

"I don't know. I think they'll still keep it to themselves. They don't want their privacy invaded. Why do you ask?"

"I was wondering . . ." Ali began, "if you'd mind if I was to write my next screenplay about a postman."

"It already sounds boring," said Supot.

"This postman falls in love with an actress, then he finds out she's a hundred-something years old."

"Bit far-fetched."

"But what do you think?"

"You want to write my story?"

"Your letters from Chiang Rai convinced me," said Ali. "All that stuff that happened here and up north. It would make a great film, don't you think?"

Supot held up two fingers for another round. "I wouldn't have to play myself, would I?"

"Nobody on this earth would pay money to watch it if you did."

Supot looked out at the motorcycles in the street jostling for gaps between the trucks.

"Then I'd be honored."

"Really?" said Ali. "That's great."

They clinked their mugs together and woo-hoo'd. An elderly couple stopped at the entrance, decided that the clientele was too raucous, and passed by instead.

"Calm it down, guys," said Tik. "You're losing me customers."

"Sorry, Tik."

"Sorry, Tik."

"You know it's going to be difficult to write it without giving away the ending," said Supot.

"Yeah, I've been thinking about that. Probably have to throw in a few red herrings."

"In fact, there might be another twist."

"Really?"

"We're sort of in one of those post-climactic scenes right now."

"We are?"

"Of course we are. If this is your movie, this is a sort of clean-up-loose-ends scene. It'll be followed by my Hollywood ending."

"You're getting your own Hollywood ending? How does that work?"

"I don't know exactly. It hasn't happened yet. I've got a sort of a modestly content ending where I'm living in a commune, fishing, picking fruit, and repairing the odd cabin. It turns out I'm handy with a hammer. I've got this old lady friend I hang out with. They tell me I was integral in her return to the community, which is odd, seeing as she did all the talking. She counseled herself better. She's not well, but she's improving. She's still certifiable in a loveable kind of way, still does a lot of embarrassing things—rips her clothes off from time to time—but we can laugh most of it off. She's less likely to knife me now."

"What about the daughter?"

"She wouldn't knife me either."

"No, idiot. I mean, where does she fit in this story?"

"She's nice. We became friends. But she'd abandoned her own aspirations to look after her mother. Once the old lady showed signs of improvement, she moved out. When she was down here looking for me, she went for auditions."

"Good for her."

"Turns out she's a pretty good actress," said Supot. "Thailand's irrevocably committed to skinny, white-skinned leading ladies, so she'll never be a love interest, but she's got the maid and funny best friend markets cornered."

"I'll look out for her."

"You don't watch television."

"I'm getting more into it. Kwang likes us to watch together in the evenings."

Supot felt a shudder climb his spine.

"What do you do to keep your artistic bent . . . bent?" Ali asked.

"I think I mentioned it in my letter. I found a skill I didn't know I had. I call it motion picture telling. It's like fortune-telling and storytelling, except I tell movies. I'm surprised how much I remember from all the films we've watched. It's as if I can't forget anything. I do regular shows for the commune, and I've done a couple for the outside community. Seems people never get too old to be told stories."

"Then that sounds like a nice way to end the movie," said Ali.

"Yes, I know. I just think the cinematic world wants something more, something bigger. They want a mega-feel-good moment. Without a Hollywood finale, I feel like I'm letting everyone down."

"So, this scene . . . our scene now . . . is finished once we pay Tik and go our separate ways?"

"It's pretty much done," said Supot. "Except for the other twist."

"The other twist. Right."

"You might not want to include it in your screenplay. I'm not even sure 'twist' really describes it. The audience might have already seen it coming."

"Does it involve me?"

"Yes."

"Tell me anyway."

Supot batted the flies away from the untouched sticky rice sweets.

"All right," he said. "It's something I should have said a long time ago, and, for that, I'm sorry. In all the years I've known you and you've known Kwang, how many negative things have I said about her?"

"You've never said anything?"

"That's right. And that's because I assumed you liked her."

"I do."

"Enough to marry her."

"Right."

"Okay, here goes. Cue viola soundtrack. Ali, if you marry that woman, you're going to be miserable for the rest of your life. She's a dog. An attractive dog admittedly, from a good Muslim family. Your parents and her parents have been close since they were young. If you marry their daughter, her parents will be delighted to get rid of her. Of course, they'd talk you out of this silly notion that you'll make something of yourself working in a video store and writing screenplays. You'll agree for Kwang's sake and take a job at Sabaijai Insurance, and you'll age rapidly. I won't even get into how kids of yours might turn out."

"Wow," said Ali.

But Supot was firing on all cylinders.

"I should have been a better friend," he continued. "I'm sorry. I think the reason you haven't dated anyone else is because you felt this unnecessary obligation to the Muslim community. Now you're a screenplay writer. You'll be hanging out with directors and other writers and actresses desperate to be in one of your movies. You're funny-looking but there are women who find that endearing. The important thing to them is that you're smart and creative and you have a great sense of humor. There are women who don't believe life revolves around money, and the fact that you aren't rich wouldn't worry them. The reason I'm not going to your wedding isn't because I don't like weddings, which, incidentally, I don't, but it's because you marrying Kwang would be like watching you step out of your fortieth-floor apartment and landing on a city bus."

Ali finally put down his untouched coffee, but his jaw remained dropped.

"Wow!" he said.

"Does that work?" asked Supot.

"As a twist?"

"Yeah."

Ali thought about it for a few seconds.

"Damn right it does," he said.

The Chiang Rai bus had arrived late at Mo Chit Bus Station, so it was only to be expected that it would be leaving late. Supot looked around at the slow-moving passengers. Nobody was ever in a hurry in a Thai bus station. Even those latecomers whose bus was already reversing out of the bay would saunter after it, not wanting anyone to think their lives were so mundane that missing a bus would make any difference. Bus terminals were the opposite of airports.

The girl stepped down from the bus with her plastic brush-and-dustpan-set in one hand and a plastic bag of discarded items and junk in the other. That was the cleaning service. There was no fumigation, no insect repellent for the seats, no bleach and Dettol for the overused, under-ventilated toilet. Whatever germs had arrived from Chiang Rai would be returning to Chiang Rai. The girl nodded at the driver, who had been sitting patiently on a concrete bench. His hooded eyes suggested he might nod off even before they reached the endless suburbs. There weren't enough bottles of Red Bull on the planet to keep a long-distance bus driver alert.

Supot had decided to be Indonesian on this trip. He certainly couldn't be Thai. If he was from the Philippines, there were those who might want to practice English with him. But nobody expected anything from an Indonesian. He just had to say "Jakarta," raise a thumb, and act dumb for the rest of the journey. Then he would be excused from twelve hours of inane conversation with people he had nothing in common with. Anyone who argued there were friends to be made on a long-distance bus was mad.

Finally, the passengers were herded onto the bus and placed in their seats. Even after the gear lever had been milled into reverse and the bus was signaled to depart, there was still a vacant seat beside Supot. The other passengers looked at him with envy. It was every man and woman's dream to be blessed with an empty seat next to them on a long-distance bus journey. They dreamed of that luxurious space upon which they could lay their aching limbs, where they could nod off in one province and wake up twelve provinces down the road. The owl-like man in front of him looked through the space between the seats and growled. Supot raised his thumb and said, "Jakarta."

They were just leaving second gear when a girl ran . . . yes, ran . . . beside the bus and banged her fist on the driver's door. He heaved his foot against the brake pedal and forty-seven passengers were a tendon away from whiplash. They didn't suffer in silence.

"Where did you learn to drive?" shouted one.

The girl walked around the front of the bus to the passenger door, and the driver yanked the lever to open it for her. She jogged up the steps. Her smile lit up the interior of the bus, or, at least, Supot thought so. She wasn't a classical beauty. She wouldn't have reached the quarterfinals of Miss Thailand World. She wore no makeup, and her hair was wet, perhaps from a late shower. She dressed simply but carried herself with confidence and elegance. She was the loveliest girl he'd ever seen.

"Almost missed it," she said to everyone and nobody, and there was that smile again. Two old ladies made sarcastic comments in the northern Thai dialect. Supot didn't understand what they said, but the girl apparently passed the banter test. Whatever she replied had the two old dears in stitches.

She walked to the back of the bus and looked at her ticket. She smiled at the man who was sitting beside her seat and threw her small pack and a heavy plastic bag onto the overhead luggage shelf. She sat and he was immediately bathed in the fragrance of kaffir lime shampoo.

He was Supot, so nothing original came into his mind for the first ten minutes as they drove through the smoky inner city. The only thing he thought about was the line, "*Unmoving, futuristic traffic clogs the street. The vehicles aren't clearly visible through the fog, but the drivers are so comatose they could be corpses.*" Fortunately, they passed a minor motorcycle accident that cheered everyone up. The two riders threatened each other with metal tire irons. The bus passengers enjoyed the show. Supot turned and smiled at his seatmate. She smiled back. He didn't want to push his luck, so he returned to the traffic, but in the window reflection he could see her face. He had an odd sensation that she was looking at him.

"You're Supot," she said.

"I . . . I know."

She laughed. She had a fine set of teeth.

"You're from the commune," she said. "I came to your moving picture telling at our elementary school. *The Wizard of Oz.*"

"You're a teacher."

"Yes."

"I don't remember you."

He chalked it up as one of his least romantic opening lines.

"I have an easily forgettable face," she said.

"Not at all," he said.

"And you were surrounded by adoring eight-year-olds. How could I compete?"

"It was a fun day," said Supot.

"You were amazing."

"Thank you."

The bus hostess arrived with a tray of unidentifiable snacks and small sealed plastic cups with a mouthful of water in each. The girl took one meal for herself and handed one to Supot.

"It's like in *The Langoliers*," she said.

"*The Langoliers?*"

"Right. The movie they made of the Stephen King story. You must have seen it. You're a movie guy. These survivors arrive at an airport and the food looks like regular food, but it has no taste."

Of course he'd seen *The Langoliers*, but it had only come out recently, and it wasn't on general release. His mind slipped off its rails.

"Where did you see it?" he asked.

"We have a sort of film club," she said. "Started at university, then just kept going after we left."

He looked out of the window and smiled. The dirty sidewalks were crowded with clueless people heading off to places they'd sooner not be. The scene reminded him of the John Wayne movie *Hatari!*, when the Jeep patiently plowed its way through a vast herd of wildebeests. The animals raised their sad faces to the passing vehicle with dreams of a better life. And here, the Bangkok inmates watched another bus make its escape from the grubby city. And through the smudged glass, they saw a happy postman staring back at them, a pretty lady by his side.

"I wonder if this is too much," he said.

"What?"

"Nothing."

# AUTHOR'S NOTE

Back in the nineties I was approached by a fledgling movie production company to write screenplays to add to their portfolio. One of these I called *Bangkok 2010*. I was living in Thailand and my research for this movie took me into areas I'd never seen and introduced me to the underbelly of Thai suburban life. It encouraged me to walk down seedy alleyways and interview street people. It re-educated me and helped me see Thailand from a different perspective.

Nothing came of the movie, but the story continued to fascinate me, and I decided to turn it into a novel with a cinematic backdrop. Thus, we arrive at *The Motion Picture Teller*, an unrequited love story about a poor Thai postman and a beautiful movie star. It delved into the lives of people whose dreams hold them together, whose only hopes are that one day they might meet someone who can change their lives.

GREAT BRITAIN
1661

BAVARIA
1806

BOHEMIA
c.1450

HUNGARY
c.1000

SWEDEN
1560

ARAGON
c.1400

BELGIUM
c.1400

PORTUGAL
1817

WURTTEMBERG
1822

# The Concise Guide to
# Kings and Queens

Peter Gibson

# The Concise Guide to Kings and Queens

## A Thousand Years of European Monarchy

*Webb & Bower*

EXETER, ENGLAND

First published in Great Britain 1985 by
Webb & Bower (Publishers) Limited
9 Colleton Crescent, Exeter, Devon EX2 4BY

Design Malcolm Couch
Production Nick Facer

Copyright © Peter Gibson 1985

**British Library Cataloguing in Publication Data**

Gibson, Peter
  The concise guide to kings and queens: a
  thousand years of European monarchy.
  1. Royal houses — Europe.     2. Europe —
  Kings and rulers
  I. Title
  929.7'094     D106

ISBN 0-86350-094-3

Typeset in Great Britain by P&M Typesetting Ltd, Exeter, Devon

Printed and bound in Great Britain

# CONTENTS

# INTRODUCTION

The *Concise Guide to the Kings, Queens Regnant, Emperors and Tsars of Europe* lists all the significant monarchs who reigned in Europe in the last thousand years. Forty-three kingdoms are examined, 688 monarchs separately identified and dated with, in most cases, biographical information. Such kings as are not included are non-starters, imposters, pretenders and over 400 minor kings in Ireland, who ruled in addition to the all-powerful ones shown.

Each country is introduced by a short history. Of the kingdoms covered twenty-one survive as sovereign states. Seven of them are still monarchies: Belgium, Denmark, Great Britain, the Netherlands, Norway, Spain and Sweden. Of those states which have either disappeared or changed their constitutions, twelve had done so by 1670, nine more by 1870 and the rest before 1970.

No duchies or principalities, no landgraviates or electorates, no counties or republics have been dealt with; though some are referred to *passim*.

Rulers' personal names provided a problem, since history is never consistent in spelling. The solution, also adopted by many history books, was to put down the name by which the King, or Queen, is most readily known. This is not always the monarch's native name. After the country entries, therefore, there is a *Conversion Table* showing the names, by which they were known in their own countries, of some 125 monarchs; names which have been 'translated' in the text.

The last portion of the book is a *Chronology* of all the rulers, showing their dates of accession, their age at that date, their kingdom(s) and the end of their reign (but not necessarily the date of their death). The list enables the reader to see very clearly what the relationships between the crowned heads of Europe was at any given moment. It also makes other statistics more easily extracted and yields largely unrealized information. To cite two examples: consider that in all the 1000 years during which forty-three countries supported nearly 700 rulers, there have only been six instances when kings of different kingdoms came to their thrones and left them in the same year as each other and only four times were two kings of the same age when they were enthroned. (The first of like *reigns* was from 1033 to 1039 when Iago of Wales ruled the same length of time as Conrad of Burgundy. The last example of like *ages at accession* was in 1481 when John became King of Denmark in May and another John, King of Portugal, the following October. Both men were twenty-six years old.)

Through its record of monarchies, many of which have disappeared, the Guide gives an idea of the changing map of Europe; the interrelationships between kingdoms and between ruling families. It gives an insight into the family feuds and conspiracies which changed the leadership of many of the countries as some moved from monarchies to republics.

# ALBANIA

A Roman province for many years, Albania was subsequently administered by Normans, Serbians and Bulgarians. It then enjoyed a brief spell of autonomy before being submerged by the all-conquering Turks. The Ottoman power reigned for nearly 500 years, until the Balkan War. In 1912 Albania was declared a principality, but this proved unsuccessful and a republic was formed in 1925, a kingdom in 1928 and then, in 1939, Italy annexed the country. 'Liberated' by Italy's defeat in 1944, it took only eighteen months before a communist republic came into being in January 1946.
Capital *TIRANA*; currency *lek*

**WILLIAM** (1876-1945), reigned 1914. Though a Prince of Wied (a German dynasty) he was intended to be king. Deprived of all support, however, both from within the country and abroad, he left the 'throne' when the outbreak of the First World War made the situation totally impossible. He never abdicated.

**ZOG,** originally Ahmed Bey Zogu (1895-1961), reigned 1928-1948. By the age of twelve he was head of his clan. Upon independence being declared, the then seventeen-year-old Zog swore to uphold that independence. When Italy invaded, however, Zog and Queen Geraldine fled to Britain, taking their newly born son, Leka, with them. (It has been claimed that Geraldine had the somewhat dubious distinction of being related to one-time American President, Richard Nixon.) After the Second World War Britain refused to help Zog back onto his throne, and he went to live in Egypt. While there, he was officially deposed. He moved to the French Riviera where he died.

**VICTOR EMANUEL III** of Italy (1869-1947), reigned 1939-1943. He assumed the throne when the Italians overran the country, but renounced it in September 1943.

# ARAGON

A small county in the north-east of Spain, Aragon was absorbed by Navarre in the tenth century. It was then established as an independent

monarchy in 1035 by SANCHO, 'The Great', of Navarre. His illegitimate son, RAMIRO, became the first king of this expanded country.

**RAMIRO I** (died 1063), reigned 1035-1063. He took the new throne the year his father, SANCHO of Navarre, died.

**SANCHO** (1037-1094), reigned 1063-1094. He was Ramiro's son and also Sancho V of Navarre.

**PEDRO** (1068-1104), SANCHO's son, reigned 1094-1104.

**ALFONSO I** (died 1134), reigned 1104-1134. PEDRO's brother, he was also ALFONSO VII, King of Leon and Castile, who conquered the Moors at Saragossa in 1118. His marriage to Urraca, a widow, was annulled by the Pope because they were third cousins. Doubtless Alfonso was pleased, since Urraca's morals were not all they ought to have been. In his will he left his kingdom to the Knights Templar, but the Aragonese chose to ignore his testamentary wishes.

**RAMIRO II**, 'The Monk', who reigned 1134-1137, was ALFONSO and PEDRO's younger brother. His chosen vocation for the cloister was delayed until the question of succession had been resolved through his marriage and the birth of a daughter. He then abdicated and went into the church.

**PETRONILLA** (1137-1163), reigned 1137-1163, the sixth and last ruler of the Navarre dynasty. She was RAMIRO's daughter (as a result of his obliging efforts to serve the state before he embraced the Church) and married Ramon, Count of Barcelona.

**ALFONSO II** of Barcelona (1152-1196), reigned 1163-1196. The son of PETRONILLA, he inherited Catalonia from his father, Ramon. Aragon and Catalonia were uneasy bedfellows. Alfonso was a spare time poet in the 'Provençal manner'.

**PEDRO II** (1174-1213), son of ALFONSO and Sancia of Castile, reigned 1196-1213. He was rather a puzzling person who hobnobbed in 'low circles', yet was a brave warrior. He was killed by Simon de Montfort's Crusaders, in a battle at Muret. An engagement sparked off by his involvement with the Albigensians. The Saracens must have been delighted.

**JAMES,** 'The Conqueror' (1208-1276), reigned 1213-1276. The son of PEDRO II, he earned his nickname honestly, by conquering Valencia, Murcia and the Balearic Islands, so creating a Mediterranean extension to his kingdom. He also founded a navy to patrol it.

**PEDRO III** (1236-1286), reigned 1276-1285. He inherited his father JAMES's military genius, conquering Sicily (which earned him the epithet 'The Great') and generally stirring up matters between the Aragonese and the Angevins in Southern Italy.

**ALFONSO III**, 'The Beneficent' or 'The Good Do-er' (1265-1291), the son of 'The Great', reigned 1285-1291. He clawed back land from the Moors, argued endlessly with the Pope and, most importantly, he granted a *Privilege of Union* which gave his subjects the right to carry arms.

**JAMES II,** 'The Just' (1260-1327), reigned 1291-1327. ALFONSO's elder brother, he became King of Sicily in 1285, but resigned in 1291. He

then married Blanca, daughter of Charles of Anjou, hoping to patch up the family's quarrels with Naples and the Angevins.

**ALFONSO IV,** 'The Good' (1299-1336), reigned 1327-1336. Good he may have been, weak he certainly was. He spent more time fighting the Genoese over the possession of Corsica and Sardinia than attending to his other affairs.

**PEDRO IV,** 'The Ceremonious' (1319-1387), reigned 1336-1387. A man of rigid etiquette who, like his father, spent most of his life fighting battles. Pedro's battles, however, were against his own nobles whom he defeated at Epila in 1348. He also regained Sicily. He married three times: Mary of Navarre, Eleanor of Portugal and Eleanor of Sicily.

**JOHN I** (1350-1395), PEDRO's son, reigned 1387-1395.

**MARTIN,** 'The Humane' (1355-1410), reigned 1395-1410. He was the son of PEDRO, who ceded Sicily to him. Obviously a bad manager, he died without leaving a will or, in the absence of heirs, any indication who should succeed him. This resulted in a two-year hiatus after his death until a specially appointed commission met and elected a king.

**FERDINAND,** 'The Just' (1379-1416), reigned 1412-1416. He was the son of JOHN of Castile and King of Sicily. For reasons of his own, he supported the anti-pope, Benedict XIII. In 1415 the Emperor Sigismund persuaded him to see the error of his ways and from then on, in the interests of church unity, he supported the orthodox establishment.

**ALFONSO V,** 'The Magnanimous' or 'The Wise' (1385-1458), FERDINAND's son, reigned 1416-1458. He was a classicist and very much in the mould of a renaissance prince. He unwisely left Aragon to take care of itself and spent most of his time sorting out his Kingdoms of Sicily and Naples (leaving the latter to his bastard son, Ferdinand).

**JOHN II** (1397-1479), ALFONSO's brother, reigned 1458-1479. He was an unscrupulous, bellicose man, who quarrelled with his first wife, Blanche of Navarre, by whom he had had a son. By his second wife, Joan Henriquez (who was often thought to have poisoned her stepson) he had another son, Ferdinand. In a marriage-making master-stroke, he arranged an alliance between Ferdinand and Isabella of Castile. He thus ensured the unity of Spain, and Ferdinand became King FERDINAND V of the whole country in January 1516.

# AUSTRIA

Originally the Eastern State – the *Oesterreich* – of Bavaria, Austria was a Duchy from the middle of the twelfth century until 'acquired' by Rudolf of

Habsburg in 1267. His descendants added bits and pieces and formed the Habsburg Empire. When the Holy Roman Empire was finally dismantled in 1806, Archduke Franz of Austria, who was the Emperor of the day, had already promoted himself to Emperor of Austria. The *Austro-Hungarian* Empire, formed in 1867, was broken up at the end of the First World War. The central section became the Austria of today and the remainder formed the basis for Hungary and Czechoslovakia, with smaller areas being absorbed by Italy, Yugoslavia, Romania and Poland.

Capital *VIENNA*; currency *schilling*

**FRANZ I** (1768-1835), reigned 1804-1835. He was the eldest son of the Archduke Leopold II of Austria whom he succeeded as Archduke on March 1, 1792. On April 11, 1804 he declared himself Emperor of Austria. From 1809, with Metternich by his side, Austria went from strength to strength and managed to come through the NAPOLEONIC struggles with credit (literally and metaphorically).

**FERDINAND** (1793-1875), eldest son of Franz, reigned 1835-1848. Sadly, he was an epileptic. His health improved slightly as he grew older and, when his father died, he was considered fit enough to rule. Luckily Metternich was still 'in the driving seat' and headed the Council of State. Ferdinand, who was sometimes, though not sarcastically, called *Der Gütige* or 'Kindly One', had some quite serious mental lapses. The revolt in Vienna forced him to take sanctuary at Innsbrück, but his health and general bearing made abdication imperative. He lived for the last 27 years of his life under close medical supervision in Prague.

**FRANZ JOSEPH I** (1830-1916), reigned 1848-1916. Although his younger brother, Francis Charles, was very much alive, the debilitated FERDINAND was 'guided to abdicate' in favour of his nephew, Franz Joseph. The latter seems to be remembered as a wise, patriarchal and bewhiskered old gentleman, yet as an Emperor, all he did was to sit back and watch as his empire was eroded around him. His vivacious wife, Elisabeth of Bavaria, found him kind but heavy-going. She moved to Corfu and left an actress called Katherina Schratt to look after him. (Even Herr Schratt co-operated.) In 1866 the *Dual Monarchy* was instituted, which effectively gave Hungary autonomy within the Austro-Hungarian Empire. Franz Joseph's son and heir, Rudolf, died at Mayerling, in a suicide pact with his eighteen-year-old, pregnant mistress. He left his nephew, Ferdinand, next in line to the throne. Ferdinand was assassinated at Sarajevo in 1914; an event which plunged Europe into the First World War. Franz Joseph died bemused, with his Empire on the brink of collapse.

**KARL** (1887-1922), reigned 1916-1918. A grand nephew of FRANZ JOSEPH, Karl was actually crowned with the ancient crown of St Stephen of Hungary in Budapest. He was to step down in November 1918, just after the end of the war that had been sparked off by the murder of his uncle Ferdinand. Though he renounced government, he never actually abdicated.

# BAVARIA

A kingdom of Southern Germany, Bavaria was once the second largest of the states of the German Empire, both in area and population. The house of Wittelsbach ruled the Duchy of Bavaria from 1375, becoming electors in 1623 and finally kings in 1805.

Capital *MUNICH*

**MAXIMILIAN I** (1756-1825), reigned 1805-1825. He was head of the Zweibrücken branch of the Wittelsbach family and had been Elector of the country since 1799. He sided with NAPOLEON and gained further territory under the Peace of Prestburg in 1805, when he declared himself King. His French connection, understandably, gave grounds for Austrian mistrust.

**LUDWIG I** (1786-1868), reigned 1825-1848. Rather confusingly many reference books style all the Ludwigs as Louis. He was MAXIMILIAN's son but, unlike his father, no admirer of NAPOLEON or the French. In 1846, Ludwig became enamoured of a dancer, Lola Montez, and the scandal caused by this liaison forced his abdication. Some reports claimed that Ludwig actually married Lola.

**MAXIMILIAN II** (1811-1864), reigned 1848-1864. He was a liberal patron of the arts, who was obliged to ascend the throne when his father, LUDWIG, abdicated.

**LUDWIG II** (1845-1886), reigned 1864-1886. He was only 18 when he came to the throne. Ludwig moved his kingdom politically closer to Prussia, but neither diplomacy nor kingship appealed to him. He formed a passionate friendship with the composer Richard Wagner, settling debts of his for 18,000 *gulden* and giving him an income of 4,000 *gulden*. The King was homosexual and his personal bodyguard were chosen as much for their good looks as their military distinction. His intellect, never very strong, eventually gave way and he was declared insane in June 1886. He drowned himself five days later in Lake Starnberg.

**OTTO** (1848-1916), reigned 1886-1913, was LUDWIG's brother and also mentally unbalanced. His uncle, Prince Luitpold, was Regent and during the years when Otto was King in name, Bavaria shared the prosperity of Germany. Otto was legally deposed in November 1913.

**LUDWIG III** (1854-1921), reigned 1913-1918. The last of the Wittelsbachs and the last King of Bavaria, he was Prince Luitpold's son (and OTTO's cousin). His reign ended by his deposition on the rise of the Independent Socialists.

# BELGIUM

For centuries Belgium was known as the Southern Netherlands. Its provinces, such as Flanders, Brabant, Limburg and Hainault, were once counties or duchies, often under German domination. In 1814 the north and south areas of the country united, but in 1830 the south broke away and the Kingdom of Belgium was formed under the Coburg family.

Capital *BRUSSELS*; currency *Belgian franc*

**LEOPOLD I** (1790-1865), reigned 1831-1865. The first King of the Belgians, he was the youngest son of the Duke of Saxe-Coburg (and a descendant of John Frederick, Elector of Saxony, who died in 1547). He married Charlotte, only daughter of GEORGE IV of Great Britain, who died in childbirth. His second wife was the daughter of King LOUIS PHILIPPE of France. Leopold refused the throne of Greece, but was *elected* King of the Belgians. He was a man of culture and judgement and has sometimes been referred to as the 'Nestor of Europe'.

**LEOPOLD II** (1835-1909), the son of LEOPOLD I, reigned 1865-1909. During his reign the Congo Free State was founded; a vast region autocratically administered by Leopold and used by him to feather his nest. His immense fortune was based on quite unspeakable cruelty and exploitation in Africa. His only son, the Duke of Hainault, died when he was just ten.

**ALBERT I** (1875-1934), reigned 1909-1934. The nephew of Leopold II, he was generally considered to have been the 'best constitutional monarch in Europe'. He died in a mountaineering accident.

**LEOPOLD III** (1901-1983), reigned 1934-1951. His first wife, Princess Astrid of Sweden, was killed in a car crash, but the sympathy engendered by the tragedy was not sufficient to efface his behaviour during the Second World War. Leopold personally ordered his army to surrender and he was 'kept prisoner' by the Germans. He did not return to his capital until 1950 and relinquished his royal prerogative almost immediately, to his twenty-year-old son, BAUDOUIN. He abdicated officially the following year.

**BAUDOUIN** (born 1930), his reign began in 1951, but he occupies a rather hollow throne. He and his Spanish wife, Fabiola de Mora y Aragon have no children.

# BOHEMIA

Most of what was Bohemia now forms a large part of Czechoslovakia. Not long after it was established as a Duchy in the ninth century, it combined with Moravia as a suzerain state of the Holy Roman Empire, becoming a kingdom in 1198. It passed through various 'families' until 1562, when the Habsburgs inherited the domain. They held on to it right up until 1918, when the State of Czechoslovakia was created from part of the Austro-Hungarian Empire.

Capital *PRAGUE*

**PREMISLAS I (OTTOCAR I)** of the House of Premysl (1150-1230), reigned 1198-1230. There had been rulers styled as kings before Premislas: Vratislav from 1085-1092 and Vladislav II who was Elector until he became King from 1140 until his death in 1173. A state of anarchy reigned from then until 1198, when Premislas was given the formal title of King by the Holy Roman Emperor, OTTO IV, and established the dynasty for himself and his descendants.

**VACLAV I** (1205-1253), son of PREMISLAS, reigned 1230-1253.

**PREMISLAS II (OTTOCAR II)** (1230-1278), reigned 1253-1278. The greatest Bohemian king, he conquered BELA of Hungary at Kressenbrunn in 1260 and then took Austria, Styria, Carinthia and Carniola. Pride, however, went before his fall. He refused to pay homage to RUDOLF of Habsburg, was eventually forced to hand over all the lands he had conquered and was killed in a skirmish with Rudolf's forces at Marchfeld.

**VACLAV II** (1271-1305), reigned 1278-1305. He was PREMISLAS's son and also King of Poland from 1296.

**VACLAV III** (1289-1306), son of VACLAV II, he was King of Hungary and, like his father, also King of Poland. He reigned for only a year, from 1305 until 1306, before he was assassinated.

From 1306 to 1310, a form of interregnum existed. Rudolf III of Austria declared himself King, and saw to it that the following year Henry V of Carinthia, son-in-law of VACLAV II, was elected King. It was an unpopular piece of 'contrived democracy' and Henry was deposed.

**JOHN,** 'Jan the Blind' (1296-1346), reigned 1310-1346. He was another son-in-law of VACLAV II and the first of the house of Luxembourg to be elected king. A more or less professional soldier, he spent most of his thirty-six-year reign fighting in Italy and elsewhere. He finally met his Waterloo at the battle of Crécy. His motto was supposed to have been *Ich Dien* – I serve.

15

**CHARLES I** (1316-1378), son of JOHN, reigned 1346-1378. He was anointed Emperor in 1347 and set about making Prague one of Europe's leading cities, lovely to look at and culturally rich.

**VACLAV IV** (1361-1419), who was also King of Germany, reigned 1378-1419.

**SIGISMUND** of Hungary and Germany (1368-1437), reigned 1419-1437.

**ALBERT,** Albert II of Germany (1384-1439), reigned 1437-1439. He was followed by a four-year interregnum.

**LADISLAS V** of Hungary (1424-1457), reigned 1443-1457. He, too, was followed by an interregnum.

**GEORGE of PODERBRAD** (1420-1471), reigned 1458-1471. A right wing Protestant, George was unique amongst the rulers of Bohemia. Firstly, he was a true native of the country (a son of Victoria of Kunslat) with estates in the north-east, secondly, he was not a Catholic. His religion made life difficult for him and, though he made many concessions, he was usually at cross purposes with either Pope Pius II or his successor, Pope Paul II, who excommunicated him. A Catholic revolt ensued, George died and his former ally, King MATTHIAS of Hungary, took over the country.

**LADISLAV JAGIELLON,** also Vladislav of Hungary (1450-1516), reigned 1471-1516. He was the son of a sister of LADISLAV V, who was the first member of the House of Jagiellon to come to the throne.

**LOUIS,** also LOUIS II of Hungary (1506-1526), reigned 1516-1526. He was JAGIELLON's son.

**FERDINAND** (1503-1564), he reigned 1526-1564 and became Ferdinand I of Germany in 1556. He was the son-in-law of LADISLAV JAGIELLON.

 # BOSNIA

A region of what is today Yugoslavia, Bosnia was ruled from the twelfth until the fourteenth century by Slavic *Bans*. In 1376 it obtained its independence from Hungary, but this lasted only until 1463, when it was conquered by the *Osmanli* Turks.

**STEPHEN TVRTKO I** (died 1391), reigned from 1376-1391. He was a nephew of Stephen Kotromanich, a grandson of Stephen Kotroman and, for good measure, a brother-in-law of LOUIS of Hungary. He assumed the heady title, '...in Christ God, King of the Serbs and Bosnia and the Coastland' and had himself crowned with the crowns of Bosnia and Serbia, at the grave of St Sava at Mileševo.

**STEPHEN DABISHA** (died 1395), reigned 1391-1395. He lost Croatia and Dalmatia to SIGISMUND of Hungary.

**HELENA** (died 1398), the widow of STEPHEN DABISHA. She ruled from 1395-1398 on behalf of the under-age STEPHEN OSTOJA.

**STEPHEN OSTOJA** (1380-1418), reigned 1398-1404. He was DABISHA's nephew and possibly the illegitimate son of TVRTKO.

**STEPHEN TVRTKO II** (died 1443), the legitimate son of TVRTKO I, reigned 1404-1408.

**STEPHEN OSTOJA** reigned again 1408-1418, after his brief deposition by his more orthodox sibling.

**OSTOJIC** (died 1421), reigned 1418-1421. Like his father, STEPHEN OSTOJA, Ostojic was unable to hold back the rising tides of dissatisfaction amongst his nobles.

**STEPHEN TVRTKO II,** nothing if not persistent, came back to the throne from 1421 to 1443. He was obliged to flee to Hungary, however, after being attacked by his own vassal, Hranić.

**STEPHEN THOMAS OSTOJICH** (died 1461), reigned 1443-1461. He was one of the illegitimate sons of STEPHEN OSTOJA.

**STEPHEN TOMASHEVICH** (died 1463), son of STEPHEN OSTOJICH, reigned 1461-1463. It was his bad luck that Mohammed of Turkey personally invaded Bosnia, executed him and took over his kingdom.

# BULGARIA

A *Khanate* called Great Bulgaria, populated by Volga Bulgars, broke up in the seventh century and the people moved into the region of the Lower Danube. The state formed there was annexed by Byzantium and remained so until the Asen family forged a powerful and independent kingdom. Unhappily, this country was overrun by the Golden Horde, the romantic sounding name given to the decidedly unromantic Mongols who dominated Eastern Europe in the thirteenth century. They were conquered by the Turks at the end of the fourteenth century. In 1879, after the Treaty of Berlin, the Principality of Bulgaria was created and the Coburg dynasty established. Bulgaria was on the losing side in 1918 and its Thracian territories were ceded to Greece. The country was invaded by Nazi Germany in the Second World War, and in 1944 Russia, too, declared war on the country. In 1946 the monarchy was officially abolished and a republic set up.

Capital *SOFIA*; Currency *lek*

**ASEN** (died 1196), reigned 1187-1196. The brothers Peter and Ivan Asen Belgun, who were Vlachs, owned the strategic fortresses at Trnovo, which controlled the north side of the country. Resentful of their masters' treatment of them, they revolted and by 1187 had broken free. Ivan was proclaimed King, having defeated the Emperor Isaac Angelos at Stara Zagora.

**PETER** (died 1197), reigned 1196-1197. He had ruled jointly with his brother Ivan. Then, after less than a year of sole rule, he was murdered by his own *boyars* who were probably egged on by his younger brother KALOJAN.

**KALOJAN** (died 1207), reigned 1197-1207. This fratricidal man was to become *Tsar* in 1204. Having disposed of PETER he began his cruel reign, during which he was known variously as *Joanitsa* and 'Whelp-John'. He conquered all Bulgaria, curried favour with Pope Innocent III (who 'loved him so much that he thought only of his interests and glory') attacked Baldwin's Crusade in 1205 and was eventually murdered at Salonika in a plot probably engineered by his Tsarina.

**BORIL,** reigned 1207-1218. He was KALOJAN's nephew. He reigned from December 1207 and was definitely dead ten years later, having been blinded and deposed. But the precise date of his final departure is not known.

**IVAN ASEN II** (died 1214), reigned 1218-1241. BORIL's cousin and son of ASEN I, he was a pious soldier and a man of genius (recognised even by the Greeks). He added Macedonia, Epirus and much of Albania to his kingdom. The Pope, however, did not figure amongst his admirers and excommunicated him.

**KOLOMAN** (died 1246), the son of IVAN, reigned 1241-1246.

**MICHAEL** (died 1257), reigned 1246-1257. KOLOMAN's brother must have been either under age or feeble, as his mother, Irene, was Regent.

**MICO,** a usurper, came to the throne for a few months in 1257. Although he was never recognized he could be considered a *de facto* ruler.

**CONSTANTINE TICH** (died 1277), reigned 1257-1277. The last of the accepted *Tsars* of the Trnova dynasty, he was killed in battle resisting the usurper IVAILO. Ivailo began his working life as a swine herd.

**IVAILO, IVAN ASEN III** and another IVAILO, three usurpers, occupied the throne from 1277 until 1280. This period of usurpation ended with the asssination of the second IVAILO.

**GEORGE I,** reigned 1280-1292. The first of the Terters, he fled after a reign of twelve years.

Two Terter usurpers followed, reigning 1292-1298. SMILITZ, a Mongol puppet King, was on the throne until 1298, when he was deposed by CAKA, a son-in-law of GEORGE, who lasted only a few months.

**THEODORE SVETOSLAV** (died 1322), son of GEORGE, reigned 1298-1322.

**GEORGE II** (died 1323), reigned 1322-1323. He was THEODORE's son and the last of the Terters.

**MICHAEL SHISHMAN** (died 1330), reigned 1323-1330. This first king

of the Shishmanovich dynasty was killed at the *Battle of Velbuzhd* fighting STEPHEN UROSH of Serbia.

**IVAN STEPHEN** (died 1331?), reigned 1330-1331. MICHAEL's son reigned, for only a few months, during a confused period, when Bulgaria was harassed by Turkey and unsettled by the Serbs.

**IVAN ALEXANDER** (died 1371), MICHAEL's nephew, reigned 1331-1371. For part of his reign, probably between 1365 and 1371, he shared the throne with his son.

**IVAN SHISHMAN** (1361-1393), reigned 1371-1393. By 1371, when his father IVAN ALEXANDER was dead and he was sole ruler, Ivan was a vassal of the Turkish Sultan, Murad I. In 1389 Trvnovo fell to the Turks after a three-month siege. Ivan's death is uncertain: Bulgarian legend has him disappear in a puff of smoke during the battle of Samokov. Ivan's brother, Ivan Stracimir, defended himself at Vidin, but when it fell in 1396, the country collapsed entirely.

From 1396-1878 Bulgaria almost 'disappeared' from the map of Europe. In 1876 revolts in Bosnia unleashed political unrest in Bulgaria until the *Treaty of San Stefano*, dictated by the Russians in 1878, established the Bulgarian throne.

**FERDINAND I** (1861-1948), reigned 1887-1918. In August 1879 the newly-formed Bulgarian Assembly elected Prince Alexander of Battenberg, an offshoot of Hesse, as Prince of the country. He was only 22 and life was difficult. In 1886 he was seized in his own palace, forced to abdicate and political regents were appointed. In July 1887 Ferdinand of Saxe-Coburg was elected by the *Grand Sobranye* and took over, despite Russian claims that he was a usurper. He was proclaimed King in October 1908. Privately he was a respected botanist and entomologist; publicly he had great dreams of power and always wanted to recapture Constantinople 'for Christianity'. His children referred to him as 'The Monarch', but not, alas, affectionately. His country's defeat in the Second Balkan War and alliance with the 'wrong side' in 1918, forced his abdication. He died in exile.

**BORIS III** (1894-1943), reigned 1918-1943. Young Boris had a head start on his father, FERDINAND, in that he could actually speak Bulgarian. Though generally popular, his very right wing attitudes provoked several attempts on his life. He was the subject of a motor ambush in 1925, followed by another assault in which the cupola of the Cathedral in Sofia was brought down by explosives, crushing 200 people to death. When he did die, aged 49, it was thought that German agents had possibly succeeded where Bulgarian anarchists had failed.

**SIMEON** (born 1937), son of BORIS, reigned 1943-1946. He began his reign under a Council of Regents. In 1945 the Communists seized power and the young King's uncle, Prince Kyril, and over 200 other influential members of the regime were executed. A heavily rigged referendum purported to show that the monarchy was no longer welcome and Simeon went into exile in Egypt in 1946. Then followed a stint (as Cadet Rylski) at Valley Forge Military Academy,

Pennsylvania. Afterwards, Simeon married and went, with his five children, to live in Spain.

# BURGUNDY

The original Burgundians were Germans who settled in the eastern part of France in the fifth century AD. They were conquered by the Franks some hundred years later. The first Burgundian King was Gundicar in 411, whose line died out with his grandson, Gundimar in 532.

**RUDOLPH II,** reigned 934–937, over a re-united Burgundy

**RUDOLPH III** (died 1032), reigned 993–1032. He was the grandson of Rudolph II, who died in 937.

**CONRAD II** (died 1039), RUDOLPH's cousin, reigned 1033–1039. He was also the Holy Roman Emperor, styled as Konrad II. As a result Burgundy began to lose its identity, was divided up and eventually absorbed by the French monarchy.

# DENMARK

The kingdom was made up of the islands of Zeeland, Lolland and Funen amongst others, the Jutland Peninsular, Bornholm, the Faroes and Greenland. This last is an island of 840,000 square miles, over 2.1 million square kilometres. Denmark is Europe's oldest kingdom. It was unified, and the first ruling dynasty, that of Gorm, 'The Old', founded, in AD 960. His descendants ruled until 1448, when a distantly related family, the Oldenburgs, took over and have been on the throne ever since.

Capital *COPENHAGEN*; currency *krone*

**SVEN I** (died 1014), reigned 986–1014. He was the grandson of Gorm, 'The Old' and son of King Harald ('Bluetooth') the King who christianized Denmark. Sven was probably Harald's illegitimate son by a peasant girl, Aesa. He was also King of England for a while and actually died in Lincolnshire, in February 1014. His second wife, a Scandinavian firebrand, was the widow of the King of Sweden, who had rejected the King of Norway because she would not submit to baptism.

**HARALD II** (died 1019), the son of SVEN, reigned 1014-1019.

**KNUT II,** 'The Great' (995-1035), reigned 1019-1035. He was better known as CANUTE, King of England from 1016, *and* as Sven Knuttson, King of Norway from 1015.

**HARDICANUTE** (1017-1042), reigned 1035-1042. Like his father, KNUT, Hardicanute was also King of England.

**MAGNUS,** 'The Good' (died 1047), reigned 1042-1047. Of the House of Norway, he was also King of Norway.

**SVEN II** (1020-1076), reigned 1047-1076. Sven was of the House of Estrith and his mother was KNUT II's sister. He re-united Denmark and kept out intrusive Norwegians.

**HARALD III** (1043-1080), SVEN's son, reigned 1076-1080.

**KNUT IV** (1086), reigned 1080-1086. He was made a saint in 1100 by Pope Paschal II, for no apparent reason other than that he was assassinated in St Alban's Church at Odense. In 1075, when he invaded their territory, Englishmen from Yorkshire would not have considered him a fit subject for canonization. He is, however, the patron saint of Denmark.

**OLAF I** (died 1095), reigned 1086-1095. The brother of HARALD and St KNUT, some authorities call him Olaf IV.

**ERIK I,** 'The Evergood' (1056-1103), son of Sven, reigned 1095-1103. ('Evergood' is a rather free translation of *Ejegod*.)

**ERIK,** 'The Memorable', reigned 1103-1104. But why 'The Memorable', when he was on the throne for less than a year and was probably the illegitimate son of ERIK I?

**NIELS** (1063-1134), another son of SVEN, reigned 1104-1134. He was engaged in civil war with Erik and died in battle.

**ERIK II** (died 1137), reigned 1134-1137. He was a legitimate son of ERIK I who, to confuse matters, was also referred to as 'The Memorable'.

**ERIK III,** reigned 1137-1147. Probably the son of ERIK II's sister, he exchanged the throne for the cloister and retired to a monastery, leaving the country gripped by civil war.

**SVEN III** (died 1157), son of ERIK II, reigned 1147-1157. His throne was challenged by KNUT V, grandson of NIELS. Knut was eventually killed by Sven's soldiers, but little time elapsed before Sven's own death at the hands of VALDEMAR.

**VALDEMAR,** 'The Great' (1131-1182), reigned 1157-1182. He was the grandson of ERIK I, emerging as sole ruler after ten years of civil unrest. Valdemar, allied with FREDERICK, 'Barbarossa', defeated the Wends, thereby adding a Baltic possession to Denmark's kingdom.

**KNUT VI** (1163-1202), reigned 1182-1202. Nominally co-ruler with his father VALDEMAR, he became sole ruler in 1182.

**VALDEMAR II** (1170-1241), reigned 1202-1241. KNUT's brother who, like his father, extended the kingdom. Having pushed as far east as Estonia, he was captured by the Germans and finally traded his conquests for his freedom.

**ERIK IV** (1216-1250), reigned 1241-1250. He may have been co-ruler with his brother VALDEMAR from 1231, both were sons of

VALDEMAR, 'The Great'. He was to be killed by another brother, ABEL.

**ABEL** (1218-1252), reigned 1250-1252. Having eliminated his brother, he himself was killed in battle, less than two years later.

**CHRISTOPHER I** (born 1219), reigned 1252-1259. He was deposed by his own son's nobles.

**ERIK V** (1249-1286), reigned 1259-1286. He was put on the throne by a political coup, but later murdered by his very followers.

**ERIK VI** (1274-1319), reigned 1286-1319. Son of the murdered ERIK V, he tried desperately to restore Denmark to its strength of the days of VALDEMAR II, 80 years before. His attempts stripped his Treasury and only resulted in more violent civil war. There followed a year's interregnum.

**CHRISTOPHER II** (1276-1333), reigned 1320-1326. He was the son of ERIK V, but only awarded the crown when he agreed to the demands of the nobles. He later withdrew his support and plunged Denmark into even bloodier warfare, resulting in the end of rule from the throne. Duke Valdemar 'assumed power', but not the title.

**VALDEMAR III** (1320-1375), reigned 1340-1375. By strength of character and military acumen he ended the internal conflicts. During his expansive reign, Denmark became the leading Baltic State.

**OLAF II** (1370-1387), also OLAF IV of Norway, reigned 1375-1387. He was grandson of VALDEMAR III, on his mother MARGARET's side.

**MARGARET** (1352-1412), reigned 1387-1412. She was OLAF II's mother and 'mother of Scandinavia' as well, being Queen of Denmark, Norway and Sweden. Her control of Sweden was overturned, but Norway and Denmark remained conjoined for 400 years.

**ERIK VII** of Pomerania (1381-1459), great-grandson of VALDEMAR III, reigned 1412-1438. He was co-ruler with MARGARET for the last fifteen years of her life. A two-year interregnum followed his deposition in 1438.

**CHRISTOPHER III** (1418-1448), reigned 1440-1448. He was the nephew of Ludwig IV, Count Palatine, son of ERIK VII's sister. A member of the House of Bavaria, he was the last of the direct Gorm family.

**CHRISTIAN I** of Oldenburg (1426-1481), reigned 1448-1481. His descent (albeit a frail one) was from VALDEMAR I, he was the son of Dietrich of Oldenburg. He was a noted 'gilded figure', a Renaissance Man. He obtained Schleswig and Holstein for Denmark, which were to become major thorns in the country's side.

**JOHN** (1455-1513), reigned 1481-1513. CHRISTIAN's elder son, he married Christina of Saxony.

**CHRISTIAN II** (1481-1559), JOHN's son, reigned 1513-1523. The same day he was crowned King of Denmark and Norway, he was also married, by proxy, to Isabella, sister of the Holy Roman Emperor, CHARLES V. But Christian refused to give up his 'bourgeois' Dutch girl friend, Dyveke. She, poor girl, was murdered in 1517 and

Christian, himself, killed her supposed murderer. He then made Sigbrit, Dyveke's shrewd mother, his Chief Counsellor. She was universally loathed and all Denmark's troubles were attributed to the '...foul-mouthed Dutch sorceress who hath bewitched the King'. He was deposed and finally imprisoned in Kalundborg Castle.

**FREDERICK I** (1471-1533), reigned 1523-1533. Although CHRISTIAN II's younger son, he preceded his elder brother for religious reasons.

**CHRISTIAN III** (1503-1559), reigned 1533-1559. A perfervid Protestant, he was passed over for FREDERICK and never stopped opposing him. Christian founded the Lutheran Church in 1536 and, within months of acceding, imprisoned any bishop who had supported Frederick.

**FREDERICK II** (1534-1588), reigned 1559-1588. One of Denmark's best loved kings, and perhaps unusual in that he was one of the few Danish monarchs who did not indulge in extra-marital liaisons.

**CHRISTIAN IV** (1577-1648), reigned 1588-1648. Since he was only eleven when his father FREDERICK II died, his reign began under a Regency of four nobles. When he was 15, he was described as '...big set...and could speak the Dutch, French and Italian tongues...'. His court was to become one of the most splendid in Europe. Under his rule, his army and the country's defences were strengthened.

**FREDERICK III** (1609-1670), reigned 1648-1670. In 1660 Frederick (CHRISTIAN IV's second son) converted the elective monarchy into an absolute one.

**CHRISTIAN V** (1646-1699), reigned 1670-1699. The son of FREDERICK III, he was the darling of the proletariat but hated by his nobles. They were delighted when he was killed in a hunting accident in August 1699.

**FREDERICK IV** (1671-1730), son of CHRISTIAN V, reigned 1699-1730. Though no firebrand, he nevertheless abolished serfdom on the royal estates.

**CHRISTIAN VI** (1699-1746), reigned 1730-1746. His career was no more distinguished than that of his undistiguished father, FREDERICK IV.

**FREDERICK V** (1723-1766), son of CHRISTIAN VI, reigned 1746-1766. Like GEORGE III of England (just his contemporary) Frederick was interested in, and did much for, agriculture.

**CHRISTIAN VII** (1749-1808), reigned 1766-1808. One of the Danish royal skeletons in the Copenhagen closet. Having had the scantest of educations, he was brutally treated by a governor and corrupted by sexually ambivalent courtiers. Though practically an idiot, he was married to Caroline, daughter of Frederick, Prince of Wales. He was not much of a husband and the pleasures denied Queen Caroline by Christian were supplied by a German born politician, Johann Struensee. Count Struensee gradually dominated Christian, introducing many reforms to Denmark, most of them unpopular. Eventually both the Queen and her Count were arrested. He confessed to 'criminal association', the royal marriage was dissolved and Struensee beheaded.

**FREDERICK VI** (1768-1839), reigned 1808-1839. He had really been

running the country since the 'Struensee affair' in 1772 and not doing too bad a job. He was not so successful in his dealings with the ever-so-wily NAPOLEON. As a result of abortive negotiations, Denmark was to lose most of her 'possessions', including Norway.

**CHRISTIAN VIII** (1786-1848), reigned 1839-1848. He was the half-brother of CHRISTIAN VII. Not a great success, he failed either to regain Norway, or stave off hostilities with Sweden. He more or less went into retirement with his second wife, Queen Caroline Amelia.

**FREDERICK VII** (1808-1863), reigned 1848-1863. He was much less autocratic than his ancestors, perhaps more like his father, CHRISTIAN VIII, and as diplomatically inept. Frederick failed to resolve the Schleswig problem or to produce a satisfactory new Danish constitution.

**CHRISTIAN IX** (1818-1906), reigned 1863-1906. He was the son of William, Duke of Schleswig Holstein-Holstein-Sonderburg-Glücksburg and greatgrandson of FREDERICK V. A modest man who lived in a modest way, his children were to colour the royal families of Europe. Frederick married the daughter of the King of Sweden, GEORGE became King of Greece, Alexandra married EDWARD VII of England, Dagmar was the Tsarina of Russia and Tyra married the Duke of Cumberland. His grandson became HAAKON VII of Norway in 1905.

**FREDERICK VIII** (1843-1912), reigned 1906-1912. During his reign, Iceland gained independence from Denmark, but retained a 'personal union' with the mother country.

**CHRISTIAN X** (1870-1947), reigned 1912-1947. In 1915 Danish women were given the right to vote – such measures were typical of the reign of this much-loved king. His courage and bearing under the stress and indignity of the German occupation of Denmark during the Second World War, were admirable. In 1943 he was imprisoned by the Nazis in his own castle at Amalienborg.

**FREDERICK IX** (1899-1972), son of CHRISTIAN X, reigned 1947-1972. In 1953 (in agreement with his brother Knud) Frederick reopened the throne to admit Queens Regnant. The move was significant as Frederick and his Queen (Ingrid of Sweden) only had two daughters.

**MARGRETHE II** (born 1940), her reign began in 1972. In 1967 she married Count Henri de Laborde de Monpézat, a French diplomat. By 1969 she had given birth to two sons, the heir, the Crown Prince Frederick, and Joachim.

# ETRURIA

Also called *Tuscia* hence the modern Tuscany, which was the northern part of this ancient kingdom. When the French expelled Ferdinand in 1800, the Grand Duchy of Tuscany was restyled as the Kingdom of Etruria and bestowed by NAPOLEON on the Crown Prince of Parma in 1801.

Capital *FLORENCE*

**LOUIS I** (1773-1803), reigned 1801-1803. The Grand Duke of Tuscany, whose family had ruled the duchy since 1531, was dispossessed by the French not long after they marched into Florence in March 1799. NAPOLEON then gave the throne to Louis of Parma. (Parma, a duchy of northern Italy, had been ceded to the Bourbon, Don Philip of Spain, in 1748.)

**LOUIS II** (1799-1849), reigned 1803-1808. The son of LOUIS I and also Charles, Duke of Parma, his reign only lasted just over four years. Upon the throne being given up, the Grand Duchy was re-invoked but, instead of being handed back to Ferdinand's family, it went to NAPOLEON's sister, Elizabeth, by then Princess of Lucca. In 1814 Ferdinand was restored, Lucca united with Tuscany and the whole state was annexed by the Kingdom of Italy in 1860.

# FRANCE

Today the largest state in Central Europe, the Kingdom of France really emerged as a result of the Carolingian Empire's disintegration. The last Carolingian, Louis V, who was killed in a hunting accident in 987, was succeeded by Hugh Capet, whose descendants ruled the kingdom until 1328. For centuries the power of the French Kings was far from consolidated in their own realm. This situation was underlined in 1340 when EDWARD III of England began to style himself *Rex Angliae et Franciae*; then in 1420 HENRY V called himself *Regens Franciae*.

Capital *PARIS*; currency *French franc*

**ROBERT II,** *Le Pieux* (970-1031), reigned 996-1031. He had been joint

25

ruler with his father Hugh, the first Capet, who died in 996. The reign was bedevilled by famine throughout the land and revolution.

**HENRI I** (1011-1060), reigned 1031-1060. His father, ROBERT, with whom he shared the throne for five years, very unwisely gave Burgundy to Henri's brother, Robert.

**PHILIPPE I** (1053-1108), reigned 1060-1108. He succeeded at the age of seven and by the time he was fourteen he was 'ruling in his own right'.

**LOUIS VI** (1081-1137), who reigned 1108-1137, was variously nicknamed 'The Fat', 'The Wideawake' and even 'The Bruiser'. Luckily the army was on his side and he was able to enlist its support against his step-mother, Bertrada, who tried to poison him.

**LOUIS VII,** *Le Jeune* (1120-1180), reigned 1137-1180. The son of LOUIS VI, he took part in the Second Crusade, which proved a disaster for him. His first wife, Eleanor of Aquitaine, married HENRY II of England. She complained that Louis was 'more like a monk than a king'.

**PHILIPPE II,** 'Augustus' (1145-1223), son of 'Le Jeune', reigned 1180-1223. He banished Jews from his kingdom and went on a Crusade (which proved more successful than his father's) with RICHARD I of England. In 1190 he was able to take possession of Normandy, Anjou, Maine and Poitou, followed by Touraine.

**LOUIS VIII,** *Le Lion* (1187-1226), reigned 1223-1226. He combined ability as a soldier with a certain religious quality. In 1216 he was offered the throne of England by a group of English barons, who were disenchanted with King JOHN. He actually invaded England, despite the manoeuvre being banned by the Pope. In any case his invading force was defeated at the *Fair of Lincoln*. He later went on the Albigensian Crusade and helped direct the brutal massacre at Marmande.

**LOUIS IX,** Saint Louis (1215-1270), reigned 1226-1270. A son of *Le Lion* he was canonized in 1297. He went on the 1249 Crusade and captured Damietta, but shortly afterwards the Ayoubite Sultan captured the entire French army. Louis was imprisoned and spent four years captive in Syria. Between this time and 1269, when Louis set off on a second Crusade, France enjoyed a sort of minor *golden age*. Upon returning to France Louis subdued his nobles and made peace with HENRY III of England and JAMES of Aragon. Domestic affairs settled, he sailed for Africa, but died of the plague at Carthage.

**PHILIPPE III,** *Le Hardi* (1245-1285), reigned 1270-1285. He was the second son of LOUIS IX. He added Toulouse to France in 1271, only to die fighting in Aragon.

**PHILIPPE IV,** *Le Bel* (1268-1314), reigned 1285-1314. Handsome, cynical and detached, this son of *Le Hardi* made many changes in France, quarrelled with the Pope and persecuted French Jews.

**LOUIS X,** *Le Hutin* (1289-1316), reigned 1314-1316. Louis was as stupid as his father, PHILIPPE, was good-looking. In 1305, he inherited Navarre from his mother, Joan. He died on June 5, when his second wife, Clemence of Hungary, was four months pregnant. During the remaining months of the pregnancy there was an interregnum until,

on November 14, a boy, JOHN, was born. Five days later he died, so his uncle, LOUIS X's brother, took the throne.

**PHILIPPE V,** *Le Long* (1293-1322), reigned 1316-1322. He finally ended the war in Flanders. He also successfully opposed the claims to the throne of his niece Jeanne, the daughter of LOUIS X. In doing so he established the fundamental difference between the French and the other European monarchies: that no woman could reign in France.

**CHARLES IV,** *Le Bel* (1294-1328), reigned 1322-1328. He was the last of the House of Capet. After his death there was another interregnum, during the last three months of his widow's pregnancy. A daughter was born and denied the throne as a result of her uncle's edict.

**PHILIPPE VI** (1293-1350), reigned 1328-1350. He was the first of the House of Valois and a nephew of PHILIPPE IV. He ruled during a bad time for France: in 1340 the plague had ravaged Europe, in 1346 EDWARD III of England defeated him at Crécy and the French navy was destroyed at Sluys.

**JOHN II,** *Le Bon* (1319-1364), reigned 1350-1364. PHILIPPE's son, he was captured at Poitiers by the English and taken to London as hostage. In 1360 he was permitted to return to try and raise the ransom. The hostage who took his place broke *parole* and John, a true gentleman, returned to London, where he died, still a prisoner.

**CHARLES V,** *Le Sage* (1337-1380), reigned 1364-1380. He recovered much of the territory lost to the English by his grandfather, PHILIPPE VI.

**CHARLES VI** (1368-1422), reigned 1380-1422. During his reign civil war was rife and then, in 1415, the English army, under HENRY V, totally defeated the French forces. Charles became wholly insane and suffered from the extremely inhibiting fixation that he was made of glass and therefore breakable if moved.

**CHARLES VII** (1403-1461), reigned 1422-1461. The son of CHARLES VI, he was not actually crowned King until 1429. During his reign the so-called *Hundred Years War* at last came to an end. With Joan of Arc's victories, national morale expanded and the English were left with only a toe-hold at Calais.

**LOUIS XI,** 'The Spider' (1423-1483), reigned 1461-1483. He established an absolute monarchy, but the last years of his life were made miserable by his obsessive fear of death. In the last tortured months, it was said, he drank warm blood from infants, hoping to stave off the Reaper.

**CHARLES VIII** (1470-1498), son of LOUIS XI, reigned 1483-1498. He just failed in his attempt to add the Kingdom of Naples to his territory.

**LOUIS XII** (1462-1515), reigned 1498-1515. The first of the Valois-Orleans dynasty and often called 'The Father of His People', he was great-grandson of CHARLES V and son-in-law of LOUIS XI.

**FRANCIS I** (1494-1547), brother of LOUIS XII, he reigned 1515-1547. A literate, athletic young man; he was a patron of the arts who was sufficient of a soldier to triumph in the Italian war and win Burgundy for France.

**HENRI II** (1519-1559), reigned 1547-1559. The son of FRANCIS, he was mortally wounded in a joust.

**FRANCIS II** (1544-1560), reigned 1559-1560. The eldest, if short-lived, son of HENRI II, whose wife was MARY, Queen of Scots.

**CHARLES IX** (1550-1574), reigned 1560-1574. He was a mentally deficient youth. On St Bartholomew's Eve, 1572, he was forced by his ogress of a mother, Catherine of Médici, to order the massacre of over 3,000 French Protestants.

**HENRI III** (1551-1589), reigned 1574-1589. He had been elected King of Poland in May 1573, but fled when his brother CHARLES providentially died. The Catholic League found even his relatively rigid anti-Protestant stance too conciliatory and he was assassinated while beseiging Paris, by a monk, called Jacques Clément. He was homosexual and was believed to have practised 'Black Magic'.

**HENRI IV** (1553-1610), reigned 1589-1610. The first Bourbon, he was also King of Navarre from 1562 and a distant descendant of LOUIS IX. He was a strong king, but had '...the morals of an alley cat'. He was eventually assassinated by a Catholic, Ravaillac.

**LOUIS XIII,** *Le Juste* (1601-1643), reigned 1610-1643. A poorly child, he quarrelled with his mother, the formidable Marie de Médici, who was Regent. Eventually he appointed Cardinal Richelieu as his Chief Minister.

**LOUIS XIV,** *Le Grand* or *Dieudonné* (1638-1715), reigned 1643-1715. He was the son of LOUIS XIII. Cardinal Mazarin was his mentor and his reign has sometimes been referred to as France's *Augustan Age* and Louis himself called 'The Sun King'. Yet, by forcing his ruling classes to become little more than lackeys at his court, he sowed the seeds of republicanism.

**LOUIS XV,** *Le Bien-Aimé* (1710-1774), reigned 1715-1774. Too well-beloved perhaps: in five years he was reputed to have given *one* of his mistresses, Madame du Barry, *180 million livres*. During his reign, France 'lost' Canada, sold Louisiana and the revolution came one step nearer. His constitution could not match his libido, so '...after a life of vice, he was seized by small pox and died unwept'.

**LOUIS XVI** (1754-1792), grandson of LOUIS XV, reigned 1774-1792. The pigeons came home to roost. The third Estate declared itself a National Assembly and a Republic was declared on September 21, 1792. Louis and his family were imprisoned and he and his Queen, the Austrian Marie Antoinette, were both beheaded.

**LOUIS XVII** (1785-1795), reigned 1793-1795. The small son of LOUIS XVI, he was declared King by exiled Royalists in January 1793. He died, still a prisoner, in the *Temple* in June 1795. He was never crowned and can hardly be counted as King of France.

The Convention ran the country from 1792 until October 1795, when the Directorate, a five-membered body, took over the country's government until 1799. In November of that year the first of the Consuls was appointed. The last consul, Charles François Lebrun, handed over to NAPOLEON on May 18, 1804.

# THE FIRST EMPIRE

**NAPOLEON BONAPARTE** (1769-1821), reigned 1804-1815. 'The Little Corporal', he was only about five feet two inches (157 centimetres) tall and had once been an army corporal. He came from a large, Corsican family, but by combining his brilliance with ruthlessness he rose to be the most powerful man in Europe. His generalship was masterful and he subdued the armies of practically all France's neighbours in a few years, even extending French dominion into Egypt. His career began to take a downward course when his armies were heavily defeated in both Russia and Spain. He abdicated on April 6, 1814 and went into exile on Elba. On March 20, 1815, he was restored. But on Sunday June 18, 1815, at the end of *The Hundred Days* he was defeated by the Allies under the Duke of Wellington at the *Battle of Waterloo*. He was exiled to the island of St Helena where he died (some suspected poisoned) six years later. Despite his tyrannical rule, Napoleon restored order to France, gave the country a Legal Code and established the National Bank.

**LOUIS XVIII** (1755-1824), reigned 1815-1824. He was the brother of the decapitated LOUIS XVI, who assumed the title of King in 1795. He 'ruled' from April 1814 to March 1815 and then re-established the Bourbon dynasty after NAPOLEON's final downfall. His last words were popularly supposed to have been, 'A King should die standing'. An interesting death bed comment from an obese man of 69, suffering terribly from gout.

**CHARLES X** (1757-1836), reigned 1824-1830. LOUIS XVIII's brother, he had been living in Scotland. He brought a reactionary outlook to the throne and set about compensating the nobility for their losses in the Revolution. This totally misjudged action caused another revolution and his abdication.

**LOUIS XIX** (1775-1844), he reigned on August 2, 1830, from breakfast until tea-time, making history by being the shortest reigning king on record. Upon the abdication of his father, he succeeded to the throne in the morning, but abdicated later the same day.

**HENRI V** (1820-1883), reigned in 1830. A contender for his uncle LOUIS XIX's record; Henri reigned from August 2 to August 9. He was the last of the Elder Bourbon line.

**LOUIS-PHILIPPE,** *Le Roi-Citoyen* (1773-1850), reigned 1830-1848. He was the great-great-great-great-grandson of LOUIS XIII, so not all that *bourgeois*. Though elected, he became so unpopular through his repressive regime that he was dethroned by yet another revolution. He died, a sedate 77, in England.

The Provisional Government of February 1848 gave way to the Constituent Assembly in June, after riots in Paris. The President, Prince Louis Napoleon, nephew of NAPOLEON I, led the body until December 1852.

## THE SECOND EMPIRE

**NAPOLEON III** *(1808-1873)* reigned 1852-1870. The ex-President and only surviving son of Louis Bonaparte, quondam King of Holland. This womanizing, wax-moustachioed, tinpot Emperor staged a coup on the anniversary of the *Battle of Austerlitz* and, having suppressed opposition, proclaimed the Second Empire, Never popular, the humiliation of the country in the Franco-Prussian War eliminated any residual support and he was deposed.
The Third Republic was proclaimed on September 4, 1870.

# GERMANY

The Romans controlled land now covered by the south and west of the country; the remainder was ruled by a number of German tribes. After the decline of Rome, the Franks, the Agilulfings and the Carolingians divided the country between them, until the Holy Roman Empire was created by Charlemagne in 800. By the early part of the second millenium, Germany was a powerful force, but split into a number of increasingly important duchies and minor states, such as Saxony, Swabia and Franconia. By the sixteenth century the Habsburgs ruled the roost. True national unity was not achieved until 1871, when the German Empire was created. After the Second World War, Germany was redivided; one part is the Federal Republic, established in September 1949, which obtained complete autonomy in May 1955. The other side of the division is the Democratic Republic, dominated by the USSR, the capital of which is East Berlin.

Capital of the Federal Republic *BONN*; currency *Deutschemark*

(HRE) after a king's name, means he was also Emperor of the Holy Roman Empire.

**OTTO III** (980-1002), reigned 983-1002 (HRE). The son of Otto II, he was chosen as his father's successor in 983, six months before Otto II actually died. Early in 984 the little King was seized by Henry, deposed Duke of Bavaria, but eventually handed back to his mother, Theophano. He was declared 'of age' in 995, crowned the following year and ruled without a Regent. A precocious boy, he was sometimes called 'The Wonder of the World'. He died whilst on a military campaign against the Romans.

**HENRY II** (973-1024), reigned 1002-1024 (HRE). He was the great-grandson of Henry, 'The Fowler' of Bavaria and called 'The Holy' or 'The Lame'. It was often supposed that he wanted to be a

monk and posthumous legend claimed that he had a 'celibate marriage'. His wife, Cunegund, would probably have disagreed, however. Henry founded the See of Bamberg and was canonized for this act of episcopal piety in 1146. His sanctity was emulated by Cunegund, who became a saint in 1200. Both Henry and she were ardent supporters of Benedictine monasticism.

**CONRAD II** of Franconia (990-1039), a grandson of Otto the Great, reigned 1024-1039 (HRE).

**HENRY III,** 'The Black' (1017-1056), Conrad's son, reigned 1039-1056 (HRE). In his reign the Holy Roman Empire was extended to include Hungary, most of southern Italy and Bohemia.

**HENRY IV** (1050-1106), reigned 1056-1106 (HRE). In 1065 he was declared of age and a year later proved it by marrying Bertha of Savoy. 'After a licentious youth', he later developed considerable (and very necessary) diplomatic skills. He had to deal not only with irritated Popes, by one of whom he was excommunicated, but with no less than three usurpers, or Anti-Kings, Rudolf, Herman and his own son, Conrad (details under Holy Roman Empire) and a faithless second wife. His usurping son finally took him prisoner and he was forced to abdicate in 1105. He escaped from custody and was trying to rally aid from England, France and Denmark when he died at Liège.

**HENRY V** (1086-1125), reigned 1106-1125 (HRE). The younger son of HENRY IV, his reign was beset with difficulties from the start – from within his family, his kingdom and the Papacy. He married MATILDA, daughter of HENRY I of England, in 1114 and lived long enough to see her recognized as heir presumptive to the English throne.

**LOTHAIR III** of Supplinburg, 'The Saxon' (1075-1137), reigned 1125-1137 (HRE). He was an elected King.

**CONRAD III** of Hohenstauffen (1093-1152), reigned 1138-1152 (HRE). The grandson, by female descent, of HENRY IV, he was never actually crowned.

**FREDERICK,** 'Redbeard', *Rotbart* (1123-1190), nephew of CONRAD, he reigned 1152-1190 (HRE). Whether by flattery, in the bestowal of titles or by flattening on the field of battle, 'Redbeard' brought Germany to heel and (temporarily at least) restored his imperial authority in the cities of Lombardy. Satisfied with matters on the home front, he set off on the Third Crusade and was drowned in Kalykadnos the following year.

**HENRY VI,** 'The Cruel' (1165-1197), reigned 1190-1197 (HRE). The son of 'Redbeard', he was also King of Sicily.

**PHILIP** (1177-1208), another of 'Redbeard's' sons, he reigned 1198-1208 (HRE). He was elected but never crowned so, technically, never king. In the ten years of his 'reign', before being assassinated, he was constantly at war with OTTO, Duke of Saxony, the second son of Henry, 'The Lion'.

**OTTO IV** of Saxony (1174-1218), reigned 1198-1215 (HRE). His grandfather was HENRY II of England, his daughter, Maud, married 'The Lion'. He was probably born at Argenton in France and King

RICHARD I of England made him Duke of Aquitaine. Both civil war and foreign campaigns made for a busy reign, but he eventually withdrew to his Brunswick domain, after being defeated at Bouvines in 1214.

**FREDERICK II** of Sicily (1194-1250), reigned 1215-1250 (HRE). The son of HENRY VI, he was also King of Sicily. During his reign he had to contend with two Anti-Kings who were both simultaneously Holy Roman Emperors, Henry Raspe and William II of Holland.

**CONRAD IV** (1218-1254), reigned 1250-1254 (HRE). He was the son of FREDERICK and never crowned, but nevertheless King of Sicily. He was followed by an interregnum.

**RICHARD** of Cornwall (1209-1269), he reigned in 1257 (HRE). The second son of King JOHN of England, he was elected but never crowned. He married three times, the last time when he was over 60.

**ALFONSO X** of Leon and Castile (1221-1284), reigned 1257-1273 (HRE). Again someone who was elected but not crowned, so technically not a king.

**RUDOLF,** Duke of Austria (1218-1291), reigned 1273-1291 (HRE). He was the first of the Habsburgs and elected but never crowned. He was followed by another short interregnum.

**ADOLF** (1250-1298), reigned 1292-1298 (HRE). He was the son of Walram, Count of Nassau. Another of the elected, uncrowned brigade, he owed his election more '…to the political conditions of the time than his personal qualities'. His electoral promises were not honoured and ALBERT of Austria was elected King. The rival monarchs met at Göllheim in July and Adolf died there, probably murdered by ALBERT's followers.

**ALBERT I** (1250-1308), reigned 1298-1308 (HRE). The son of RUDOLPH, he was a stern man who, unusually for his day, had considerable sympathy for the serfs and offered protection to persecuted Jews. This side of him does not seem to have been in evidence in Switzerland, where he is remembered as despicable and cruel. He was murdered by his nephew, John (afterwards, incorrectly, called 'The Parricide') whilst on his way to suppress yet another revolt.

**HENRY VII** (1270-1313), reigned 1308-1313 (HRE). He was also Henry IV of Luxembourg. He died in Italy, on his way to attack Naples in fact, but had obviously already made his mark in Italian literary circles. Dante honoured him in his poem *Il Paradiso*. There followed a short interregnum.

**LUDWIG,** the Bavarian (1286-1347), reigned 1314-1347 (HRE). He found himself in opposition to the Anti-King, Frederick, 'The Fair' of Austria, whom he took prisoner during the *Battle of Mühldorf* in 1322.

**CHARLES IV** of Luxembourg (1316-1378), reigned 1347-1378 (HRE). He was the son of JOHN, King of Bohemia. In 1356 he published the *Golden Bull* (so called because of its golden seal) which laid down the rule by which a Holy Roman Emperor could be elected. He thus managed to extract the institution from the grasp of the Vatican. In 1349 Charles had to cope with the Anti-King Günther.

**VACLAV** (1361-1419), reigned 1378-1400 (HRE). The son of CHARLES, he was deposed from the German throne in 1400, but allowed to continue as VACLAV of Bohemia. In the last year of his German reign, FREDERICK of Brunswick-Luneburg, an anti-king, made his brief appearance.

**RUPERT III** of the Palatinate (1352-1410), reigned 1400-1410 (HRE). (Frederick, Duke of Brunswick, had been elected, but was assassinated immediately after the votes had been counted.)

**SIGISMUND** (1361-1437), reigned 1410-1437 (HRE). The son of CHARLES and brother of VACLAV, he was also King of Bohemia and Hungary. During his reign, John Huss, the Bohemian religious reformer, was burned to death as a heretic at Constance, despite having been given a personal 'safe conduct' by Sigismund. The last of the Anti-Kings, Jobst of Moravia, made his appearance during the first year of Sigismund's reign.

**ALBERT II** (1397-1439), reigned 1437-1439 (HRE). He was also Albert V of Austria, the great-great-grandson of ALBERT I and King of Bohemia and Hungary. A short interregnum followed his rule.

**FREDERICK III** (1415-1493), ALBERT's brother, reigned 1440-1493 (HRE). On March 16, 1452, he married Leonora of Portugal in Rome and three days later he was crowned Emperor of the Holy Roman Empire by Pope Nicholas V. He was the last Emperor to go to Rome for his coronation, all his successors assumed the title immediately upon their election.

**MAXIMILIAN** (1459-1519), reigned 1493-1519 (HRE). He was FREDERICK's son and Archduke of Austria. In 1495 he declared a *Perpetual Peace* (as likely, one imagines, as 'Perpetual Motion') and divided Germany into six parts. In 1513, assisted by HENRY VIII of England, he defeated the French at Guinegate, in the *Battle of the Spurs* a reference to the precipitate flight of the French, who spurred their horses from the field.

**CHARLES V** (1500-1558), reigned 1519-1556 (HRE). The son of Philip of Austria and Joan of Castile, he had ruled Spain as CHARLES I since 1516. An ill and nervous man, he abdicated from all his kingdoms in 1555 and 1556 and retired to a monastery at Yuste in Spain. (It was during his reign that the Spaniards conquered Mexico and Peru.)

**FERDINAND I** (1503-1564), brother of CHARLES, reigned 1556-1564 (HRE). In 1521 he married Anna. In 1526, on the death of his brother-in-law, LOUIS, he was elected to the thrones of Bohemia and Hungary. He and Charles inherited the Austrian dominions in 1519, but he handed his shares to his brother three years later.

**MAXIMILIAN II** (1527-1576), reigned 1564-1576 (HRE). He was a mild, ecumenically-minded son of FERDINAND. He negotiated a treaty with Selim of Turkey in 1568 and brought a degree of peace to the Roman Empire.

**RUDOLF II** (1552-1612), son of MAXIMILIAN, reigned 1576-1612 (HRE). He was scholarly, absent-minded and very much the puppet of the court of Spain. He gave the Bohemian Protestants their

religious freedom in 1609 and conceded the Hungarian throne to his younger brother, MATTHIAS, two years later.

**MATTHIAS** (1557-1619), reigned 1612-1619 (HRE). A far more worldly man than his elder brother RUDOLF, he plotted against him continuously. He had no legal children and so, having acquired the Hungarian throne, he arranged for his cousin FERDINAND of Styria to succeed him.

**FERDINAND II** (1578-1637), reigned 1619-1637 (HRE). He was MATTHIAS's cousin and fellow 'throne fixer'. Their joint machinations rebounded on him and he was deposed from the Bohemian throne by Protestant elements, in 1619. He took his revenge a year later and virtually 'abolished' the religion.

**FERDINAND III** (1608-1657), reigned 1637-1657 (HRE). He succeeded his father, FERDINAND II, as Holy Roman Emperor and King of Germany, Hungary and Bohemia, having been an involved witness to the total defeat of the Swedish army at the *Battle of Nördlingen* three years before.

**LEOPOLD I** (1640-1705), reigned 1658-1705 (HRE). FERDINAND's second son, he spent most of his forty-seven-year reign at war. Through his Spanish family connections he became caught up in the *War of Spanish Succession* which had a profound effect on the history of Europe as a whole and on its monarchies in particular. The war arose out of a dispute over who should succeed CHARLES II. It waged from 1701 until 1713, when it was finally settled by the *Peace of Utrecht*.

**JOSEPH I** (1678-1711), reigned 1705-1711 (HRE). LEOPOLD's son carried on the *War of Spanish Succession* though he did not live to see its conclusion as he died of smallpox in Vienna, when he was only 32.

**CHARLES VI** (1685-1740), reigned 1711-1740. He was JOSEPH's brother and, as CHARLES III, Pretender to the Spanish throne. In 1713 he issued a *ukase* now called *The Pragmatic Sanction*. It decreed that all Austrian territory should remain undivided and, if there were no male heirs, that these lands should devolve upon his daughters, which, importantly in this case, meant his daughter MARIA THERESA.

**MARIA THERESA** (1717-1780), reigned 1740-1780. Her right to the throne was supported by England (the right having been stipulated in her father, CHARLES's, *Pragmatic Sanction*). She was, of course, now Archduchess of Austria and probably contributed more than any other man or woman to the creation of modern Austria. Her grandson, FRANZ, was created Emperor of Austria in 1806, the year the Holy Roman Empire ceased to exist. She ruled Austria alone from October 1740 until August 1765 and jointly with her eldest son, Joseph II, father of FRANZ, until her death.

# GERMAN EMPIRE

In 1871 the Hohenzollern family, who controlled practically all northern Germany, brought all the different states together and formed a united

kingdom for the first time. WILLIAM I, a Hohenzollern, who had been King of Prussia for ten years, was persuaded to accept the title of Emperor. It was against his better judgement, for, unlike his grandson WILLIAM II, he had little use for titles. All three Emperors retained the subsidiary title of King of Prussia.

**WILLIAM I** (1797-1888), reigned 1871-1888. He had been King of Prussia since 1861. As a young man, and a Captain in the army, he was awarded the *Iron Cross* for bravery shown at Bar-sur-Aube in 1815. Politically he was an ultra-Conservative; a suitable outlook for a German Field Marshall in 1854. Four years later he became his brother's Regent. He had a good friend in Bismarck and any impetus the Emperor lacked may have been counterbalanced by Bismarck's not entirely discreet encouragement. It was during the siege of Paris that William announced the adoption of his title, Emperor of Germany, and in March 1871, he opened the first Imperial Parliament.

**FREDERICK III** (1831-1888), reigned in 1888. In contrast to his father, WILLIAM, Frederick was very much a Liberal. He married the Princess Royal, eldest daughter of Queen VICTORIA of England, in 1858. He was understandably opposed to Bismarck and the policies fostered by that political prince. In his early fifties Frederick developed cancer of the throat and became mortally ill. An English throat specialist, Morell Mackenzie, was summoned, over the heads of the Crown Prince's medical advisers. Mackenzie was unable to prolong his royal patient's life, indeed, through his ineptitude, he probably shortened it. By the time his ninety-year-old father, WILLIAM, had breathed his last in Berlin on March 9, Frederick had only days to live.

**WILLIAM II** (1859-1941), reigned 1888-1918. In 1901 Queen VICTORIA, his grandmother, died in his arms – literally. Yet just over 13 years later, he led his country in war against his cousin, GEORGE V, another of Victoria's grandchildren. William was born with a foreshortened left arm. Amateur psychologists would no doubt argue that he compensated for this disability by an over aggressive attitude and a passion for military uniforms and splendid regalia. William blamed his advisers for the First World War and it is recorded that on August 1, 1914, as he signed the order for German mobilization, he said to the Assembly, 'Gentlemen, you will live to rue the day that you made me do this'. Whether or not they did is moot; he certainly did. On November 10, 1918, the Emperor William slipped into Holland and became a private citizen. Here, at Doorn, he spent the last 23 years of his life, living long enough to shake hands with Nazi soldiers, who had trampled over the Netherlands only a few weeks before.

# GREAT BRITAIN

In order to consider the monarchy of the British Isles, the history of the nation has been divided into four periods. First, from 959, when Edgar, 'The Pacific', was crowned *King of All England* in Bath Abbey, to 1307. Second, from 1307, when EDWARD II came to the throne as the first Prince of Wales and was accordingly the *King of both England and Wales*, until 1603. Third, JAMES VI of Scotland came to the throne of England on the death of ELIZABETH, the last of the Tudors, so uniting both countries and becoming *King of England, Wales and Scotland*. This position was maintained more or less informally until the the fourth period: the reign of his great-granddaughter, ANNE. During her reign there was an *Act of Union* (May 1, 1707) which officially united the kingdoms of England and Scotland. (There was a further statute of January 1, 1801, which united Great Britain with Ireland, but it seems unnecessarily complicated to dwell on that formality.)

Capital of the kingdom since AD 43 *LONDON*; currency *pound sterling*

## ENGLAND

**ETHELRED II,** 'The Unready' (from *Redeless*: without a council) (968-1016), reigned 978-1016. He came to the throne when his half-brother, Edward, 'The Martyr', was murdered. Ethelred developed the system of paying Danish invaders not to invade, in preference to meeting them in battle. He fled to Normandy in 1013, but was restored to the throne the following year.

**EDMUND,** 'Ironside' (989-1016), reigned in 1016, being murdered after less than a year on the throne.

**CANUTE I** (995-1035), reigned 1016-1035. He had already received Mercia, East Anglia and Northumbria by treaty and seized the throne of all England upon EDMUND's death. In 1028 he became CANUTE II of Norway, by right of conquest. One of his first acts was to have the most powerful English chieftains, his potential rivals, put to death.

**HAROLD I,** 'Harefoot' (1017-1040), reigned 1035-1040. He was the younger of CANUTE's two sons.

**HARDICANUTE** (1018-1042), reigned 1040-1042. HAROLD's half-brother and King of Denmark from 1035, he was *elected* King of All England.

**EDWARD,** 'The Confessor' (1004-1066), reigned 1042-1066. Son of ETHELRED, the last Anglo Saxon king, he was also elected by the

*Witanagemot* (the national assembly of superior churchmen and laymen of the 'upper classes'). He was a saintly man and was canonized by Pope Alexander III in 1161. In 1268, his body was enshrined in Westminster Abbey, the church he founded in 1040.

**HAROLD II** (1022-1066), reigned in 1066. He was the Earl of Wessex, whose sister had married EDWARD 'The Confessor' in 1045. On October 14, 1066, Harold was killed at the *Battle of Hastings* (in Sussex) – the battle which changed the blueprint of English history.

**WILLIAM I,** 'The Conqueror' (1025-1087), reigned 1066-1087. He was the bastard son of Robert II, 'The Devil', of Normandy, by his mistress, Harlette. He defeated HAROLD's army in October and was crowned in Westminster Abbey on Christmas Day. It has been written of William that: 'He may worthily take his place as William the Great alongside Alexander and Constantine...'.

**WILLIAM II,** 'Rufus' (1056-1100), 'The Conqueror's' son, he reigned 1087-1100. William of Malmesbury wrote that at William's court '...the model for young men was to rival women in delicacy of person, to mince their gait, to walk with loose gesture and half naked'. He was killed (probably murdered by William Tirel) in the New Forest and buried without ceremony in Winchester Cathedral.

**HENRY I** (1068-1135), reigned 1100-1135. By his first wife, Matilda, this fourth son of 'The Conqueror' had a daughter, MATILDA (sometimes called the Empress Maud) who was recognized as heiress presumptive to the English throne in 1119. Matilda was to carry on a civil war against her cousin STEPHEN for a number of years. R.W. Southern said of Henry: 'He contributed nothing to the theory of kingship or to the philosophy of government. He created men'.

**STEPHEN** (1096-1154), reigned 1135-1154. He was the third son of Adela ('The Conqueror's' sister) by the Count of Blois. At one stage (April to November 1141) MATILDA secured the throne for herself, but was never crowned and eventually renounced her claims entirely. Stephen was the last of the Norman kings.

**HENRY II** (1133-1189), reigned 1154-1189. The first of the Plantagenets, he was the son of MATILDA and Geoffrey Plantagenet. He married Eleanor of Aquitaine, the divorced wife of LOUIS VII of France. His nickname was 'Curthose' (or 'Curtmantle') as he affected a short 'continental' cloak.

**RICHARD I** *Coeur de Lion* (1157-1199), the second son of HENRY II, he reigned 1189-1199. Only a few weeks of his reign did he actually spend in his own kingdom. He was either almost permanently crusading, or else a prisoner of Duke Leopold in Austria. He was eventually killed at the siege of Chalus. He married Berengaria of Navarre in 1191, but the union was never consummated.

**JOHN,** 'Lackland' (1167-1216), reigned 1199-1216. He was RICHARD's younger brother and generally thought of as 'a bad king'. (See, particularly, the *Robin Hood* legend.) John, someone said, was '...the very worst of all our kings, a man whom no oaths could bind, no pressure of conscience, no consideration of policy restrain from evil; a faithless son, a treacherous brother, an ungrateful master; to his people

a hated tyrant'. In 1209 he was excommunicated by Pope Innocent III. At Runnymede in June 1215, he did, however, sign the *Magna Carta* for his people.

**HENRY III** (1206-1272), reigned 1216-1272. A Regency, under Hubert de Burgh, operated until Henry, son of JOHN, was 21, when he declared himself King. His wife, Eleanor of Provence, died as a nun in 1291.

**EDWARD I,** 'Longshanks' (1239-1307), HENRY's eldest child, reigned 1272-1307. He is buried in Westminster Abbey, despite his wish that his bones were to be carried by his son until the Scottish people had been totally subdued. On his tomb is inscribed *Eduardus primus, Scotorum malleus hic est* – Here is Edward, hammer of the Scots. A great King, who said of himself, 'I should not be a better one however splendidly I was dressed'.

# ENGLAND AND WALES

**EDWARD II** (1284-1327), reigned 1307-1327. In 1301, the fourth son of EDWARD I, was officially made Prince of Wales. He was given to making much of young men, in particular Piers Gaveston. After a troubled reign he was murdered in an obscene manner by Gurney and Maltravers. His murder was commissioned by Lord Berkeley (in whose castle in Gloucestershire the king was prisoner) at the behest of Edward's unscrupulous Queen, Isabella, and her lover, Roger Mortimer.

**EDWARD III** (1312-1377), reigned 1327-1377. EDWARD II's son, the father of 'The Black Prince', and husband of Philippa of Hainault, he founded the *Order of the Garter*. He was the first king to speak English as his chosen language.

**RICHARD II** (1366-1399), reigned 1377-1399. He was the son of 'The Black Prince', who had died in 1376. His strife-torn reign ended in his deposition, then murder, in Pontefract Castle, Yorkshire. (Legend had it that he in fact escaped, insane, to France.)

**HENRY IV** (1366-1413), reigned 1399-1413. With Henry, son of John of Gaunt and usurper of the throne, begins the House of Lancaster. He is the only king to be buried in Canterbury Cathedral.

**HENRY V** (1397-1422), reigned 1413-1422. The eldest of the usurper's four sons, Henry has been immortalized by Shakespeare. Yet, according to Bowle, he was '...not the bluff patriot of Shakespeare's plays; he was a dour and martial fanatic obsessed by religion and his legal rights'.

**HENRY VI** (1421-1471), reigned 1422-1471. The son of HENRY V, he became a religious fanatic and most certainly mentally unbalanced. He founded Eton College in 1440. In 1461 he was deposed and treated very shabbily. Nine years later he was restored to the throne for a brief period, only to be deposed a second time, by his cousin, EDWARD. He was murdered whilst at his prayers in the Tower of London.

**EDWARD IV** (1442-1483), the first king of the House of York reigned 1461-1483. The *Wars of the Roses* the civil war which raged beween the

Yorks and the Lancasters, spelt misery for the country. Edward first seized the throne from HENRY in 1461 and was deposed in 1470, before regaining the throne in 1471. Besides which, during most of his reign England was having trouble with its territorial interests in France.

**EDWARD V** (1470-1483), son of EDWARD IV, reigned in 1483. He succeeded in April, when his father died, but was placed in the Tower of London for 'safety', on the instructions of his uncle Richard, Duke of Gloucester. His younger (and only surviving) brother, the ten-year-old Richard, was imprisoned with him in the Tower. Neither were seen outside their prison alive. They were probably both suffocated, on June 23, 1483, in the so-called 'Bloody Tower' and the murder was almost certainly countenanced by their uncle.

**RICHARD III** (1452-1485), reigned 1483-1485. The 'wicked uncle' was reputedly hunch-backed, but was more probably slightly deformed, having been clumsily delivered at birth – a 'breach' baby, possibly. He was killed at the *Battle of Bosworth Field* in his fight with Henry Tudor. During the battle Richard literally lost his crown and his body was probably buried in a common soldier's grave.

**HENRY VII** (1457-1509), reigned 1485-1509. RICHARD was the last of the Yorks and Henry, the first of the Tudor kings, took the crown of England, but his blood right to the throne must be suspect. He married Elizabeth of York, daughter of EDWARD IV, finally ending the family feuding between the Houses of Lancaster and York. He was shrewd and parsimonious. 'Men feared him, admired him, depended on him, but they did not love him.'

**HENRY VIII** (1491-1547) reigned 1509-1547. The second son of HENRY VII, Henry took Katherine of Aragon, the widow of his elder brother, Arthur, Prince of Wales (d.1502) as the first of his six wives. In a letter to Erasmus, Lord Mountjoy wrote of the young Henry, upon his accession: 'This king of ours is no seeker after gold, or gems, or mines of silver. He desires only the fame of virtue and eternal life'. Henry was to have five more wives, two of whom he had executed, separate his country from the Church of Rome and still, despite all his faults, set England on its path to glory.

**EDWARD VI** (1537-1553), reigned 1547-1553. Edward was HENRY's only legitimate son. His mother was Henry's third wife, Queen Jane Seymour, who died two days after the boy's birth at Hampton Court. A sickly boy and 'militant protestant', he died, probably of tuberculosis, before he was sixteen.

**LADY JANE GREY** (1537-1553), reigned in 1553. She did have some title to the throne, but her supporters' motives were solely selfish or political. She 'reigned' for only nine days. She was beheaded on a February afternoon in the Tower of London, her young husband having been beheaded on Tower Hill that morning.

**MARY I** (1516-1558), reigned 1553-1558. The rabidly Catholic daughter of HENRY VIII, by Katherine of Aragon, Mary was to marry King PHILIP II of Spain and wage a 'Holy War' against English Protestants.

**ELIZABETH I** (1533-1603), reigned 1558-1603. MARY's half-sister, she

was HENRY VIII's daughter by his second wife, Anne Boleyn. Under Elizabeth, England destroyed the might of Spain's naval power and began to colonize the *New World*. She never married and was the last of the Tudors.

# ENGLAND, WALES AND SCOTLAND

**JAMES I** (1566-1625), reigned 1603-1625. The son of MARY, Queen of Scots, James had been King JAMES VI of Scotland since the age of one. The first Stewart king, he came to the throne of England, because he was the great-great-grandson of HENRY VII, the first of the Tudors. He was a very complex person, fonder of the company of young men than was prudent and saddled with a profligate, Danish wife. He was a passionate huntsman and considered tobacco sinful. At his post-mortem, his head was found to be '...very full of brains'.

**CHARLES I** (1600-1649), reigned 1625-1649. The second son of JAMES, he was married to Henrietta, daughter of HENRY IV of France. He believed in the 'Divine Right of Kings', fell foul of his Parliament and so precipitated the Civil War. The war began with the *Battle of Edgehill* on October 23, 1642. It ended seven years later with his trial before Parliament, followed by judicial beheading in Whitehall on January 29, 1649.

**THE COMMONWEALTH,** 1649-1660. A republic was established by Oliver Cromwell, who was made 'Protector', though not until December 1653. All traces of the monarchy were destroyed, even to the extent of removing statues of CHARLES (and replacing at least one of them with an inscription which began, *'Exit Tyrranus Regum Ultimus...'*). Cromwell died in September 1658, aged 59, and was succeeded by his son Richard. He had none of his father's greatness and moves were soon afoot to restore the monarchy. Before long CHARLES's eldest son rode into London in triumph (actually on his thirtieth birthday).

**CHARLES II** (1630-1685), reigned 1660-1685. 'The Black Boy' or 'Old Rowley' (as he was called amongst other nicknames) was a libertine. The pleasures he took in life were exactly in keeping with the nation's reaction after nearly eleven years of excessively rigorous, Puritanical rule. The king had at least seven official mistresses (by whom he had thirteen illegitimate children, all of whom were supported by Parliamentary allowances and some of whom were given titles which descend to this day). By his mousey little Portuguese wife, Catherine of Braganza, he had no children at all. Pepys recorded of Charles's lady friends that, the 'King doth spend most of his time in feeling them and kissing them naked all over their bodies...but this lechery will never leave him'. Charles, however, was not all sensualist. He had a genuine interest in the Arts and the Sciences and he founded the now internationally prestigious Royal Society. He died a Catholic.

**JAMES II** (1633-1701), reigned 1685-1688. He was possessed of morals as

loose as those of his elder brother CHARLES. According to Pepys he, '...in all things but his *amours* was led by the nose by his wife'. His second wife was the Catholic, Mary of Modena, by whom he was to become the grandfather of 'Bonnie Prince Charlie', the *Young Pretender*. It was his public adoption of catholicism which made him unacceptable to his people and Parliament and led to the so-called *Bloodless Revolution*. He was ousted by his Dutch son-in-law and died an exile in France.

**WILLIAM III** (1650-1702) and **MARY II,** reigned 1688-1702. William of Orange married Mary, elder daughter of JAMES II (by his first wife) in 1677, when she was 25 years old. They were both devout Protestants and so totally acceptable to the majority of their subjects. They were crowned (uniquely) simultaneously and accorded parallel powers. William, shorter than his wife, was asthmatic and stooped:

> Breathless and faint he moves
> (Or rather stumbles,)
> Silent and dull he sits
> And snorts or grumbles. (Anon)

They had no children and Mary died in 1694. Lonely and unloved, William reigned on for six more years.

## UNITED KINGDOM OF GREAT BRITAIN

**ANNE** (1665-1714), reigned 1702-1714. The corpulent, younger sister of MARY was the last of the Stewarts. By her Danish husband (as fond of the bottle as she) she conceived eighteen children, none of whom survived for long. A few died at birth, some lasted only days. The longest lived was William, Duke of Gloucester, but even he only just saw his eleventh birthday. Macaulay wrote that Anne was, '...when in good humour, meekly stupid and when in a bad humour was sulkily stupid'.

**GEORGE I** (1660-1727), reigned 1714-1727. He was the first Hanover and King of Great Britain, by virtue of being the great-grandson of JAMES I. (Queen ANNE died on August 1, 1714. Sophia, George's mother, died on June 8. Had she lived 54 days longer, she would have been Queen Sophia of England.) George did little to advance the monarchy; 'a dull, stupid king full of drink and low conversation...'.

**GEORGE II** (1683-1760), son of GEORGE I, he reigned 1727-1760. The historian Hallam described the period of George's reign as being '...the most prosperous period that England had ever known'. George, 'this strutting Turkey-cock of Herrenhausen', died whilst sitting on a water-closet and was the last king to be buried in Westminster Abbey.

**GEORGE III** (1738-1820), the grandson of GEORGE II, he reigned 1760-1820. 'In character and convictions he was the average Briton of his day, or what the average Briton aspired to be. He *was* John Bull.' His plain, but fertile wife, Charlotte, presented him with fifteen children over 21 years. (Incredibly, they produced only one legitimate

and acceptable heir, even though ten of them married.) George was afflicted by *porphyria* and was declared insane in 1811. His eldest son was made Regent.

**GEORGE IV** (1762-1830), reigned 1820-1830. This large and brutish man was the eldest son of GEORGE III with whom, in the best Hanoverian tradition, he enjoyed the worst of relationships. In 1785, contrary to the *Royal Marriage Act* of 1772, George married a Catholic, Maria Fitzherbert, a twenty-nine-year-old widow. He was subsequently forced to marry Princess Caroline of Brunswick-Wolfenbüttel (she too was a widow, but one who did not consider cleanliness next to Godliness). He had one daughter by her, Charlotte, who died giving birth to a still-born son in 1817. Charlotte's husband, LEOPOLD, became King of the Belgians in 1831. Lord Aberdeen, one-time Prime Minister, recorded that George was '...certainly a sybarite, but his faults were exaggerated'.

**WILLIAM IV** (1765-1837), reigned 1830-1837. The younger brother of GEORGE IV, he was amiable, nautical, but not overbright. By his mistress, Mrs Jordan, he had a quiverful of children. Yet, when he eventually married Adelaide of Saxe Meiningen in 1818, he was only able to sire two daughters, both of whom died in infancy.

**VICTORIA** (1819-1901), reigned 1837-1901. She was the daughter of Edward Duke of Kent, fourth son of GEORGE III, who had been plucked from the arms of his long-standing mistress to marry the widowed Victoria Mary of Saxe-Saalfeld Coburg in 1818. Edward responded to the call and expired from a chill eight months after Victoria was born. On her uncle William's death, little Victoria became Queen of Great Britain, a month after her eighteenth birthday. She was to reign for 64 years and become the head of the largest Empire in the world. She was the last of the Hanovers, but she disliked the thought of her predeceased relations so much, the style of Hanover was not used at her coronation. She married her cousin, Albert of Saxe-Coburg and Gotha, had nine children by him and was desolated when he died from typhoid in 1861, just 42 years old. In November 1858, she was proclaimed in India as the Queen of the 'United Kingdom of Great Britain and Ireland and the colonies and dependencies thereof in Europe, Asia, Africa, America and Australia'. In 1877 she was declared Empress of India itself, in Delhi.

**EDWARD VII** (1841-1910), reigned 1901-1910. VICTORIA's eldest son, he was the first of the House of Saxe-Coburg and Gotha. He was nearly sixty when he finally eased his not inconsiderable weight onto the throne, having spent the intervening years as a roly-poly play-boy because VICTORIA denied him practically all access to State Papers. He married the beautiful Princess Alexandra of Denmark, of whom he was very fond, though this did not inhibit him from maintaining a number of *petites amoureuses*. He came to be loved by his people and even admired by the French. 'He wasn't clever;' said Admiral, Lord Fisher, 'but he always did the right thing, which is better than brains.'

**GEORGE V** (1865-1936), reigned 1910-1936. The second son of

EDWARD VII, he inherited his father's lack of intellectual stamina. He had had a naval training and retained a nautical vocabulary. In 1917 he changed the family name from Saxe-Coburg and Gotha to the ultra-British, Windsor. 'Thank God I am an optimist', he once said of himself.

**EDWARD VIII** (1894-1972), reigned in 1936. Like his namesake and ancestor, EDWARD V, Edward was never crowned. He met, and wished to marry, Wallis Simpson, a twice-divorced American. (She was still married to Ernest Simpson when she first met Edward.) A morganatic marriage was not possible and Edward chose to abdicate rather than create a constitutional crisis, or give up the woman he loved. He was styled as HRH the Duke of Windsor, but his wife, much to his annoyance and her chagrin, was not allowed the dignity of 'Her Royal Highness'.

**GEORGE VI** (1895-1952), reigned 1936-1952. The second son of GEORGE V, he was happy to remain the Duke of York, until forced onto the throne by the abdication of his brother, EDWARD. He was a retiring man with a pronounced stammer, but his resolution and the support of his wife (née Bowes-Lyon) helped him to overcome the handicap. In the beleaguered and dark days of the Second World War, his kingship was tested and found to triumph. George was the last Emperor of India, the country being granted independence in 1947. He died of cancer at his favourite home, Sandringham House, in Norfolk.

**ELIZABETH II** (born 1926), her reign began in 1952. The elder of the two daughters of GEORGE VI, she married the ex-Prince Philip of Greece, Philip Mountbatten, who was created Duke of Edinburgh. They have four children; the eldest, Charles, Prince of Wales, being heir to the throne. Elizabeth's reign has seen winds of change blow across monarchies and empires in Europe, but the throne of Great Britain proved itself adaptable.

# GREECE

After centuries of turbulent history, Greece succeeded in overthrowing the oppressive Ottoman Turkish rule, in a series of bloody skirmishes in the 1820s. The new kingdom, formed in 1829, was recognized by London protocol in 1830.

Capital *ATHENS*; currency *drachma*

**OTHO I** (1815-1867), reigned 1832-1862. The second son of LUDWIG I of Bavaria, he was chosen to be the King of the Hellenes. He took

personal control of the country's government in 1835, when he was only twenty. He was markedly odd and totally Bavarian in outlook. Not surprisingly, he was not popular with his adopted countrymen and fled in the revolution of 1862.

**GEORGE I** (1845-1913), reigned 1863-1913. The Greeks now changed from the House of Wittelsbach to Oldenburg and elected the son of CHRISTIAN IX of Denmark to their throne. The fact that he was brother-in-law to Edward Albert, Prince of Wales, was not overlooked. In 1867 he married the Russian Grand Duchess Olga and, though his reign was partially successful, it was turbulent and he was assassinated by a Greek called Schinas.

**CONSTANTINE I** (1868-1923), reigned 1913-1922. The son of GEORGE I, he led the Greek army to victory in the Balkan Wars of 1912-1913. In 1917, he was forced to abdicate by Venizelos (who persuaded the Allies that Constantine was pro-German). He was later re-instated, but finally deposed when Turkey defeated Greece in 1922. When he was 49 years old, an American woman wrote of him, 'he had a childlike appeal which few women can resist'.

**ALEXANDER I** (1893-1920), reigned 1917-1920. He succeeded his father, when CONSTANTINE was first deposed. Alexander was married to a commoner, by whom he had one daughter. He died from blood poisoning, having been bitten by a pet monkey.

**GEORGE II** (1890-1947), reigned 1922-1947. Although CONSTANTINE's eldest son, George had been passed over in favour of ALEXANDER, because he was thought to be pro-German (he probably was) in the First World War. He succeeded to the throne after his father's second deposition. After yet another revolution in 1923, George quit Greece, was voted off the throne in 1924, but restored (by plebiscite) in 1935. When the Germans invaded in 1941 he fled to Egypt and then Britain. He was restored to his throne, again by plebiscite, in 1946.

**PAUL** (1901-1964), GEORGE's younger brother, reigned 1947-1964. He served in the Greek Navy in 1922, went into exile with his brother, in 1924, and then lived in London during the Second World War.

**CONSTANTINE II** (born 1940), PAUL's son, reigned 1964-1967. He was obliged to leave the country after a coup in 1967. The Greek government allowed him to keep his 80,000 acre (32,300 hectares) estate at Tatoi near Athens, and the family 'home', *Mon Repos*, on Corfu.

# HANOVER

The German spelling of this kingdom (which once belonged to the Dukes of Brunswick) has two 'n's, Hannover, and the French call it Hanovre. These, with the English spelling, appeared indiscriminately. It once formed part of Saxony and was raised to a kingdom by the *Treaty of Vienna* in 1814.

Capital *HANNOVER*

**GEORGE-WILLIAM-FREDERICK** (1738-1820), reigned 1814-1820. He was the country's first king, as the rulers had been styled Electors, since 1692. George-William is much better known as GEORGE III of Great Britain.

**GEORGE-AUGUSTUS-FREDERICK** (1762-1830), reigned 1820-1830. He was the son of GEORGE, who had been Prince Regent during the last nine years of his father's life and was, of course, GEORGE IV of Great Britain from 1820.

**WILLIAM-HENRY** (1765-1837), reigned 1830-1837. He was fat GEORGE's brother and King WILLIAM IV of Great Britain.

**ERNEST-AUGUSTUS** (1771-1851), reigned 1837-1851. The younger brother of GEORGE and WILLIAM, he was also the Duke of Cumberland. Hanover was separated from Britain when William died, making Ernest the first real king of a more or less autonomous country. Unlike his royal brothers, he was tall, once thin, as uncommunicative as they were talkative and an arch conservative. He had been seriously wounded at the Battle of Tournai in 1794, which left his face badly scarred. (Having been damaged, his left eye later went blind and he was probably fitted with an artificial eyeball. His left arm was crippled, too.) In May 1810, the Duke's valet, Sellis, was murdered in St James's Palace – under very strange circumstances. The Duke's thumb was practically severed that night and there were many who thought that he had killed Sellis himself. His wife was the twice-married Princess of Solms-Braunfels. She had jilted his younger brother, the Duke of Cambridge, between her first and second marriages.

**GEORGE V** (1819-1878), reigned 1851-1866. Cumberland's son and the last King of Hanover. The kingdom was annexed to Prussia in 1866 and George went into exile in Paris. His son, who was to become Queen Alexandra's brother-in-law (Queen Alexandra was the wife of EDWARD VII of Great Britain) was deprived of all British honours because he fought for the German Army in 1919.

# HOLY ROMAN EMPIRE

The Empire was never a physical state (or collection of states) in the way other kingdoms discussed in this book are, or were. It was more a state of *mind*. By the end of the eighth century, the Church of Rome realized that the great centralized power it had enjoyed for eight hundred years was declining and admitted the Papacy no longer had the 'muscle' to impose its will, let alone extend it. It needed to add temporal to spiritual strength. In Charlemagne, King of the Franks, it saw a man of personal strength, who ruled a kingdom with material strength which, if allied to the spiritual strength the Church abrogated to itself, could forge the omnipotent union they sought. Accordingly, Charlemagne was invited to fill the newly-created vacancy. On Christmas Day, AD 800, the fifty-eight-year-old king was crowned *Emperor of the Romans* at the Basilica of St Peter in Rome. The theory of Holy Empire, an ecclesiastical theory which embodied actual power, became fact. Fact which lasted over 1000 years. Charlemagne became Charles I and was styled as *Emperor of Romans* which was changed to *Holy Roman Emperor* on the death of Henry, 'The Fowler', in 936. Otto, 'The Great', was the first of the House of Saxony and the first to bear the revised title.

**OTTO** (980-1002), reigned 983-1002. He was grandson of Otto, 'The Great', and King of Germany.

**HENRY II,** of Bavaria (973-1024), reigned 1002-1024. The great-grandson of Otto, 'The Great', he was also King of Germany.

**CONRAD II,** of Franconia (990-1039), reigned 1024-1039. He was the great-great-grandson of Otto, 'The Great', and King of Germany.

**HENRY III** (1017-1056), reigned 1039-1056. The son of CONRAD, he was also King of Germany.

**HENRY IV** (1050-1106), reigned 1056-1105. The son of HENRY III and King of Germany, his reign was plagued by Anti-Kings.

**RUDOLF** (1039-1080), reigned 1077-1080. The son of Kuno, Count of Rheinfelden, Rudolf was the first of a number of challengers to both the throne of Germany and the seat of the Emperor. He married HENRY IV's sister, Matilda, in 1059 and was made administrator of Burgundy. When his brother-in-law was excommunicated by Pope Gregory VII, Rudolf was recognized and crowned at Mainz in March 1077. Constantly engaged in warfare with HENRY's factions, Rudolf finally died from wounds he received in one of these encounters, at Hohenmolsen, in October 1080.

**HERMAN** (died 1088), reigned 1081-1088. The son of Giselbert of Luxemburg, he was the second of the Anti-Kings. Herman, Count of

Luxemburg, had been elected king by the opponents of HENRY IV. In 1086, Henry was defeated at Wurzburg, but two years later Herman voluntarily withdrew from the power struggle and left the field to Henry. Herman was also Count of Salm, a small county in the Ardennes, between Luxemburg and Liège.

**CONRAD,** reigned 1093-1098. He was the son of HENRY V by his first wife, Bertha of Savoy and the third Anti-King to emerge in less than fifteen years. He plotted with his father's second wife, the Russian princess, Praxedis (later called Adelaide) and was actually crowned King of Germany in 1087 and King of Italy in 1093, at Monza. He was deposed in 1098.

**HENRY V** (1081-1125), son of HENRY IV and King of Germany, reigned 1106-1125.

**LOTHAIR III,** of Supplinburg (1075-1137), reigned 1125-1137. He was an elected King of Germany.

**CONRAD III,** of Hohenstauffen (1093-1152), reigned 1138-1152. He was a grandson of HENRY IV and King of Germany.

**FREDERICK I** (1123-1190), Duke of Swabia and King of Germany, he reigned 1152-1190.

**HENRY VI** (1165-1197), reigned 1190-1197. He was the son of FREDERICK and King of both Germany and Sicily.

**PHILIP** (1177-1208), reigned 1198-1208. The brother of HENRY VI, he was also King of Germany.

**OTTO IV,** of Saxony (1174-1218), reigned 1198-1215. Although not an Anti-King, he was 'in competition' with PHILIP. Otto was a grandson of King HENRY II of England, whose daughter, Maud, married Otto's father, Henry, 'The Lion', Duke of Saxony. Otto was probably born at Argenton in France. RICHARD I of England made him Duke of Aquitaine. In 1214, after more than fifteen years of infighting, Otto was defeated at Bouvines and withdrew gracefully to his Brunswick domain.

**FREDERICK II,** of Sicily (1194-1250), reigned 1212-1250. A son of HENRY VI, Frederick had to cope with two Anti-Kings.

**HENRY RASPE,** of Thuringia (1202-1247), reigned 1246-1247. An Anti-King, he was the son of Herman of Thuringia and brother of Louis, whose widow, St Elizabeth of Hungary, he expelled in 1227. In April 1246, Pope Innocent (he was hardly that) recommended that Henry Raspe should be elected in place of Frederick. Fortunately, a year later, Raspe expired, leaving a wife but no child, and was the last of the line.

**WILLIAM,** of Holland (1227-1256), reigned 1247-1256. He succeeded as Count of Holland in about 1234 and was chosen as King of Germany, in opposition to FREDERICK II, and actually crowned in 1248. He was, nevertheless, considered an Anti-King. He died in battle.

**CONRAD IV** (1218-1254), reigned 1250-1254. The son of FREDERICK II, he was King of Sicily.

**RICHARD,** of Cornwall (1209-1272), reigned 1257-1272. The second son of King JOHN of England (and brother of HENRY III) Richard was elected Emperor by a very narrow margin. His second wife, Sancha,

was the sister of Eleanor, Henry III's wife. Richard took Henry's side in the civil war against Montfort, was captured by the parliamentary forces and held prisoner until Montfort's death in 1265. His own death, in April 1272, was said to have been hastened by the grief occasioned over the murder of his eldest son, Henry of Almain, by Montfort's sons.

**ALFONSO X,** of Leon and Castile (1221-1284), reigned 1257-1273. Alfonso marked the first appearance of Spanish runners in the Holy Roman race.

**RUDOLF,** of Habsburg (1218-1291), King of Germany, reigned 1273-1291.

**ADOLF,** of Nassau (1250-1298), King of Germany, reigned 1292-1298.

**ALBERT I** (1250-1308), reigned 1298-1308. He was the son of RUDOLF and King of Germany.

**HENRY VII** (1270-1313), reigned 1308-1313. Apart from being King of Germany, he was also Count Henry of Luxemburg.

**LUDWIG,** 'The Bavarian', of Upper Bavaria (1286-1347), reigned 1314-1347. He found himself in conflict with the Anti-King, FREDERICK, 'The Fair', of Austria, who was exactly the same age as he.

**FREDERICK,** 'The Fair' (1286-1330), reigned 1314-1330. Though the second son of ALBERT, he had been denied the Bohemian throne and German crown and made to pay 50,000 marks for Moravia. Frederick considered his treatment very unfair. Despite a majority electing LOUIS king (whom Frederick had beaten in battle) Frederick was crowned at Bonn, thereby beginning a seven-year quarrel. He was imprisoned at Trausnitz from 1322 to 1325.

**CHARLES IV,** of Luxemburg (1316-1378), another King of Germany, reigned 1346-1378.

**GUNTHER,** of Schwarzburg (1304-1349), reigned in 1349. The shortest of the Anti-King reigns, he was elected King of Germany on January 30 and died three weeks later. He was a son of Henry, Count of Blankenburg.

**VACLAV,** of Bohemia (1361-1419), reigned 1378-1400. He was the son of LUDWIG, 'The Bavarian' and King of Germany.

**FREDERICK,** of Brunswick-Lüneburg (dates unknown), reigned in 1400. He was one of the three grandsons of Magnus of Brunswick (died 1369) who refounded the Wolfenbuttel branch of the House in 1345.

**RUPERT III,** of the Palatinate (1352-1410), reigned 1400-1410. He was King of Germany and son of the Elector, Rupert II, and Beatrice of Sicily.

**JOBST,** Margrave of Moravia (1350-1411), reigned 1410-1411. The last of the Anti-Kings, he was nephew of CHARLES IV and grandson of JOHN, 'The Blind', of Bohemia. He was elected in October, a few days after SIGISMUND's election, but died three months later.

**SIGISMUND** (1368-1437), reigned 1410-1437. He was the King of Germany, Bohemia and Hungary.

**ALBERT II,** 'The Great' (1397-1439), King of Germany, he reigned 1437-1439.

**FREDERICK III,** Duke of Austria (1415-1493), reigned 1440-1493. Crowned in Rome in 1452, he was the last Holy Roman Emperor to be so anointed. All his successors automatically became emperors *de facto* on election. He was also King of Germany.

**MAXIMILIAN I** (1459-1519), reigned 1493-1519. The son of FREDERICK III, he was Archduke of Austria, and King of Germany.

**CHARLES V** (1500-1556), reigned 1519-1555. He was also CHARLES I of Spain, grandson of MAXIMILIAN and King of Germany.

**FERDINAND I** (1503-1564), reigned 1558-1564. The brother of CHARLES, Archduke of Austria, He was King of Bohemia and Germany.

**MAXIMILIAN II** (1527-1576), reigned 1564-1576. He was the son of FERDINAND and King of Germany.

**RUDOLF II** (1552-1612), the son of MAXIMILIAN and King of Germany, he reigned 1576-1612.

**MATTHIAS** (1557-1619), reigned 1612-1619. RUDOLPH's brother, he was King of Germany, too.

**FERDINAND II,** of Styria (1578-1637), reigned 1619-1637. He was the nephew of MAXIMILIAN II and King of Germany and Hungary.

**FERDINAND III** (1608-1657), reigned 1637-1657. He was the son of FERDINAND II and King of Germany.

**LEOPOLD I** (1640-1705), reigned 1658-1705. He was FERDINAND III's son and King of Germany.

**JOSEPH I** (1678-1711) reigned 1705-1711. He was LEOPOLD's son and King of Germany.

**CHARLES VI** (1685-1740), reigned 1711-1740. JOSEPH's brother and King of Germany, he was 'Pretender' to the Spanish throne.

**CHARLES VII** (1697-1745), reigned 1742-1745. The son-in-law of JOSEPH I, he succeeded his father, Maximilian Emmanuel, Elector of Bavaria, in 1726. When the *War of Austrian Succession* broke out in 1740, Charles entered into the spirit of the thing and was made King of Bohemia in 1741.

**FRANCIS,** of Lorraine (1708-1765), reigned 1745-1765. He was the son-in-law of CHARLES VI and Grand Duke of Tuscany. His election was largely due to his wife, MARIE THERESA, who made him co-regent to her not inconsiderable dominions. Francis was quite happy to let the Empress 'look after the shop'. Whilst so doing, she also bore Francis sixteen children, the most famous being Marie Antoinette who, as Queen of France, was to fall victim to the French Revolution.

**JOSEPH II** (1741-1790), reigned 1765-1790. One of FRANCIS's litter, he was also Archduke of Austria. He co-ruled with his capable mother, becoming sole ruler of the Habsburg domains in 1780. The following year he proclaimed the *Edict of Tolerance* and abolished serfdom.

**LEOPOLD II** (1747-1792), reigned 1790-1792. He was JOSEPH's brother, MARIE THERESA's third son and Grand Duke of Tuscany from 1765-1790. He formed an alliance with Prussia in February 1792,

to take up arms against France. Six months previously his sister, Marie, was taken prisoner by her husband's subjects, who were in revolt. She died only a few days later, before hostilities were joined.

**FRANCIS II** (1768-1835), reigned 1792-1806. The last Roman Emperor, this son of LEOPOLD II was the first Emperor of Austria. By the time he came to the throne, the Holy Roman Empire was an empty vessel: it was certainly not Holy, neither was it Roman and there was not really an Empire. His own kingdom was widely scattered and vulnerable to attack from a number of directions. In 1806, under NAPOLEON's protection, the Confederation of the Rhine States was formed. Such a substantial, concerted, potential enemy could not be ignored and Francis abdicated from the throne of the Holy Roman Empire. As there was no logical successor, the 'institution' came quietly to an end, after a lifetime of 1006 years.

 # HUNGARY

The Roman province of Pannonia covered the Hungarian plain south of the Danube. After the Roman retreat, in the fifth century, various barbaric tribes occupied the land until the empire of Attila the Hun was centred here. By the middle of the tenth century the bellicose Magyars had taken over and in 1095 Croatia was included (taking the Hungarian border to the Adriatic). The Arpad family were the rulers until 1301. The Turks came to power 200 years later, but by the end of the seventeenth century the Habsburgs had taken over. This family remained in the ascendant until the Austro-Hungarian Empire was broken up in 1918.

Capital *BUDAPEST*; currency *forint*

**STEPHEN** (997-1038), reigned 1000-1038. He succeeded as Duke of Hungary, before being crowned, with a royal crown from Pope Silvester, in 1001. He worked hard to convert his people. In 1083, he became the patron saint of the country, when he was canonized, and his remains enshrined. His only son, Emeric, who was killed in a hunting accident, was also revered as a saint.

**PETER** (1012-1047) reigned 1038-1041. Called Orseolo, the nephew of St STEPHEN, he was deposed in 1041.

**ABA** (died 1044), reigned 1041-1044. The son-in-law of Duke Geza, father of St STEPHEN (d.997) Aba deposed PETER.

**PETER** made a short-lived comeback, 1044-1047, before being deposed again, blinded and killed.

**ANDREW I** (1014–1060), reigned 1047–1060. The great-grandson of Taksony (St STEPHEN's grandfather) he, too, was murdered.

**BELA I** (1016–1063), reigned 1060–1063. He suppressed the last pagan uprisings and introduced financial reforms. He was killed by a falling tower.

**SALOMON** (1052–1087), reigned 1063–1074. The son of ANDREW, he was deposed in 1074 by his cousin, GEZA.

**GEZA I** (died 1077), reigned 1074–1077. BELA's eldest son, he was 'both righteous and generous'.

**LADISLAS I** (1040–1095), reigned 1077–1095. The brother of GEZA, Ladislas deposed SALOMON, but had to deal with him once more, when he invaded the country with Cuman forces. Ladislas acquired Croatia for Hungary and christianized it. He also introduced a legal code in his enlarged kingdom. Whilst preparing to go on the First Crusade, he died. He was canonized and his relics are enshrined in the cathedral he founded at Nagyvarad.

**KOLOMAN** (1070–1116), reigned 1095–1116. He was the son of GEZA by a Greek concubine and spent his youth in Poland. He returned to seize the crown when uncle LADISLAS died. In 1113 he imprisoned and blinded his half brother, Almos, the legitimate son of GEZA. Despite this obvious lack of the finer aspects of family feeling, Koloman was reputed to be a wise and farseeing king.

**STEPHEN II** (1100–1131), reigned 1116–1131. The son of KOLOMAN and known as *Le Foudre* and also *Eclair*.

**BELA II** (1108–1141), reigned 1131–1141. STEPHEN's nephew, he was blinded by the opposition. His plucky little wife avenged her husband's mutilation by having a few members of the Diet blinded too.

**GEZA II** (1131–1161), reigned 1141–1161. BELA's son, he spent most of his twenty-year reign at war with his Byzantine cousin, Emperor Manuel Commenus.

**STEPHEN III** (1148–1172), reigned 1161–1172. The son of GEZA II, he had to contend with his nephews (sons of BELA II) LADISLAS II and STEPHEN IV, who deposed him twice. Anarchy was the order of the day. The younger sprigs were seen off by 1165 and Stephen ruled on, not very happily, for seven more years.

**BELA III** (1150–1196), reigned 1172–1196. The son of GEZA II, he was brought up in the Byzantine court. After the troubles of his brother STEPHEN's reign, he became 'the most powerful and respected of rulers'. His first father-in-law, the crusader Renaud, had the privilege of being beheaded by Saladin personally. His second wife was sister of PHILIPPE II of France.

**EMERIC** (1174–1204), reigned 1196–1204. The son of BELA III (by his first wife, the Duchess of Antioch) he was crowned as a baby.

**LADISLAS III** (died 1205), reigned 1204–1205. He was EMERIC's son. He reigned for only six months and was probably murdered.

**ANDREW II** (1175–1235), reigned 1205–1235. It is likely he cleared his pathway to the throne by murdering his brother EMERIC's son. He ruined the country's finances and, through weakness, was forced by

his nobles to sign *The Golden Bull* of 1222 (Hungary's *Magna Carta*) which gave all lords the right to disallow any royal act.

**BELA IV** (1206-1270), reigned 1235-1270. He was ANDREW's son, who colonized and christianized Transylvania. He was driven from his country by the Mongol invasion of 1241 and fled to Dalmatia. (Something like half the population of Hungary were killed by the invading armies.) He eventually managed to re-establish himself and finally defeated the Tartar, Nogai Khan, in 1261. Bela had two sons and seven daughters, the most famous being St Margaret of Hungary.

**STEPHEN V** (1239-1272), reigned 1270-1272. The son of BELA IV, he resisted the invasion of the Bohemian, PREMISLAS. But he was then murdered (probably) upon setting out to find his son, LADISLAS, who had been kidnapped.

**LADISLAS IV** (1262-1290), reigned 1272-1290. The son of STEPHEN, he lived in a ferment. He ill-treated his wife, Elizabeth of Anjou, and spent the last year of his reign as a fugitive, before being murdered by Cumans in July 1290. (His mother was born a Cuman, the Cumans being an Ugric tribe who invaded Hungary in the late tenth century.)

**ANDREW III**, 'The Venetian' (1264-1301), reigned 1290-1301. He was the grandson of ANDREW II and the last of the Arpads.

**VACLAV** (1289-1305), reigned 1301-1305. He was also VACLAV III of Bohemia and Poland, and not considered a real King of Hungary.

**OTTO** (died 1309), reigned 1305-1309. A descendant of STEPHEN V and Duke of Bavaria, again he was not considered a king

**ROBERT,** of Anjou (1275-1342), reigned 1309-1342. The great-grandson of STEPHEN V, he was King of Naples and Sicily. He became very attached to Hungary and did much that was good for the country.

**LOUIS I,** 'The Great' (1326-1382), reigned 1342-1382. In 1370, this son of ROBERT was elected King of Poland.

**MARY** (1370-1395), reigned 1382-1395. The daughter of LOUIS I, although Queen Regnant, she was called 'King Mary'. She was deposed for a few months, in 1385, by CHARLES III of Naples. Then in February 1387, her husband, SIGISMUND, whom she had married in 1385, joined her as co-ruler.

**SIGISMUND** (1368-1437), reigned 1395-1437. The King of Bohemia and Holy Roman Emperor, he was not popular in Hungary.

**ALBERT** (1397-1439), reigned 1437-1439. He was also King of Bohemia and Germany. His father was Albert IV, Duke of Austria and of the House of Habsburg. He spent the two years of his Hungarian reign defending the country against the Turks.

**VLADISLAV** Jagiellon (1424-1444), reigned 1439-1444. The King of Poland, he was killed by the Turks at the *Battle of Varna*. There followed an interregnum. Later John Hunniades became Regent until 1458.

**LADISLAS V** (1440-1457), reigned 1444-1457. The son (born posthumously) of ALBERT, he continued to fend off the Turks. He was probably poisoned.

**MATTHIAS CORVINUS**, 'The Great' (1443-1490), reigned 1458-1490. The son of John Hunniades, Matthias introduced the Renaissance into

central Europe. His virtues, his introduction of learning and his sense of justice are better remembered than his despotic attitudes or his introduction of crippling taxation. From 1464 he was also King of Bohemia.

**VLADISLAV II** (1450-1516), reigned 1490-1516. He was called 'I agree' and elected by the nobles because he could be guaranteed to do so. He was also King of Bohemia.

**LOUIS II** (1506-1526), reigned 1516-1526. He was the son of VLADISLAV and also King of Bohemia. He was drowned fleeing from the *Battle of Mohács* where the Magyars were completely crushed by the Turks.

**JOHN ZAPOLYA** (1487-1540), reigned 1526-1540. He was the *Waivode* of Transylvania, elected by the Hungarians and supported (as their puppet) by Turkey.

The next eleven rulers of Hungary, listed below, who reigned 1540-1780, were Archdukes of Austria and Kings of Germany, under which country more details can be found. The dates beside them are dates of accession to the Hungarian throne only and may not, in all cases, be the same date as the rulers' accession to the German throne.

**FERDINAND I,** 1540
**MAXIMILIAN II,** 1564
**RUDOLPH,** 1576
**MATTHIAS II,** 1608
**FERDINAND II,** 1618
**FERDINAND III,** 1637
**FERDINAND IV,** 1647
**LEOPOLD I,** 1657
**JOSEPH I,** 1705
**CHARLES III,** 1711
**MARIA THERESA,** 1740

**JOSEPH II** (1741-1790), reigned 1780-1790. He was the eldest son of MARIA THERESA and Archduke of Austria. He had ruled jointly with his mother since 1765, but not harmoniously. Many of the reforms instituted during their joint reign have been claimed as his, but, in fact, most of the really beneficial ones were originally her ideas. He was married twice: his first wife, Isabella of Parma died in 1763 and his second marriage (a politically arranged misalliance) was very unhappy. There were no children by either union.

**LEOPOLD II** (1747-1792), reigned 1790-1792. The younger brother of JOSEPH, he had a short and perilous reign. He was troubled by CATHERINE of Russia to the east and France to the west. France, where his sister, Marie Antoinette, was Queen, was in the throes of a revolution.

**FRANCIS I** (1768-1835), reigned 1792-1835. The son of LEOPOLD, he became Emperor FRANZ I of Austria in 1804. (The Emperor's three successors were also technically kings of Hungary, the last, Charles I, abdicating in 1918.

# IRELAND

From about AD 500 until 900, there were a few major 'kingdoms' in Ireland. The modern names for them are Donegal, Londonderry, Armagh and Monaghan, Antrim and Down, Connaught, Munster (which used to be known as *Muma*) Meath and, lastly, Leinster. The occupants of these various 'thrones' are really too numerous to list in a book of this nature. (To afford some idea of the size of the problem: there were 49 High Kings of Tara before BRIAN BORUMA, 67 kings of Cashel and Munster between 450 and 1194, 72 kings of Ulster between 500 and 1201, 68 kings of Leinster between 436 and 1171, 64 kings of Connaught between 450 and 1224, 53 kings of Meath from 466 until 1173, 52 of Ailech from 466 to 1170 and 25 of Dublin from 856 to 1170. There were 401 kings in all!) The review of the Irish monarchy has been restricted to the *Kings of all Ireland* after BRIAN BAROMY (or *Borum* or *Boru*) had forced the 'High King' MAEL SECHMAIL II to submit to him in 1002. In the ninth century AD the Vikings subdued the country and founded small kingdoms centred on Dublin and other parts of the country. Their thrall held until 1014, when they were vanquished by Brian Baromy at Clontarf. The Normans destroyed the resulting Irish kingdoms and from 1170 the island was a *lordship* until becoming attached to the English crown in 1541. A Free State of Ireland was created in 1921 and the country is now known as Eire.

Capital *DUBLIN*; currency *Irish pound*

**BRIAN BAROMY,** of Munster (926-1014), reigned 1002-1014. During the closing stages of Brian's consolidation, the armies of Dublin and Leinster joined with the Norse Viking army and a battle was fought at Clontarf on Good Friday 1014. Brian gained a decisive victory, but was stabbed in the back (in his tent) by a Viking chief, who had taken refuge in a wood to the rear of the Irish troops.

**MAEL SECHMAILL II,** of Meath (died 1022), reigned 1014-1022. Subdued by BRIAN in 1002, this king had already reigned for some seventeen years before his overthrow. Confusion, though no lack of kings, followed his demise and the next confirmed monarch was probably BRIAN's grandson.

**TURLOUGH O'BRIEN,** of Munster (died 1086), reigned 1072-1086. His name was also spelt *Tairrdelbach*. He held court in Limerick.

**MURTOUGH O'BRIEN,** also spelt *Muirchertach* (died 1114), reigned 1086-1114. The son of TURLOUGH, after him came another spell of comparative kinglessness until DONNELL O'LOUGHLIN.

The apparent inconsistency between the dates of MURTOUGH and DONNELL (below) is caused by a very Irish situation. Several times

during this period, either one or other of these 'High Kings' was not accepted by the *majority* of the provinces mentioned in the preamble. Whichever king was out of favour, was referred to as a 'King-in-Opposition'. Even in a book devoted solely to a history of the Irish Monarchy between 1090-1114, the list of their periods of technical sovereignty, would be voluminous.

**DONNELL O'LOUGHLIN** (died 1121), reigned 1090-1118. The great-great-great-great-great-grandson of a king of Tara, called Aed Findliath, who died in 879.

**TURLOUGH O'CONNOR,** of Connaught (died 1156), reigned 1118-1156. Pope Adrian IV 'allowed' HENRY II of England to invade Ireland in 1156.

**MURTOUGH MACLOUGHLIN,** of Ailech (died 1166), reigned 1156-1166. He was DONNELL's grandson.

**RORY O'CONNOR,** alternatively *Ruaidri Ua Conchobar* (died 1186), the son of TURLOUGH, reigned 1166-1186. In 1177, HENRY II had created his son, JOHN, *Dominus Hibernie* at the Council of Oxford. JOHN visited Ireland in 1185 and under his *Lordship* Ireland was united with the English crown.

# ITALY

After the fall of the Roman Empire, a *Scirian Kingdom* centred on Rome lasted until the end of the fifth century. It was followed by the Ostrogoths before the country became part of the Byzantine Empire for a brief period. From 951, the title of King of Italy was used by the Holy Roman Emperor. Before 250 years had passed, the country had been divided into a number of small states, such as; Guastalla, Modena, the Duchy of Milan and so on. Napoleonic Italy began to have a political meaning, but the country was only truly unified in 1860, under the House of Savoy.

The capital was declared to be *ROME* in 1871; currency *lira*

**VICTOR EMANUEL II** (1820-1878), reigned 1861-1878. Called the 'Honest King', he was the son of CHARLES-ALBERT of Sardinia and had been King of Sardinia since 1849. He encouraged Garibaldi in his efforts to dislodge the Bourbons and openly encouraged the Duchies to rebel.

**UMBERTO I** (1844-1900), reigned 1878-1900. VICTOR's eldest son, he was assassinated at Monza by an anarchist, called Bresci. An attempt to murder this good-humoured man, had already been made near Rome, by a thug called Acciarito, in April 1897.

**VICTOR EMANUEL III** (1869-1947), reigned 1900-1946. He and his

advisers completely failed to appreciate the threat that Mussolini and his Fascists posed to the monarchy. Twenty-five years later, with Mussolini dead and Allied Armies driving German Nazi troops north through his country, Victor Emanuel misjudged events again. He abdicated too late to give the Italian monarchy even the remotest chance to make a comeback in defeated Italy.

**UMBERTO II** (born 1904), reigned in 1946. His father, VICTOR EMANUEL III, abdicated on May 9, 1946 and on June 13 a national referendum clearly showed that the Italian people wanted no more kings. Umberto (and his descendants) were barred from Italy forever. He did not, however, abdicate.

# LEON AND ASTURIAS

Leon, an ancient north-western Spanish city, derives its name from the *Legio Septima Gemina* of Galba, stationed here by the later Roman Emperors. It capitulated to the Moors in 717 and became a Spanish kingdom under Garcia, in about 910.

**ALFONSO** (994-1028), reigned 999-1028. He attempted to spread Christianity throughout his kingdom and died whilst besieging the Mohameddans in Northern Portugal.

**VERMUDO III** (1016-1037), reigned 1028-1037. Son of ALFONSO and brother-in-law FERDINAND of Castile who killed him in battle at Tamaron.

# LEON AND CASTILE

(★ indicates King of Castile only.)

**FERDINAND I,** *El Magno* (died 1065), reigned 1035-1065. The son of SANCHO III of Navarre, he became King, by conquest, of Leon and Asturias in 1037. In 1056 he declared himself 'Emperor of Spain', having disposed of his cousin Garcia in 1054.

**SANCHO II★,** 'The Strong' (1038-1072), reigned 1065-1072. The son of FERDINAND, he was assassinated.

**ALFONSO,** *El Bravo* (1040-1109), reigned 1072-1109. SANCHO II's brother, he became a sort of 'hero of the people', as a result of his resistance to Moorish invasion.

**URRACA** (1080-1126), reigned 1109-1126. She was the daughter of ALFONSO, 'The Brave', and divorced from ALFONSO, of Aragon, with whom she was at loggerheads. She did not see eye to eye with their son either.

**ALFONSO VII** (1104-1157), reigned 1126-1157. Despite the war waged with his mother, URRACA, Alfonso happily took her throne and nine years later announced himself as Emperor of Spain.

**SANCHO III★,** 'The Beloved' (1134-1158), reigned 1157-1158. ALFONSO's son, he married Blanca of Navarre.

**ALFONSO VIII★** (1155-1214), reigned 1158-1188. He was King of Castile alone, because Leon was separated from it in 1157, under FERDINAND II. He married Eleanor, daughter of HENRY II of England, and founded the university of Palencia in 1209 – the first of the Spanish universities.

**FERDINAND II** (1145-1888), King of Leon 1157-1188. ALFONSO VIII's brother, he defeated his father-in-law, ALFONSO I of Portugal, at Badajoz in 1167 and took him prisoner.

**ALFONSO IX** (1166-1230), reigned 1188-1230. He was FERDINAND's son. The Pope declared both his marriages invalid for being 'within the degrees of affinity'. Well might the Pope be worried: Alfonso was called 'The Slobberer' and used to foam at the mouth.

**HENRY I★** (1203-1217), reigned 1214-1217. The son of ALFONSO VIII and, like his father, King of Castile.

**FERDINAND III★** (1200-1252), reigned 1217-1252. He was canonized by Clement X in 1671, but on what grounds it is hard to imagine. He captured Cordoba and Seville from the Moors and, under him, Leon was permanently united with Castile. He married the daughter of ALFONSO VIII.

**ALFONSO X,** 'The Wise' (1221-1284), reigned 1252-1282. The son of FERDINAND III, he was also known as 'The Astronomer'. Under his control the *Alphonsine Tables* were drawn up. He had the Bible translated into Castilian and so created the national language. Although never crowned, he was elected Holy Roman Emperor. He was unseated by his second son.

**SANCHO IV** (1258-1295), reigned 1282-1295. He was called 'The Great and the Brave', because he conquered the Moors at Jarifa. Having usurped his father's throne, he was troubled by the claims of the true king, his nephew.

**FERDINAND IV,** 'The Summoned' (born 1285), reigned 1295-1312. He was the son of SANCHO IV.

**ALFONSO XI** (1311-1350), reigned 1312-1350. The son of FERDINAND IV, he was a ferocious man sometimes known as 'The Avenger'. He dispensed justice arbitrarily, neglected his Portuguese wife and had a large, publicly acknowledged, illegitimate brood by his mistress Leonora. It was the Black Death that eventually killed him.

**PEDRO,** 'The Cruel' (1334-1369), reigned 1350-1366 and again from

1367-1369. With the help of 'The Black Prince' (the Prince of Wales, son of EDWARD III of England) Pedro defeated his illegitimate brother, Henry, and deposed him at Najera in 1367. Two years later the tables were turned and Henry took Pedro prisoner at Montiel and put him to death.

**HENRY II** (1333-1379), reigned 1366-1367 and again from 1369-1379. The illegitimate son of ALFONSO XI, he seized PEDRO's throne, but occupied it only until the *Battle of Najera* a year later. In 1369 he returned to the fray and had PEDRO murdered. Ten years later he was poisoned by a monk. Henry was probably crueller than 'The Cruel', Pedro, yet he was nicknamed 'The Gracious'.

**JOHN I** (1358-1390), reigned 1379-1390. The son of HENRY II, he united Biscay with Castile.

**HENRY III** (1379-1406), reigned 1390-1406. The poorly son of JOHN, he was called 'The Sufferer'.

**JOHN II** (1405-1454), reigned 1406-1454. He was the son of HENRY III.

**HENRY IV** (1425-1474), reigned 1454-1474. The son of JOHN, '...weak and vacillating in character...his reign was marked by incidents of the most ignominious kind'. He was nicknamed 'The Impotent' and there was not a little speculation as to whether the daughter produced by Joan of Portugal, his wife, was (or could have been) his.

# NAPLES

Naples was once part of ROGER II's Kingdom of Sicily. When the Anjous were evicted from Sicily, after the *Sicilian Vespers* in 1282, they kept Naples for themselves. From December 1816, both Naples and Sicily were absorbed into the Kingdom of Italy.

**ROGER** (1093-1154), reigned 1130-1154. Having been King of Sicily for a year, he became King of Naples. The nine kings who followed him, down to CHARLES of Anjou, were all Kings of Sicily (see Sicily).

**CHARLES II** (1245-1309), reigned 1285-1309. He was the son of CHARLES of Anjou and called 'The Lame', possibly as a result of a childhood injury.

**ROBERT**, 'The Wise' (1275-1343), reigned 1309-1343. The son of CHARLES II, he unwisely tried to recover his grandfather's Sicilian throne.

**JOANNA I** (1326-1382), reigned 1343-1382. She was ROBERT's granddaughter. Since a handy divorce was not easily available, Joanna arranged for the disposal of her first husband, Prince Andrew of Hungary. For this she was expelled by LOUIS of Hungary, in 1345. A

year later she married Louis of Taranto. Her bothersome reign ended with her death by suffocation, at the hands of her successor.

**CHARLES III** (1345-1386), reigned 1382-1386. Charles was of the Durazzo branch of the House of Anjou and also King of Hungary. He was murdered in Buda.

**LADISLAS** (1377-1414), reigned 1386-1414. The son of CHARLES III, he tried to unite all Italy. He only succeeded in expelling Pope John XXIII in 1413. (John was, in fact, an *Anti-Pope*).

**JOANNA II** (1371-1435), reigned 1414-1435. She was LADISLAS's sister. When she died, she bequeathed her crown to Regnier, of Anjou, who was then twenty-six. He reigned in name only until eventually ALFONSO, of Aragon, took over the kingdom which Joanna had left him in her will. Regnier never relinquished his claim to the throne.

**ALFONSO I,** 'The Wise' (1385-1458), reigned 1442-1458. From 1416 he was also ALFONSO V of Aragon.

**FERDINAND I** (1424-1494), reigned 1458-1494. He was ALFONSO's illegitimate son. Not only was he kept busy by a barons' revolt, but Regnier continued to press his claims.

**ALFONSO II** (1448-1495), reigned 1494-1495. He was the son of FERDINAND and Isabella. Having made himself totally obnoxious, he abdicated when the French invaded in January 1495.

**FERDINAND II** (1469-1496), reigned 1495-1496. The son of ALFONSO II, he drove out the French, helped not a little by FERDINAND of Castile's General de Cordova, and recovered his kingdom.

**FREDERICK IV** (1452-1504), reigned 1496-1501. The son of FERDINAND I, he was deposed after an invasion of French and Aragonese troops. There followed an interregnum, while France and Aragon discussed the future of Naples. After two years, Spain became master of the kingdom and remained so until the advent of the House of Savoy in 1713.

**VICTOR-AMADEUS** (1666-1732), reigned 1713-1718. He was King of Sardinia and had received the island of Sicily under the *Treaty of Utrecht* but was obliged to hand it back to Spain. In 1734, the *Treaty of the Escurial* between France, Spain and Savoy (against Austria) was signed and CHARLES III of Spain became king.

**CHARLES IV** (1716-1788), reigned 1734-1759. In 1738 he was recognized as King of the Two Sicilies and Spain renounced all claim. He succeeded to the Spanish crown in 1759 and abdicated in favour of his son.

**FERDINAND I** (1751-1825), reigned 1759-1806. CHARLES's son, he was born in Naples, fled the kingdom in 1806 and ruled over Sicily alone until 1815. In 1815 he returned to Naples (see after JOACHIM MURAT).

**JOSEPH BONAPARTE** (1768-1844), reigned 1806-1808. The elder brother of NAPOLEON, he was a trained lawyer whom the Emperor sent to Naples to expel the Bourbons. He set about trying to tackle the mountainous fiscal problems of the Neapolitans and stayed there for

two years. All the while he fended off British attacks, until his brother 'posted' him to Spain in May 1808.

**JOACHIM MURAT** (1771-1815), he reigned 1808-1815. A French general, he was Marshal of France and NAPOLEON's brother-in-law. With his 'black hair flowing in curls over his shoulders: his hat gorgeous with plumes: his whole dress carrying an air of masquerade', this lascivious innkeeper's son cut a conspicuous figure. He had been more than helpful in the 1799 *coup d'état*. Napoleon, however, found him a little too zealous on the throne of Naples. When his brother-in-law fell, Murat behaved true to form and deserted the French cause, hastily turning his coat again during the 'Hundred Days'. He was finally captured and shot in Calabria.

**FERDINAND I,** reigned 1815-1825. Now 64 years old, he was none other than the Ferdinand who first came to the throne before the Bonapartists in 1759. Once again he reconsolidated Sicily and Naples. From 1825-1861 FERDINAND's grandson and great-grandson ruled (details of whom may be found under the *Two Sicilies*). On September 7, 1860, Garibaldi entered Naples to a rapturous welcome and a plebiscite finally amply demonstrated the desire to dismantle the Kingdom of Naples. It became part of VICTOR EMANUEL's Italy in 1861.

# NAVARRE

In the eleventh century, SANCHO, 'The Great', began to rule a region of northern Spain which had been a kingdom since the Mohammedan conquest of the Visigoths. Sancho created Leon and Castile, leaving Navarre out on its own. Relatively undeveloped, it was taken over by the Counts of Champagne, until practically all of it was drawn into Spain in 1516. Today Navarre is a province of Spain.

Capital *PAMPLONA*

**SANCHO III** (992-1035), reigned 1000-1035. A king of Pamplona who, having pushed back the Moors, proclaimed himself Emperor. He then weakened his rule by dividing his kingdom.

**GARCIA IV** (died 1054), SANCHO's son reigned 1035-1054.

**SANCHO IV** (born 1038), reigned 1054-1076. The son of GARCIA, he was deposed by the 'Aragon branch'. The date of his death is unknown.

**SANCHO V** (1037-1094), the nephew of Garcia III, reigned 1076-1094.

**PEDRO** (1068-1104), son of SANCHO V, reigned 1094-1104.

**ALFONSO** (died 1134), reigned 1104-1134. He was the brother of PEDRO and ALFONSO I of Aragon.

**GARCIA V** (died 1150), reigned 1134-1150. The first of the House of Navarre, he was chosen by the nobles of the country.

**SANCHO VI,** 'The Wise', reigned 1150-1194. He (wisely) chose to be styled as King of Navarre rather than Pamplona.

**SANCHO VII,** 'The Strong' (died 1234), reigned 1194-1234. He was both a dashing Spaniard and the last full-blooded one to be King of Navarre. His various successors were more Gallic than Iberian.

**THEOBALD I,** 'The Posthumous', of Champagne (1201-1253), reigned 1234-1253. He was a nephew of SANCHO VII by Sancho's sister. Later he married Sancho's daughter who would have been his first cousin – yet the marriage was not banned.

**THEOBALD II** (1207-1270), reigned 1253-1270. He was the son of THEOBALD I, by his marriage to his uncle's daughter.

**HENRY I** (1210-1274), reigned 1270-1274. THEOBALD II's brother, he was called Henry 'Crassus'.

**JOANNA I** (1273-1305), HENRY's daughter reigned 1274-1305. She married PHILIPPE IV of France, so Navarre passed to the French and Philippe became FELIPE I of Navarre until he died in 1314.

**LOUIS I** (born 1289), reigned 1314-1316. He was also LOUIS X, *Le Hutin* of France, son of JOANNA and Felipe.

**PHILIPPE II** (1293-1322), reigned 1316-1322. He was LOUIS's brother and PHILIPPE, 'The Tall', King of France.

**CHARLES I** (1294-1328), reigned 1322-1328. Also CHARLES IV of France, he was the brother of LOUIS and PHILIPPE and the last of the Capets.

**JOANNA II** (1311-1349), reigned 1328-1349. The daughter of LOUIS X of France, she ruled with her husband, Philip of Evreux. Under them, Navarre became an independent kingdom once again.

**CHARLES II** (1332-1387), reigned 1349-1387. He was known, deservedly, as 'The Bad'. Forever untrustworthy, Charles, finding an ally in England, tried to enlarge his kingdom, but du Guesclin put an end to that in 1364.

**CHARLES III,** 'The Noble' (born 1361), reigned 1387-1425. Although a contrast to his father, 'The Bad', he was not really very noble.

**BLANCHE** (1405-1441), reigned 1425-1441. The daughter of CHARLES III, she ruled with her husband, JOHN.

**JOHN,** of Aragon (1397-1479), reigned 1441-1479. BLANCHE's second husband, he ruled alone after her death.

**ELEANOR** (died 1479), reigned in 1479. The daughter of JOHN and BLANCHE, she was the last of the House of Trastamara.

**FRANCIS-PHOEBUS,** of Foix, ELEANOR's grandson, reigned 1479-1483.

**CATHERINE** (died 1512), reigned 1483-1512. The sister of FRANCIS-PHOEBUS, she ruled for one year alone and then together with her husband, JOHN Albret.

**JOHN III** (died 1516), CATHERINE's widower, reigned 1512-1516.

During his reign, Aragon seized the Spanish portion of the country, leaving a small Basque 'kingdom' nestling in the Pyrenees.

**HENRI II** (1503-1555), reigned 1516-1555. The son of CATHERINE and JOHN, he was a man of taste and culture.

**JOANNA** (1528-1572), reigned 1555-1572. HENRY's daughter and a devout Huguenot, she ruled with her husband, Anthony de Bourbon, who died in 1562. Her religious beliefs led her to become involved in the religious wars being fought in France. Their son became HENRY IV of France in 1589.

# THE NETHERLANDS

The Netherlands is the correct name for the country of which Holland is part. In medieval times the country was divided into states (the county of Holland being the most important). Most of them eventually passed to Burgundy, then to the Austro-Spanish Empire, until the people of the Netherlands revolted against PHILIP II. In 1579 the United Provinces came into being. This lasted until 1795, when the French invaded and established the Batavian Republic, which became the Kingdom of Holland under Napoleon.

Capital *AMSTERDAM* but the seat of government is at The Hague; currency *gulden*

**LOUIS BONAPARTE** (1778-1846), reigned 1806-1810. One of NAPOLEON's numerous brothers, he was made King of Holland not long after the splendid French victory at Austerlitz. Napoleon meant his brother to be little more than a puppet king, but Louis took the job more than seriously. He tried to prevent the Emperor from annexing Holland (to stop trade with the hated English) but Napoleon invaded the Dutch capital. Louis fled, having abdicated, and on July 9 1810, Holland was annexed. Louis settled in Rome and watched the progress of his sons with some pride. His youngest son, Louis (by the lovely Hortense de Beauharnais, daughter, by her first marriage, of Napoleon's second wife, Josephine) became the Emperor NAPOLEON III in 1852.

**NAPOLEON-LOUIS BONAPARTE** (born 1804), reigned in 1810, for all of five days, after his father fled before his uncle's invading army.

**WILLIAM I** (1772-1844), reigned 1815-1840. The son of the dismissed *Stadtholder* (William V, who died in 1806) William was in command of the army beaten by NAPOLEON's French army in 1810. The House of Orange was restored in 1813, with William as *Stadtholder*. He was

promoted to king after the extinction of the Napoleonic Empire. William married a Belgian Catholic and this religious miscegenation so offended the low church lowlanders, that he felt he had to abdicate. He retired to Silesia for the last four years of his life.

**WILLIAM II** (1792-1849), reigned 1840-1849. The son of WILLIAM I, he served under Wellington in the *Peninsular War* in Spain. He had a liberal outlook, instigated many reforms and granted the country a democratic constitution.

**WILLIAM III** (1817-1890), reigned 1849-1890. He continued his father's reformation, creating more liberal conditions.

**WILHELMINA** (1880-1960), reigned 1890-1948. She was the daugher of WILLIAM III and his second wife, Emma. At one time she was reputed to be the 'richest woman in the world', she was certainly one of the plainest. She abdicated in favour of her daughter.

**JULIANA** (born 1909), reigned 1948-1980. She eventually inherited much of her mother's wealth, as well as her kingdom. In 1930, before her marriage, which produced four daughters, she graduated with a law degree from Leyden University.

**BEATRIX** (born 1938), her reign began in 1980. She is the eldest daughter of JULIANA, who abdicated in her favour when she came of age. Beatrix married Claus van Amsberg, a German. Not a diplomatic choice, perhaps, in the light of the German occupation of her country from 1940 to 1944.

 # NORWAY

In the ninth century, Harald, 'The Fairhair', *Jarl* of Westfold, became king of a more or less united country. Despite much fighting and squabbling, his descendants ruled until 1319. Then in 1387, MARGARET of Denmark became Queen. The two countries were joined by having a common sovereign for 400 years. This lasted until 1814, when Sweden took the country over. By 1905, independence had been negotiated and the Oldenburgs were back on the throne.

Capital *OSLO*; currency *krone*

**OLAF I,** of the Tryggvesson family (965-1000), reigned 995-1000. Great-grandson of Harald, 'The Fairhair', his father Trygve was murdered and his mother, Astrid, expelled. Educated in Russia, Olaf became a Viking. He put himself on the throne at the end of a twenty-five-year interregnum, following the death of Harald II in 970. He was killed, probably drowned, in a naval battle against his

own disaffected *jarls* fighting with the Swedes and the Danes. There followed a fifteen-year interregnum.

**OLAF II,** St Olaf (995-1030), reigned 1015-1028. As a teenager he was fighting for King ETHELRED in England against the Danes. He returned a Christian. Though canonized he spread the gospel in a very unsaintlike manner, using both bribery and strongarm tactics. All this caused such unpopularity, he was driven from the country by the Anglo Danish CANUTE. In trying to get back to power, he was killed at the *Battle of Stiklestad* on the Trondheim fjord. Rather confusingly he is patron saint of Norway and enshrined in the Cathedral of Nidaros.

**CANUTE,** King of England (1016-1035), reigned 1028-1035.

**MAGNUS I,** 'The Good' (1024-1047), reigned 1035-1047. St OLAF's son, he ruled alone until 1046, when he ruled jointly with HARALD III for a year, before being killed in battle.

**HARALD III,** *Hardrada* (meaning a stern man in council) (1015-1066), reigned 1047-1066. He was sole ruler from 1047, having shared the throne since the age of twenty. He was killed by HAROLD II of England at the *Battle of Stamford Bridge*.

**MAGNUS II** (1048-1069), reigned 1066-1069. The son of HARALD III, he was co-ruler with OLAF III.

**OLAF III** (1050-1093), reigned 1066-1093. He was called *Kyrre* meaning man of peace. He ruled with his brother MAGNUS II.

**MAGNUS III,** 'The Barefoot' (1073-1103), reigned 1093-1103. The son of OLAF III, he ended up another battle casualty.

**OLAF MAGNUSSON** (1091-1115), reigned 1103-1115. He was the son of MAGNUS III and co-ruler with his two brothers.

**EYESTEIN I** (1089-1122), reigned 1103-1122. He ruled in fraternal concord with OLAF MAGNUSSON and SIGURD I.

**SIGURD I** (1090-1130), reigned 1103-1130. The longest ruling of the happy band of brothers. He was the first Norwegian king to go on a Crusade.

**MAGNUS IV** (1115-1139), reigned 1130-1135. SIGURD's son, he ruled with HARALD IV (who could have been his illegitimate half-brother) until he was blinded and deposed. He eventually died in battle.

**HARALD IV** (1103-1136), reigned 1135-1136. He claimed to be the bastard son of MAGNUS III, but at this distance it seems doubtful.

**SIGURD II** (born 1134), the son of HARALD IV, reigned 1136-1155.

**INGE I,** 'The Hunchback' (1135-1161), reigned 1136-1161. He ruled with his half-brother, SIGURD, until 1155, and then alone until he was killed in 1161.

**EYESTEIN II** (1125-1157), reigned 1142-1157. He was possibly a brother of the last two, but he claimed to be a by-blow of HARALD IV's. Not really to be counted.

**HAAKON II** (born 1147), reigned 1161-1162. The son of SIGURD, he was co-ruler with MAGNUS V.

**MAGNUS V,** Erlingsson (1156-1184), reigned 1161-1184. Co-ruler with HAAKON II, he was a grandson, through female descent, of SIGURD I. He was killed in battle by a cousin called SVERRE.

**SVERRE,** Sigurdsson (1152-1202), reigned 1184-1202. He was possibly a son of SIGURD II. A priest from the Faroes, he sufficiently forgot his calling to kill poor young MAGNUS. He did, however, start to restore order. Part of his campaign was to bridle the power of the bishops. He was so successful at this that they complained to Rome and Sverre was excommunicated.

**HAAKON III,** Sverresson (1177-1204), reigned 1202-1204. His short reign ended when he was poisoned by his stepmother, SVERRE's second wife.

**INGE II,** Baardsson (1195-1217), reigned 1204-1217. He was a grandson of SIGURD II and a nephew of SVERRE.

**HAAKON IV,** 'The Old' (1204-1263), reigned 1217-1263. He was the son of HAAKON III, who died before the boy was born. The baby was placed in the care of INGE. He ruled well, ended the civil war and established Norway as a commercial and maritime power of consequence.

**MAGNUS VI,** 'The Law Mender' (1238-1280), reigned 1263-1280. He was the son of HAAKON IV.

**ERIK II,** Magnusson (1268-1299), the son of MAGNUS VI, reigned 1280-1299.

**HAAKON V** (1270-1319), reigned 1299-1319. He was ERIK II's brother. His commercial policies in relation to the *Hanseatic League* had damaging long-term effects on Norwegian trade.

**MAGNUS VII** (1316-1374), reigned 1319-1355. The grandson, on his mother's side, of HAAKON V, he was also MAGNUS IV of Sweden.

**HAAKON VI,** Magnusson (1340-1380), reigned 1343-1380. He was co-ruler with his father, MAGNUS VII, from 1343-1345 and King of Sweden from 1362.

**OLAF IV** (died 1387), reigned 1380-1387. He was HAAKON VI's son and OLAF V of Denmark.

**MARGARET** (1352-1412), reigned 1387-1412. The mother of OLAF IV, she was also Queen of Denmark.

From 1412 until 1814, the Kings of Denmark were also Kings of Norway. For the record, they are listed below, with the dates of accession only beside them. Further details can be found under Denmark.

**ERIK VII,** 1412
(Interregnum 1438)
**CHRISTOPHER III,** 1440
**CHRISTIAN I,** 1448
**JOHN,** 1481
**CHRISTIAN II,** 1513
**FREDERICK I,** 1523
**CHRISTIAN III,** 1533
**FREDERICK II,** 1559
**CHRISTIAN IV,** 1588
**FREDERICK III,** 1648
**CHRISTIAN V,** 1670

**FREDERICK IV,** 1699
**CHRISTIAN VI,** 1730
**FREDERICK V,** 1746
**CHRISTIAN VII,** 1766

**FREDERICK VI,** 1808. Frederick continued to reign in Denmark until 1836, but in 1814 Norway was united in a *Personal Union* with Sweden and the next five Kings were also Kings of Sweden. Fuller details of these will be found under Sweden.

**CHARLES I,** 1814
**CHARLES II,** 1818
**OSCAR I,** 1844
**CHARLES III,** 1859

**OSCAR II,** 1872. Oscar renounced the Norwegian throne on June 7, 1905 and the Oldenburg line was reintroduced to Norway.

**HAAKON VII** (1872-1951), reigned 1905-1951. He was the second son of FREDERICK VIII, of Denmark, and the first elected king. He did not accept the crown until a Norwegian plebiscite had been held and the people themselves had shown him to be 'suitable'. He was crowned at Trondheim in June. In July 1896, he had married the twenty-seven-year-old Princess Maud, daughter of King EDWARD VII of England (and his cousin). His genuine simplicity endeared him to his new subjects and their loyalty was strengthened by his demeanour, while exiled from Norway, during the Second World War.

**OLAF V** (born 1903), whose reign began in 1951. The only son of HAAKON and Maud, he was born at Sandringham House, the home of his English grandfather, and christened Alexander. It was not until 1905 (when his father became King of Norway and changed his name to Haakon) that he was called Prince Olaf. He is a fine yachtsman, a first class skier and a great Anglophile.

# POLAND

A dynasty, established by the legendary Piast, ruled Poland in the tenth century. It was a major power in Eastern Europe. By the first quarter of the fourteenth century, a new kingdom had been created. In 1370 the throne passed to the Angevins then to a Lithuanian dynasty, who formed an immense country; an all-powerful state, holding sway until the end of the Jagiellons in 1572. Under the Vasas the crown was elective and powerful, but was declining by the eighteenth century. In 1795 the great area was split up between Austria, Russia and Prussia. NAPOLEON established a Grand Duchy, which Russia overran in 1813. As the Russian

Tsars called themselves Kings of Poland, a truly independent country did not emerge until 1918. It was partitioned again in 1939, between Nazi Germany and Russia. The final 'surgery' took place in December 1948, when Russia effectively took control. The republic was given a new constitution in July 1952, which was finally modified in February 1976.

Capital *WARSAW*; currency *zloty*

**BOLESLAV I,** 'The Brave' (966-1025), reigned 992-1025. He had been Duke of Great Poland from his accession until he was declared 'king' in 1024. He was the son of Mieszko, Prince of Poland.

**MIESZKO II** (990-1034), reigned 1025-1034. He was BOLESLAV's brother. In 1031 another brother, Bezrin, appeared on the scene for a year or so.

**KASIMIR I** (born 1016), reigned 1034-1058. He was called 'The Restorer', 'The Peaceful' or even 'The Monk'. In 1037 he was deposed. Two years later he was restored and rebuilt the country, mostly on a Christian base.

**BOLESLAV II,** 'The Intrepid' (1039-1079), reigned 1058-1079. KASIMIR's son, he was finally excommunicated and fled the country with his sons. He died in Hungary.

**VLADISLAV I,** 'The Careless' (1043-1102), reigned 1079-1102. The son of KASIMIR, he abdicated and died in the same year.

**BOLESLAV III,** 'Wrymouth' (1085-1138), reigned 1102-1138. He was the son of VLADISLAV. He waged war unsuccessfully against Hungary and Bohemia.

**VLADISLAV II,** 'The Exile' (1104-1159), reigned 1138-1145. He was deposed by his brothers, all sons of BOLESLAV.

**BOLESLAV IV,** 'Curly' (1127-1173), reigned 1146-1173. Deposed, like his brother VLADISLAV, he died within months.

**MIESZKO III,** 'The Old' (1126-1202), reigned 1173-1177. The last of the brothers and, in turn, also deposed. He returned to the throne from 1198 to 1202.

**KASIMIR II,** 'The Just' (1138-1194), reigned 1177-1194. He introduced laws which protected the peasantry from the nobles.

**LESZEK I,** 'The White', of Mazoria (1185-1227), reigned 1194-1198. KASIMIR's son, he was deposed, but returned 1202-1227.

**BOLESLAV V** (1221-1279), reigned 1227-1279. He was LESZEK's son and called 'The Chaste'.

**LESZEK II,** 'The Black' (died 1289), reigned 1279-1289. He was the Duke of Sieradz and great-grandson of KASIMIR II.

**VLADISLAV** (born 1260), reigned 1289-1290. He was deposed in 1290, restored in 1306 and made king in 1320 (see below).

**PRZEMISLAV** (died 1296), reigned 1290-1296. He was Duke until 1295, when he was made king, but assassinated soon afterwards.

**VACLAV I** (1271-1305), reigned 1296-1305. The son-in-law of PRZEMISLAV, he was also VACLAV II, King of Bohemia.

**VACLAV II** (1289-1306), reigned 1305-1306. The son of VACLAV I, he was VACLAV III of Bohemia.

**VLADISLAV I** (see above), reigned 1306-1333. He was finally made

King of Poland on January 20, 1320, when, for some reason, the Vladislavs were renumbered. He strengthened his country and made effective political marriages for his children.

**KASIMIR III,** 'The Great' (1310-1370), reigned 1333-1370. Diplomatically, culturally and judicially, he was a great man. He befriended the Jews and built extensively; '...he found a country of wood and left a country of stone'.

**LOUIS** (1326-1382), reigned 1370-1382. The son of KASIMIR's sister, Elizabeth, he was also King LOUIS of Hungary. A two-year interregnum followed his reign.

**JADWIGA** (1373-1399), reigned 1384-1399. LOUIS's daughter, she married VLADISLAV, who ruled with her from 1386. He was Duke of Lithuania. Her *election* to the throne (being a younger daughter) set a pattern for an elective monarchy in the future.

**VLADISLAV II** (1350-1434), reigned 1386-1434. He continued to rule alone after JADWIGA's death and was the first of the Jagiellon dynasty. He brought Lithuania into the kingdom, so Poland now had the Baltic on the west and stretched as far as the Ukraine in the east.

**VLADISLAV III** (1424-1444), reigned 1434-1444. He was also King VLADISLAV of Hungary. Killed in battle, a three-year interregnum followed his rule.

**KASIMIR IV** (1427-1492), reigned 1447-1492. VLADISLAV's brother, he acquired large land holdings in Bohemia, Silesia and Hungary, and drove the Turks out of Moldavia.

**JOHN I,** Albert (1459-1501), reigned 1492-1501. He was the fourth son of KASIMIR and elected to the throne.

**ALEXANDER** Jagiellon (1461-1506), reigned 1501-1506. An impoverished reign, funds were lacking to support an army and Russians roamed Poland, more or less at will.

**SIGISMUND I** (1467-1548), reigned 1506-1548. The son of KASIMIR, he ruled alone until 1530, when he was joined by his ten-year-old son and became referred to as 'The Old'.

**SIGISMUND II** (1520-1572), reigned 1530-1572. The last male Jagiellon, he co-ruled with his father, SIGISMUND I, for eighteen years. The last twenty years of his reign are sometimes called Poland's *Golden Age*. A year's interregnum followed his death.

**HENRY** (1551-1575), reigned 1573-1575. He was also HENRY III of France.

**STEPHEN BATORY,** of Transylvania (1522-1586), reigned 1575-1586. He was the son-in-law of SIGISMUND II. A year's interregnum followed.

**SIGISMUND III,** Vasa (1566-1632), reigned 1587-1632. the grandson of SIGISMUND I, he was SIGISMUND of Sweden for some of his ruling years.

**VLADISLAV IV** (1595-1648), son of SIGISMUND, reigned 1632-1648. He defended Poland brilliantly against attack from his father's erstwhile Swedish subjects, as well as keeping Russia and Turkey at bay.

**JOHN II,** Kasimir (1609-1668), reigned 1648-1668. The brother of

VLADISLAV, he was a Cardinal and lived in France until summoned to the throne when nearly forty. Poland was at a low ebb, hit by the plague, religious schism, crop failures and marauding neighbours. Eventually John could take no more and abdicated.

**MICHAEL WISNIOWIECKI** (1638-1673), reigned 1669-1673. It took a year to arrive at a unanimous vote electing him king. His father was a large landholder and acquired a good record for stemming waves of invading Cossacks.

**JOHN III,** Sobieski (1629-1696), reigned 1674-1696. With good French connections, both politically and through marriage, John became the greatest king Poland ever had. He was a general of genius. In 1683 he 'rescued' Vienna and destroyed the Turkish presence.

**AUGUSTUS** (1670-1733), reigned 1697-1704. Augustus was one of eighteen candidates for the throne when JOHN died. Technically he was Augustus II because SIGISMUND II was also referred to as Augustus I (see below).

**STANISLAV I,** Leszozynski (1677-1733), reigned 1704-1709. His pro-French attitude worried the Poles and he was deposed, but 'given' Lorraine, in France, as ample compensation. He returned to the Polish throne for eight months in 1733.

**AUGUSTUS II,** returned to the throne, 1709-1733, after STANISLAV had forced his abdication in 1704.

**AUGUSTUS III** (1796-1763), reigned 1733-1763. He was also Elector of Saxony and supported Prussia in the first Silesian War. He changed sides for the second Silesian conflict and had to pay Prussia an indemnity of one million rix-dollars.

**STANISLAV II** (1732-1798), reigned 1764-1795. He had once been one of CATHERINE of Russia's many lovers and succeeded to the throne of Poland through her influence. He was double-crossed by Catherine and Russia invaded Poland twice. Prussia, too, took action and by 1795, the country was virtually torn apart. In the November of that year, Stanislav abdicated. He died, virtually a prisoner, in Russia.

# PORTUGAL

Though colonized by the Romans, Portugal did not become established as a kingdom until the end of the eleventh century. It was then under French domination, through the Burgundian House of Capet. Gradually it pushed southwards, driving the Moors out of the country as it expanded. The sixteenth century saw massive overseas growth and Portugal became an international power, with staggeringly rich colonies in India and Brazil. In 1580. all this wealth fell into the laps of the Spanish Habsburgs, who

retained power until the emergence of the Braganzas in 1640. The Braganzas held the throne until the abolition of the monarchy in 1910. A republic was declared in August 1911.

Capital *LISBON*; currency *escudo*

**ALFONSO I** (1094-1185), reigned 1112-1185. His father, Count Henry of Burgundy, married the illegitimate daughter of ALFONSO of Leon. This strong-minded young woman brought her husband Portugal as her dowry. The seven-foot-tall (2.13 metres) Alfonso was styled as 'king' in 1139, having pushed the Moors back south of the river Tagus and Lisbon.

**SANCHO I** (1154-1211), reigned 1185-1211. In 1184 Sancho had to be rescued by his ninety-year-old father, ALFONSO, having landed in trouble besieging the Moors at Santarem.

**ALFONSO II** (1185-1223), son of SANCHO, reigned 1211-1223. In his avarice, he attempted to appropriate church revenues, which led him to be excommunicated by Pope Honorius III. Alfonso, 'The Fat', was as rotund as his grandfather was tall.

**SANCHO II** (1209-1248), reigned 1223-1248. As civil war boiled, Sancho had so little authority that the Pope let his brother, ALFONSO, depose him. When the unrest died down, Sancho went into exile for the last two years of his life, leaving Alfonso Regent.

**ALFONSO III** (1210-1279), reigned 1248-1279. He carried on ALFONSO II's campaign of Moor expulsion and added the Algarve region to the kingdom.

**DIONSIUS,** *Diniz* (1261-1325), reigned 1279-1325. The son of ALFONSO III, he founded the University of Coimbra.

**ALFONSO IV** (1291-1357), reigned 1325-1357. A spiteful man, he 'hastened' the death of his father, DIONSIUS, and organized the barbarous murder of his daughter-in-law, Inez.

**PEDRO I** (1320-1367), reigned 1357-1367. He revenged his wife's murder by devastating large tracts of the country between the Douro and Minho rivers, before being reconciled with his sadistic sire.

**FERDINAND I,** 'The Gentleman', *El Gentil* (born 1345), reigned 1367-1383. As a great-great-grandson of SANCHO II, he became a claimant to the throne of Castile and became involved in wars which lasted for twelve years, from 1370. The, eventual, *Peace of Badajoz* stipulated that his daughter, BEATRICE, should marry JOHN of Castile. Ferdinand was the last of the Portuguese Burgundian kings.

**BEATRICE** (dates unknown), reigned 1383-1385. The daughter of FERDINAND, she was the *de jure* Queen of Portugal. Her 'reign' ended when her faction was roundly defeated at Aljubarrota by JOHN's forces. Beatrice 'faded away' and no more is known of her.

**JOHN,** of Aviz (1357-1433), reigned 1385-1433. He was the illegitimate son of PEDRO and the father of Henry, 'The Navigator'. John established a relationship with England, which lasted so long that, in the twentieth century, Portugal is often referred to as 'Britain's oldest ally'.

**EDWARD** (1391-1438), son of JOHN, reigned 1433-1438.

**ALFONSO V** (1432-1481), reigned 1438-1481. He was called 'The African', as he extended his fight against the Moors into Africa itself – with mixed success. In 1475 he invaded Castile. He completely over-reached himself and abdicated in favour of his son, JOHN, who refused the crown, leaving his father to carry on for another two years. In 1478 it all became too much for him and he retired to a monastery at Cintra.

**JOHN II** (1455-1495), reigned 1481-1495. 'The Perfect Prince' seemed perfectly lacking in scruples. He was the ruthless son of ALFONSO. During his reign his subject, Diaz, discovered the Cape of Good Hope and Portuguese colonization began on the Gold Coast of Africa.

**MANUEL I** (1469-1521), reigned 1495-1521. The nephew of ALFONSO V, he claimed Brazil for Portugal, created rich trade, through Goa, with India and established a Congolese kingdom.

**JOHN III** (1502-1557), son of MANUEL, reigned 1521-1557. He was dominated by the Church and the commercial effect on his country was disastrous.

**SEBASTIAN** (1554-1578), JOHN's grandson, reigned 1557-1578. He was killed while 'crusading' in Morocco. His slightly mysterious life started a sort of 'Fake Sebastian' industry. Men masquerading as Sebastian appeared regularly for years after 1578. One such, '...a queer youth of humble birth', the son of a potter, who travelled around Portugal in 1584 peddling rosaries, told innkeepers that he was King Sebastian and 'obtained gratuitous hospitality'.

**HENRY** (1512-1580), reigned 1578-1580. He was the last of the Aziz dynasty. He effectively ended the line upon being made a cardinal in 1542. He may have been a pillar of the Church, but he was a broken reed of state. A Council of Regency was appointed and ruled after his death for five months.

**PHILIP I** (1527-1598), reigned 1580-1598. JOHN III's son-in-law, he was PHILIP II of Spain and husband of Queen MARY of England.

**PHILIP II** (1578-1621), reigned 1598-1621. He was PHILIP III of Spain.

**PHILIP III** (1605-1640), reigned 1621-1640. The son of PHILIP II (or III of Spain) he was PHILIP IV of Spain and the last Portuguese Habsburg.

**JOHN IV**, 'The Fortunate' (1604-1656), reigned 1640-1656. The first of the Braganzas, he was the great-great-grandson of MANUEL I.

**ALFONSO VI** (1643-1683), reigned 1656-1683. The son of JOHN, he suffered from a particularly nasty form of insanity. For the last 27 years of his life his wife and brother had him committed to confinement on the island of Terceira. There he became so fat, he had to be rolled along the passages of his house.

**PEDRO II** (1648-1706), reigned 1683-1706. He was the brother of the regrettable ALFONSO and had married Alfonso's wife after arranging a trumped-up, nullity divorce.

**JOHN V** (1689-1750), reigned 1706-1750. Despite the truly immense flow of silver coming in from Brazil, PEDRO's son managed to spend it all, and more, on the Portuguese contemporary equivalent of wine, women and song.

**JOSEPH** (1714-1777), reigned 1750-1777. The son of the fleshly JOHN, Joseph was a withdrawn, indolent man. He was more than happy to leave matters of state to his statesman, Pombal, who, in 1750, aged 51, was at the height of his power.

**MARIA I** (1734-1816), reigned 1777-1816. JOSEPH's daughter, most of the time she was mentally unbalanced. Her husband, PEDRO III, the son of her uncle JOHN, ruled with her until 1786, when he died aged 69. In 1807, she was removed to Brazil and Portugal was administered by the Duke of Wellington and his diplomatic staff.

**JOHN VI,** Prince of Brazil (1767-1826), reigned 1816-1826. The son of MARIA and PEDRO II, he had been his demented mother's regent since 1799. He ruled Portugal from Brazil until 1822, then stayed in Lisbon for the last four years of his reign. He granted Brazil independence in 1825.

**PEDRO IV** (1798-1834), reigned in 1826. The elder son of JOHN VI, he was King of Portugal for only sixty days. He became PEDRO I, Emperor of Brazil.

**MARIA II** (1819-1853), reigned 1826-1853. She was the eldest daughter of PEDRO IV, but was deposed by her uncle MIGUEL, after less than two years on the throne. She returned after MIGUEL's death in 1834 and reigned, as the last Braganza, until 1853.

**MIGUEL** (1802-1866), reigned 1828-1834. The younger son of JOHN VI, a dashing man, deposed his niece MARIA II (for whom he was Regent). He was deposed himself in 1834 and died in Germany, thirty-two years later.

**PEDRO V** (1837-1861), reigned 1853-1861. The eldest son of MARIA and her husband FERDINAND (of Saxe-Coburg).

**LUIS** (1838-1889), PEDRO V's brother, reigned 1861-1889. During his longish reign, the growth of republicanism became more evident than ever before.

**CHARLES** (1863-1908), reigned 1889-1908. Despite the growing radical element and Charles's 'flamboyant' behaviour, LUIS's elder son was popular. It could not last, however, and in February 1908 he and his son and heir, Luis, were assassinated as they drove through Lisbon in an open carriage.

**MANUEL II** (1889-1932), reigned 1908-1910. The younger son of CHARLES, Manuel fled to Gibraltar, and from thence to England, when revolution broke out after the general election of 1910. He died in Twickenham.

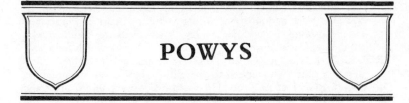

# POWYS

From the sixth century, Powys was a principality in north central Wales. Some 300 years later it was united with Gwynedd, gaining a form of independence in 1075. It split into north and south in 1160 and was ruled by the grandsons of Bleddyn, until the death of Gruffydd Maelor in 1269.

**BLEDDYN AP CYNFYN** (c.1025-1075), reigned 1063-1075. He was the half-brother of Prince Gruffyd ap Rhys, who, as a prince, was Ruler of All Wales. (Gruffyd was murdered in 1063 and his head sent to the Anglo Saxon Earl, HAROLD, as a present.) Bleddyn ruled together with his brother Rhiwallon, who was killed in 1073. He ruled alone for a further two years before he, too, was cut down and the kingdom passed to his son, Madog ap Bleddyn, who reigned as a prince, not king.

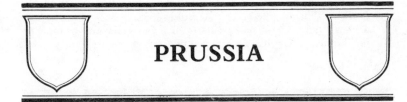

# PRUSSIA

Geographically, what was once the Baltic coastal region of Prussia now lies largely in Poland. Once it was the most powerful element in the German Empire. At the Reformation, the last Grand Master of the Teutonic Knights became a Lutheran and created himself Duke of Prussia in the east. In 1618, the territory of Brandenburg was added and the Hohenzollerns became leaders of a whole kingdom in 1701.

Capital *BERLIN*

**FREDERICK I** (1657-1713), reigned 1701-1713. The son of the Elector of Brandenburg, Frederick William, whom he succeeded as Frederick III in 1688, he was crowned first King of Prussia in 1701. He founded the University at Halle and the Academy of Sciences, yet he lived grandiosely. He supported a vastly oversized standing army and further bankrupted his treasury by having to maintain splendid palaces.

**FREDERICK-WILLIAM I** (1688-1740), reigned 1713-1740. As careful

over expenditure as his father, FREDERICK I, had been lavish, he expanded his kingdom by acquiring Stettin and part of Pomerania, under the *Peace of Stockholm* in 1720. It was Frederick-William who laid the foundation for the military might of Prussia which followed.

**FREDERICK II,** 'The Great' (1712-1786), reigned 1740-1786. This military genius (who looked anything but a soldier) was the grandson of GEORGE I of England. He raised his country into a great and respected European power. He was also a friend of Voltaire and published a number of books. By the last decade of his reign, gout and '...infirmities almost inseparably attendant on his period of life, ...indeed enfeebled his legs'.

**FREDERICK-WILLIAM II** (1744-1797), reigned 1786-1797. The nephew of FREDERICK, 'The Great', in an otherwise unmemorable reign, he formed an alliance with Austria in 1792.

**FREDERICK-WILLIAM III** (1770-1840), reigned 1797-1840. Luckily, this nervy son of FREDERICK-WILLIAM II had three strong councillors in Scharnhorst, Stein and Hardenburg to help him cope with the aggressive NAPOLEON, against whom war was declared in 1806. Princess Catherine Radziwill wrote that Frederick-William '...could never have been a handsome man but in age he was imposing'.

**FREDERICK-WILLIAM IV** (1795-1861), reigned 1840-1861. He succeeded his father, but was not as highly strung as he. He was compelled to grant a constitution in 1848. Not long after, he became so physically incapacitated, he was obliged to hand over to his brother, William, who became Regent in 1858.

**WILLIAM I** (born 1797), reigned 1861-1871. Ten years after he came to the throne, the German Empire was established.

 # ROMANIA

Spelt Romania by its present masters, it was previously spelt Roumania or Rumania. An ethnic curiosity, Romanians can probably claim Roman ancestry. The people who made up a Wallachian state in this territory, in the late 1200s, were a migrant, mix-blooded lot. They were joined to Moldavia, the second state, established about a hundred years later. The governors of these little principalities were called *Voivodes*. The country suffered the fate of most Balkan states, when the Turks took over in the 16th century. They were eventually forced to grant the country autonomy. A Hohenzollern prince was elected Prince of Roumania, and recognized by the *Treaty of Berlin* in July 1878. After 1918, Romania was greatly enlarged

when Transylvania was added to it. Russia retrieved the latter in 1940 and by 1947 the communist takeover was completed. The country became the Romanian People's Republic.

Capital *BUCHAREST*; currency *leu*

**CAROL I** (1839-1914), reigned 1881-1914. He was Prince Charles of Hohenzollern-Sigmaringen, first Prince of Roumania in 1886 and King in 1881.

**FERDINAND I** (1865-1927), reigned 1914-1927. The nephew of CAROL, he was at the head of his armies in the *Bulgarian Campaign* of 1913. It was during his reign that universal suffrage was introduced.

**MICHAEL** (born 1921), reigned 1927-1930. His father, CAROL II, renounced the throne, so the six-year-old Michael was placed upon it and a Regent appointed.

**CAROL II** (1893-1953), reigned 1930-1940. The eldest son of FERDINAND (and a great-grandson of Queen VICTORIA) Carol was a wilful, dissolute man. He made a morganatic marriage to Jeanne Lambrino, a general's daughter, before marrying Helen of Greece, by whom he had MICHAEL, in 1921. In 1925 he eloped with his mistress, Magda Lupescu, and renounced the throne. But in 1920, exhibiting typical impetuosity, he came back to Bucharest and deposed Michael. The pressures were too great. In 1940 he abdicated and seven years later married Lupescu in Brazil. He died in Lisbon; she lasted another 24 years.

**MICHAEL** returned to the throne, 1940-1947. After 1945, having played a part in overthrowing Antonescu, who had been head of state during the Nazi occupation, Michael, by then 25, found the communist regime intolerable. Before he could be deposed, he abdicated. He was granted Romanian citizenship and US$100,000. He married Anne of Bourbon-Parma in 1948 and they had five daughters. His money did not last long and at one stage, he was a salesman for the Lockheed Aircraft Company.

# RUSSIA

The USSR of today is very much larger than even the vast territory which formed the kingdom of the last Tsar in 1917, the year he was deposed. During the ninth century, the state of Kiev grew powerful, having been a focal colonizing area for the Slavic tribes which moved across the land adjoining the Caspian, Black and Baltic seas. Gradually the emphasis moved north to Moscow, which was the eventual nucleus of Russia. A

state based on Moscow was clearly in evidence by the reign of Alexander Nevsky (1238-1252) the first ruler of the Rurik dynasty. IVAN, 'The Terrible', was from the same house, at the time the Russian Princes became Russian Tsars, in 1547.

Capital (today) *MOSCOW*; currency *rouble*

**IVAN IV,** 'The Terrible' (1530-1584), reigned 1533-1584. The only son of Basil III, he became Tsar in 1547. Orphaned at seven, Ivan was brought up in a brutal atmosphere and grew to live a brutal life. Despite fearful rages (during one of which he killed his beloved son, Ivan, in 1580) savage sexual lust and a psychopathic nature, he would listen to the case for the 'underdog' with patience. He had (definitely) seven wives, but only two sons survived. While his fifth wife was still alive he was negotiating his marriage to Mary Hastings, one of the ladies of the court of Queen ELIZABETH of England. Despite his mental imbalance, he had political foresight (almost anticipating the idealistic PETER, 'The Great') and was, at heart, a cultured and hard-working man.

**FEODOR** (1557-1598), reigned 1584-1598. The son of IVAN, he was the last of the House of Rurik. During his reign the Russian Church was split from Constantinople and a Russian Patriarchate established. To put it mildly, Feodor was very feeble-minded.

**IRINA** (1560-1603), reigned in 1598. FEODOR's widow, she reigned in name only from January 7-17, 1598. She became a nun. She is significant in that BORIS GODUNOV was her brother.

**BORIS GODUNOV** (1552-1605), reigned 1598-1605. He was the first of the House of Godunov. The chief member of the Regency, which had been a necessity during the reign of the idiotic FEODOR, although he was elected to rule, he was never really regarded as anything but an upstart. There was a strong possibility that Boris had a hand in disposing of the *Czarevitch* Dmitri, Feodor's son and heir.

**FEODOR II** (1589-1605), reigned in 1605. The son of BORIS, he was brutally murdered by a Moscow mob, only two months after succeeding his father.

**DIMITRI** (1581-1606), reigned 1605-1606. He was usually called 'The False Dimitri'. He claimed to be the son of IVAN, 'The Terrible'. Impostor or not, he led the revolt against BORIS and, in the eleven months of his reign, at least *suggested* a number of humanitarian reforms.

**VASILI IV,** Shuisky (1552-1612), reigned 1606-1610. The one and only Shuisky Tsar, he led the revolt which unseated DIMITRI. He fared no better. In 1610 he, too, was deposed and he died in a monastery two years later. He was the son of Prince Dimitri III of Nizhny Novgorod.

**MICHAEL** (1596-1645), reigned 1613-1645. He was the first of the Romanovs. IVAN, 'The Terrible's' first wife was a Zakharina-Koshkina, a surname later known as Romanov. Michael was a great nephew of the Tsarina Anastasia.

**ALEXEI** (1629-1676), reigned 1645-1676. His warlike reign showed a net gain of Eastern Siberia. He codified the laws of many Russian

provinces and gradually began to introduce 'civilizing touches' from western Europe.

**FEODOR III** (1661-1682), reigned 1676-1682. He was the son of ALEXEI. An undistinguished man, he did not live long enough to keep his disastrous younger brother off the throne.

**IVAN V** (1666-1696), reigned 1682-1696. FEODOR's half-brother was a half blind, half-witted, drooling degenerate. He was used as a tool to keep his brother PETER off the throne and allow the power to be in the hands of Ivan's half-sister, Sophia. Despite his handicaps, Ivan married and fathered five daughters.

**PETER I,** 'The Great' (1672-1725), reigned 1682-1725. Technically he was the last Tsar, as he became Emperor in 1721. From the very beginning of his full-brother, IVAN's reign, it was obvious that the older boy was totally incapable and Peter was accepted as co-ruler, though he was never officially a regent. He was, by any standards, a remarkable man. When he was 26, he went to London to study (and roister). He was described, on that visit, as being tall but had '...convulsions, sometimes of the eyes, sometimes in his arms and sometimes in his whole body...Then he has spasms in his legs so that he can hardly stand still in one place'. He, like so many things Russian, was a complex of contrasts. He introduced much 'Western culture' – yet had his own son, a pale, poor fellow of 28, beaten to death in prison; he founded the superb city of St Petersburg – yet ruled by terror. He defeated Sweden at Poltava in 1709 and under him the giant that was Russia began to come awake.

**CATHERINE** (1679-1727), reigned 1725-1727. The widow of PETER, née Skowronska, she rose from Lithuanian laundrywoman to Tsar's consort, before becoming Empress. The style of Emperor was adopted in 1721 and PETER was, in name, the last Tsar. A bawdy, young woman, she became PETER's mistress in 1703 and was married to him four years later. She later founded the Russian Academy of Sciences.

**PETER II** (1715-1730), reigned 1727-1730. He was the son of 'The Great's' murdered son, Alexis.

**ANNE** (1693-1740), reigned 1730-1740. The youngest surviving daughter of IVAN V and sister of PETER I, she was elected by the Secret High Council on the understanding that they called the tune. She double-crossed them and it was a German ('of low birth') called Biren who really called the tune. The Secret High Council members – eight of the chief nobles of Russia – all 'disappeared'.

**IVAN VI** (1740-1764), reigned 1740-1741. ANNE adopted the eight-week-old boy, her great-nephew, just twelve days before she died, and named him her heir. ANNE's lover, Biren, was ousted from a Regency in less than a month. Ivan's own mother, Leopoldovna of Mecklenburg, handed the authority to vice-Chancellor Osterman. The whole family were imprisoned and a *coup d'état* put ELIZABETH on the throne. Poor Ivan was kept chained in solitary confinement for twenty years, lost his reason (not unnaturally) and was eventually murdered on CATHERINE, 'The Great's', orders.

**ELIZABETH** (1709-1762), reigned 1741-1762. She was PETER, 'The Great's', only surviving daughter. Fleshy and fashionable, Elizabeth founded the University of Moscow. In 1760, her armies pressed FREDERICK, 'The Great', of Prussia right back into Berlin.

**PETER III** (1728-1762), reigned in 1762. Grandson of PETER, 'The Great', and born at Kiel, he ought more properly to be called Karl Peter Ulrich. He married CATHERINE in 1745, made peace with FREDERICK, 'The Great', and was murdered for his pains after only a few months on the throne. This left a clear field for the not over-scrupulous Catherine.

**CATHERINE II** (1729-1796), reigned 1762-1796. The object of her marriage to PETER was to produce an heir for Russia. Since PETER was mad, impotent and/or sterile, Catherine was not, at first, successful. She did produce a son in 1755, but the father was probably Sergei Saltykov, one of the first of her procession of lovers. Catherine was probably the worst thing to happen to Russia since the Flood, although Voltaire, commenting on her influence, said that 'light now comes from the north'. She disposed of the country of Poland almost as effectively as she disposed of her lovers (which she continued to take until she was well over 60).

**PAUL** (1754-1801), reigned 1796-1801. He was CATHERINE's son (by PETER?). His legitimacy had only a short period in which it could be put to the test, since he was assassinated less than five years after succeeding.

**ALEXANDER I** (1777-1825), reigned 1801-1825. He was PAUL's son. He abolished serfdom in the Baltic provinces and introduced many ameliorating reforms. It was his Russia that put an end to NAPOLEON's expansion eastwards. As a result he has sometimes been referred to as the 'Liberator of Europe'.

**NICHOLAS I** (1796-1855), reigned 1825-1855. PAUL's third son was concerned with improving Russia by introducing a good railway system, improving hospitals, and liberating serfs. Privately, he was a devoted family man. Compared to his predecessors, Nicholas would appear to be a positive paragon. He was, however, very autocratic and surprisingly intolerant. He lived long enough to see his country fighting England in the senseless *Crimean War*.

**ALEXANDER II** (1845-1881), reigned 1855-1881. At the second attempt, the Anarchists managed to murder him. This was really a self-inflicted misfortune, as this plump and friendly man was about to grant a very liberal (by Russian standards) new constitution to his people.

**ALEXANDER III** (1845-1894), reigned 1881-1894. Despite the swelling tide of revolution and Alexander's hardly benevolent attitude to his subjects, his reign saw general material prosperity in the country and less evidence of terrorist and anarchistic activity, than in his father's foreshortened reign.

**NICHOLAS** (1868-1918), reigned 1894-1918. ALEXANDER's eldest, amiable and inept son bore a most striking physical resemblance to GEORGE V of Great Britain. (George's mother, Alexandra, was a

princess of Denmark. Her sister, Dagmar, married Nicholas's father, making George and Nicholas first cousins.) Whatever had held the revolution in check during his father's reign broke loose in the first years of the twentieth century. Nicholas was dominated by his wife, Alexandra Feodorovna, and she was completely absorbed in the health of their only son, the haemophiliac heir to the throne. (The haemophilia came through Queen VICTORIA: the Tsarina was Alix of Hesse, Victoria's granddaughter.) The family fell into the hands of the licentious monk, Rasputin, who seemed to be able to alleviate the little boy's sufferings somewhat. A disastrous war with Japan, in 1904, fed the flames and in 1917, the Tsar and his family were placed under house arrest at Tsarskoe Selo. In April 1918, they were all taken to Ekaterinburg in the Urals and there, probably on July 17, the entire family were shot, without trial, and their bodies burnt.

# SARDINIA

In 1720, the Duchy of Savoy, to which the island had just been ceded, permitted a kingdom to be created under the Treaty of London. So Sardinia was joined to Nice, Savoy and Piedmont, Liguria being added after the Napoleonic Wars. In 1859 and 1860, Lombardy, the Two Sicilies, the Papal Legations and the Central Duchies were attached and the Kingdom of Italy came into being.

**VICTOR AMADEUS II,** of Savoy (1666-1732), reigned 1720-1730. He was the first King of Sardinia. His father, Duke Charles, died when he was nine and he was brought up by his bossy mother, Jeanne (*Madama Reale*) and began to govern Savoy himself, when he was sixteen. By the *Treaty of Utrecht* in 1713, the Kingdom of Sicily was given to Victor, but three years later, he was obliged, by the *Quadruple Alliance* to exchange Sicily for Sardinia. Widowed, he remarried, but his second wife caused trouble between him and his son CHARLES, who actually had his father arrested after his abdication. He died at Moncalieri, where his son had him imprisoned.

**CHARLES-EMANUEL III** (1701-1773), reigned 1730-1773. Victor's unfilial first-born spent his reign involved in almost continuous conflict. He led his armies against, amongst others, Austria. As a result, he was able to pass on a powerful, expanding and wealthy kingdom to his son.

**VICTOR AMADEUS III** (1726-1796), reigned 1773-1796. He lost Savoy and Nice in 1792 and, by the end of his reign, was obliged to make a disadvantageous peace with NAPOLEON.

**CHARLES-EMANUEL IV** (1751-1819), reigned 1796-1802. He succeeded his father, VICTOR, on a 'slippery throne' and, before six years were out, had abdicated it to his younger brother and become a monk.

**VICTOR-EMANUEL I** (1759-1824), reigned 1802-1821. In 1814 he returned to Turin and the *Congress of Vienna* granted him the Genoese territory. However, he was unable to deal with an aristocratic rebellion and, having no sons of his own, abdicated in favour of his younger brother.

**CHARLES-FELIX** (1765-1831), reigned 1821-1831. Supported by Austria, he restored the stability of his throne and set about making a number of improvements (including many new roads) in the kingdom. He died without male issue and the throne passed to a cousin of the Carignano branch of the family.

**CHARLES ALBERT** (1798-1849), reigned 1831-1849. He was a collateral relative of CHARLES-FELIX (actually a grandson, five times removed, of Charles Emanuel I of Savoy, who died in 1630). He failed to defeat the Austrians over Lombardy and abdicated, dying in Oporto four months later.

**VICTOR-EMANUEL** (born 1820), reigned 1849-1861. The son of CHARLES ALBERT, he became the first King of Italy in 1861.

 # SAXONY

The 'home of the Saxons', literally, this region of northern Germany was conquered by Charlemagne. Its eventual rulers (who were styled Dukes) obtained the Imperial crown in the tenth century. It became an electorate in 1423, was split between two branches of the Wettin family in 1485, reunited in 1547 and elevated to a kingdom in 1806.

Capital *DRESDEN*

**FREDERICK AUGUSTUS I** (1750-1827), reigned 1750-1827. He was the son of FREDERICK II, King of Poland and grandson of Augustus, Elector of Saxony ('...an indolent prince'). Frederick Augustus paid six million florins for the land which became his kingdom. He increased its area after the *Treaty of Posen* by an alliance with France. When he was 28, someone wrote of this King-to-be: 'Coldness and inanimation characterize his behaviour...he displays none of the gracious and communicative disposition which...characterize...his three contemporaries'.

**ANTHONY CLEMENT** (1755-1836), brother of FREDERICK, reigned 1827-1836.

**FREDERICK AUGUSTUS II** (1797-1854), reigned 1836-1854. He had been Regent to his uncle ANTHONY since 1830.

**JOHN** (1801-1873), reigned 1854-1873. FREDERICK's brother and a notable Dante scholar, he published his translation of the *Divina Commedia* in 1839.

**ALBERT** (1828-1902), reigned 1873-1902. The son of JOHN, he commanded an army corps in the Franco-German War while Crown Prince.

**GEORGE** (1832-1904), reigned 1902-1904. The younger brother of ALBERT, he married Dona Maria, the Infanta of Portugal.

**FREDERICK AUGUSTUS III** (born 1865), reigned 1904-1918. The last king of Saxony, he was dethroned in 1918 and given compensation of 300,000 marks.

# SCOTLAND

Scotland became a kingdom in 843, when Kenneth, who had been King of Dalradia for two years, became King of the Picts and therefore of Scotland. Before him there had been Kings of *Alba* and the very first Scottish dynasty was called Alba rather than MacAlpin, his family name. The king was 'King of the Scots', rather than 'King of Scotland', which was only used briefly by Balliol between 1292 and 1306.

Capital *EDINBURGH*; currency *pound sterling* but some Scottish banks produce their own currency.

**MALCOLM II** (born 954), reigned 1005-1034. He was actually the sixteenth King of the Scots and still of MacAlpin descent, being a son of Kenneth II, who died in 995. In his reign, Scotland achieved approximately the same territorial size as its area today.

**DUNCAN I** (died 1040), reigned 1034-1040. MALCOLM's brother, he was murdered by MACBETH, his cousin.

**MACBETH** (died 1057), reigned 1040-1057. He was eventually killed by DUNCAN's son near Aberdeen. He had been defeated by Siward at Dunsinane and was the model for Shakespeare's *Macbeth*. Although his real wife, Gruoch, granddaughter of Kenneth II, was almost certainly neither a sleepwalker nor a murderess.

**LULACH** (died 1058), reigned 1057-1058. Called 'The Simple', he was MACBETH's stepson and was also disposed of by MALCOLM.

**MALCOLM III** (1031-1093), Duncan's son, reigned 1058-1093. Having

made his way to the throne by disposing of his two predecessors, he spent most of his long reign fighting border wars. He was known as *Canmore* which meant 'Great Chief'. His wife, Margaret, the daughter of EDMUND of England, influenced Malcolm considerably and her virtue led her to be canonized as a Saint in 1250. He invaded England and was killed in battle at Alnwick.

**DONALD III,** called *Donald Bane* (1033-1099), reigned 1093-1094. He was MALCOLM III's younger brother and sneakily deposed by his nephew DUNCAN II. He died five years later, having been blinded by another nephew, EDGAR.

**DUNCAN II** (1060-1094), reigned in 1094. He was murdered at the behest of his half-brother, EDMUND (their father, MALCOLM, had been twice married).

**EDMUND** (dates unknown), reigned 1094-1097. He ruled jointly with a restored DONALD until they were both deposed by EDGAR, MALCOLM III's seventh son. He became a monk and died some years later.

**EDGAR** (1074-1107), reigned 1097-1107. He only managed to secure the throne with the strong support of the English, whose vassal he became.

**ALEXANDER** (1077-1124), reigned 1107-1124. He was yet another of MALCOLM's sons. He was a vassal of HENRY I of England and married, Sybilla, Henry's illegitimate daughter.

**DAVID I** (1080-1153), reigned 1124-1153. The ninth and youngest son of MALCOLM he became St David. His feast day is on March 24. Very anglicized, David founded Abbeys, gave vast tracts of land to the Church (which was why he was canonized) and introduced a sound 'money economy' to Scotland.

**MALCOLM IV** (1142-1165), reigned 1153-1165. The grandson of St DAVID, he was obliged to hand Northumbria and Cumbria back to England after his surrender to HENRY II at Chester in 1157. He was so effeminate, he was called 'The Maiden' behind his back. (Despite this he fathered one illegitimate son.)

**WILLIAM I,** 'The Lion' (1145-1214), reigned 1165-1214. He invaded England, but was no more successful than brother MALCOLM. He was captured, forced to pay homage to HENRY II and released in 1175.

**ALEXANDER II** (1198-1249), reigned 1214-1249. 'The Lion's' son, he married King JOHN's daughter and renounced all Scottish claims to Cumbria and Northumbria.

**ALEXANDER III** (1241-1286), reigned 1249-1286. The last MacAlpin, he was ALEXANDER's son by his second marriage. He secured the Western Isles from Norway, but on March 19, 1286, while looking out to sea at Kinghorn in Fife, he dismounted from his horse rather carelessly and fell over a cliff to his death.

**MARGARET,** 'The Maid of Norway' (1283-1290), reigned 1286-1290. She was ALEXANDER's granddaughter, by his only daughter and ERIK II of Norway. She is almost certainly the only monarch in the world to have died from seasickness. In September 1290, she set sail

from Norway to take over her new kingdom, but the convoy had to put into the Orkneys, as the child Queen was too ill to sail on, and there she died.

From September 1290-1292, came the first of two interregnums. King EDWARD I of England, 'The Hammer of the Scots', asked for claimants to the throne and thirteen men stepped forward. Eventually Edward chose JOHN BALLIOL, as he hoped that he would be a puppet king for him in this troublesome region.

**JOHN BALLIOL,** or Baliol (1250-1313), reigned 1292-1296. He was the great-great-great-grandson of DAVID I. His father and mother, Devorguilla, founded Balliol College, Oxford, in about 1265. In 1296 he was obliged to surrender the throne and went to live in Normandy. From July 1296 to March 1306, there was a second interregnum. The Scots, under William Wallace (who was executed in London in 1305) led the nationalists against the English efforts to subdue the country. The struggle was continued by ROBERT after Wallace's death.

**ROBERT I,** 'The Bruce' (1274-1329), reigned 1306-1329. He was the first of the Bruce dynasty. After early setbacks, Robert completely routed the English army at the *Battle of Bannockburn* in June 1314. In 1328, England renounced all claims to Scotland and Robert rebuilt his nation. As active off the throne, as on it, he sired at least five bastards, but had only one legal son who survived. He died mysteriously, probably of leprousy. His heart was cut out and taken to the Holy Land, but later brought back and buried in Melrose Abbey. (The rest of him lies in Dunfermline.)

**DAVID II** (1324-1371), reigned 1329-1371. Compared to his father, ROBERT, David grew to be a mean man, lacking courage. He was deposed by EDWARD BALLIOL in 1332 and six years of civil war followed. David first fled to France, then invaded England in 1346. He was captured and imprisoned for eleven years, before being ransomed. (At his otherwise unceremonious coronation, he was anointed with Holy Oil; the first time such a ritual had been enacted in Scotland. The oil was sent by Pope John XXII, who charged 12,000 florins for it.) David's first wife was daughter of JOHN of England.

**EDWARD BALLIOL** (died 1363), reigned 1332-1338. He was the son of JOHN BALLIOL. With English support, Edward was able to depose DAVID. Civil war continued in Scotland and Edward fled in 1338. DAVID returned in 1340 and ruled (more or less) until his death.

**ROBERT II** (1316-1390), reigned 1371-1390. A grandson of ROBERT, 'The Bruce' (and a half-brother of DAVID II) he was the first of the Steward dynasty. He was nicknamed 'The Steward' and later 'King Bleare', because of his bloodshot eyes. A weak man, his kingdom collapsed around him.

**ROBERT III** (1337-1406), reigned 1390-1406. He was born about ten years before his father, ROBERT II, married his mother, and was christened John. Already a bit weak in the head, a kick from a horse loosened the rest up there and Scotland sank lower than it ever had

during the reign of his incompetent father. He was popularly supposed to have died of shock on being told that his son James, who was sent to France for safety, had been captured by the English en route.

**JAMES I** (1396-1437), reigned 1406-1437. Unwittingly the cause of his father's death (though the rumour was probably started by the Scots as anti-English propaganda) James was ransomed in 1423. A good ruler and a man of the arts, in a few years he achieved much. He was murdered by his uncle, the Earl of Atholl.

**JAMES II** (1430-1460), reigned 1437-1460. Having regained much ground lost by his father, JAMES I, James was accidentally killed by a prematurely exploding cannon, whilst his army was trying to repossess the town of Roxburgh from the English. His nickname was 'Fiery Face'.

**JAMES III** (1452-1488), reigned 1460-1488. Bad luck, a disastrous famine and bad management attended the reign. He was killed whilst fleeing the field, having been defeated by rebellious Scottish lords at Sauchieburn.

**JAMES IV** (1473-1513), reigned 1488-1513. The son of JAMES III, he was killed with the 'Flowers of the Forest' (in other words most of the better elements of the Scottish hierarchy) at the bloody *Battle of Flodden Field* on September 9. He had married Margaret, daughter of HENRY VII of England, a significant alliance.

**JAMES V** (1512-1542), reigned 1513-1542. The only surviving son of JAMES V, he could not control his nobles. He married Madeline, daughter of FRANCIS I of France.

**MARY,** 'Queen of Scots' (1542-1567), reigned 1542-1567. The oversexed, unscrupulous and only daughter of JAMES V, she married the Dauphin of France. He became King FRANCIS in 1559 and died seventeen months later, leaving Mary an eighteen-year-old widow. Now the Dowager Queen of Catholic France, she returned to Scotland and, in 1565, married the thin-legged Lord Darnley, by whom she had a son. On February 10, 1567, she contrived her stupid husband's murder, by having blown him up in his bed. She then married Earl Bothwell, the man who had murdered him. Her way of life alienated her from her people. She went south to England, where she was equally unwelcome and a threat to the security of the English throne of Queen ELIZABETH. She was imprisoned and, after numerous escapades, which have been shamefully romanticized over the intervening 400 years, was eventually beheaded in Fotheringay Castle.

**JAMES VI** (1566-1625), reigned 1567-1625. The son of Mary, he was the last king of a separate Scotland. He became JAMES I of England in 1603, when ELIZABETH, the last Tudor, died (see Great Britain).

# SERBIA

A region of Yugoslavia, it was established as a kingdom before 1200 by the Nemanjich family, who had thrown off the oppressive Byzantines. They stayed in power until 1389, when the Ottoman Turks poured in and instituted a regime. This lasted, more or less, until 1804, when Czerny George drove them out. They returned eight years later and Milosh Obrenovitch (who became the Prince in 1817) drove them out again in 1815 and Serbia became practically independent. After the First World War, Serbia merged with other Slavic peoples to form Yugoslavia.

Capital *BELGRADE*

**STEPHEN NEMANYA** (died 1196), reigned 1168-1196. He became the *Grand Zhupan* of Rashka and united the various states, except Bosnia, under his rule, though he never styled himself as king. He abdicated and became monk Simeon in the monastery on Mount Athos.

**STEPHEN NEMANYA II** (died 1227), reigned 1196-1227. He was also Grand Zhupan and then declared King in 1217.

**STEPHEN RADOSLAV III** (died 1234), reigned 1227-1234.

**STEPHEN VLADISLAV IV** (died 1243), reigned 1234-1243.

**STEPHEN UROSH I** (died 1277), reigned 1243-1276. He was christened Dragoslav. He gave up his throne and retired to a monastery for the last year of his life.

**STEPHEN DRAGUTIN VI** (1243-1317), reigned 1276-1282. He was deposed and, in exile, chose to become the Duke of Mačra.

**STEPHEN UROSH MILUTIN II** (died 1321), reigned 1282-1321. He was the son of STEPHEN UROSH I and Helen of Constantinople.

**STEPHEN UROSH III** (died 1331), the son of MILUTIN, reigned 1321-1331.

**STEPHEN UROSH DUSHAN IV** (1308-1355), reigned 1331-1355. (*Dushan* is a term of endearment derived from *dusha* the soul.) Stephen was illegitimate. A great soldier, in 1345 he proclaimed himself Emperor by conquest.

**STEPHEN UROSH V** (died 1371), reigned 1355-1371. DUSHAN's only son, he was the last of the Nemanjichs. The country drifted under Turkish rule and remained a *pashalik* of that oppressive empire, for nearly 350 years.

**MILAN I** (1854-1901), reigned 1882-1889. The third of the Obrenoviches, Milan was amoral, neurasthenic and two-faced. His public quarrels with Queen Natalie weakened a frail position and he was forced to abdicate.

**ALEXANDER I** (1876-1903), reigned 1889-1903. As he was only 13

when his father MILAN abdicated, his reign began under a regency of three generals. Alexander ejected this military trio when he was 17. He was a short, sulky, myopic man, who married his mistress, an engineer's widow. His people had no use for their king, so murdered him, his Queen Draga *and* her brother, for good measure. A cabinet of regicides was then formed to try and run the country.

**PETER I** (1844-1921), reigned 1903-1918. The eldest son of Alexander Karageorgevitch he had been elected Prince of Serbia in 1842. In 1918 he was elected PETER I of Yugoslavia.

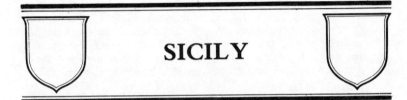

# SICILY

In very ancient times the island was controlled both from Carthage and Greece, but early in the ninth century AD, the Muslims took over from the Byzantines. This power broke up more or less naturally and the Hautevilles moved in. By 1130, King Roger was controlling Southern Italy, as well as Sicily. In 1194, the Hohenstauffens gained dominance. Then the kingdom fell to the French Angevins, but a rebellion in 1282 installed the Aragonese. They also acquired the Kingdom of Naples and both kingdoms passed to the Habsburgs, until their Spanish branch dwindled, when they passed to the Spanish Bourbons. The kingdom was finally absorbed by Italy.

Capital *PALERMO*

**ROGER II** (1095-1154), reigned 1130-1154. Having been Count of Sicily for 25 years, Roger was the first leader to be styled as 'King'. By skill and diplomatic *finesse* he built up the Kingdom of the Two Sicilies, incorporating Naples, and created an enviable bureaucratic service, staffed with Arabic personnel.

**WILLIAM I,** 'The Bad' (1120-1166), despite being ROGER's son, he was badly served by his favourite minister, Admiral Majone.

**WILLIAM II,** 'The Good' (1154-1189), reigned 1166-1189. 'The Good', like his father, 'The Bad', supported Pope Alexander III in his running fight with FREDERICK 'Barbarossa' – the Holy Roman Emperor.

**TANCRED** (died 1194), reigned 1189-1194. The illegitimate son of ROGER II's son, Roger, and styled the Count of Lecce.

**WILLIAM III** (1184-1194), reigned in 1194. TANCRED's son, he only ruled for ten months, under the regency of his mother, Queen Sibylla, and was probably murdered. He was the last of the Hauteville dynasty.

**HENRY VI** (1165-1197), reigned 1194-1197. King of Germany and

Emperor of the Holy Roman Empire, he ruled jointly with Queen Constanza, 'The Cruel'.

**FREDERICK I** (1194-1250), reigned 1197-1250. He became FREDERICK II of Germany in 1215. Frederick took over from his mother Constanza. In 1208, he began to rule 'in the Norman manner', but under the guardianship of Pope Innocent III. At the age of 13, Frederick was observed to have been given by 'the Universal Author of Nature...robust limbs and a strong body with which his vigorous spirit can achieve whatever he undertakes...'.

**CONRAD I** (1228-1254), reigned 1250-1254. He was also CONRAD IV of Germany and King of Jerusalem. (Upon Conrad's death there was much Papal manoeuvring. Eventually Pope Urban managed to place MANFRED on the throne, despite CONRAD's perfectly legitimate son, Conrad, who was only two years old. This poor lad was eventually beheaded at Naples in 1268.)

**MANFRED** (1232-1266), reigned 1258-1266. He was FREDERICK's illegitimate son, who had the throne secured for him only to be defeated by Charles of Anjou and killed by his agency. He was the last Hohenstauffen.

**CHARLES OF ANJOU** (1226-1285), reigned 1266-1282. The son of LOUIS VIII of France, he was the first and last of the Angevin dynasty of Naples. The Pope having given him the island, Charles lost it again during an uprising now called the *Sicilian Vespers*. He was deposed.

**PETER I** (1236-1285), reigned 1282-1285. MANFRED's son-in-law, he was offered the crown after the *Sicilian Vespers* affair. He was the first Aragon of the Sicilian dynasty.

**JAMES** (1260-1327), reigned 1285-1295. He became JAMES II of Aragon.

**FREDERICK II** (1272-1337), reigned 1295-1337. The third son of PETER, he was elected king by the Sicilian Parliament.

**PETER II** (died 1342), FREDERICK's son, reigned 1337-1342.

**LOUIS** (1338-1355), PETER's son, reigned 1342-1355.

**FREDERICK III,** 'The Simple' (1341-1377), reigned 1355-1377. He was another of PETER's sons.

**MARY** (died 1402), reigned 1377-1402. She was FREDERICK's (not so simple) daughter, who reigned alone until 1391 and then with her husband.

**MARTIN I** (died 1409), reigned 1402-1409. He ruled jointly with his wife, MARY, until her death in 1402 and then alone for a further seven years.

**MARTIN II** (died 1410), reigned 1409-1410. Rather confusingly, Martin II was MARTIN I's *father*. He was also MARTIN II of Aragon. A two-year interregnum followed his rule.

**FERDINAND I,** 'The Just' (1373-1416), reigned 1412-1416. He was also FERDINAND of Aragon and a nephew of MARTIN II. Since the kingdom was now under Spanish rule, he sent the Infante Don Juan to govern the island.

**ALFONSO** (1385-1458), reigned 1416-1458. The son of FERDINAND,

he recalled the Infante and despatched a Viceroy, so beginning a long and usually unhappy history of viceregal government.

**JOHN** (1397-1479), reigned 1458-1460. He was ALFONSO's brother and King of Aragon as well. He ceded Sicily to FERDINAND.

**FERDINAND II,** 'The Catholic' (1452-1516), reigned 1460-1516. In 1500, the Treaty of Granada divided the kingdom between Ferdinand and LOUIS XII of France. Three years later the French were expelled and Spain had total power over the island until 1707. He was also Ferdinand V of Castile.

**JOANNA** (1479-1555), reigned 1516-1555. Called *La Loca* 'The Mad', of Spain, she married PHILIP I in 1496. She was the last of the House of Trastamara. Having, in effect, been certified mad in 1506, Philip was given full powers to act for her.

The Habsburg Kings of Spain then reigned for nearly 200 years. Details of the following five monarchs will be found under Spain. The dates are dates of accession only.

**CHARLES I,** 1516
**PHILIP II,** 1556
**PHILIP III,** 1598
**PHILIP IV,** 1621
**CHARLES II,** 1665

**PHILIP V** of Spain pressed his claims to Sicily from 1700 until 1735, though he continued a (broken) Spanish reign until 1746. He was a Bourbon king.

**JOSEPH** (1678-1711), reigned 1707-1711. He was Archduke of Austria, a Habsburg, King of Germany and Hungary and Emperor of the Holy Roman Empire.

**CHARLES III** (1685-1740), reigned 1711-1713. He was JOSEPH's brother and holder of the same titles.

**VICTOR AMADEUS,** of Savoy (1666-1732), reigned 1713-1718. By a complicated arrangement, under the *Treaty of Utrecht* he 'exchanged' Savoy for Sicily, then swapped Sicily for Sardinia in August 1718.

**CHARLES III** reigned again 1718-1735, during which time Naples was reunited with Sicily. He was the last Habsburg.

**CHARLES IV** (1716-1788), reigned 1735-1759. This Charles was a Bourbon Spaniard and also CHARLES III of Spain. Austria withdrew and eventually the Kingdom of the Two Sicilies came into being, under the control of Charles's son.

**FERDINAND I** (1751-1825), reigned 1759-1825. The first King of the Two Sicilies, he gave way to the Bonapartes in 1806. Details of these two Frenchmen can be found under Naples. After the fall of MURAT in 1815, Ferdinand came back to 'both thrones' for ten years.

**FRANCIS I** (1777-1830), reigned 1825-1830. The son of FERDINAND, he was born in Naples and died there.

**FERDINAND II** (1810-1859), reigned 1830-1859. He was the king whom Gladstone, the British Prime Minister, called 'The Negation of God'. Coarse, cruel and debauched, his fondness for allowing his troops the indiscriminate use of bombs to suppress the few small

voices which objected to his tyrannical regime, caused him to be labelled 'Bomba'. Much to everyone's surprise, after the Revolt of 1848, he pardoned most of the ringleaders of the uprising.

**FRANCIS II** (1836–1894), reigned 1859–1860. Sicily was annexed by Italy in 1860, but this son of FERDINAND held out against Garibaldi's 'Thousand' troops, even though the King's battles and his realm were lost. He died in exile in Austria and Sicily became part of united Italy.

# SPAIN

The marriage of ISABELLA of Castile to FERDINAND of Aragon and the subsequent conquest of Granada, at the end of the fifteenth century, created a united country, with the exception of Navarre, which was included later. The first king of virtually all Spain was of the House of Trastamara. The house ruled until the Habsburgs came to the throne in 1504. They stayed until 1700, when the Bourbons arrived. The line remained, despite interruptions from the Emperor NAPOLEON and the dictator Franco. (Rulers of parts of Spain have been covered under Aragon, Leon and Asturias, Leon and Castile and Navarre.)

Capital *MADRID*; currency *peseta*

**FERDINAND V** (1452–1516), reigned 1479–1516. The son of JOHN II of Aragon, he was also King of Naples, FERDINAND II of Aragon and King of Castile. He married ISABELLA, the sister of King HENRY IV of Leon and Castile, in October 1469. On the death of the feeble King Henry in 1474, the Kingdoms of Castile and Aragon were united.

**ISABELLA I** (1451–1504), reigned 1474–1504. The wife of FERDINAND, like her husband, she was known as 'The Catholic'. She and her confessor, Ximenes, spread Catholicism forcibly and expelled some Spanish Jews. It was FERDINAND and she who financed Christopher Columbus in 1491.

**JOANNA,** *La Loca* (1479–1555), reigned 1504–1516. The daughter of FERDINAND and ISABELLA, she married Archuduke Philip of Austria in 1496. A passionate woman, given to jealous fits over her husband's (often unfaithful) behaviour, she became insane in about 1502. On the death of her mother, PHILIP ruled for her. He died in September 1506, having been officially given full royal power only the month before, and Joanna, now completely deranged, refused to leave his corpse for days. FERDINAND then took over the throne. He died in 1516.

**CHARLES I** (1500-1556), reigned 1516-1555. JOANNA's son (who did not, luckily, inherit her mental problems) was also Emperor of Germany and, in his time, probably the most powerful man in Europe. Despite vast territories both in Europe and the 'New World', Charles expressed a preference for his Flemish subjects and only spent seventeen of the forty years of his reign actually in Spain. Tired of power, partly disillusioned, he abdicated and retired to a monastery.

**PHILIP II** (1527-1598), reigned 1556-1598. He was the son of CHARLES I and King of Portugal. He is best remembered as the beloved husband of MARY Tudor, of England. He was hated by the English and used as a sort of 'frightener', in both English and Dutch nurseries, to scare young children into behaving. Philip was not as black as he was painted, but his grandiose thinking led Spain along the perilous path to bankruptcy.

**PHILIP III** (1578-1621), reigned 1598-1621. He was the son of PHILIP II, by his fourth and final wife, Anne of Austria. During his reign, the Moors (*Moriscos*) were finally cleared from Spain's mainland.

**PHILIP IV** (1605-1665), reigned 1621-1665. Despite the ability of his minister, Olivares, the young king could only watch his country slide further downhill. A revolt in Catalonia gave Portugal the chance to re-establish its independence.

**CHARLES II** (1661-1700), reigned 1665-1700. He was the son of PHILIP IV and the last of the Habsburgs. His childlessness precipitated the *War of the Spanish Succession*.

**PHILIP V** (1683-1746), reigned 1700-1746. The first Bourbon, he was the grandson of LOUIS XIV of France. He lost Gibraltar in 1704 and, by the *Treaty of Utrecht*, Spain was obliged to give away the Spanish Netherlands, Sicily and Naples. He abdicated in favour of his son LOUIS in January 1746, but the boy, only seventeen years old, died on September 6. Philip took back the crown for 22 more years.

**FERDINAND VI,** 'The Wise' (1712-1759), reigned 1746-1759. He married the dominant Barbara of Portugal, who died in 1758 and he followed her, insane, less than two years later.

**CHARLES III** (1716-1788), reigned 1759-1788. The brother of FERDINAND and fifth son of PHILIP V, he was King of the Two Sicilies, King of Naples and Duke of Parma. He built the Prado, in Madrid. His efforts to reform the Church in Spain, resulted in the expulsion of the Jesuits.

**CHARLES IV** (1748-1819), reigned 1788-1808. He was the second son of CHARLES III and had a greater affinity to painters than ships. Thus, he was Goya's patron, but failed to prevent the English, under Nelson, destroying his fleet at Trafalgar, in 1805. His wife, Maria Louisa, ran rings around him and was flauntingly faithless with the politician, Godoy. It was Godoy's despicable peace with France that eventually led to Charles's first abdication in March, 1808. After less than three months, during which the hapless twenty-four-year-old FERDINAND VII was on the throne, Charles restored himself. He stayed until the end of 1808, when he handed over to NAPOLEON.

**JOSEPH BONAPARTE** (1768-1844), reigned 1808-1813.

NAPOLEON's elder brother, he was also King of Naples. He made little impression on Spain and was deposed.

**FERDINAND VII** (1784-1833), 1813-1833. The eldest (surviving) son of CHARLES IV, he had been a prisoner of the French, an experience which coloured his subsequent behaviour. He ruled despotically and foolishly, losing the South American colonies in 1820. From none of his four wives could he produce a son, so he changed the laws of succession in order that his daughter, ISABELLA II, could become Queen Regnant. Such legislative manipulation infuriated his brother Charles and the *Carlist Wars* began.

**ISABELLA II** (1830-1904), reigned 1833-1868. The daughter of FERDINAND, she was the unwitting cause of the *Carlist Wars*. Though only thirteen, she assumed control of the Government in 1843. As if matters were not already difficult enough for her, in 1846 she married her half-witted, impotent cousin, Don Francisco de Bourbon and revolt raised its ugly head. She was deposed in a coup, led by an ex-lover, Serrano.

**AMADEUS** (1820-1890), reigned 1870-1873. His rule followed a two-year regency. The second son of VICTOR EMANUEL II of Italy, he was elected King of Spain. Kingship was not to his liking and he abdicated as soon as he could.

A republic was declared in February 1873 only to end, five presidents later, in December 1874.

**ALFONSO XII** (1857-1885), reigned 1874-1885. He was ISABELLA's son, but by whom? He died without an heir.

**MARIA CHRISTINA** (1858-1929), reigned 1885-1886. Three months pregnant by ALFONSO when he died, she filled in as a 'child-bearing Regent' for six months. She was tactful and politically capable. Her son was born into a much more stable Spain on May 17, 1886.

**ALFONSO XIII** (1886-1941) reigned 1886-1931. He was a true courtier and obviously something of a curiosity. (The last time a child had been *born* a king was in 1316 in France, when LOUIS X died five months before his short-lived son, JOHN, was born.) Alfonso's life was one of nervous excitement. In 1906, he married Queen Victoria's granddaughter, Princess Ena of Battenberg. They narrowly escaped being killed when a bomb, intended for the royal couple, killed the horses drawing the bridal carriage away from the church after the wedding ceremony. The assassination attempt was only one of several. In 1931, civil war threatened when the Republicans gained a majority. Alfonso left the country, though he refused to abdicate. (General Franco, who became the Spanish dictator in October 1936, reinstated the king as a 'private citizen' and restored his confiscated property.) He never went back to Spain alive; he died in Rome in February 1941.

**JUAN CARLOS** (born 1938), his reign began in 1975. He was ALFONSO XIII's grandson and restored after Franco's death (though Spain was theoretically restored as a kingdom in March 1947). Juan Carlos was created the Prince of Spain in 1961 and officially declared

heir to the throne in 1971. He married Sophia, daughter of King PAUL of Greece and their third child, Philip, born in 1968, is heir to the throne.

# SWEDEN

Written Swedish history can only be relied on from the tenth century AD, though saga and legend provide a colourful past record long before then. The Skoldung family, followed by the Folkungs in the mid-thirteenth century, occupied the throne, which was united with both Denmark and Norway by Queen MARGARET of Denmark in 1387. Power ebbed and flowed until revolt brought the Vasa family to the top of the tree and they created a powerful Sweden. The Wittelsbachs, who succeeded them, suffered badly and, in 1751, a weakened country came under the Oldenburgs. They lasted until 1818, when the ex-Marshall Bernadotte, a Frenchman who had been chosen as Crown Prince, became KARL XIV. His family still occupies the throne.

Capital *STOCKHOLM*; currency *krona*

**OLAF SKOTKONUNG,** 'The Infant' (died 1022), reigned 995-1022. Prior to Olaf, the kings had been styled 'Kings of Upsal'. He united the Swedes with the Goths and during his reign Christianity was spread through the newly-created Swedish kingdom.

**ANUND JAKOB** (died 1050), the son of Olaf, he reigned 1022-1050.

**EMUND** (died 1060), reigned 1050-1060. ANUND's half-brother, called 'The Old', he actually *was* older than Anund.

**STENKIL RAGNVALDSON** (died 1066), reigned 1060-1066. He was the son-in-law of EDMUND and a noble from Vastergotland. An interregnum, lasting until 1078, followed.

**HALSTEN** (died 1099), reigned 1079-1099. STENKIL's son, he was a co-ruler with INGE and possibly with BLOT SVEN.

**INGE I** (died 1112), reigned 1080-1112. Until 1099, with one short break, he shared the throne with his brother, HALSTEN. He was overthrown by BLOT SVEN, but later killed him and returned to the throne.

**BLOT SVEN** (died 1083), reigned 1081-1083. He was probably the brother-in-law of INGE, whom he overthrew when leading a recrudescence of pagan feeling against national Christianity.

**PHILIP** (died 1118), reigned 1112-1118. INGE's son, he co-ruled with his brother.

**INGE II** (1125), reigned 1112-1125. He shared the throne with PHILIP.

**MAGNUS I** (died 1134), reigned 1129-1134. He was the son of NIELS of

Denmark by a daughter of INGE I.

**SVERKER I** (died 1156), reigned 1134–1156. He consolidated the union between Goths and Swedes, begun by OLAF some 150 years before. Sverker was one step out of the family lineage, being BLOT SVEN's grandson.

**ERIC IX,** St Eric (died 1160), reigned 1156–1160. He tried to convert Finland to Christianity, but only succeeded in getting himself killed at Upsala by an invading Danish prince leading a band of Swedish rebels. His memory was perpetuated by his son, Eric, and he was canonized, becoming Sweden's patron saint. His saintly and kingly record both leave room for doubt.

**MAGNUS II** (died 1161), the great-grandson of INGE I, reigned 1160–1161.

**KARL VII** (died 1167), reigned 1161–1167. The son of SVERKER I, he was killed by his cousin KNUT I.

**KNUT I,** Ericssen (died 1196), reigned 1176–1196. He was the first of three kings of the House of Jedvardssen.

**SVERKER II** (died 1210), reigned 1196–1208. The son of KARL VII, he was deposed by KNUT's son ERIC.

**ERIK X** (died 1216), son of KNUT I, reigned 1208–1216.

**JOHN I,** Sverkerssen (died 1229), reigned 1216–1222. Like his father, SVERKER II, he was deposed.

**ERIK XI** (died 1250), reigned 1222–1250. The last of the Jedvardssens, he was deposed by Knut II (of very doubtful origin) in 1229. He was returned to the throne in 1234.

**VALDEMAR I** (1238–1302), reigned 1250–1275. He was the son of ERIC XI's sister and, as he was only twelve years old on his accession, his father, Birger Jarl, ruled for him. Birger was one of the great medieval statesmen and has often been called 'King' by historians, though he never assumed the title. He founded Stockholm and ruled Sweden autocratically. His lasting achievements were the measures he instituted which led the way to the abolishment of serfdom. MAGNUS, who deposed Valdemar, extended Birger's successes.

**MAGNUS III,** Ladulas (1240–1290), reigned 1275–1290. He was the brother of VALDEMAR, whom he deposed. He set about the slightly risky process of creating a number of almost independent Swedish duchies.

**BIRGER** (1280–1321), reigned 1290–1318. He was the son of MAGNUS and so grandson of Birger Jarl, but he was not 'Birger II' as he has sometimes been erroneously styled. He was usurped by his brothers Erik and Valdemar, though they never formally assumed kingship.

**MAGNUS IV,** Smek (1316–1374), reigned 1319–1365. The nephew of BIRGER, he had an 'on-off' reign until his deposition in 1365. In 1356 he was joined by ERIK XII, who co-ruled with him for two years. He was also MAGNUS VII of Norway.

**ERIK XII** (1339–1359), reigned 1356–1359. He co-ruled with his father, MAGNUS, whom he forced into co-operation.

**ALBERT OF MECKLENBURG** (1340–1412), reigned 1365–1389. He was the son of a sister of MAGNUS IV. He was put up, as a puppet

king, by a group of nobles. They soon discovered the puppet did not respond to their manipulation, but had a mind of his own. He was deposed by the now wiser group of nobles and replaced by Queen MARGARET of Denmark.

The Danish monarchs ruled over Sweden until 1523. The list which follows shows their dates of accession only and more detail will be found under Denmark.

**MARGARET,** 1389 (1387 in Norway)
**ERIC XIII,** 1412
**CHRISTOPHER,** 1440
**CHARLES VIII,** 1448, deposed
**CHRISTIAN I,** 1457
**CHARLES VIII** resumed the throne in 1464.
Interregnum, 1470, under a regent, Sten Sture, the Elder
**JOHN II,** 1497, deposed
Interregnum, 1501, under three different Stures
**CHRISTIAN II,** 1520, deposed

**GUSTAV I** (1496-1560), reigned 1523-1560. A man who had been brought up to mistrust the Danes and all things Danish, he was taken prisoner to Denmark by King CHRISTIAN in 1516. He returned to his native land and, between 1521-1523, proceeded to expel the Danes. He was crowned, as an elected king, on June 6, 1523. He broke with the *Hanseatic League* and, despite a stern, nearly cruel style of kingship, created a strong Swedish monarchy. He was an imposing figure with '...a ruddy countenance...and a body as fitly and well proportioned as any painter could have painted it'.

**ERIC XIV** (1533-1577), reigned 1560-1568. He was GUSTAV's elder son (by one of his three marriages) and the second king of the Vasa dynasty. Eric disposed of the Stures, quarrelled with his half-brothers and made his mistress Queen Consort. Not popular (understandably) he was deposed, when it was alleged he was insane. He was probably as sane as his accusers.

**JOHN III** (1537-1592), reigned 1568-1592. The brother of ERIC XIV, he was theologically inclined but dynastically weak.

**SIGISMUND** (1566-1637), reigned 1592-1599. The son of JOHN III, he became a Catholic and was elected King of Poland. He was deposed.

**CHARLES IX** (1550-1611), JOHN's brother, reigned 1599-1611. Having deposed his nephew SIGISMUND, Charles, by using unpopular means, began to bring the country back into line with his Calvinistic views. He also marched the Swedish army as far as Moscow and the Russian throne was offered to his son, GUSTAV. He attacked Poland, Denmark and Finland, leaving three nicely simmering wars for his son to cope with when, unmourned, he died aged 61.

**GUSTAV ADOLF II** (1594-1632), reigned 1611-1632. The son of CHARLES IX, he was a brilliant general, a fluent Latinist and was possessed with foresight. His involvement in the *Thirty Years War* had a long-term non-military consquence: Protestantism was unshakeably established in North Germany. He created a small empire for Sweden

and opportunities for the country it did not have the ability to exploit. He was killed fighting the Germans at the *Battle of Lutzen*.

**CHRISTINA** (1626-1689), reigned 1632-1654. She was only six when her father GUSTAV was killed and the fine Swedish statesman, Axel Oxenstierna, acted as Regent. When Christina was allowed to act for herself, she advanced Swedish awareness of culture and depleted the treasury. Illegally, she became a Catholic and was averse to any attentions paid by potential suitors. 'Her countenance was sprightly, but somewhat pale...and though her person was of smaller size, yet her mien and carriage was very noble.' She refused to marry, abdicated and lived in exile in Rome, where Scarlatti and Bernini were amongst her friends.

**CHARLES X** (1622-1660), reigned 1654-1660. Prince Carl of the Palatinate, he was grandson of CHARLES IX. His short reign was warlike, but otherwise undramatic.

**CHARLES XI** (1655-1697), reigned 1660-1697. His widowed mother was one of six regents. He restored the armed forces and reduced the national debt from about 44 million to 15 million *thalers*.

**CHARLES XII** (1682-1718), reigned 1697-1718. He was declared of age when only fifteen, although 'addicted to wild pranks and perilous sports'. He was, despite such high spirits, a great patriot. He lost the *Battle of Poltava* to the Russians (having defeated Poland) and was forced into exile from 1709-1714. He was killed by a bullet whilst in Norway looking for allies to help him fight back against Russian-aided Denmark.

**ULRIKA** (1688-1741), reigned 1718-1720. CHARLES's sister and married to Frederick of Hesse Cassel, she was elected to the throne. Two years later, she abdicated and passed the crown to her husband.

**FREDERICK** (1676-1751), reigned 1720-1751. When he acquired the throne, upon his wife, ULRIKE's, abdication, he found the country to be bankrupt.

**ADOLF FREDERICK** (born 1710), reigned 1751-1771. The Prince of Holstein-Gottorp, he was elected king as a result of pressure from a political group called *The Hats*. His wife wore the breeches, however.

**GUSTAV III** (1746-1792), reigned 1771-1792. During his reign the government 'nationalised' the distillation of alcohol, a pastime which had previously been a source of pleasure and profit to the peasants. His mother tried to interfere during Gustav's reign as she had done during his father, ADOLF's. The king was murdered at an Opera House Ball in Stockholm, by an army captain.

**GUSTAV IV** (1772-1837), reigned 1792-1809. He was the son of GUSTAV III. His stubbornness led to an army coup in March 1809. The king was taken prisoner and forced to abdicate.

**CHARLES VIII** (1748-1818), reigned 1809-1818. An uncle of GUSTAV IV, he came to the throne after a three-month interregnum. Charles was childless and in 1810 he 'adopted' a French Marshal, Count Jean-Baptiste Bernadotte, who was 47 years old. Bernadotte was a shrewd man and, in any case, Sweden wished to keep the friendship of the all-victorious NAPOLEON. Bernadotte changed his name to

Charles John and became the Crown Prince. A special ordinance was passed so that he became heir to the throne.

**CHARLES XIV** (1763-1844), reigned 1818-1844. He was the first Bernadotte. He dropped all Swedish claims to Finland and managed to acquire Norway as compensation. Considering he never learned to speak Swedish, Charles/Bernadotte ruled the country well, if a little cautiously.

**OSCAR I** (1799-1859), reigned 1844-1859. A more gifted, if less strong-minded man than his father, CHARLES, Oscar pursued a number of lines of small reforms. During his reign, the decision to build the main railway lines as nationalised concerns, was taken.

**CHARLES XV,** (1826-1972), reigned 1859-1872. He had been virtually ruler of the country for the last two years of his father, OSCAR's reign.

**OSCAR II** (1829-1907), reigned 1872-1907. The third son of OSCAR I, he was a writer and a musician who made his feelings about his dual kingdom of Sweden and Norway perfectly clear. Trouble brewed and Oscar finally laid down his Norwegian crown on October 26, 1905.

**GUSTAV V** (1858-1950), reigned 1907-1950. The dignified and retiring eldest son of OSCAR II, he kept Sweden neutral during both the World Wars.

**GUSTAV VI,** Adolf (1882-1973), reigned 1950-1973. He was an archaeologist, an expert on porcelain and the last Swedish king to have any real constitutional power.

**CARL XVI,** Gustav (born 1946), his reign began in 1973. The grandson of GUSTAV VI, he married a commoner, Fraülein Renate Sommerlath, in 1976. They have three children.

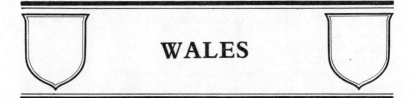

# WALES

After the Romans withdrew from Britain (a gradual evacuation, completed by AD 436) a number of Welsh principalities were formed, which were briefly united by Rhodri in the ninth century. He was killed by the Angles in 878. The Norman kings never really subdued Wales, but finally, in 1542, the country was formally joined with England.

Capital (today) *CARDIFF*

**LLYWELYN AP SEISYLL** (died 1023), reigned 999-1023. He was King of Deheubarth and great-grandson of Anarawd, who had been Prince of Gwynedd 878-916. Gwynedd was the northern 'kingdom' of the country and embraced the region of Snowdonia.

**RHYDDERCH AB IESTYN** (died 1033), reigned 1023-1033. He was also King of Deheubarth.

**IAGO AB IDWAL** (died 1039), reigned 1033-1039. He was the great-grandson of Idwal Foel, who had been Prince of Gwynedd after Anarawd. Iago's own men split his head open with an axe.

**GRUFFYDD AP LLYWELYN** (died 1063), reigned 1039-1063. The son of LLYWELYN, he became King of All Wales after his victory at the battle of Tywi. He, too, was murdered.

**BLEDDYN AP CYFYN** (died 1075), reigned 1063-1075. He was a half-brother to GRUFFYDD and a grandson, through a daughter, to Maredudd of Gwynedd (d.999).

**TRAHAERN AP CARADOG** (died 1081), reigned 1075-1081. He was a cousin of BLEDDYN and yet another victim of a murderous plot.

**GRUFFYDD AP CYNAN** (1055-1137), reigned 1081-1137. The ruler of north Wales, he spent the first twelve years of his reign imprisoned in England by order of King WILLIAM, 'The Conqueror'. His imprisonment continued during the first six years of the reign of WILLIAM, 'Rufus'. He was succeeded by his sons, the younger one first, but they were styled as princes not kings.

 # WESTPHALIA

This kingdom was created by the Emperor NAPOLEON in 1807. It formed nearly all Hesse-Cassel, all Brunswick and large parts of Prussia, Hannover and Saxony. It ceased to exist in 1813, after the battle of Leipsic.

Capital *CASSEL*

**JEROME BONAPARTE** (1784-1860), reigned 1807-1813. Like his elder brother, NAPOLEON, Jerome was born in Ajaccio, Corsica. He was the most dissolute of the Emperor's dissolute bunch of siblings. He married a Miss Elizabeth Patterson of Baltimore in 1803 but, having been created king of a puppet kingdom, he took Princess Catherine of Wurttemberg as his consort. After he fled in 1813, he married Giustina Pecori – for her money.

# WURTTEMBERG

It was formerly called Wirtemberg. A southern German kingdom and a state in the Empire, it was bounded by Bavaria on three sides and Lake Constance in the south. Having been ruled by the same family for over 700 years, it became a kingdom on December 26, 1805.

Capital *STUTTGART*

**FREDERICK I** (1754–1816), reigned 1805–1816. Having become Duke Frederick II when his father died in 1797, he was elector in 1803 and king two years later. As a second wife, he took Charlotte, the Princess Royal, daughter of GEORGE III of Great Britain. He formed an advantageous alliance with NAPOLEON and gained further territory. However, in 1813, he deserted the Emperor and joined the Allies.

**WILLIAM I** (1781–1864), reigned 1816–1864. The son of FREDERICK (by his first wife) William abolished serfdom in the kingdom. In 1862 he became the oldest living sovereign, dying two years later, four months before his eighty-third birthday.

**CHARLES** (1823–1891), reigned 1864–1891. WILLIAM's only son, he saw his country absorbed by the German Empire only seven years after he came to the throne. Despite the 'takeover', Wurttemberg controlled a number of its own services autonomously.

**WILLIAM II** (1848–1921), reigned 1891–1918. He was FREDERICK's great-grandson. The constitution was revised in 1906, but the revolution broke out soon after the First World War and William resigned. A republican constitution was adopted in 1919.

# YUGOSLAVIA

The country became a republic in November 1945. It is made up of the Socialist Republics of Serbia, Croatia, Slovenia, Montenegro, Bosnia and Herzegovina, Macedonia. It is one of the more 'free-thinking' satellite countries of the communist bloc.

Capital *BELGRADE* currency *dinar*

**PETER I** (1844-1921), reigned 1918-1921. The son of Alexander, Prince of Serbia, Peter lived in exile from 1858. He joined the French army in 1870 and later fought against the Turks under the name of Mrkonjić. He was elected the first King of the Serbs, Croats and Slovenes, having been King of Serbia since 1903. Ill health required him to entrust the Crown Prince with the regency and he died in retirement at Topola.

**ALEXANDER I** (1888-1934), reigned 1921-1934. Dissident elements within the kingdom forced him to adopt a dictatorial role. The unpopularity this created, led to his assassination in Marseilles by a gunman hired by a secret society of Croatian nationals. His Queen, Marie, was the great-granddaughter of Queen VICTORIA of Great Britain.

**PETER II** (1923-1970) reigned 1934-1945. He was exiled when Tito came to power and left his country promising to '...liberate Yugo-Slavia from tyranny...'. This, of course, he could not do. Eventually he moved to the United States and died in Denver, Colorado. (His son, born in 1945, uses the family name of Karageorgevitch. Until 1984, he was the fifty-fourth in line of succession to the throne of Great Britain.)

# Conversion Table

## Chronology of Monarchs

# The names of monarchs used in the book showing their national variants

| Name as in Text | Denmark | France | Germany | Hungary | Italy |
|---|---|---|---|---|---|
| ALBERT | | | Albrecht | | |
| ALEXANDER | | | | | |
| ALFONSO | | | Alfons | | |
| AMADEUS | | | | | |
| ANDREW | | | | Andras | |
| ANTHONY | | | | | |
| | | | | | |
| BEATRICE | | | | | |
| BLANCHE | | | | | |
| BOLESLAV | | | | | |
| | | | | | |
| CATHERINE | | | | | |
| CHARLES | | | Carl/Karl | | Carlo |
| CHRISTIAN | | | | | |
| CHRISTOPHER | | | | | |
| CONRAD | | | Konrad | | Corrado |
| CONSTANTINE | | | | | |
| CONSTANTINE TICH | | | | | |
| | | | | | |
| EDWARD | | | | | |
| ELEANOR | | | | | |
| ELIZABETH | | | | | |
| ERIK | | | | | |
| ERNEST-AUGUSTUS | | | | | |
| | | | | | |
| FEODOR | | | | | |
| FERDINAND | | | | | Ferdinando |
| FRANCIS | | François | Franz | Ferenc | Francesco |
| FRANCIS-PHOEBUS | | | | | |
| FREDERICK | Frederik | | Friedrich | | Federico |
| | | | | | |
| GEORGE | | | Georg | | |
| | | | | | |
| HENRY | | Henri | Heinrich | | Enrico |
| | | | | | |
| INGE | | | | | |
| | | | | | |
| JEROME | | | | | |
| | | | | | |
| JAMES | | | | | Giacomo |

| Norway Sweden | Poland | Russia | Spain | Other variants |
|---|---|---|---|---|
| | Olbracht | | | Albrekt (Bohemia) |
| | | Aleksandr | | Alexandros (Greece) |
| | | | | Afonso (Portugal) |
| | | | Amadeo | |
| | | | | Anton (Saxony) |
| | | | | Beatriz (Portugal) |
| | | | | Blanca (Navarre) |
| | Boleslaw | | | |
| | | Ekaterina | | |
| Carl/Karl Kristian Kristofer | | | Carlos | |
| | | | | Konstantinos (Greece) |
| | | | | Konstantin Tikh (Bulgaria) |
| | | | | Duarte (Portugal) |
| | | | | Eléonore (Navarre) |
| | | Elisaveta | | |
| Eirik | | | | Ernst-August (Hanover) |
| | | Fyodor | | |
| | | | Fernando | Ferrante (Naples) |
| | | | | Francisco-Febo (Navarre) |
| Fredrik | | | | |
| | | | | Giorgios (Greece) Jiri (Bohemia) Georgi (Bulgaria) |
| | | | Enrique | Enrique (Portugal) |
| Ingi | | | | |
| | | | | Hieronymus (Westphalia) |
| | | | Jaime | |

# CONVERSION TABLE

| Name as in Text | Denmark | France | Germany | Hungary | Italy |
|---|---|---|---|---|---|
| JOACHIM | | | | | |
| MURAT | | | | | |
| JOANNA | | | | | Giovanna |
| JOHN | Hans | Jean | Johann | János | Giovanni |
| JOSEPH | | | | Jószef | Giuseppe |
| KASIMIR | | | | | |
| KNUT | Knud | | | | |
| LADISLAS | | | | | |
| LADISLAV | | | | Laszló | |
| LOTHAIR | | | Lothar | | |
| LOUIS | | | | Lajos | Lodovico |
| MANUEL | | | | | |
| MARGARET | Margarethe | | | | |
| MARTIN | | | | | Martino |
| MATTHIAS | | | | Mátyás | |
| MICHAEL | | | | | |
| MIESZKO | | | | | |
| NICHOLAS | | | | | |
| OLAF | | | | | |
| OSCAR | | | | | |
| OTHO | | | | | |
| PAUL | | | | | |
| PETER | | | | | Pierro |
| PHILIP | | Philippe | Philipp | | Filippo |
| PREMISLAS | | | | | |
| ROGER | | | | | Ruggiero |
| RUDOLPH | | Rodolphe | Rodolf | | |
| SEBASTIAN | | | | | |
| SIGISMUND | | | | | |
| STEPHEN | | | | István | |
| SVERRE | | | | | |
| THEOBALD | | Thibaut | | | |
| THEODORE | | | Theodor | | |
| VACLAV | | | Wenzel | | |
| VICTOR-EMMANUEL | | | | | Vittorio-Emanuele |
| VLADISLAV | | | | | |
| WILLIAM | | | Wilhelm | | Guglielmo |

| Norway Sweden | Poland | Russia | Spain | Other variants |
|---|---|---|---|---|
| Johann | Jan | | Juana Juan | Gioacchino Napoleone (Naples) João (Portugal) Ján (Bohemia) |
| Cnud | Kazimierz | | | |
| | | | | Laslo (Naples) Vladislav (Bohemia) |
| | Ludwik | | Luis | Ludvik (Bohemia) |
| Margrete/ Margaretha | | | | Manoel (Portugal) |
| | Michal Mieczyslaw | Mikhail | | Mihail (Bulgaria) Mihai (Romania) |
| | | Nikolai | | |
| Olav/Olof Oskar | | | | |
| | | | | Othon (Greece) |
| | | Pavel | Felipe | Pavlos (Greece) Petur (Bulgaria) Felippe (Portugal) Premysl (Bohemia) |
| | Zygmunt Stefan | | | Sebastão (Portugal) Stepan (Serbia) |
| Sverrir | | | | |
| | | | | Todor (Bulgaria) |
| | Waclaw | | | |
| | Wladyslaw | | | |
| | | | | Willem (Netherlands) |

# List of monarchs from AD 978 to the present

KEY
HRE  Emperor of the Holy Roman Empire
(J)  Jointly, as a co-ruler
(AK)  Anti-king
(LK)  Last king of that kingdom
(LQ)  Last queen of that kingdom

| Date of Accession | Age at Accession | Monarch | Kingdom(s) | Date Reign Ended |
|---|---|---|---|---|
| 978 | 10 | ETHELRED | England | 1016 |
| 983 | 3 | OTTO | HRE | 1002 |
| 986 | – | SVEN | Denmark | 1014 |
| 992 | 26 | BOLESLAV I | Poland | 1025 |
| 993 | – | RUDOLPH III | Burgundy | 1032 |
| 995 | 31 | OLAF | Norway | 1000 |
| 995 | – | OLAF, Skotkonung | Sweden | 1022 |
| 996 | 16 | OTTO III | Germany, HRE | 1002 |
| 996 | 26 | ROBERT II | France | 1031 |
| 999 | – | LLYWELYN AP SEISYLL | Wales | 1023 |
| 999 | 5 | ALFONSO | Leon and Asturias | 1028 |
| 999 | | Silvester II (Gebert) was elected Pope. He was popularly supposed to have introduced Arabic numerals into Europe and to have invented clocks. | | |
| 1000 | 8 | SANCHO III | Navarre | 1035 |
| 1000 | 23 | STEPHEN I | Hungary | 1038 |
| 1002 | 74 | BRIAN, Boruma | Ireland | 1014 |
| 1002 | 29 | HENRY II | Germany, HRE | 1024 |
| 1005 | 53 | MALCOLM II | Scotland | 1034 |
| 1014 | – | HARALD II | Denmark | 1019 |
| 1014 | | BRIAN, King of Ireland was killed at the *Battle of Clontarf* (April 23) whilst defeating the Danes. | | |
| 1014 | – | MAEL, Sechmaill, II | Ireland | 1022 |
| 1015 | 20 | SAINT OLAF II | Norway | 1030 |
| 1016 | 27 | EDMUND | England | 1016 |
| 1016 | 22 | CANUTE | Norway, England, Denmark | 1035 |
| 1022 | – | ANUND JACOB | Sweden | 1050 |
| 1023 | – | RHYDDERCH AB IESTYN | Wales | 1033 |
| 1024 | 34 | CONRAD II | Germany, HRE | 1039 |
| 1025 | 35 | MIESZKO II | Poland | 1034 |
| 1028 | 12 | VERMUDO III | Leon and Asturias | 1037 |
| 1031 | 20 | HENRI I | France | 1060 |
| 1033 | – | IAGO AB IDWAL III | Wales | 1039 |
| 1033 | – | CONRAD II (LK) | Burgundy | 1039 |
| 1034 | 18 | KASIMIR I | Poland | 1058 |
| 1034 | – | DUNCAN I | Scotland | 1040 |

| Date of Accession | Age at Accession | Monarch | Kingdom(s) | Date Reign Ended |
|---|---|---|---|---|
| 1035 | 11 | MAGNUS I (J) | Norway | 1047 |
| 1035 | 18 | HAROLD | England, Denmark | 1040 |
| 1035 | – | GARCIA IV | Navarre | 1054 |
| 1035 | – | FERDINAND | Leon and Castile | 1065 |
| 1035 | – | RAMIRO I | Aragon | 1063 |
| 1038 | 26 | PETER | Hungary | 1047 |
| 1039 | 22 | HENRY III | Germany, HRE | 1056 |
| 1039 | – | GRUFFYDD AP LLYWELYN | Wales | 1063 |
| 1040 | – | MACBETH | Scotland | 1057 |
| 1040 | 22 | HARDICANUTE | England, Denmark | 1042 |
| 1041 | – | ABA | Hungary | 1044 |
| 1042 | 38 | EDWARD, 'The Confessor' | England | 1066 |
| 1042 | 24 | MAGNUS | Denmark, Norway | 1047 |
| 1047 | 27 | SVEN II | Denmark | 1076 |
| 1047 | 34 | ANDREW I | Hungary | 1060 |
| 1047 | 15 | HARALD III (J) | Norway | 1066 |
| 1050 | – | EMUND | Sweden | 1060 |
| 1054 | 16 | SANCHO IV | Navarre | 1076 |
| 1056 | 6 | HENRY IV | Germany, HRE | 1106 |
| 1057 | – | LULACH | Scotland | 1058 |
| 1058 | 27 | MALCOLM III | Scotland | 1093 |
| 1058 | 19 | BOLESLAV II | Poland | 1079 |
| 1060 | – | STENKIL | Sweden | 1066 |
| 1060 | 44 | BELA I | Hungary | 1063 |
| 1060 | 7 | PHILIPPE I | France | 1108 |

| 1061 | | POLAND overran HUNGARY | | |
|---|---|---|---|---|

| 1063 | 38 | BLEDDYN AP CYFYN (LK) | Wales | 1075 |
|---|---|---|---|---|
| 1063 | 26 | SANCHO IV | Aragon | 1094 |
| 1064 | 12 | SALOMON | Hungary | 1074 |
| 1065 | 27 | SANCHO II | Castile | 1072 |

| 1066 | | The *Battle of Hastings* was fought on October 14. William of Normandy defeated and killed HAROLD II of England. | | |
|---|---|---|---|---|

| 1066 | 44 | HAROLD II | England | 1066 |
|---|---|---|---|---|
| 1066 | 39 | WILLIAM I | England | 1087 |
| 1066 | 18 | MAGNUS (J) | Norway | 1069 |
| 1066 | 16 | OLAF III (J) | Norway | 1093 |
| 1072 | 32 | ALFONSO VI | Leon and Castile | 1109 |
| 1072 | – | TURLOUGH O'BRIEN | Ireland | 1086 |
| 1074 | – | GEZA I | Hungary | 1077 |
| 1075 | – | TRAHAERN AP CARADOG | Wales | 1081 |
| 1076 | 39 | SANCHO V | Navarre | 1094 |
| 1076 | – | HARALD III | Denmark | 1080 |
| 1077 | 37 | LADISLAS | Hungary | 1095 |
| 1079 | – | HALSTEN (J) | Sweden | 1099 |
| 1079 | 36 | VLADISLAV I | Poland | 1102 |
| 1080 | – | INGE I (J) | Sweden | 1112 |
| 1080 | – | KNUT IV | Denmark | 1086 |

| Date of Accession | Age at Accession | Monarch | Kingdom(s) | Date Reign Ended |
|---|---|---|---|---|
| 1081 | 26 | GRUFFYDD AP CYNAN (LK) | Wales | 1137 |
| 1081 | – | BLOT SVEN | Sweden | 1083 |
| 1081 | | WILLIAM, 'The Conqueror' of England invaded Wales. | | |
| 1086 | – | MURTOUGH O'BRIEN | Ireland | 1114 |
| 1086 | – | OLAF I | Denmark | 1095 |
| 1087 | 31 | WILLIAM II | England | 1100 |
| 1090 | – | DONNELL O'LOUGHLIN | Ireland | 1118 |
| 1093 | 33 | DONALD III (J) | Scotland | 1094 |
| 1093 | 20 | MAGNUS III | Norway | 1103 |
| 1093 | – | CONRAD (AK) | HRE | 1098 |
| 1094 | 34 | DUNCAN II | Scotland | 1094 |
| 1094 | – | EDMUND (J) | Scotland | 1097 |
| 1094 | 26 | PEDRO | Navarre, Aragon | 1104 |
| 1095 | 25 | KOLOMAN | Hungary | 1116 |
| 1095 | 39 | ERIK I | Denmark | 1103 |
| 1097 | 23 | EDGAR | Scotland | 1107 |
| 1099 | | On July 15, the First Crusade ended with the capture of Jerusalem and Godfrey of Bouillon was established as king. | | |
| 1100 | | The estimated population of Europe was 44 million. | | |
| 1100 | 32 | HENRY I | England | 1135 |
| 1102 | 17 | BOLESLAV III | Poland | 1138 |
| 1103 | 12 | OLAF, Magnusson (J) | Norway | 1115 |
| 1103 | 15 | EYESTEIN I (J) | Norway | 1122 |
| 1103 | 13 | SIGURD I (J) | Norway | 1130 |
| 1103 | – | ERIK | Denmark | 1104 |
| 1104 | – | ALFONSO I | Navarre, Aragon | 1134 |
| 1104 | 41 | NIELS | Denmark | 1134 |
| 1106 | 25 | HENRY V | HRE, Germany | 1125 |
| 1107 | 29 | ALEXANDER I | Scotland | 1124 |
| 1108 | 27 | LOUIS VI | France | 1137 |
| 1109 | 29 | URRACA | Leon and Castile | 1126 |
| 1112 | – | PHILIP (J) | Sweden | 1118 |
| 1112 | 18 | ALFONSO I | Portugal | 1185 |
| 1116 | 14 | STEPHEN II | Hungary | 1131 |
| 1118 | – | INGE II | Sweden | 1125 |
| 1118 | – | TURLOUGH O'CONNOR | Ireland | 1156 |
| 1124 | 44 | SAINT DAVID | Scotland | 1153 |
| 1125 | 50 | LOTHAIR III | Germany, HRE | 1137 |
| 1126 | 22 | ALFONSO VII | Leon and Castile | 1157 |
| 1129 | – | MAGNUS I | Sweden | 1134 |
| 1130 | 15 | MAGNUS IV | Norway | 1135 |
| 1130 | 35 | ROGER II | Sicily, Naples | 1154 |
| 1131 | 23 | BELA II | Hungary | 1141 |
| 1134 | – | GARCIA V | Navarre | 1150 |
| 1134 | – | SVERKER I | Sweden | 1156 |
| 1134 | – | RAMIRO II | Aragon | 1137 |

| Date of Accession | Age at Accession | Monarch | Kingdom(s) | Date Reign Ended |
|---|---|---|---|---|
| 1134 | – | ERIK II | Denmark | 1137 |
| 1135 | 32 | HARALD IV | Norway | 1136 |
| 1135 | 39 | STEPHEN | England | 1154 |
| 1136 | 2 | SIGURD II (J) | Norway | 1155 |
| 1136 | 1 | INGE I (J) | Norway | 1161 |
| 1137 | – | ERIK III | Denmark | 1147 |
| 1137 | 1 | PETRONILLA | Aragon | 1163 |
| 1137 | 17 | LOUIS VII | France | 1180 |
| 1138 | 45 | CONRAD III | Germany, HRE | 1152 |
| 1138 | 34 | VLADISLAV II | Poland | 1145 |
| 1141 | 10 | GEZA II | Hungary | 1161 |
| 1142 | 17 | EYESTEIN II | Norway | 1157 |
| 1146 | 19 | BOLESLAV IV | Poland | 1173 |
| 1147 | – | SVEN III | Denmark | 1157 |
| 1150 | – | SANCHO VI | Navarre | 1194 |
| 1152 | 29 | FREDERICK I | Germany, HRE | 1190 |

| 1152 | Nicholas Breakspear, the Vatican Legate and to become the only English Pope (as Adrian IV) founded the Archbishopric of Trondheim in Norway. |
|---|---|

| 1153 | 11 | MALCOLM IV | Scotland | 1165 |
|---|---|---|---|---|
| 1154 | 34 | WILLIAM I | Sicily | 1166 |
| 1154 | 21 | HENRY II | England | 1189 |
| 1156 | – | MURTOUGH | Ireland | 1166 |
| 1156 | – | SAINT ERIK IX | Sweden | 1160 |

| 1156 | Pope Adrian 'permitted' HENRY II of England to invade Ireland. |
|---|---|

| 1157 | 26 | VALDEMAR | Denmark | 1182 |
|---|---|---|---|---|
| 1157 | 23 | SANCHO III | Castile | 1158 |
| 1157 | – | FERDINAND II | Leon | 1188 |
| 1158 | 3 | ALFONSO VIII | Leon and Castile | 1188 |
| 1160 | – | MAGNUS II | Sweden | 1161 |
| 1161 | – | KARL VII | Sweden | 1167 |
| 1161 | 14 | HAAKON II (J) | Norway | 1162 |
| 1161 | 6 | MAGNUS V | Norway | 1184 |
| 1161 | 13 | STEPHEN III | Hungary | 1172 |
| 1163 | 11 | ALFONSO II | Aragon | 1196 |
| 1165 | 22 | WILLIAM I | Scotland | 1214 |
| 1166 | 12 | WILLIAM II | Sicily | 1189 |
| 1166 | – | RORY O'CONNOR (LK) | Ireland | 1186 |
| 1167 | – | KNUT | Sweden | 1196 |

| 1167 | The *Lombard League* was formed. It consisted of the towns of Milan, Venice, Pavia and other important centres in northern Italy; uniting to resist the power of the German Emperor. |
|---|---|

| 1168 | – | STEPHEN I, Nemanya | Serbia | 1196 |
|---|---|---|---|---|
| 1172 | 22 | BELA III | Hungary | 1196 |
| 1173 | 47 | MIESZKO III | Poland | 1202 |

| Date of Accession | Age at Accession | Monarch | Kingdom(s) | Date Reign Ended |
|---|---|---|---|---|
| 1177 | 39 | KASIMIR II | Poland | 1194 |
| 1180 | 15 | PHILIPPE II | France | 1223 |
| 1181 | 19 | KNUT VI | Denmark | 1202 |
| 1184 | 34 | SVERRE | Norway | 1202 |
| 1185 | 31 | SANCHO I | Portugal | 1211 |
| 1187 | – | ASEN | Bulgaria | 1196 |
| 1188 | 22 | ALFONSO IX | Leon and Castile | 1230 |
| 1189 | 32 | RICHARD I | England | 1199 |
| 1189 | – | TANCRED | Sicily | 1194 |
| 1190 | 25 | HENRY VI | HRE, Germany | 1197 |
| 1191 | | On June 23, due to a total eclipse of the sun, stars were shining brightly over England at ten in the morning. | | |
| 1194 | 10 | WILLIAM III | Sicily | 1194 |
| 1194 | 29 | HENRY VI | Sicily, HRE, Germany | 1197 |
| 1194 | 9 | LESZEK I | Poland | 1227 |
| 1194 | – | SANCHO VI | Navarre | 1234 |
| 1196 | – | STEPHEN II, Nemanya | Serbia | 1227 |
| 1196 | – | SVERKER II | Sweden | 1208 |
| 1196 | 22 | EMERIC | Hungary | 1204 |
| 1196 | – | PETER (J) | Bulgaria | 1197 |
| 1196 | 22 | PEDRO II | Aragon | 1213 |
| 1197 | – | KALOJAN | Bulgaria | 1207 |
| 1197 | 4 | FREDERICK I | Sicily | 1250 |
| 1198 | 21 | PHILIP | HRE, Germany | 1208 |
| 1198 | 24 | OTTO IV | HRE | 1215 |
| 1198 | 48 | PREMISLAS I | Bohemia | 1230 |
| 1199 | 32 | JOHN | England | 1216 |
| 1200 | | The estimated population of Europe was about 58 million. | | |
| 1202 | 25 | HAAKON III | Norway | 1204 |
| 1202 | 32 | VALDEMAR II (J) | Denmark | 1241 |
| 1204 | 9 | INGE II | Norway | 1217 |
| 1204 | 5 | LADISLAS III | Hungary | 1205 |
| 1205 | 30 | ANDREW II | Hungary | 1235 |
| 1207 | – | BORIL | Bulgaria | 1218 |
| 1208 | 34 | OTTO IV | Germany, HRE | 1215 |
| 1208 | – | ERIK X | Sweden | 1216 |
| 1211 | 26 | ALFONSO II | Portugal | 1223 |
| 1212 | 18 | FREDERICK II | Sicily, HRE, Germany | 1250 |
| 1213 | 5 | JAMES I | Aragon | 1276 |
| 1214 | 16 | ALEXANDER II | Scotland | 1249 |
| 1214 | 11 | HENRY I | Castile | 1217 |
| 1215 | | On June 15, King JOHN of England was forced by his barons to sign the *Magna Carta* at Runnymede. | | |
| 1216 | – | JOHN | Sweden | 1222 |

| Date of Accession | Age at Accession | Monarch | Kingdom(s) | Date Reign Ended |
|---|---|---|---|---|
| 1216 | 9 | HENRY III | England | 1272 |
| 1217 | 3 | HAAKON IV | Norway | 1263 |
| 1217 | 17 | FERDINAND III | Leon and Castile | 1252 |
| 1218 | – | IVAN ASEN II | Bulgaria | 1241 |
| 1219 | | Gengis Khan invaded India. By the time he died in 1227, aged 65, his empire extended from the Black Sea to the Pacific. | | |
| 1222 | – | ERIK XI | Sweden | 1250 |
| 1223 | 14 | SANCHO | Portugal | 1248 |
| 1223 | 36 | LOUIS VIII | France | 1226 |
| 1226 | 11 | LOUIS IX | France | 1270 |
| 1227 | – | STEPHEN III, Radoslav | Serbia | 1234 |
| 1227 | 6 | BOLESLAV V | Poland | 1279 |
| 1230 | 25 | VACLAV I | Bohemia | 1253 |
| 1234 | – | STEPHEN IV, Vladislav | Serbia | 1243 |
| 1234 | 33 | THEOBALD | Navarre | 1253 |
| 1235 | 29 | BELA IV | Hungary | 1270 |
| 1241 | 25 | ERIK IV (J) | Denmark | 1250 |
| 1241 | – | KOLOMAN | Bulgaria | 1246 |
| 1243 | – | STEPHEN I, Urosh | Serbia | 1276 |
| 1246 | 42 | HENRY RASPE | HRE | 1247 |
| 1246 | – | MICHAEL ASEN | Bulgaria | 1257 |
| 1247 | 20 | WILLIAM (AK) | HRE | 1256 |
| 1248 | 38 | ALFONSO III | Portugal | 1279 |
| 1249 | 8 | ALEXANDER III | Scotland | 1286 |
| 1250 | 12 | VALDEMAR I | Sweden | 1275 |
| 1250 | 22 | CONRAD IV | HRE, Germany, Sicily | 1254 |
| 1250 | 32 | ABEL | Denmark | 1252 |
| 1252 | 31 | ALFONSO X | Leon and Castile | 1282 |
| 1252 | 33 | CHRISTOPHER I | Denmark | 1259 |
| 1253 | 46 | THEOBALD II | Navarre | 1270 |
| 1253 | 23 | PREMISLAS II | Bohemia | 1278 |
| 1257 | – | CONSTANTINE TICH | Bulgaria | 1277 |
| 1257 | 48 | RICHARD | HRE | 1272 |
| 1257 | 36 | ALFONSO X | HRE, Leon and Castile | 1273 |
| 1258 | 26 | MANFRED | Sicily | 1266 |
| 1259 | 10 | ERIK V | Denmark | 1286 |
| 1260 | | The capital city of Sweden, Stockholm was founded. | | |
| 1263 | 35 | MAGNUS VI | Norway | 1280 |
| 1265 | | In May, Dante Alighieri was born in Florence. He died in Ravenna fifty-six years later. | | |
| 1266 | 45 | CHARLES of Anjou | Sicily, Naples | 1282 |
| 1270 | 60 | HENRY CRASSUS I | Navarre | 1274 |
| 1270 | 41 | STEPHEN V | Hungary | 1272 |
| 1270 | 25 | PHILIPPE III | France | 1285 |

| Date of Accession | Age at Accession | Monarch | Kingdom(s) | Date Reign Ended |
|---|---|---|---|---|
| 1272 | 10 | LADISLAS IV | Hungary | 1290 |
| 1272 | 33 | EDWARD I | England | 1307 |
| 1273 | 55 | RUDOLF | HRE, Germany | 1291 |
| 1274 | 1 | JOANNA (J) | Navarre | 1305 |
| 1275 | 35 | MAGNUS III | Sweden | 1290 |
| 1276 | 40 | PEDRO III | Aragon | 1285 |
| 1276 | 33 | STEPHEN VI, Dragutin | Serbia | 1282 |
| 1278 | 7 | VACLAV II | Bohemia, Poland | 1305 |
| 1279 | | The University at Coimbra, Portugal, was founded. | | |
| 1279 | – | LESZEK II | Poland | 1289 |
| 1279 | 18 | DIONYSIUS | Portugal | 1325 |
| 1280 | 12 | ERIK II | Norway | 1299 |
| 1280 | – | GEORGE, Terter | Bulgaria | 1292 |
| 1282 | – | STEPHEN II, Urosh Milutin | Serbia | 1321 |
| 1282 | 46 | PEDRO I | Aragon, Sicily | 1285 |
| 1282 | 24 | SANCHO IV | Leon and Castile | 1295 |
| 1282 | | On March 30, the Sicilians, having become violently resentful toward the French citizens on the island, rose up (on Easter Monday) and slew an estimated 8,000 French residents in a massacre called the *Sicilian Vespers*. | | |
| 1285 | 20 | ALFONSO III | Aragon | 1291 |
| 1285 | 40 | CHARLES II | Naples | 1309 |
| 1285 | 15 | JAMES | Sicily | 1295 |
| 1285 | 17 | PHILIPPE IV | France | 1314 |
| 1286 | 4 | MARGARET | Scotland | 1290 |
| 1286 | 12 | ERIK VI | Denmark | 1319 |
| 1286 | | Konigsberg became the capital city of Prussia. | | |
| 1289 | 29 | VLADISLAV I | Poland | 1333 |
| 1290 | 10 | BIRGER II | Sweden | 1318 |
| 1290 | – | PRZEMISLAV | Poland | 1296 |
| 1290 | 26 | ANDREW III | Hungary | 1301 |
| 1291 | 31 | JAMES | Aragon | 1327 |
| 1291 | | The eighth (and last) Crusade ended with the Christians being driven out of Acre. | | |
| 1292 | 42 | JOHN BALLIOL | Scotland | 1296 |
| 1292 | 42 | ADOLF | HRE, Germany | 1298 |
| 1295 | 10 | FERDINAND IV | Leon and Castile | 1312 |
| 1295 | 23 | FREDERICK II | Sicily | 1337 |
| 1298 | – | THEODORE | Bulgaria | 1322 |
| 1298 | 48 | ALBERT I | Germany, HRE | 1308 |
| 1299 | 29 | HAAKON V | Norway | 1319 |
| 1300 | | The estimated population of Europe was about 79 million. | | |
| 1305 | – | OTTO | Hungary | 1309 |

| Date of Accession | Age at Accession | Monarch | Kingdom(s) | Date Reign Ended |
|---|---|---|---|---|
| 1305 | 26 | VACLAV II | Bohemia, Poland | 1306 |
| 1306 | – | RUDOLPH | Bohemia | 1307 |
| 1306 | 32 | ROBERT I | Scotland | 1329 |
| 1307 | | Declaration of Independence for Switzerland, freeing the country of Austrian rule. (Maximilian did not recognize the state until 1499.) | | |
| 1307 | 23 | EDWARD II | England and Wales | 1327 |
| 1307 | – | HENRY | Bohemia | 1310 |
| 1308 | 38 | HENRY VII | HRE, Germany | 1313 |
| 1309 | | Pope Clement V took up residence officially at Avignon in France. | | |
| 1309 | 34 | ROBERT | Sicily, Hungary, Naples | 1343 |
| 1310 | 14 | JOHN | Bohemia | 1346 |
| 1312 | 1 | ALFONSO XI | Leon and Castile | 1350 |
| 1314 | 28 | FREDERICK (AK) | HRE | 1330 |
| 1314 | 28 | LUDWIG | HRE, Germany | 1347 |
| 1314 | 25 | LOUIS X | France, Navarre | 1316 |
| 1316 | 0 | JOHN I | France | 1316 |
| 1316 | 23 | PHILIPPE V | France, Navarre | 1322 |
| 1319 | 3 | MAGNUS VII (J) | Norway, Sweden | 1365 |
| 1320 | 44 | CHRISTOPHER II | Denmark | 1326 |
| 1320 | | In Germany a monk, known as Bertholdus, was credited with having invented gunpowder. | | |
| 1321 | – | STEPHEN III, Urosh | Serbia | 1331 |
| 1322 | – | GEORGE II | Bulgaria | 1323 |
| 1322 | 28 | CHARLES IV | France, Navarre | 1328 |
| 1323 | – | MICHAEL SHISHMAN | Bulgaria | 1330 |
| 1325 | 34 | ALFONSO IV | Portugal | 1357 |
| 1327 | 15 | EDWARD III | England and Wales | 1377 |
| 1327 | 28 | ALFONSO IV | Aragon | 1336 |
| 1328 | 17 | JOANNA | Navarre | 1349 |
| 1328 | 35 | PHILIPPE VI | France | 1350 |
| 1329 | 5 | DAVID II | Scotland | 1371 |
| 1330 | – | IVAN STEPHEN (J) | Bulgaria | 1331 |
| 1331 | – | IVAN ALEXANDER (J) | Bulgaria | 1371 |
| 1331 | 23 | STEPHEN Dushan | Serbia | 1355 |
| 1332 | – | EDWARD BALLIOL | Scotland | 1346 |
| 1333 | 23 | KASIMIR III | Poland | 1370 |
| 1336 | 19 | PEDRO IV | Aragon | 1387 |
| 1337 | – | PETER II | Sicily | 1342 |
| 1340 | 20 | VALDEMAR III | Denmark | 1375 |
| 1340 | | The plague of the *Black Death* killed thousands in Italy. | | |
| 1342 | 4 | LOUIS | Sicily | 1355 |
| 1342 | 16 | LOUIS | Hungary, Poland | 1382 |
| 1343 | 3 | HAAKON VI (J) | Norway, Sweden | 1380 |

| Date of Accession | Age at Accession | Monarch | Kingdom(s) | Date Reign Ended |
|---|---|---|---|---|
| 1343 | 17 | JOANNA | Naples | 1382 |
| 1346 | 30 | CHARLES I | Germany, Bohemia, HRE | 1378 |
| 1347 | | On August 4, Edward III of England took Calais after a year's siege. The use of cannons by the English, was recorded for the first time. | | |
| 1347 | 33 | CHARLES IV | Germany, HRE | 1378 |
| 1349 | 45 | GUNTHER (AK) | HRE | 1349 |
| 1349 | 17 | CHARLES II | Navarre | 1387 |
| 1350 | | An English farm labourer at this time would have been paid about one penny (less than half a new penny) a day. This wage would double in the course of the next hundred years. | | |
| 1350 | 31 | JOHN II | France | 1364 |
| 1350 | 16 | PEDRO | Leon and Castile | 1369 |
| 1355 | – | STEPHEN V, Urosh | Serbia | 1371 |
| 1355 | 14 | FREDERICK III | Sicily | 1377 |
| 1356 | 17 | ERIK XII (J) | Sweden | 1359 |
| 1357 | 37 | PEDRO | Portugal | 1367 |
| 1364 | 27 | CHARLES V | France | 1380 |
| 1365 | 25 | ALBERT | Sweden | 1389 |
| 1366 | 33 | HENRY II | Leon and Castile | 1379 |
| 1367 | 22 | FERDINAND I | Portugal | 1383 |
| 1370 | 44 | LOUIS | Poland, Hungary | 1382 |
| 1371 | 6 | IVAN SHISHMAN (J) | Bulgaria | 1393 |
| 1371 | 55 | ROBERT II | Scotland | 1390 |
| 1375 | 5 | OLAF II | Denmark, Norway | 1387 |
| 1376 | – | STEPHEN TVRTKO I | Bosnia | 1391 |
| 1377 | – | MARY (J) | Sicily | 1402 |
| 1377 | 11 | RICHARD II | England and Wales | 1399 |
| 1378 | 17 | VACLAV IV | HRE, Germany, Bohemia | 1419 |
| 1379 | 21 | JOHN I | Leon and Castile | 1390 |
| 1380 | – | OLAF IV | Norway, Denmark | 1387 |
| 1380 | 12 | CHARLES VI | France | 1422 |
| 1382 | 37 | CHARLES III | Naples, Hungary | 1386 |
| 1382 | 12 | MARY (J) | Hungary | 1395 |
| 1383 | – | BEATRICE | Portugal | 1385 |
| 1384 | 11 | JADWIGA (J) | Poland | 1399 |
| 1385 | 28 | JOHN I | Portugal | 1433 |
| 1386 | 36 | VLADISLAV II | Poland | 1434 |
| 1386 | 9 | LADISLAS | Naples | 1414 |
| 1387 | 37 | JOHN I | Aragon | 1395 |
| 1387 | 35 | MARGARET | Norway, Sweden, Denmark | 1412 |
| 1387 | 19 | SIGISMUND (J) | Hungary, Bohemia, HRE | 1437 |
| 1387 | 26 | CHARLES III | Navarre | 1425 |

| Date of Accession | Age at Accession | Monarch | Kingdom(s) | Date Reign Ended |
|---|---|---|---|---|
| 1390 | 50 | ROBERT III | Scotland | 1406 |
| 1390 | 11 | HENRY III | Leon and Castile | 1406 |
| 1391 | – | STEPHEN DABISHA | Bosnia | 1395 |
| 1395 | –. | HELENA (R) | Bosnia | 1398 |
| 1395 | 40 | MARTIN (J) | Aragon, Sicily | 1410 |
| 1398 | 18 | STEPHEN OSTOJA | Bosnia | 1418 |
| 1399 | 33 | HENRY IV | England and Wales | 1413 |
| 1400 | – | FREDERICK | HRE | 1400 |
| 1400 | 48 | RUPERT III | HRE, Germany | 1410 |
| 1402 | – | MARTIN I | Sicily | 1409 |
| 1404 | – | STEPHEN TVRTKO II | Bosnia | 1443 |
| 1406 | 1 | JOHN II | Leon and Castile | 1454 |
| 1406 | 12 | JAMES I | Scotland | 1437 |

| 1406 | | The plague killed more than 30,000 people in London. The population of Europe in 1400 has been estimated to have been about 60 million. Between 1347 and 1353 the plague, the *Black Death*, had killed between one quarter and one third of the people in Europe. | | |

| 1409 | – | MARTIN II | Sicily | 1410 |
| 1410 | 60 | JOBST (AK) | HRE | 1411 |
| 1412 | 31 | ERIK VII | Denmark, Sweden, Norway | 1438 |
| 1412 | 33 | FERDINAND II | Aragon, Sicily | 1416 |
| 1413 | 26 | HENRY V | England and Wales | 1422 |
| 1414 | 43 | JOANNA | Naples | 1435 |

| 1415 | | On October 25, Henry V of England defeated the French army at Agincourt; 10,000 French soldiers died. | | |

| 1416 | 31 | ALFONSO V | Sicily, Aragon, Naples | 1458 |
| 1418 | – | OSTOJIC | Bosnia | 1421 |
| 1419 | 41 | SIGISMUND | HRE, Germany, Bohemia, Hungary | 1437 |

| 1420 | | Tomas de Torquemada, the Spaniard, who organized the *Spanish Inquisition* was born. He died in 1498. | | |

| 1422 | 18 | CHARLES VII | France | 1461 |
| 1422 | 1 | HENRY VI | England and Wales | 1471 |
| 1425 | 20 | BLANCHE (J) | Navarre | 1441 |

| 1429 | | On April 29, Joan of Arc drove the English army out of Orléans leading the army of CHARLES II of France. She was burned at the stake by the English in May 1431. | | |

| 1433 | 42 | EDWARD | Portugal | 1438 |
| 1434 | 10 | VLADISLAV III, Jagiellon | Poland, Hungary | 1444 |
| 1437 | 40 | ALBERT II | HRE, Hungary, Bohemia, Germany | 1439 |
| 1437 | 7 | JAMES II | Scotland | 1460 |
| 1438 | 6 | ALFONSO V | Portugal | 1481 |

115

| Date of Accession | Age at Accession | Monarch | Kingdom(s) | Date Reign Ended |
|---|---|---|---|---|
| 1440 | 25 | FREDERICK III | Germany, HRE | 1493 |
| 1440 | 22 | CHRISTOPHER III | Norway, Denmark, Sweden | 1448 |
| 1440 | 16 | LADISLAV V | Bohemia, Hungary | 1457 |

| 1440 | | Copenhagen became the capital city of Denmark. | | |
|---|---|---|---|---|

| 1441 | 44 | JOHN II (J) | Navarre | 1479 |
|---|---|---|---|---|
| 1443 | – | STEPHEN THOMAS | Bosnia | 1461 |
| 1447 | 20 | KASIMIR IV | Poland | 1492 |
| 1448 | 22 | CHRISTIAN I | Denmark, Norway | 1481 |

| 1452 | | On September 21, Girolamo Savanarola was born at Ferrara. Morally and religiously, but *not* theologically, Savanarola was perhaps the real initiator of the Reformation. He died in Florence in 1498. | | |
|---|---|---|---|---|

| 1454 | 19 | HENRY IV (LK) | Leon and Castile | 1474 |
|---|---|---|---|---|

| 1456 | | The Turks, under Mahomet II, conquered Athens and a large area of Greece. | | |
|---|---|---|---|---|

| 1458 | 61 | JOHN II (LK) | Aragon, Sicily | 1479 |
|---|---|---|---|---|
| 1458 | 38 | GEORGE | Bohemia | 1471 |
| 1458 | 15 | MATTHIAS CORVINUS | Hungary, Bohemia | 1490 |
| 1458 | 34 | FERDINAND | Naples | 1494 |
| 1460 | 8 | FERDINAND V | Sicily, Castile | 1516 |
| 1460 | 8 | JAMES III | Scotland | 1488 |
| 1461 | 20 | EDWARD IV | England and Wales | 1483 |
| 1461 | 38 | LOUIS XI | France | 1483 |
| 1461 | – | STEPHEN (LK) | Bosnia | 1463 |

| 1466 | | Athens was taken by the Venetians. | | |
|---|---|---|---|---|

| 1471 | 19 | LADISLAV JAGIELLON | Bohemia, Hungary | 1516 |
|---|---|---|---|---|
| 1474 | 23 | ISABELLA | Spain | 1504 |

| 1477 | | The fifty-five-year-old William Caxton published the first printed book in London, *The Dictes or Sayengis of the Philosophres.* | | |
|---|---|---|---|---|

| 1479 | 27 | FERDINAND II | Aragon, Spain | 1516 |
|---|---|---|---|---|
| 1479 | – | FRANCIS-PHOEBUS | Navarre | 1483 |
| 1479 | – | ELEANOR de Foix | Navarre | 1479 |
| 1481 | 26 | JOHN II | Portugal | 1495 |
| 1481 | 26 | JOHN | Norway, Denmark, Sweden | 1513 |
| 1483 | 13 | EDWARD V | England and Wales | 1483 |
| 1483 | 31 | RICHARD III | England and Wales | 1485 |
| 1483 | – | CATHERINE (J) | Navarre | 1512 |
| 1483 | 13 | CHARLES VIII | France | 1498 |
| 1485 | 28 | HENRY VII | England and Wales | 1509 |

| Date of Accession | Age at Accession | Monarch | Kingdom(s) | Date Reign Ended |
|---|---|---|---|---|
| 1487 | | The thirty-seven-year-old Bartolomeu Diaz, a navigator of King John of Portugal's court, discovered the Cape of Good Hope at the southernmost tip of Africa. | | |
| 1488 | 15 | JAMES IV | Scotland | 1513 |
| 1490 | 40 | VLADISLAV II | Hungary, Bohemia | 1516 |
| 1492 | 33 | JOHN I | Poland | 1501 |
| 1492 | | On April 17, Christopher Columbus set sail on the voyage during which he discovered West Indies. | | |
| 1493 | 34 | MAXIMILIAN | HRE, Germany | 1519 |
| 1494 | 46 | ALFONSO II | Naples | 1495 |
| 1495 | 26 | MANUEL I | Portugal | 1521 |
| 1495 | 28 | FERDINAND II | Naples | 1496 |
| 1496 | 44 | FREDERICK IV | Naples | 1501 |
| 1497 | | Vasco da Gama discovered the Passage to India. | | |
| 1498 | 36 | LOUIS XII | France | 1515 |
| 1500 | | The estimated population of Europe was about 81 million | | |
| 1500 | | In April Pedro Alvarez Cabral discovered Brazil and claimed the country on behalf of the King of Portugal. | | |
| 1501 | 40 | ALEXANDER JAGIELLON | Poland | 1506 |
| 1504 | 15 | JOANNA (J) | Sicily, Spain, Naples | 1555 |
| 1504 | | Leonardo da Vinci, aged 52, painted The Mona Lisa. | | |
| 1506 | 39 | SIGISMUND I (J) | Poland | 1548 |
| 1509 | 20 | HENRY VIII | England and Wales | 1547 |
| 1512 | – | JOHN III | Navarre | 1516 |
| 1513 | 1 | JAMES V | Scotland | 1542 |
| 1513 | 32 | CHRISTIAN II | Norway, Denmark, Sweden | 1523 |
| 1515 | 21 | FRANCIS I | France | 1547 |
| 1516 | 16 | CHARLES I | Spain, Germany, HRE | 1556 |
| 1516 | 13 | HENRY II | Navarre | 1555 |
| 1516 | 10 | LOUIS II | Hungary, Bohemia | 1526 |
| 1521 | 19 | JOHN III | Portugal | 1557 |
| 1521 | | On April 17, Martin Luther was excommunicated by the Diet at Worms, seat of the Holy Roman Empire. | | |
| 1523 | 27 | GUSTAV I | Sweden | 1560 |
| 1523 | 52 | FREDERICK I | Denmark, Norway | 1533 |
| 1526 | | The forty-eight-year-old Francisco Pizarro began to explore Peru. (He had been with Balboa in 1509, when the Pacific Ocean was discovered.) | | |

| Date of Accession | Age at Accession | Monarch | Kingdom(s) | Date Reign Ended |
|---|---|---|---|---|
| 1526 | 39 | JOHN ZAPOLYA | Hungary | 1540 |
| 1530 | 10 | SIGISMUND (J) | Poland | 1572 |
| 1533 | 3 | IVAN | Russia | 1584 |
| 1533 | 32 | CHRISTIAN III | Denmark, Norway, Sweden | 1559 |
| 1534 | | HENRY VIII of England parted company with the Church of Rome, establishing the Church of England. | | |
| 1540 | 37 | FERDINAND I | Germany, Hungary | 1563 |
| 1542 | 1 wk | MARY | Scotland | 1567 |
| 1547 | | On October 9, Miguel de Cervantes, author of *Don Quixote*, was born. He died in Madrid in 1616. | | |
| 1547 | 28 | HENRI II | France | 1559 |
| 1547 | 10 | EDWARD VI | England and Wales | 1553 |
| 1551 | | The Protestant religion was officially established in Iceland. (The island had been Danish since 1397.) | | |
| 1553 | 16 | Lady JANE Grey | England and Wales | 1553 |
| 1553 | | On May 20, Sir Hugh Willoughby sailed from London to try and find a north-east passage to China. | | |
| 1554 | 38 | MARY | England and Wales | 1558 |
| 1555 | 17 | JOANNA (LQ) | Navarre | 1572 |
| 1556 | 39 | PHILIP II | Spain, Portugal | 1598 |
| 1556 | 53 | FERDINAND I (LK) | Bohemia, Germany, HRE | 1564 |
| 1557 | 3 | SEBASTIAN | Portugal | 1578 |
| 1558 | 25 | ELIZABETH I | England and Wales | 1603 |
| 1559 | 15 | FRANCIS II | France | 1560 |
| 1559 | 25 | FREDERICK II | Norway, Denmark, Sweden | 1588 |
| 1560 | 27 | ERIK XIV | Sweden | 1568 |
| 1560 | 10 | CHARLES IX | France | 1574 |
| 1564 | | April 23 (Saint George's Day) William Shakespeare was born at Stratford-upon-Avon and died there in 1616. | | |
| 1564 | 37 | MAXIMILIAN II | Germany, Hungary, HRE | 1576 |
| 1567 | 1 | JAMES I | England and Scotland | 1625 |
| 1568 | 31 | JOHN III | Sweden | 1592 |
| 1573 | 22 | HENRI III | France, Poland | 1589 |
| 1575 | 53 | STEPHEN BATORY | Poland | 1586 |
| 1576 | 24 | RUDOLPH II | Germany, HRE, Hungary | 1612 |
| 1578 | | King SEBASTIAN of Portugal was killed at the battle of Alcazar, in Morocco. | | |
| 1578 | 66 | HENRY I | Portugal | 1580 |

| Date of Accession | Age at Accession | Monarch | Kingdom(s) | Date Reign Ended |
|---|---|---|---|---|
| 1579 | | IVAN, 'The Terrible', of Russia sought to marry Queen ELIZABETH I of England. | | |
| 1582 | | Pope Gregory XIII published the *New Style Calendar* and October 5 became October 15. It was adopted by France, Italy, Spain, Denmark, Holland and Portugal the same year; by Germany and Switzerland in 1584 and Hungary in 1587. Great Britain did not come into line until 1751, when September 3 became September 14. | | |
| 1584 | 27 | FEODOR I | Russia | 1598 |
| 1587 | 21 | SIGISMUND III | Poland, Sweden | 1632 |
| 1588 | | Between July 21-27, the *Armada* of PHILIP of Spain was completely defeated by the English navy under Drake, Howard and Hawkins. | | |
| 1588 | 11 | CHRISTIAN IV | Denmark, Sweden, Norway | 1648 |
| 1589 | 36 | HENRI IV | France | 1610 |
| 1592 | 26 | SIGISMUND | Sweden, Poland | 1599 |
| 1594 | | On February 2, the composer, Giovanni Pierluigi da Palestrina, died in Rome, aged 70. | | |
| 1598 | 20 | PHILIP III | Spain, Portugal | 1621 |
| 1598 | 47 | BORIS GODUNOV | Russia | 1605 |
| 1599 | 49 | CHARLES IX | Sweden | 1611 |
| 1600 | | The estimated population of Europe was about 100 million. | | |
| 1605 | 16 | FEODOR II | Russia | 1605 |
| 1605 | 24 | DMITRI II | Russia | 1606 |
| 1606 | 54 | VASILI IV | Russia | 1610 |
| 1606 | | In March the Dutch discovered Australia. (Portugal had claimed discovery in 1601). | | |
| 1606 | | On July 15, Rembrandt van Rijn was born in Leyden. He died in Amsterdam in October 1669. | | |
| 1608 | 55 | MATTHIAS II | Germany, Hungary, HRE | 1619 |
| 1610 | | On January 8, the forty-five-year old Galileo Galilei discovered the planet Jupiter in his Paduan observatory. | | |
| 1610 | 9 | LOUIS XIII | France | 1643 |
| 1611 | 17 | GUSTAV ADOLF II | Sweden | 1623 |
| 1613 | 17 | MICHAEL | Russia | 1645 |
| 1619 | 41 | FERDINAND II | Germany, Hungary, HRE | 1637 |
| 1621 | 16 | PHILIP IV | Spain, Portugal | 1665 |

| Date of Accession | Age at Accession | Monarch | Kingdom(s) | Date Reign Ended |
|---|---|---|---|---|
| 1624 | | The Dutch founded Manhattan, now called New York. | | |
| 1625 | 25 | CHARLES I | England, Wales and Scotland | 1649 |
| 1628 | | Aged 50, William Harvey made public his 'discovery' of the circulation of the blood. | | |
| 1632 | 6 | CHRISTINA | Sweden | 1654 |
| 1632 | 37 | VLADISLAV IV | Poland | 1648 |
| 1634 | | Cardinal Richelieu organized the Académie de France. | | |
| 1637 | 29 | FERDINAND III | Germany, Hungary, Bohemia, HRE | 1657 |
| 1640 | 36 | JOHN IV | Portugal | 1656 |
| 1643 | 5 | LOUIS XIV | France | 1715 |
| 1645 | 16 | ALEXEI | Russia | 1676 |
| 1648 | 37 | FREDERICK III | Denmark, Norway, Sweden | 1670 |
| 1648 | 39 | JOHN II | Poland | 1648 |
| 1654 | 32 | CHARLES X | Sweden | 1660 |
| 1656 | 13 | ALFONSO VI | Portugal | 1667 |
| 1658 | 17 | LEOPOLD I | Germany, Hungary, HRE | 1705 |
| 1658 | | On September 3, Oliver Cromwell, Lord Protector and Head of State during the English Commonwealth, died. Soon after the country was beginning to show its monarchist sympathies again. | | |
| 1660 | 5 | CHARLES XI | Sweden | 1697 |
| 1660 | 30 | CHARLES II | England, Wales and Scotland | 1685 |
| 1662 | | Bombay was ceded to England as part of the dowry of Catherine of Braganza, when she married CHARLES II. | | |
| 1665 | 4 | CHARLES II | Spain | 1700 |
| 1669 | 31 | MICHAEL WISNIOWIECKI | Poland | 1673 |
| 1670 | 24 | CHRISTIAN V | Denmark, Sweden, Norway | 1699 |
| 1674 | 35 | JOHN SOBIESKI | Poland | 1696 |
| 1676 | 15 | FEODOR III | Russia | 1682 |
| 1682 | 16 | IVAN V (J) | Russia | 1696 |
| 1683 | 35 | PEDRO | Portugal | 1706 |
| 1685 | 52 | JAMES II | England, Wales and Scotland | 1688 |
| 1689 | 27 | MARY II (J) | England, Wales and Scotland | 1694 |
| 1689 | 39 | WILLIAM III (J) | England, Wales and Scotland | 1702 |

| Date of Accession | Age at Accession | Monarch | Kingdom(s) | Date Reign Ended |
|---|---|---|---|---|
| 1689 | | Warsaw became the seat of the Polish Government. | | |
| 1696 | 24 | PETER I | Russia | 1725 |
| 1697 | 15 | CHARLES XII | Sweden | 1718 |
| 1697 | 27 | AUGUSTUS II | Poland | 1733 |
| 1699 | 27 | FREDERICK IV | Denmark, Sweden, Norway | 1730 |
| 1700 | | The estimated population of Europe was about 120 million. | | |
| 1700 | 17 | PHILIP V | Spain, Sicily | 1746 |
| 1701 | 44 | FREDERICK | Prussia | 1713 |
| 1702 | 37 | ANNE | Great Britain | 1714 |
| 1703 | | On June 28, John Wesley, founder of the Methodist religion was born at Epworth, Lincolnshire. He died in London in 1791. | | |
| 1704 | 27 | STANISLAV I | Poland | 1709 |
| 1704 | | On August 2, the French and Bavarian armies were heavily defeated by the English forces and their allies, under John Churchill, first Duke of Marlborough, at Blenheim, on the river Danube in Bavaria. | | |
| 1705 | 9 | JOSEPH I | Sicily, Germany, Hungary, HRE | 1711 |
| 1706 | 17 | JOHN V | Portugal | 1750 |
| 1709 | | On July 8, PETER, 'The Great', of Russia vanquished the Swedish army, under CHARLES XII, at Pultowa. | | |
| 1711 | 27 | CHARLES III | Sicily, Germany, Hungary, HRE | 1740 |
| 1713 | 25 | FREDERICK-WILLIAM I | Prussia | 1740 |
| 1713 | 47 | VICTOR AMADEUS II | Sicily, Naples, Sardinia | 1730 |
| 1714 | 54 | GEORGE I | Great Britain | 1727 |
| 1715 | 5 | LOUIS XV | France | 1774 |
| 1717 | | On January 4, the *Triple Alliance* was ratified, whereby Great Britain, Holland and France were to be united against Spain. | | |
| 1718 | 30 | ULRICA ELEANORA | Sweden | 1720 |
| 1720 | 44 | FREDERICK I | Sweden | 1751 |
| 1725 | 46 | CATHERINE | Russia | 1727 |
| 1727 | 44 | GEORGE II | Great Britain | 1760 |
| 1727 | 12 | PETER II | Russia | 1730 |
| 1730 | 29 | CHARLES-EMANUEL III | Sardinia | 1773 |
| 1730 | 37 | ANNE | Russia | 1740 |
| 1730 | 31 | CHRISTIAN VI | Denmark, Sweden, Norway | 1746 |

| Date of Accession | Age at Accession | Monarch | Kingdom(s) | Date Reign Ended |
|---|---|---|---|---|
| 1733 | 37 | AUGUSTUS III | Poland | 1763 |
| 1734 | 18 | CHARLES IV | Spain, Naples | 1788 |
| 1740 | 0 | IVAN VI | Russia | 1741 |
| 1740 | 28 | FREDERICK II | Prussia | 1786 |
| 1740 | 24 | MARIA THERESA | Hungary, Germany | 1780 |
| 1741 | 32 | ELIZABETH | Russia | 1762 |
| 1742 | 45 | CHARLES VII | HRE, Bohemia | 1745 |
| 1745 | 37 | FRANCIS | HRE | 1765 |
| 1746 | 23 | FREDERICK V | Denmark, Norway | 1766 |
| 1746 | 34 | FERDINAND VI | Spain | 1759 |

| 1746 | | On March 31, the painter, Francisco Goya y Lucientes, was born near Saragossa. He died at Bordeaux in 1828. | | |
| 1749 | | On August 28, Johann Wolfgang von Goethe was born at Frankfort. He died at Weimar in 1832. | | |

| 1750 | 36 | JOSEPH | Portugal | 1777 |
| 1751 | 41 | ADOLPH FREDERICK | Sweden | 1771 |

| 1759 | | On September 13, General Wolfe defeated the French at Quebec and British rule was established in eastern Canada. | | |

| 1759 | 8 | FERDINAND I | Naples, Two Sicilies | 1825 |
| 1759 | 43 | CHARLES III | Spain, Two Sicilies | 1788 |
| 1760 | 22 | GEORGE III | Great Britain, Hanover | 1820 |
| 1762 | 34 | PETER III | Russia | 1762 |
| 1762 | 33 | CATHERINE II | Russia | 1796 |

| 1763 | | FREDERICK, 'The Great', established village schools in Prussia. | | |

| 1764 | 32 | STANISLAV II (LK) | Poland | 1795 |
| 1765 | 24 | JOSEPH II (J) | HRE | 1790 |
| 1766 | 17 | CHRISTIAN VII | Norway, Denmark, Sweden | 1808 |

| 1770 | | On December 16, Ludwig van Beethoven was born at Bonn. He died in Vienna, aged 57. | | |

| 1771 | 25 | GUSTAV III | Sweden | 1792 |
| 1773 | 47 | VICTOR-AMADEUS II | Sardinia | 1796 |
| 1774 | 20 | LOUIS XVI | France | 1792 |

| 1776 | | On July 4, the *American Declaration of Independence* was carried by Congress. (New Orleans and the Louisiana Territory – named after LOUIS XIV – belonged to France, until America bought the land in April 1803). | | |
| 1777 | | On October 17, the British Army (of 6,000 men) surrendered to the American General Gates at Saratoga. | | |

| 1777 | 27 | MARIA (J) | Portugal | 1816 |
| 1780 | 39 | JOSEPH II | Hungary, Austria | 1790 |

| Date of Accession | Age at Accession | Monarch | Kingdom(s) | Date Reign Ended |
|---|---|---|---|---|
| 1784 | 16 | FREDERICK VI | Denmark, Norway, Sweden | 1839 |
| 1786 | 42 | FREDERICK-WILLIAM II | Prussia | 1797 |
| 1787 | | Sierra Leone, in Africa, was settled by English colonists. | | |
| 1788 | 40 | CHARLES IV | Spain | 1808 |
| 1790 | 43 | LEOPOLD II | Hungary, Austria, HRE | 1792 |
| 1791 | | In July the revolutionary *Reign of Terror* began in France. King Louis XVI was guillotined eighteen months later. | | |
| 1792 | 14 | GUSTAV IV | Sweden | 1809 |
| 1792 | 24 | FRANCIS I (LK) | Hungary, Austria, HRE | 1835 |
| 1792 | | On September 20, the French army, under Kellerman, defeated the Duke of Brunswick's Prussian forces at Valmy, in north eastern France. | | |
| 1793 | 8 | LOUIS XVII | France | 1795 |
| 1796 | 44 | CHARLES-EMANUEL IV | Sardinia | 1802 |
| 1796 | 42 | PAUL | Russia | 1801 |
| 1797 | 25 | FREDERICK-WILLIAM III | Prussia | 1840 |
| 1798 | | On August 1, Admiral Horatio Nelson destroyed the French Fleet at the *Battle of the Nile* (Aboukir). | | |
| 1799 | 32 | JOHN VI | Portugal | 1826 |
| 1800 | | The estimated population of Europe was 180 million. | | |
| 1801 | | On January 1, the *Union Jack* became the official flag of the United Kingdom of Great Britain, incorporating the crosses of Saints George, Andrew and Patrick. | | |
| 1801 | 24 | ALEXANDER | Russia | 1825 |
| 1801 | 28 | LOUIS I | Etruria | 1803 |
| 1802 | 43 | VICTOR-EMANUEL I | Sardinia | 1821 |
| 1803 | 14 | LOUIS II | Etruria | 1808 |
| 1804 | 35 | NAPOLEON BONAPARTE | France | 1815 |
| 1804 | 36 | FRANZ I | Austria | 1835 |
| 1805 | 49 | MAXIMILIAN | Bavaria | 1825 |
| 1805 | 51 | FREDERIC I | Wurttemberg | 1816 |
| 1806 | 56 | FREDERICK AUGUSTUS I | Saxony | 1827 |
| 1806 | 28 | LOUIS BONAPARTE | Netherlands | 1810 |
| 1806 | 38 | JOSEPH BONAPARTE | Naples, Spain | 1808 |
| 1807 | 23 | JEROME BONAPARTE (LK) | Westphalia | 1813 |
| 1808 | 40 | FREDERICK VI | Denmark | 1839 |
| 1808 | 37 | JOACHIM MURAT | Naples | 1815 |
| 1809 | 61 | CHARLES VIII | Sweden, Norway | 1818 |
| 1813 | 29 | FERDINAND VII | Spain | 1833 |

| Date of Accession | Age at Accession | Monarch | Kingdom(s) | Date Reign Ended |
|---|---|---|---|---|
| 1813 | | On May 22, Richard Wagner, composer, was born at Leipsic. He died in Venice in 1883. | | |
| 1814 | 60 | LOUIS XVIII | France | 1824 |
| 1815 | | On Sunday, June 18, the Allies, under the Duke of Wellington, defeated NAPOLEON's 72,000 strong army at Waterloo, in Belgium. | | |
| 1815 | 65 | FERDINAND I | Naples, Two Sicilies | 1825 |
| 1815 | 43 | WILLIAM I | Netherlands | 1840 |
| 1816 | 35 | WILLIAM I | Wurttemberg | 1864 |
| 1816 | 49 | JOHN VI | Portugal | 1826 |
| 1818 | 55 | CHARLES XIV | Sweden, Norway | 1844 |
| 1819 | | The S.S. Savannah a 350 ton ship steamed across the Atlantic in 26 days. | | |
| 1820 | 58 | GEORGE IV | Great Britain, Hanover | 1830 |
| 1821 | 56 | CHARLES-FELIX | Sardinia | 1831 |
| 1824 | 67 | CHARLES X | France | 1830 |
| 1825 | 39 | LUDWIG I | Bavaria | 1848 |
| 1825 | 58 | FRANCIS I | Two Sicilies | 1830 |
| 1825 | 29 | NICHOLAS I | Russia | 1855 |
| 1826 | 28 | PEDRO IV | Portugal | 1826 |
| 1826 | 7 | MARIA | Portugal | 1853 |
| 1827 | 62 | ANTHONY | Saxony | 1836 |
| 1828 | 26 | MIGUEL | Portugal | 1834 |
| 1829 | | The Nile rose 26 cubits (15.8 metres) during its annual flood, rather than the necessary minimum of 16 cubits and 30,000 Egyptians were drowned. | | |
| 1830 | 65 | WILLIAM IV | Great Britain, Hanover | 1837 |
| 1830 | 20 | FERDINAND II | Two Sicilies | 1859 |
| 1830 | 55 | LOUIS XIX | France | 1830 |
| 1830 | 10 | HENRI V | France | 1830 |
| 1830 | 57 | LOUIS-PHILIPPE | France | 1848 |
| 1830 | | On September 15, Huskisson, an English politician, became the first person in the world to be killed in a railway accident. | | |
| 1830 | 33 | CHARLES-ALBERT | Sardinia | 1849 |
| 1831 | 41 | LEOPOLD I | Belgium | 1865 |
| 1832 | 17 | OTHO I | Greece | 1862 |
| 1833 | 3 | ISABELLA II | Spain | 1870 |
| 1835 | 42 | FERDINAND I | Austria | 1848 |
| 1836 | 39 | FREDERICK AUGUSTUS II | Saxony | 1854 |
| 1837 | 66 | ERNEST AUGUSTUS | Hanover | 1851 |
| 1837 | 18 | VICTORIA | Great Britain | 1901 |

| Date of Accession | Age at Accession | Monarch | Kingdom(s) | Date Reign Ended |
|---|---|---|---|---|
| 1839 | | The fifty-year-old, Louis Jacques Mandé Daguerre perfected his photographic process. | | |
| 1839 | 53 | CHRISTIAN VIII | Denmark | 1848 |
| 1840 | 45 | FREDERICK-WILLIAM IV | Prussia | 1861 |
| 1844 | 48 | WILLIAM II | Netherlands | 1849 |
| 1844 | 45 | OSCAR I | Sweden, Norway | 1859 |
| 1847 | | Sir James Simpson first used chloroform as an anaesthetic. | | |
| 1848 | 18 | FRANZ JOSEPH I | Austria | 1916 |
| 1848 | 37 | MAXIMILIAN II | Bavaria | 1864 |
| 1848 | 40 | FREDERICK VII | Denmark | 1863 |
| 1849 | 32 | WILLIAM III | Netherlands | 1890 |
| 1849 | 29 | VICTOR-EMANUEL II (LK) | Sardinia, Italy | 1878 |
| 1851 | 32 | GEORGE V (LK) | Hanover | 1866 |
| 1852 | 44 | NAPOLEON III (LK) | France | 1870 |
| 1853 | 16 | PEDRO V | Portugal | 1861 |
| 1854 | 53 | JOHN | Saxony | 1873 |
| 1855 | 37 | ALEXANDER II | Russia | 1881 |
| 1859 | 23 | FRANCIS II (LK) | Two Sicilies | 1860 |
| 1859 | 33 | CHARLES XV | Sweden, Norway | 1872 |
| 1859 | | Charles Darwin published his revolutionary *Origin of Species by Natural Selection. Descent of Man* followed in 1871. | | |
| 1861 | 64 | WILLIAM I (LK) | Prussia, German Empire | 1888 |
| 1861 | 23 | LUIS | Portugal | 1889 |
| 1863 | 18 | GEORGE I | Greece | 1913 |
| 1863 | 45 | CHRISTIAN IX | Denmark | 1906 |
| 1863 | | The population of Lisbon was 224,000. In 1860 that of Athens was 47,000 and Copenhagen 155,000. In 1862 Naples was 418,000, Palermo 167,000, Madrid 475,000, Munich 167,000 and Vienna 560,000. In 1866, Warsaw was 243,000, Konigsberg 104,000, Brussels 189,000, Stockholm 138,000, Christiana (Oslo) 57,000 and Paris 1.8 million. In 1867, Amsterdam was 264,000, Dublin 319,000, Rome 215,000 and London 3 million. | | |
| 1864 | 41 | CHARLES I | Wurttemberg | 1891 |
| 1864 | 19 | LUDWIG II | Bavaria | 1886 |
| 1865 | 30 | LEOPOLD II | Belgium | 1909 |
| 1867 | | On June 19, the Emperor Maximilian of Mexico was shot, after trial, by the Mexicans. He was the brother of the Austrian Emperor and son-in-law of the King of Belgium. | | |
| 1869 | | On November 17, the Suez Canal was opened, bringing the Far East 'weeks nearer' to Europe. | | |

| Date of Accession | Age at Accession | Monarch | Kingdom(s) | Date Reign Ended |
|---|---|---|---|---|
| 1870 | 25 | AMADEUS | Spain | 1873 |
| 1872 | 43 | OSCAR II | Sweden, Norway | 1907 |
| 1873 | 45 | ALBERT | Saxony | 1902 |
| 1874 | 17 | ALFONSO XII | Spain | 1885 |
| 1878 | 34 | UMBERTO I | Italy | 1900 |
| 1881 | 36 | ALEXANDER | Russia | 1894 |
| 1881 | 42 | CAROL | Romania | 1914 |
| 1882 | 28 | MILAN I | Serbia | 1889 |
| 1885 | 27 | MARIA CHRISTINA | Spain | 1886 |
| 1885 | | Karl Benz built a single cylinder petroleum powered motor car engine. | | |
| 1886 | 0 | ALFONSO XIII | Spain | 1931 |
| 1886 | 38 | OTTO | Bavaria | 1913 |
| 1887 | 26 | FERDINAND | Bulgaria | 1918 |
| 1888 | 57 | FREDERICK III | German Empire | 1888 |
| 1888 | 29 | WILLIAM II (LK) | German Empire | 1918 |
| 1889 | 26 | CHARLES | Portugal | 1908 |
| 1889 | 13 | ALEXANDER I | Serbia | 1903 |
| 1890 | 10 | WILHELMINA | Netherlands | 1948 |
| 1891 | 43 | WILLIAM II (LK) | Wurttemberg | 1918 |
| 1894 | 26 | NICHOLAS II (LK) | Russia | 1918 |
| 1895 | | Guglielmo Marconi invented Wireless Telegraphy. Wireless messages were transmitted from England to Newfoundland in 1901. | | |
| 1900 | | The estimated population of Europe was 390 million. | | |
| 1900 | 31 | VICTOR-EMANUEL III | Italy, Albania (LK) | 1946 |
| 1901 | 59 | EDWARD VII | Great Britain | 1910 |
| 1902 | 70 | GEORGE | Saxony | 1904 |
| 1903 | | On December 17, the Wright brothers made the first successful flight in a petrol-engined aeroplane. | | |
| 1904 | 39 | FREDERICK-AUGUSTUS III | Saxony (LK) | 1918 |
| 1905 | 33 | HAAKON VII | Norway | 1957 |
| 1906 | 63 | FREDERICK VIII | Denmark | 1912 |
| 1907 | 49 | GUSTAV V | Sweden | 1950 |
| 1908 | 19 | MANUEL II (LK) | Portugal | 1910 |
| 1909 | 34 | ALBERT I | Belgium | 1934 |
| 1910 | 45 | GEORGE V | Great Britain | 1936 |
| 1912 | 42 | CHRISTIAN X | Denmark | 1947 |
| 1913 | 45 | CONSTANTINE I | Greece | 1917 |
| 1913 | 59 | LUDWIG III (LK) | Bavaria | 1918 |
| 1914 | | On June 28, Archduke Francis Ferdinand of Austria was assassinated at Sarajevo in Bosnia. This murder led to the outbreak of the First World War on August 4. | | |
| 1914 | 49 | FERDINAND I | Romania | 1927 |

| Date of Accession | Age at Accession | Monarch | Kingdom(s) | Date Reign Ended |
|---|---|---|---|---|
| 1914 | 38 | WILLIAM I | Albania | 1914 |
| 1916 | 29 | KARL (LK) | Austria | 1918 |
| 1917 | 23 | ALEXANDER I | Greece | 1920 |
| 1918 | 24 | BORIS III | Bulgaria | 1943 |
| 1918 | 74 | PETER I | Yugoslavia, Serbia (LK) | 1921 |
| 1921 | 33 | ALEXANDER | Yugoslavia | 1934 |
| 1922 | 32 | GEORGE II | Greece | 1947 |

| 1926 | | On January 26, John Logie Baird demonstrated his invention of television, in London. | | |
|---|---|---|---|---|

| 1927 | 6 | MICHAEL (LK) | Romania | 1947 |
|---|---|---|---|---|

| 1927 | | On May 20/21, Charles Lindbergh flew from New York to Paris in 37 hours. | | |
|---|---|---|---|---|

| 1928 | 33 | ZOG I | Albania | 1948 |
|---|---|---|---|---|
| 1930 | 37 | CAROL II | Romania | 1940 |
| 1934 | 33 | LEOPOLD III | Belgium | 1951 |
| 1934 | 11 | PETER II (LK) | Yugoslavia | 1945 |
| 1936 | 42 | EDWARD VIII | Great Britain | 1936 |
| 1936 | 41 | GEORGE VI | Great Britain | 1952 |

| 1939 | | On September 3, the United Kingdom and France declared war on Germany and the Second World War (second in 21 years) began. | | |
|---|---|---|---|---|

| 1943 | 6 | SIMEON (LK) | Bulgaria | 1946 |
|---|---|---|---|---|

| 1945 | | On August 6, America dropped an atomic bomb on Hiroshima, followed by a second, on Nagasaki, three days later. Japan surrendered unconditionally. | | |
|---|---|---|---|---|

| 1946 | 42 | UMBERTO II (LK) | Italy | 1946 |
|---|---|---|---|---|
| 1947 | 48 | FREDERICK IX | Denmark | 1972 |
| 1947 | 46 | PAUL | Greece | 1964 |
| 1948 | 39 | JULIANA | Netherlands | 1980 |
| 1950 | 62 | GUSTAV VI | Sweden | 1973 |

| 1950 | | The population of Europe was about 490 million. In 1975 it was about 635 million and the forecast for AD 2000 is in excess of 710 million. | | |
|---|---|---|---|---|

| 1951 | 54 | OLAF V | Norway | |
|---|---|---|---|---|
| 1951 | 21 | BAUDOUIN | Belgium | |
| 1952 | 26 | ELIZABETH II | Great Britain | |
| 1964 | 24 | CONSTANTINE II (LK) | Greece | 1967 |
| 1972 | 32 | MARGARETHE | Denmark | |
| 1973 | 27 | CARL GUSTAV XVI | Sweden | |
| 1975 | 27 | JUAN CARLOS | Spain | |
| 1980 | 42 | BEATRIX | Netherlands | |

AUSTRIA
*1804*

PRUSSIA
*1889*

GREECE
*1862*

DENMARK
*1671*

RUSSIA
*1762*

NORWAY
*1814*

ITALY
*1805*

FRANCE
*1804*

NETHERLANDS
*1831*